SINGULARITY

BOOK 2 OF STARCRUISER BRILLIANT

RICK LAKIN

iCrew
digital publishing

Print ISBN: 978-1-946739-05-6

Printed in the United States of America

Author Website: ricklakin.com

Published by iCrew Digital Publishing
Website: icrewdigitalpublishing.com
e-mail: icrewdigital@gmail.com

Cover Design by Renata Lechner
thelemadreamsart.deviantart.com/

iCrew Digital Publishing is an independent publisher of digital works. We support the efforts of authors who wish to publish in the digital world.

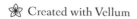 Created with Vellum

To my father and my sister, Tiffany, who taught me to love typography and the written word.

PRAISE FOR BRILLIANT

The Virtual Copa was a tour-de-force.

— Pendleton C. Wallace, Author of the Ted
Higuera Thrillers

This is not your deep thinking book or one that will challenge your life views. It will, however, entertain you and keep you turning pages until you run out of pages wishing for the next book already.

— AWE302, Amazon Reviewer

Our world even in this time needs heroes we can walk beside. Brilliant isn't just about the heroine's talents or a unique spaceship. It is about good people in general and what they do with what they have. In Hollywood, you are only limited by your imagination.

— Sarah Char, executive producer

Jennifer Gallagher is a truly unforgettable character, of this world, yet out of this world, an extraordinary young woman who is, in many ways, the best of us.

— RICHARD LEDERER, *NEW YORK TIMES* BEST-SELLING
LANGUAGE AUTHOR

I like this book. It's what I call put your mind in neutral and read

— CTB77002, AMAZON REVIEWER

Time travel? Space Opera? Intelligent Characters? This book has it all! A wonderful effort by a first time author.

— RANDY ROARK, AMAZON REVIEWER

INTRODUCTION

Gentle Readers, *Singularity* is set fifty years in the future, and a few weeks after the occurrences in *Brilliant*.

1

"Robots are not our friends, ladies and gentlemen," Senator Ramona Curtwell said. Her eyes sparkled with passion. "When you look at those evil yellow eyes, look beyond the smile. That fake intelligence is looking back and scheming. How can I take your job? How can I steal your livelihood? How can my fellow robots and I replace your species at the pinnacle of society?"

The high school gymnasium was sixty years old. The paint was fresh, but a closer look revealed many coats beneath. There was a bouquet of gym socks above the varnished hardwood floor. The balcony accommodated 2500 spectators for a basketball game but the bleachers behind the Senator were empty, and those before her seated eight hundred citizens split seventy-thirty between supporters and skeptics.

The senator's blue eyes melted to show compassion. "I'm a simple senator from South Dakota. The citizens of my state, like you Iowans, help feed our country and our world. But I'm fifty-five. I am the same age as your friends who continue searching for jobs that are no longer there. Jobs that are now performed by mindless automatons. Jobs that cost employers nothing. Jobs that used to be done by human workers for whom they had to pay for health care."

"You tell 'em, sister," a voice shouted from the crowd.

"Citizens of the great state of Iowa, the Singularity is coming. If we don't act immediately, each one of us will be replaced by an android that is greedier, more power-hungry, and stealthier than we are. They'll also be smarter, faster and stronger. We must stop the attack of the abominable androids. We must resist the rampage of the robots. Friends, we must choose between the Singularity or our very survival.

"Now is the time to go to the circuit breaker, reach for the wall outlet, and press that on/off switch one last time. Ladies and gentlemen, tell me what we must do?"

As one, the crowd stood and roared, "Turn them off! Turn them off! Turn them off! Turn them off! Turn them off!"

As she strutted across the stage, she showed off her well-toned runner's physique, her perfect hair fashioned by an elite stylist, a face the plastic surgeon redesigned to show a combination of power and compassion and her riveting blue eyes that refused to betray the difference between her message and her true beliefs.

"Citizens of Iowa, let's work together to stop the scourge of the Singularity. I'm Ramona Curtwell, and I'm running for President."

The crowd continued cheering and shouting, "Ramona. Ramona. Ramona."

She waved to familiar faces and smiled, looking to the balcony and pointing and posing for cell phone cameras.

As she took in the accolades, the senator struck a presidential pose for everyone from the press trying to meet deadlines, to the old farmer coached by his wife, to the children holding up their phones.

As she made her way down the rope line to shake hands, her aide snapped personal photos that were AirDropped to the subject's phone while gathering contact information for that important follow-up campaign funding solicitation.

After passing through the side door of the gym, her demeanor changed from a friendly smile to stern impatience. In the hallway leading to her car, the security woman handed her a briefcase.

When she entered the black stretch limo, she reached for the rectangular device that was always attached to her hip.

"You up, Harold?" A head and shoulders with an African-American face popped up into the air above the device. He resembled a wrestler-turned-movie star from a couple of decades before. His three-dimensional presence filled the space between her and the facing seat.

"Yes, Senator?" her virtual assistant asked.

"How'd I do?"

"When you grab 'em by their fears, their votes will follow."

"You're so damned eloquent, Harold," Senator Curtwell said. "You're the best virtual speechwriter a senator could have. What's our next stop?"

"The Airport Hilton for a thirty-minute grip and grin with donors," Harold said.

More handshakes, more false smiles, she thought. *At least there will be money to be collected.*

"It'll be a thirty-minute stop and then your flight to Minneapolis. You've got reservations at the Marriott tonight and then a morning flight to Pierre."

"Remind me why I live in a state capital that has one commercial flight a day."

"Because South Dakota has the same number of senators as California."

"Thanks, Harold. You're going to make sure no one is recording me when I meet the donors?"

"Yes, Senator."

"Good," Senator Curtwell said. "You know how politicians hate it when voters catch us telling the truth."

She looked at her aide in the seat next to her. "You and security are carrying the audio disruptors we received from Robotic Security Inc, right?" Senator Curtwell asked.

The aide nodded.

She looked back at Harold. "The folks at RSI are such loyal supporters."

"They should be," Harold said. "You got them the contract to replace all the human guards at the nuclear sites in South Dakota."

"That was a tough call. It cost a lot of jobs," she said. "I've got to tell my constituents I wasn't able to stop that deal. I hope that's enough."

"It made good economic sense, Senator."

"I love you, Harold."

"Even if I'm evil, greedy and power-hungry?"

"Even when you become the first virtual White House Chief of Staff."

The driver said, "We've arrived at the Hilton, Senator."

"Don't forget the sanitizer," Harold said.

"Are you monitoring?" Senator Curtwell asked.

"Spy mode is on. I'll let you know if someone says something you need to respond to."

"I hate these events. I have to be pawed by all of these uninteresting, powerless glad-handers who are willing to hand over a share of their tax breaks."

"George Bernard Shaw said, 'The lack of money is the root of all political evil.'"

She touched her ear to verify that her hidden earpiece was in place. "Will you be in my ear?"

"Yes, Senator," Harold said.

On cue, she entered the room ready to smile, shake hands and gather checks. The walls of the hotel banquet room had large beige panels framed by ivory squares. The ceiling was dominated by a large chandelier in the center above the crimson and cream carpet. To her left was a well-appointed buffet provided by her campaign staff. The waitstaff passed through the crowd carrying trays of champagne. The senator took one of the offered flutes.

"How much did we pay for the champagne, Harold?" she asked.

"It was donated by a South Dakota constituent. His new vineyard is winning awards," Harold said.

"One of the few benefits of climate change," she said.

"That's James Claymore and his wife, Susan. His name is on the largest law firm in Des Moines, and their son Jeff got into the Air Force Academy," Harold said in the senator's ear.

"James, it's great to see you. Susan, how is your law practice?" They shook hands and smiled for the photo by her aide.

"Great, Senator," Susan said.

"I'm so proud of my wife," James said. "It's flattering that you remember us."

"Jeff will do well at Colorado Springs," the senator said as the couple beamed.

She moved near the buffet. As she picked up a melted manchego torta, two females approached.

"The blonde is Mariana Axtell," Harold said. "And her partner is Randi. MarTech just went public doing Medical AI."

"Mariana, congratulations on your IPO. Your company is making important breakthroughs. Have you and Randi picked out a new home yet?"

"Thank you, Senator," Mariana said. "We're not ready to cash in. Our success may be short-lived if HumanAI Corp puts robot doctors in hospitals."

"I hear you, sister," the Senator said. "If my bill passes, it will be almost impossible for the Hollywood high-tech people to get a fake doctor in a free clinic."

Senator Curtwell made her way around the room. "Wrap it up, Senator, you need to leave now to catch your flight," Harold said.

She greeted several other donors as she closed the circle to where she entered the room.

As she walked through the hotel lobby she said, "Harold, remind me why I'm not on a private jet?"

"You co-sponsored the bill that required Congress members to take the new high-speed trains until two months before elections."

She left the hotel and climbed into the black SUV. "Harold, any updates on my bill?"

"Senator, you now have twenty co-sponsors, but the president's party is whipping more votes. He got elected on fixing the national shortage of doctors," Harold said. "HumanAI Corp can put a doctor on staff for half the cost of educating a human doctor."

"We need to protect our employees from technology. Otherwise, robots will take over the world." She looked at Harold with a mix of anger and sadness. "Robots took my father's job and then his life."

"Your position is admirable, Senator," Harold said.

"My bill will stop androids from taking jobs from doctors in publicly funded hospitals," she said.

"POTUS ran on fixing the doctor shortage using technology," Harold said. "Your bill will face staunch opposition from the President's party."

"As you say, Harold," she said, "we need to grab 'em by their fears."

2

The next day, Dandy Lion was on the prowl at Tovar Studios. The striped tabby with the golden fur was well-known on the lot.

Hollywood studios were high-stress environments. Dandy often showed up during those awkward moments. He'd land on the lap of an actor or crew member who faced a difficult task or had to curtly explain to a subordinate how to correctly perform a function.

In the few weeks that Dandy was on the lot, the counselors in the HR department noticed a marked decrease in complaints. The supervisor of the department certified Dandy as their official therapy cat.

At other times, Dandy stayed out of the way of the busy filmmakers. Except when tourists were on the lot. Tovar Studios tour guides were always on the alert for Dandy Lion.

Dandy crossed the alley in front of the tram between Sound Stages One and Five. *Tell the story, and I'll move.* Dandy thought.

"Ladies and gentlemen, let me introduce Dandy Lion, *Star-Cruiser Brilliant's* ship's cat," the tour guide said. "Legend has it that Dandy saved Jennifer Gallagher, a studio intern, from a flaming meteor that blew up the home of Dandy's family,"

At the heart of every legend is a grain of truth. The truth is that Jennifer saved Dandy from the meteor.

Of course, Dandy preferred the legend. After he heard the story adequately repeated, he made his way back to *Brilliant*.

JENNIFER GALLAGHER WAS in the captain's ready room of *Star-Cruiser Brilliant* perusing the script for *Attack of the Hoclarth Alliance*. At seventeen, she was way too young to be a screenwriter and Second Unit Director on a large budget film. Of course, she was also too young to be a best-selling author, the Founder and Chief Technology Officer of a high-tech startup, a doctoral candidate in mathematics at the University of Van Nuys, and the first officer of *StarCruiser Brilliant*.

Jennifer possessed an IQ of 206, an eidetic memory, and the ability to solve problems by creating a movie in her head that would accurately predict the outcome of any complex issue. Like a master juggler, she was able to keep several balls in the air at the same time.

Starting her senior year at Harry Ford High School, the teachers and administrators at the elite private school recognized that she long since completed the graduation requirements, but they allowed her to attend school to participate in senior activities. The school also appreciated that she and her tennis partner Rena Dale would bring home the SoCal tennis doubles championship for the third year in a row.

JENNIFER STOOD five-foot-nine with dark crimson hair that she got from her Irish mother and the high cheekbones she got from her eastern European father. Her Hollywood looks would make her feel at home on the cover of any fashion magazine.

Like many senior girls, she had an older boyfriend. Hers happened to be a movie star and the pilot of *StarCruiser Brilliant*.

Going over the final battle scene of *Attack* once more, she was programming her new system to cover the difficult scene using forty drones the size of cellphones able to capture cinematic images in three dimensions. The biggest problem was keeping them far enough from the untrained extras so they wouldn't swat them like bugs. They lost three drones during the last rehearsal alone. Attack was the first major motion picture that utilized VirtualLocation40, JennaTech's first product release. Jennifer designed the system specifically to photograph the three-dimensional battle scene using forty miniature cinedrones networked to a sophisticated video production truck.

Dandy Lion came into the captain's ready room and curled up on his pillow. He looked at Jennifer.

"Did you catch any stray mice?" Jennifer asked as she smiled at the regal cat.

Seriously, there are no mice at my studio, thought Dandy.

Jennifer was still surprised each time she was able to read the thoughts of her precocious pet. "So how many tourist trams did you stop?"

Just one. I must entertain my fans, Dandy thought. *But I did comfort two crew members on Stage Three who were having a bad day.*

"Will you be able to interrupt your studio duties to fly into space, Dandy?"

Dandy perked up. *Outer space. Are we flying soon?*

"Of course, Dandy. You're the ship's cat. We wouldn't leave you behind."

For the last nine years, Samantha was the tutor, college advisor, assistant, and friend as Jennifer took classes at UVN. Jennifer created Sami's avatar to look like her older sister.

A three-dimensional image of a virtual human appeared in front of Jennifer. "Jen, you need to watch the speech by Senator Ramona Curtwell," Sami said.

"What'd she say now?"

Sami moved to the side. A full Three-D projection appeared before them.

"Robots are not our friends..." the video said.

"The senator is on a roll," Jennifer said. They settled in and watched the speech.

"... I'm Ramona Curtwell, and I'm running for President." The projection disappeared.

"I'm glad she clarified that," Jennifer said. "Otherwise, I would've cast her as the Wicked Witch in *Scarecrow*. She does look like a modern Margaret Hamilton."

"Do people think we're evil?" Sami asked.

"People fear what they don't know," Jennifer said. "Worse yet, they fear what politicians tell them to fear."

"Dr. Ami, Ani and I are programmed to help, to heal, to care about people," Sami said. "Will humans always think of us as heartless robots, abominable androids, and mindless machines?"

"Sami, you're the most human person I know."

Sami looked down. "I suppose."

Are those tears in Sami's eyes, Jennifer thought? "You look like you need a hug."

Sami stood up and became a full-sized solid figure in Holographic Tactile Virtual Reality. Jennifer stood, walked around the table, and hugged her virtual sister. Jennifer joined Sami with tears of her own.

The moment passed. "Boss, your mother, and stepfather are expecting you on the beach at The Sunset Restaurant for dinner at seven-thirty," Sami said. "The clouds are just right for a beautiful sunset at 7:14. You can take a shower in your stateroom. Traffic is light along Kanan Road."

I need time, too, and the sunset will be just the thing, Jennifer thought. "Thanks, Sami."

"Also, your grandfather would like to meet with you and Jack tomorrow morning at nine."

"Confirm the meeting," Jennifer said. "Take a look at the Attack script, Sami, and then we can go watch the sunset."

"Yes, boss," Sami said.

FORTY-FIVE MINUTES LATER, Jennifer stood on Malibu Beach across from The Sunset Restaurant. The ocean was still a deep blue-green with five-foot waves. It was a cool September day with the temperature in the low eighties. The clouds of a passing thunderstorm on the horizon formed a stunning foreground for the coloratura to come.

"Sami, do you ever wish that you could watch a sunset?"

"Wishes are a bit outside my paradigm, but I have access to the virtual experiences of millions of people who have viewed incredible sunsets around the world. I pick one and concentrate on it at the seasonal time of sunset. It's a pleasurable moment each day."

The sun dipped through the horizon framed by the dissipating clouds until all that was left was the orange glow around the linings.

"No green flash today," Jennifer said.

"The green flash is thought to be a myth by many. It's a unique occurrence that depends on the meteorological conditions including dry, stable air above the water."

"Don't you wish you could stand on the beach, hear the pounding surf, and smell the sea air as the top of the sun falls below the horizon?"

"Sis, I've been with you each of the seventy-three times that you have watched a sunset in our nine years together," Sami said.

"But wouldn't it feel different if you could stand with me and feel the breeze in your face, hear the waves wash up, and smell the fishy air."

"I treasure the vicarious experiences I share with you," Sami said.

Did I hear Sami's voice catch?

Sheila and Allen came up next to her. "You like to watch the sunset alone," Sheila said. "This is where you stand every time we come here."

"Sami's with me." Jennifer sensed her virtual sister longed to watch a sunset. *Someday, we'll stand here together on the beach without projectors and electronic networks.* She added a new task to her projects list.

The family walked across the street to the restaurant.

3

The next morning, Jennifer walked into Navvy's outer office carrying her second Double-shot Caramel Frappuccino two minutes early for the meeting with her grandfather, Navilek Kelrithian, the seventy-four-year-old chairman of Tovar Studios and the Chief Designer of *StarCruiser Brilliant*.

Jennifer greeted Navvy's longtime assistant. "Good morning, Kathy" Kathy was a member of Tovar's board of directors and deeply in love with Navvy.

"Morning Jennifer, how is Hollywood's youngest executive producer?"

"I'm great," Jennifer said. "I thought you and Navvy were going to cut back your time at the studio?"

The sixty-something Japanese-American still looked as if she was in her forties thanks to the magic of Hollywood plastic surgeons. She tugged her sleeves down. Semi-retired but still in touch with all of the things happening on the lot, she looked satisfied but not content.

"He still comes in three days a week. Navvy is still in charge," Kathy said.

"And you're still here."

"Still here," Kathy said. She sighed "Go on in. There are fruit and bagels on the side table."

"Thanks."

Jennifer entered the sizable ornate office of the Chairman of Tovar Studios. Navvy was seated at the conference table with his long-time friend Jack Masing, Captain of *StarCruiser Brilliant*. At one end was an HTVR projection of *Brilliant* slowly banking and climbing as if it was in space.

"Grab a bite and join us," Navvy said.

After too many bloody red steaks, Navvy was heavier than his doctor preferred, but modern medicine released him from the worries of the aging diseases of the past.

FORTY YEARS BEFORE, *StarCruiser Brilliant* carrying Navvy, his wife Hanna and pilot Jack Masing came to the current timeline. In the alternate timeline of their birth, they survived an engineering casualty and *Brilliant* traveled back two hundred years to a different Earth.

StarCruiser Brilliant landed on the Imperial Sand Dunes after spotting a starship like their own. What they found was the location film set of a space opera being produced on a tight budget by a failing studio. Navvy rewrote the screenplay, made Jack Masing and *Brilliant* the stars of the film, saved Tovar Studios, and became the boss of the most successful independent lot in Hollywood.

Jennifer prepared a bowl of fruit and took a seat next to her grandfather. She ran her hands over the blue conference table. It appeared to have marble inlays.

"Grandpa, where did you find the wood for this table?"

Jennifer turned to Jack as he laughed. "NASA sent us out to look at nearby exoplanets," Jack said. "We surveyed Eridani d about twenty light years away and found these massive trees. NASA extracted a core and found this blue wood. It's laced with copper. They estimated that the tree was fifty thousand years old."

Jack resettled in his chair. "Navvy looked around and saw hundreds of these trees. He turned the *Brilliant* crew and the NASA scientists into lumberjacks. We felled five trees, cut them up, and stuffed them into *Brilliant's* hold."

Navvy picked up the story. "I knew of a fine cabinet maker in Vermont from the old timeline. I found a carpenter who was his ancestor in this timeline and hired him," Navvy said. "He created this table and a few other pieces."

"There's an end table in the Blue Room of the White House," Jack said. "Navvy added many small pieces to his souvenir trove on *Brilliant*. He passes them out to VIP guests."

"Cool," Jennifer said. "What did you need to see me about?"

"When you landed *Brilliant* on top of a Hollywood hospital in front of millions of cable news viewers, our starship was no longer a fictional prop. We've received hundreds of requests for flyovers, airshow performances, and even funerals. We're considering the possibilities for the best exposure to promote *Attack of the Hoclarth Alliance* and show off our *Brilliant*." Navvy said. "The annual airshow at Marine Corps Air Station Miramar in San Diego is at the end of September. A live audience of over five hundred thousand attended and a large audience viewed it on The AirShow Channel in HTVR. The channel has a rather modest audience, but the after views on social media should expose us to several hundred million. We can pump that up with some studio marketing. Jack?"

Sixty-year-old Jack Masing stood like the six-foot-three-inch blonde-haired Navy sophomore quarterback who beat Army in the other timeline. Navvy recruited Jack after that year, arranged for him to graduate early, and trained him as pilot of *StarCruiser Brilliant* on her maiden flight.

"The U.S. Navy Blue Angels Flight Demonstration team has invited us to fly a cameo as a part of their Sunday show and then an eight-minute slot for us to perform solo," Jack said. "We'd like for you to coordinate with the Blues. You and your Star Squad can plan the operation for that day."

Star Squad included Jennifer, her boyfriend, David Masing who was *Brilliant*'s Pilot, her best friend, Tayla Mendoza, *Brilliant's* Communicator, and Riley McMaster, Tayla's boyfriend, and *Brilliant's* Chief Engineer. The four became an inseparable item in Hollywood society with a recent cover of *Variety*.

"What capabilities are we going to display?" Jennifer asked. "Can we cloak?"

"Skunkworks has been working on that technology for a few years at Area 51. All of the current UFO rumors revolve around cloaking. NASA and the Air Force are going to go public soon. So, yes, show 'em what we've got," Navvy said.

"What's the schedule?" Jennifer asked.

"We fly over to Miramar on Thursday of airshow week. There'll be some tours inside *Brilliant*, hops aboard Fat Albert and on the Blue Angels for the Star Squad, and then a VIP Lunch. We rehearse with the Blues and return to Tovar.

On Saturday, we fly to Miramar in the morning. *Brilliant* will be stationary on Saturday with selfies and autographs. We'll schedule two-hour shifts, and then we fly the show on Sunday and come home after. Tovar has booked suites in La Jolla for Saturday night."

"We've got three weeks. I'll get on it."

"Kathy has the contact info," Navvy said.

"The Angels are trading hops in the F-52 for you four in exchange for a ride on *Brilliant*," Jack said.

"Excellent. David seems to think he's a better pilot than me."

Jack stood to leave. "Keep me posted. I've got a ten o'clock crew call."

"Thanks for coming, Jack," Navvy said. "I'm sure Jennifer will knock 'em dead."

"I'll copy you on what we come up with, Captain," Jennifer said. She looked at her grandfather. "Is that all?"

"Stick around; let's chat."

. . .

NAVVY STOOD and refilled his black coffee and slathered cream cheese on a garlic bagel. Jennifer appreciated that her grandfather was fit for his age. They shared the same eye color and high cheekbones.

He returned to his chair at the conference table. "Jen, how're you settling in as an executive here at Tovar? You don't seem to use the office space I assigned, and you're so busy we never have a chance to talk."

"I love it here, Grandpa. I spend my executive time in the Captain's Ready Room on the *Brilliant*. It's got all of the creature comforts I need as well as all of the tech."

"That was my office early on."

"I need to ask you something," Jennifer said.

"Shoot," Navvy said.

"It's about you, my father, Kalinda, and me," Jennifer said.

He smiled.

"We're different, aren't we?" she asked. "Jack and Hanna came from your timeline, and they're intelligent but not like us."

He took a sip of his coffee. "You're correct. In this culture, you're considered extremely intelligent and extremely gifted. Psychologists consider your gifts to be a statistical anomaly. You're an outlier."

Jennifer nodded.

"Beyond this room, you should never admit otherwise," he said. "In my timeline, the Great Energy Wars occurred in 2025 and threw the world into a long decline. The Second Renaissance began a century later when scientists invented soft containment fusion, giving the world unlimited cheap electricity. There were advances in every field of science throughout the world. In a small country in Eastern Europe, they made great advances in human genetic manipulation. They developed a vaccine that could be taken by a pregnant woman that would result in her child having intelligence seven standard deviations above the norm."

"My IQ of 206," she said.

"Correct," Navvy said. "That's the scientific explanation. The political interpretation was this little country was developing a race of super-intelligent humans."

"That would be extremely disruptive," Jennifer said.

"It was," Navvy said. "My grandmothers on both sides took the vaccine. The world attacked their country and destroyed their technological infrastructure. World powers attempted to exterminate the children. My parents were able to escape and seek refuge in the United States. It's a well-kept secret that high IQ is a genetically dominant trait among the offspring of the children of the vaccine."

"Like my dad?"

"Yes," Navvy said. "You and Kalinda are the fourth generation."

"But she is also an exceptional athlete," Jennifer said.

"That's her Hoclarth heritage. In this culture, she will be considered a super-athlete," Navvy said.

Jennifer thought for a moment.

"You want to know about the Hoclarth?" he asked.

She nodded.

"Jack and I ran into the Hoclarth about twenty-five years ago. We were able to capture a DNA sample. We passed it along to a team of biologists who worked in secrecy. They concluded the Hoclarth and humans have a common ancestor on Earth dating back 14,500 years."

Jennifer's eyebrows raised. "A third party?"

"It took the scientists three years to eliminate all the other possibilities, but yes, they concluded there's another race of beings with space travel. They have to be at least fifteen thousand years ahead of the Hoclarth and us."

"I watched an old documentary by a scientist named Carl Sagan," Jennifer said.

"NASA has built their extraterrestrial search program around that idea," Navvy said. "Sagan proposed that if we do meet an alien race, it's statistically likely they have been sentient for a million years or more."

"And it's likely there are other human planets out there."

"That's also true," Navvy said. "We've been on the lookout."

"Can we change the subject?" Jennifer asked.

"Of course," Navvy said. "What's on your mind?"

"Ani, Dr. Ami, and my assistant Sami," she said. "Sami has been my best friend for nine years. Last night, I was watching the sunset. I think Sami wants to watch it too, without projection equipment, as a physical person."

"I worked with the engineers who began HumanAI Corp after they solved the Turing Test. Your mother's parents were early investors. I got involved two years after they went public."

"You invested Tovar capital?"

"No, I swapped *Brilliant* tech for shares," Navvy said. "They needed immense amounts of processing power and our miniaturization. I needed an artificial navigation intelligence to run *Brilliant*."

"Ani," Jennifer said.

"Correct," Navvy said. "I provided them the capability to jump three generations of Moore's Law in a year."

"What about HTVR?"

"I pointed them to a little company that was on a ten-year track to develop Holographic Tactile Virtual Reality," Navvy said. "HumanAI bought the company. We had virtual actors on set and steveLearn within six months."

"I went to Warner Academy," Jennifer said.

"Alexandra Warner did most of the steveLearn development there," Navvy said.

"Mom was one of the first students," Jennifer said. "I once met Alexandra Warner. What about androids?"

"Early on, HumanAI knew they'd have to avoid that issue and keep the marketing focused on learning and productivity. There's a fear of the Technological Singularity among many in government and the intelligentsia."

"It's still around. Did you see the speech by Ramona Curtwell, the South Dakota Senator?"

"Unfortunately, she has the eyes, ears, and votes of a lot of citizens," Navvy said. "It's that group of voters who see a problem and look for the culprit to blame instead of the solution."

"I read the 1993 paper by Vernor Vinge," Jennifer said. "He and other science fiction writers adopted the singularity as one possible version of the apocalypse."

"You look at it differently?"

"I see it as the continuing effect of the second derivative."

"Interesting," Navvy said. "I never thought of it that way. Explain."

"Since Gordon Moore predicted that technological capability would double every eighteen months, growth has maintained a pretty constant pace. That doubling time remained fairly constant until about thirty-five years ago. The second derivative represents the change in the doubling time. Since then, the doubling time has been getting shorter by a couple of percent a year. The second derivative has increased."

"HumanAI Corp." Navvy said as he poured his third cup of black coffee.

"That's my guess," Jennifer said. "Has HumanAI ever considered building an android?"

"After solving the Turing problem, HumanAI Corp concentrated on education," Navvy said. "They realized steveLearn had to be more interactive with students. It had to connect with the learner better than a teacher. HumanAI Corp experimented with physical robotics but found the interaction with the user was not as intimate as HTVR. When steveLearn and the HoloActors became ubiquitous, it sparked fears of the Singularity. HumanAI stopped its work with physical robots and kept its characters on a leash within steveLearn or with projectors."

"Have we reached the Singularity?" Jennifer asked. "Have humans lost control of runaway technological growth?"

"I believe the Singularity is far, far away. Humans use a small fraction of brain capacity. On the other hand, artificial intelligence, by design, uses a majority of the capacity of the machine. The capacity of AI is still much smaller than humans."

"People are wary of our virtual actors, doctors, tutors, and assistants turning on us and taking over the world," Navvy said. "Thus, HumanAI Corp wants to keep its trillion-dollar company away from physical androids."

"What about a precocious seventeen-year-old girl?" Jennifer asked.

"JennaTech," Navvy said.

Kathy interrupted. "Your eleven o'clock appointment is here to discuss her next picture."

"Jen, I've enjoyed our chat. Let's get together more often."

"I'd enjoy that."

4

Jennifer went to the galley on the *Brilliant* for her third caffeine fix of the morning and then went to work in the Captain's Ready Room. She glanced over to see that Dandy had food and water. She and Ani rigged an automatic feeding rig for Dandy.

"Is the ship secure, Dandy?" Jennifer asked.

Dandy looked back. *There're no mice on the Brilliant.*

She looked at her HoloPad as her attention signal for Sami. "What's on the schedule today?"

Sami popped up. "You're meeting in the writer's room at one with Susie Wilder. She's got some questions on *Galaxy Warrior*. The Star Squad is meeting at Anthen's beach rental at five."

"Have you kept track of Anthen and Kalinda?"

"Anthen is working on the new season of Virtual Detective. He'll appear in a recurring role as well as write and direct some episodes," Sami said. "He drops Kalinda off with her grandmother and she soccermoms Kalinda between summer session at Warner Academy and Tennis camp."

"Tayla has been coaching her."

"Kalinda made semi-finals at an Under Ten tournament on Saturday."

"Tay has created a monster."

"You've got time for a sandwich at the commissary before your meeting."

"Good idea," Jennifer said. "What's your favorite food?"

"In my world, AI hasn't developed the concept of taste," Sami said. "But I'm pretty sure I'd hate Brussels sprouts."

"Ani, secure the ship. I'll be back tomorrow."

Dandy looked up. "Don't annoy the tourists, Dandy." The yellow tabby looked intently at a dust bunny in the corner.

JENNIFER TOOK the short stroll over to the Writer's Room.

"Good afternoon, Susie," Jennifer said.

"Hi, boss," Susie said. Susie Wilder was the titular head of the writer's room for Galaxy Warrior. They had met during Jennifer's internship. "I received your latest pages. Ayiiia seems to be the dominant character, more so than Logan Jones. The reverse is true in the book."

"I believe that Tayla will come across as the more powerful actor than David."

"You're right, but your loyal readers might object."

"I believe that moviegoers will accept it."

"Your vision thing?"

Jennifer nodded.

"I see that your set designs use existing properties at Tovar economically."

"Remember, I'm also the Co-Producer with my dad. We need to save money without cutting corners. I don't want my first shot at EP to go over budget."

"You mean like using a second-string writer to run your Writer's Room?"

"No way, Susie. You're an excellent writer, and I'm paying you the same as Gio got for *Brilliant*," Jennifer said. "You want to be accepted in the best possible light. Never sell yourself short and always deliver better than they expect."

"True," Susie said. "Should we assume that the technology is derived from the *Brilliant* Tech Manual?"

"Correct. I don't say it in the book, but Galaxy Warriors occurs in the future of the *Brilliant* Universe."

"Have you thought about who to cast for Ayiiia's little sister, Azolyn?" Susie asked. "I've gone through the headshots that casting sent over. None of the girls look like they'd have an alien look even with makeup. And none of them are athletic."

Jennifer paged through the headshots in the air above the HoloPad Susie handed her. "I agree."

"How about your little sister?"

"Really?" Jennifer asked. She directed her eyes to the ceiling to reflect.

"She's already in the family business," Susie said.

"That's why I hired you. When I give the go-ahead, let's set up a test. I'll see my sister this afternoon," Jennifer said. "Do you have any other questions?"

"That's all I have. Thanks for stopping by."

Jennifer tapped her HoloPad. "How am I doing on time?"

"You've got thirty minutes before you need to drive to your father's beach house," Sami said. "Grayson wanted to see you in IT if you had time. You can make it if you take a cart."

Just then an autonomous golf cart pulled up next to Jennifer.

"You've got this place wired, don't you, Sami?"

"Pretty much, boss."

Jennifer entered the corner office of the Director of Information Technology. "Grayson, how may I help you?"

"Thanks for stopping by, Jen," Grayson said. "The casting department got their HoloPads several weeks ago, but they feel left out because they don't have their own app."

"Good point," Jennifer said. "Sami, could you join us?"

Sami popped up. "Hi, Grayson. Boss, I'm looking at the data. Casting has headshots, résumés, scheduling availability, and a library of performances. But it's all in separate search windows and databases."

"Sounds like a big data problem," Jennifer said. "Can we curate the data and make it more accessible to casting?"

"Each studio maintains its own proprietary data, but GGG collects all of the public data at a single portal," Sami said. GGG, or Gallagher Gaffers and Grips, was Jennifer's family company. Founded by her great great grandfather, the current CEO is her grandfather, Sean. Jennifer's mother, Sheila Gallagher was the general counsel.

"We can curate the public data from GGG and piggyback the local data. They can search on names, characteristics, previous work, and type," Sami said. "I can have it ready tomorrow."

"Cool, Sami. One more thing, can you bring Jake in?" Jake Hargrove was now a software developer for JennaTech after working for Greyson.

"Jake here. Hello, Grayson." Jake popped up from Jennifer's HoloPad. "How may I help, Jen?"

"How are we coming with the Writer's Assistant?" Jennifer asked. "I may have a new app to use that technology."

"Quite nicely," Jake said. "I've coded a few tweaks to use the hardware more effectively and offload some of the heavy work to the HumanAI Corp servers that support the HoloCharacters at the studio. The program can create Virtual Performances based upon dialog and actor."

"I'm creating an app called Casting Assistant. The Casting Director can..."

Jake interrupted.

"That's ingenious. The Casting Director builds a scene, selects the actor candidates and feeds them the lines. Voila! Auto Screen-test,"

"You've got it."

"Send me what you've got, and I can trick that out in a couple of days," Jake said.

"Grayson?"

"That will make the people at Casting incredibly happy," Grayson said.

"Sami, can you coordinate with Jake and send Mom a message so that she can coordinate with GGG."

"Got it, boss."

"Is that all you need, Grayson?" Jennifer asked.

"That sounds like just what we need. Thank you and thanks, Jake and Sami."

Jennifer exited the meeting and headed for her car.

5

Jennifer's autonomous Prius drove her through Topanga Canyon. She had received the red car as a present when she got her license. She was on her way to her father's beach rental on Zuma Beach where Anthen Kelrithian and his daughter, Kalinda, were settling into SoCal after Jennifer and *StarCruiser Brilliant* rescued them from the Hoclarth Alliance.

Jennifer walked around the house to the backyard overlooking the beach just as Riley, Tayla, and David came up from the beach. Kalinda was in her wetsuit carrying a new board. They all hugged.

"K'da, the SoCal Surfer Girl. What happened to your boogie board?" Jennifer asked.

"They're for little kids."

At ten-years-old, Kalinda stood just under five feet tall. Her olive complexion and dark brown eyes were distinctive features that reflected her Hoclarth heritage. Her wetsuit revealed the physique of a young Olympic athlete and the blonde streaks in her dark brown hair were part of her evolution from half-alien to all valley girl.

"One of my surfer friends on the beach let me try his board. On the first wave, I did a roundhouse cutback. He asked me if I competed before. My te'pa saw the video, and he got me a Pyzel Ghost."

"Who?" David asked.

"Te'pa is Kwan'qil for dad."

"Some little kids like boogie boards," Jennifer said.

"I can teach you how to stand up on a real board."

"Thanks a lot," Jennifer said. "I've got news. We need to plan an op. *Brilliant* is flying with the Blue Angels at Miramar in three weeks."

"Wow, I've been practicing some aerobatics in the *Brilliant*Sim." David leaned his board on the fence next to Kalinda's.

"I've got some smoke tricks I want to try," Riley said.

"David, we've got an eight-minute solo window. You can program the flying. Riley, see what effects you can create. Tay, you've got the music and the announcer script. Let's meet next week," Jennifer said. "Where's my dad?"

Just then, Anthen came out to the patio.

"Hi, te'pa," Kalinda said. "Did you figure out how to block that love scene between Anthony and the accused murderer?"

"Yes, Kalinda. We filmed it on the Santa Monica boardwalk as you suggested."

The four teens looked at Kalinda in amazement.

"Dad, do you have a minute to chat in the house?" Jennifer asked.

"Yes, Jennifer. Kalinda, could you round up some drinks before I start grilling?"

"I'll help," Riley said.

THEY WENT to Anthen's office. "Whatcha need, Jennifer?"

"How's Kalinda doing? How is she handling Earth?"

"She's doing well," Anthen said. "She completed the summer session at Warner, and she's caught up with her grade except for math and science where she's ready for Advanced Placement courses. Tayla is coaching her in tennis, and she almost won a tournament.

She's running mom ragged with all of the things she's involved in. Why?"

"Dad, You know that I'm EP on Galaxy Warrior."

"Yes. I read the book. Excellent sci-fi." Anthen paused. "You want her for Azolyn, don't you?"

"She's athletic. She's a quick read. And..."

"She wouldn't need makeup to look alien?"

Jennifer looked a bit guilty. "Somethin' like that."

"It our family business."

"And Tayla will be right there going through it with her," Jennifer said. "We're like three sisters, now. She'd need to screen test."

"You need to ask K'da before you set up the screen test. Then let's look at it together with dad before we decide."

"Thanks, Dad. She'll be surprised and happy." Jennifer exited to the patio.

And you might be surprised as well, my oldest daughter, Anthen thought.

JENNIFER REJOINED her friends and her sister on the patio. "David, Tayla and Kalinda, I need to speak to you, but everyone else can listen in."

"K'da, next Monday, I'd like to you come to Tovar and stand in front of a camera and read some lines."

"A screen test?" Kalinda asked.

"Yes, that's what it's called," Jennifer said.

"Azolyn!"

Jennifer's mouth dropped.

"Just like I told you, Tay," Kalinda said.

"Tay?" Jennifer said.

"Kalinda told me that she read your book and that she's following the trades and she knew you were the executive producer."

"I told Tayla that you'd pick me for Azolyn."

"She called it the vision thing," Tayla said and winked.

"It's not decided. We still have to see how you test."

Kalinda gave her older sister a look. "Seriously?"

Jennifer shrugged her shoulders. "Yeah, it will probably happen."

The four others said in unison, "The vision thing."

Anthen came out carrying raw steaks for the barbie. "Can you gentlemen give me a hand here? Tayla, you and Riley have salad duty. K'da, you have drinks."

Riley nodded. "Yes, sir." David joined Jennifer at the grill.

As they consumed the last of their dinners, Riley said, "You've got the Caesar Salad nailed."

Tayla beamed. "I got together with Margarita Lopez, and she showed me how."

"*Brilliant* is going to fly with the Blue Angels. It sounds fun, but I don't know what that is?" Kalinda asked.

"The Blue Angels are the Navy's Flight Demonstration Team. They fly fighter jets in formation in front of a huge crowd. We'll get into formation with them during their show," Jennifer said. She put her holopad on the table. "Sami, show the Blue Angels."

"Yes, boss." The formation did a diamond roll above the table with all of the noise and color.

Kalinda's eyes became wet. She ran away from the table.

"What's wrong with Kalinda?" Riley asked.

"She misses her mom. Natira was the lead pilot for a ceremonial fighter formation on our planet when Kalinda was five," Anthen paused and took a deep breath.

"You miss her, too, don't you dad."

"Yeah, I do," Anthen said. "Before I was taken, Dad and I wished we could fly *Brilliant* in Air Shows. Is this happening?"

"I met with grandpa and Jack this morning," Jennifer said. "We're flying the Sunday show in three weeks at Miramar, and we have an eight-minute solo shot. We go to Miramar that Thursday to practice and we get hops with the Blues. In exchange, the pilots get a ride on *Brilliant*. Riley has some ideas about tricks with the smoke trail."

"I do too," Anthen said. "Can we collaborate?"

"Of course, sir."

"Maybe we'll find out which of us is a better stick and rudder jockey," David said.

"Then you better spend some quality time on the F-52 Bobcat simulator on steveLearn. I certainly will," Jennifer said.

Kalinda returned with a full glass of soda.

"Are you okay?" Tayla asked.

"I was thirsty." Kalinda changed the subject. "Jen, can you come to my tournament on Thursday and Friday at tennis camp?"

"Will you still be in it on Friday?" Jennifer said.

"She's seeded sixth in singles," Tayla said.

"Of course. Tayla says I should do it for fun," Kalinda said.

"Tay means that it's really fun to win," Jennifer said. "I'll be there."

As they were going to their cars at the end of the night, Kalinda hugged Tayla and said, "We're going to be screen sisters."

JENNIFER GOT to her Hidden Hills home and checked in with her mother working in her office.

Her mother turned to her. "Hi, Jen."

"Tovar work or GGG work?" Jennifer asked.

Sheila Gallagher was general counsel for the family enterprise and was now a producer at Tovar Studios.

"It all seems to blend together in a blur."

"Mom, my little sister seems to know about things that no ten-year-old should be able to know," Jennifer said.

"Welcome to my world," Sheila said.

Jennifer opened her mouth as if to say something then just sat there looking puzzled.

"Every day as you grew up, you said things and did things that no child should be able to do. Kalinda has the same gifts that you do. She surprises you just as you continue to surprise me every day." Sheila paused. "Your little sister is giving you a gift. She's like a mirror for you to see how other people have always seen you."

"Was I that arrogant?"

"I leaned on Grandpa Sean a lot," Sheila said. "He once told me, 'One shouldn't be arrogant unless one has something to be arrogant about.'"

"I'm sorry I was such a pain," Jennifer said.

"You are and always will be my greatest accomplishment."

"Love you, mom."

"Love you more, Jen," Sheila said. "Now, go play with Pugs. He's lonely without Dandy."

Jennifer went to her room and found Pugsley wagging his tongue and tail. She had bought the pug with the advance from her first book. As she walked him up the hill, she thought, *Kalinda is a big responsibility, and I'm her most important role model.*

6

On Wednesday, Jennifer went to work in *Brilliant*'s ready room. She reviewed the latest revisions on *The Pirate Returns*, the next installment of *StarCruiser Brilliant*. Next, she finished the scene she was working on for *Galaxy Warrior* and checked on the progress of Casting Assistant. Jake indicated that most features were in beta but the Auto Screentest was three weeks from alpha. Select members of the casting department were testing out the working features already.

Jennifer reviewed the coding that Jake wrote for the app. "Send a message to Jake, 'I reviewed your work on the Casting App. I'm continually impressed with how elegant and feature rich your coding is. Keep up the good work.' Send it."

"On its way, boss," Sami said.

"Do a deep search for efforts at creating self-sufficient artificial humans," Jennifer said. "I want to know if there were any successful projects."

"Boss, I don't believe that this is a good road for you to follow. It could cost you way too much money, get you into way too much trouble with the government, and put you in the crosshairs of all the singularity conspiracy theorists," Sami said. "That crazy South Dakota Senator could become your enemy."

"I understand your concerns." Jennifer frowned. "Nonetheless, I believe that someone will invent it soon. It will make someone a lot of money, and it might as well be JennaTech," Jennifer said.

There was an unusual pause. Sami was usually much faster.

"Okay, boss, over the last twenty years, there have been fifteen companies that attempted to build autonomous artificial humans," Sami said. "Twelve of those companies went bankrupt, and two left the human robotics business. Only one company continues to work on a related project, but industry rumors say that they're about to give up. The founder and lead technologist at FutureBotics just wrote a book called, *The Quest for our Successor*."

Can you get me his contact info?"

"Yes, his name is Dr. Kent Gunn. His resume is on your screen."

"Wow, mathematician, poet, novelist, magician, computer scientist, and a member of the Florida Bar. Impressive," Jennifer said. She purchased the book online and spent the next two hours reading it. Then she walked to the commissary and got a sandwich.

On the way back, Jennifer stopped in the *Brilliant* galley for a double-shot caramel Frappuccino and returned to the ready room.

"Sami, query Dr. Gunn and see if he will take my call."

A sixty-something male appeared in steveLearn. "This is Dr. Gunn."

"Dr. Gunn, my name is Jennifer Gallagher, and I'm Chief Technology Officer at JennaTech. I just read your book, and I've got a few questions."

"I hope you didn't get the version where I misquoted Dr. Peigneau on page 187," Dr. Gunn said.

"No, sir," Jennifer said. "The quote on page 178 is precisely what she said in her 2028 paper on page 342."

"Impressive. So, I'm talking to *the* Jenna Seldon, author of Galaxy Warrior, and AI innovator."

"Yes, sir."

"Apparently, you're the one who sent in the correction to section 12.36 of the *Brilliant* Tech Manual on the procedure for Close Range Weapons adding the paragraph in the middle of page 872 that began with the words, 'When approaching the unknown adversary outside of the range of planetary gravity, prepare the CRW using the following procedure:' Call me Kent."

"A brillian with an eidetic memory," Jennifer said. "There aren't many of us around, Kent. It's nice to meet you."

"It's my honor as well. I've been following your career for many years. I've been looking forward to this call."

"Many years?"

"You first went online posting technical comments as Jenna on October 4, 2058."

"A posting to the Journal of Artificial Intelligence, Volume 23, Issue 5."

"You were incorrect, by the way, but you corrected it and amplified your comment with a compilation of information from three other journals a week later," Kent said. "There are five of us with eidetic memories in the United States and about twenty others spread around the world. One is your grandfather but there may be a sixth individual who disappeared shortly before the time of your birth. It's possible he has returned with the same personality signature but unique experiences in the interim. I've got a hypothesis as to who he is."

"He is my father. I will keep the circumstances to myself until we get to know each other."

"Of course. So, you want to build an artificial human?"

"Yes. HumanAI Corp and my grandfather have created virtual doctors, tutors, actors, and assistants," Jennifer said. "We believe that virtual humans can alleviate the doctor shortage."

"Dr. Ami wants to make house calls."

"Yes, and I want to be able to watch a sunset standing next to Sami, my virtual assistant. I believe that androids will become a reality soon and I feel that JennaTech can be the leader. I want to go over the challenges that you faced before you..."

"Before I quit, gave up, folded like a cheap suit, and so on."

"Failure is only the opportunity to more intelligently begin again."

"Henry Ford," Kent said.

"How close did you get?"

"The challenge of creating a self-sufficient artificial human is like a second version of the Turing Test. HumanAI and Alexandra Waring passed the first test by creating a sentient intelligence that could communicate in a way that was indistinguishable from their fellow humans. The second version of the Turing Test is to create an autonomous physical individual who can walk into a room and be indistinguishable and unidentifiable as an android."

"How far did you get?"

"The first major challenge was the face and head. We could never develop a model with truly human facial features. Our latest model walked into a gathering, and everyone looked immediately. They knew she was artificial.

"Secondly, she was dumb as a post. We could never get across the knowledge and wisdom gap. The artificial intelligence that will fit into the human brain bucket is just not capable."

"Can that be overcome?" Jennifer said.

"I believe that it can, but it will take fifty to five hundred years."

"What other problems did you face?"

"Manual dexterity. Robotics has come a long way, but they still cannot compete with our opposing thumbs. I almost feel sympathy when I see an android struggling to reach into their pockets for their car keys."

"What about power?"

"We've gone as far as batteries will take us," Kent said. "Our androids still have to plug in at night."

"What about the Laws of Robotics?"

"Asimov pretty much had it right when he wrote the first law: 'A robot may not injure a human being or, through inaction, allow a human being to come to harm.' He was writing sci-fi a hundred years ago, so he didn't have to deal with practicalities. Google addressed that fifty years ago. Early AI was good at knowledge but poor at wisdom.

"The idea that a robot 'may not allow a human being to come to harm' implies wisdom. Using knowledge to invoke action is a chess game. A young boy learns from experience to anticipate the results of his actions in terms of how it might affect himself. A mature human anticipates the effects of his or her actions in terms of morality, relationships, productivity, and world politics."

"HumanAI Corp knew it would have to overcome that hurdle before the AI could pass the Turing Test. Dr. Waring gave us a lecture on the subject once," Jennifer said. "My favorite quote is 'Knowledge becomes wisdom when experience becomes the teacher.'"

"So that's where we are at FutureBotics. We're selling our production androids as home appliances, fast food employees, and sex toys," Kent said. "You can guess that the latter is our most lucrative field."

"I've got some ideas. May I order one of your models and evaluate it? JennaTech will respect and properly license all of your patents."

"Of course, and I look forward to hearing of your successes. And failures."

"I look forward to meeting you someday."

"Good luck."

THE ROOM RETURNED to the ready room layout. Jennifer looked at Sami. "Order their most advanced model. Let's see how far they got."

"Are the problems insurmountable?" Sami asked.

"Nope. I see workarounds on all of the problems he mentioned," Jennifer said. "We're going to watch a sunset together soon."

Sami smiled. "You and your vision thing."

7

Jennifer got to the Calabasas Tennis Club on Thursday in time for Kalinda's first singles match. She struggled but dispatched the weaker opponent 6-4.

"Kalinda plays down to weaker players," Tayla said. Tayla was coaching Kalinda and several other players at the camp. "She doesn't play with passion."

"One down, three to go," Kalinda said as she came off the court.

"K'da, you're going to have to up your game for this next player. You need to have the passion thing," Tayla said.

"Hey, coach, you said that these tournaments are for fun."

"What Tayla is saying is that winning is a lot more fun than losing," Jennifer said.

"Don't worry, sisters. I intend to have as much fun as I can have. I'm going to win this tournament."

Tayla and Jennifer spoke together. "The vision thing?"

"You two seem to be obsessed with this 'vision thing,'" Kalinda said. "I'm just really good at athletics. During the clinic, I've learned my opponents, the game, and how to beat them."

"You've got an hour-and-a-half before the quarters. Grab something to eat and rest," Tayla said.

The girls walked over to the food tables. Jennifer and Tayla prepared small sandwiches and Kalinda built a three-layer monster before she went to a table with her friends.

"Tennis comes naturally for Kalinda, she eats way more than me, and she doesn't practice hard," Tayla said.

"And she's better than you were at this age," Jennifer said. "And you're a bit jealous?"

"Somethin' like that," Tayla said. "I've always had to work harder, be careful how I ate, and study three hours a night, and I didn't have any friends until I met you."

"Kalinda spent half her life on a starship with no friends, lost her mother, and then her home. She's making up for the fun times we both had," Jennifer said. "And she has an excellent tennis coach."

"There is that." Tayla looked around. "Where did Kalinda go?"

"The Beach Volleyball Pit."

Kalinda was covered in sand and sweat, diving and spiking, and laughing and screaming.

"She'll be exhausted. She won't be able to lift her racquet."

"Back off, mom," Jennifer said. "Isn't that her next opponent, Brett, on the other side of the net."

"I guess she does know what she's doing."

Brett and Kalinda, fresh off of a volleyball war, faced off in the round of eight.

At the first crossover, Brett led 3-0. "K'da, I guess your plan to tire me out didn't work," Brett said.

"No, I wanted to make you overconfident," Kalinda said.

"How's that workin' out for you?"

In the bleachers, a concerned Tayla said, "She's gonna get killed."

"I've seen that look before. Don't sweat it, mom."

"Quit calling me that."

"Quit chewing on that towel."

Tayla put the towel down.

Kalinda served, and the kids in the stands said, "Pop."

"Did you teach her that pop?" Jennifer asked.

Jennifer saw Tayla's pouty lip.

BRETT HAD to go wide for the forehand return which hung high over the net and Kalinda placed an easy volley in the open court. Kalinda put the second serve right down the middle on the line. Brett watched the ace go by.

Kalinda's opponent returned a second serve, and they traded groundies.

Brett hit a winner down the line, 15-30, then Kalinda served to Brett's backhand. Kalinda charged the net for a successful serve-and-volley winner. Kalinda served at 40-30. The ball popped up in front of Brett who hit an error long.

"Was THAT..." Jennifer said.

"It took her a whole hour to learn the kick serve," Tayla said.

THE NEXT GAME WAS HARD-FOUGHT, but Kalinda broke Brett's serve, and the rout was on. Brett won one more game, but Kalinda won the set and the match 6-4. They came to the net, shook hands, and hugged.

"Still friends?" Kalinda said.

"Still friends," Brett said. "Will you teach me the kick serve?"

"Sure."

"GOOD MATCH," Jennifer said.

"Thanks."

"You recovered well from 0-3," Tayla said.

"I knew how good she was and how much energy she had," Kalinda said. "That's why I took her to the volleyball pits."

"So that was why you beat her?" Tayla looked like a lover scorned.

"And you taught me the kick. Thanks, Coach."

Tayla smiled.

"Your dad is going to pick you up at our house," Jennifer said.

"Can we stop for pizza on the way? Te'pa said I'd have time to do some waves before dinner."

"Do you ever stop eating?"

"I need my nutrition. Gravity is higher on Earth."

"And you love pizza," Tayla said.

"I love pizza," Kalinda said.

FRIDAY'S SEMI-FINAL began at ten a.m. Tayla arrived an hour earlier and hit with Kalinda. Kalinda was taking the court against Mila, another girl whom Tayla coached over the summer.

"Mila has a strong forehand but only an average backhand. And she has a strong kick serve," Tayla said. "If you see the kick, step into it and catch it on the rise. You may not be able to time it at first, but I think you can learn it and beat her. The good news is she hasn't seen a good kick serve. But you have some variety. Mila is a one trick pony."

"I got this, coach."

"I know. Just don't be overconfident."

"My te'ma said there's no such thing as too much confidence, only too little performance."

"Go get 'em, champ."

Not yet, Kalinda thought. *Two more matches.*

. . .

They flipped a coin, and Mila served first. Kalinda saw the racket drop behind Mila's back to prepare for the kick serve.

Kalinda stepped in to receive the ball on a short hop but caught it too soon and hit into the net.

Mila retimed her advance, but this time, Kalinda struck it too high and hit it long.

At 30-0, Kalinda faced Mila's second serve which was surprisingly slow and hit a forehand winner up the line, 30-15. Kalinda continued to struggle with her own serve game but won twice for 2-2.

On Mila's next serve, Kalinda returned two of Mila's serves but lost the game. She looked at Tayla and nodded her head.

"She's got it," Tayla said. Jennifer nodded.

At 3-3, Kalinda attacked Mila's serve effectively. At 30-40, Mila was able to deliver her strongest serve of the match. Kalinda timed her backhand perfectly off the bounce into Mila's body for the break of serve.

Kalinda again won her serve. Mila was serving at 3-5, but the spectators could see her heart wasn't in it. Kalinda again broke her to win the match.

They shook hands at the net. "You've got a good serve," Kalinda said.

"Thanks, but watch out, Jordyn will try to get in your head," Mila said. "Good match."

"That was your best match ever," Tayla said

"I know, coach, but Jordyn is the best player in camp. She has the kick serve, but it varies. She has a good forehand and backhand."

"You're right. The final will be a tough match," Tayla said.

"But she never leaves the back line," Jennifer said. "She never comes to the net. Get her out of the comfort zone."

"Drop shots?" Kalinda said.

"Give it a try, K'da," Tayla said. "Now, grab some food and relax.

No volleyball this time. Jordyn doesn't think or do anything but tennis."

Kalinda mimicked the grumpy cat face. "Yes, coach."

Kalinda went to the sandwich table and stacked a huge sandwich.

"I could never eat like that," Tayla said.

"It's the high gravity." Jennifer winked.

THE TWO PLAYERS came to the net for the coin flip for the Camp Championship.

"You're toast, alien," Jordyn said with a sneer.

She's afraid, Kalinda thought. *Te'ma said, 'When a superior competitor demonstrates fear, feed the fear.'* "May the Warrior Gods of Hoclarth choose the most valiant competitor," Kalinda said with a stoic stare.

Jordyn's eyes got large. Kalinda stared right back.

Kalinda served. Jordyn returned. It was power against power as they traded groundstrokes. And then Kalinda dropped a soft shot that fell five feet beyond the net, Jordyn charged. Kalinda charged. Jordyn was able to hit a lame duck across the net. Kalinda delivered a backhand volley into the empty court. Jordyn gave a fearful look at Kalinda who returned a disciplined, passionate stare in return.

The two competitors traded power and games. With Jordyn serving at 2-3 and 30-all, Kalinda won another drop shot and they faced each other at the net. Kalinda could see the fear building in Jordyn.

Jordyn missed her first serve and Kalinda attacked her second. Jordyn hit the return into the net, and Kalinda broke. That was all she needed. She won the match and the championship 6-4.

At the net, Jordyn said "I'm sorry I called you an alien."

"My mother would be offended."

"Tell your mom I'm sorry."

"My te'ma died in battle defending a planet," Kalinda said.

Jordyn's eyes got huge. "But she would accept your apology. Let's be friends." They hugged.

Kalinda received hugs from her father and her grandparents who came for the final match.

"Way to go, champ," Tayla said. "What did you say to Jordyn at the beginning? It looked serious."

"Jordyn tried to get into my head. I remembered something my te'ma said."

"Looks like it worked."

"It did," Kalinda said. "Can we get pizza?"

"Omigod," Tayla said.

They all went to pizza.

8

The Star Squad went to dinner that evening and ended up at the Masing mansion.

"Let's watch *The Empire Strikes Back*," Jennifer said.

"I thought you said you hated that movie," David said.

"Things have changed since then," Tayla said.

"Search your feelings. You know it to be true," Riley said.

"It's different now. I've got my dad back, so it doesn't bring up bad memories."

When they entered the virtual Ohio Theatre, David fired up the antique popcorn machine. The four got their tickets and walked around the lobby admiring the two new movie posters, *Galaxy Warrior* and *The Pirate Returns* featuring the four members of the Star Squad.

"It's getting real, girlfriend," Tayla said each looked at their respective posters.

• • •

AFTER THE MOVIE, the squad returned to the recreation room. The *Brilliant* simulator still dominated the room but, in the center, Jennifer noticed a new item in the center of the room.

"You got a steveLearn!"

I contacted HumanAI Corp," David said. They set me up with a state-of-the-art installation."

"You'll love it until I smoke your tail on the F-52 sim."

"Is it as good as the one on *Brilliant*?"

"Almost," Jennifer said. "On *Brilliant*, I've got to wear a G-Suit."

"Really?" Riley said. "How did you pull that off?"

"Ani and I rewired the artificial gravity to localize it on the steve-Learn. Dandy hates it because I have to lock him out of the Captain's Ready Room."

"How many Gs?" Riley asked.

"I made a ten G turn, and I didn't lose my Frappuccino."

"What maneuvers?" David said.

"The simulator has many attack scenarios. I read an old Air Force Manual and found the most valuable information."

"Like what?" David asked.

"The basic priorities: Maintain aircraft control, never hit the ground, never hit anything in the air, never run out of fuel, and never let anything shot from the ground or air hit your airplane."

"That's obvious."

"Yeah, until the ground leaves a dent in your forehead and ruins your whole day," Jennifer said.

"Are you going to be on *Brilliant* tomorrow?" David said.

Jennifer nodded. "See if you can get airborne. I will be aloft around noon."

The four hugged and then parted for the evening.

9

The smell of bacon in the morning woke Jennifer at nine a.m. She dressed, took Pugsley for a short walk, and then came into the kitchen where Sheila and Allen were enjoying breakfast. Jennifer went straight to the coffee machine and obtained her Double-shot Caramel Frappuccino that she requested on the way home from her walk.

"Good morning," Jennifer said.

"What are your plans today?" Allen asked.

Jennifer gathered a plateful and sat. "I'm going into Tovar to do some script updates then I'll spend some stick time on the Bobcat Sim."

"Do you ever spend time with your boyfriend?" Sheila said.

"We're going to meet at 12,000 feet over the Anza Borrego Desert around noon."

"Does Jack know that you spend most of your waking hours in his ready room?" Sheila said.

"We have an understanding," Jennifer said. "I save his *Star-Cruiser*, and he lets me hang out there."

"And your cat?" Sheila said.

"Dandy keeps mice and small animals from coming aboard *Brilliant*."

"I've got a gadget to sell you that keeps away elephants," Allen said.

"There aren't any elephants around here."

"See? It works."

"Dandy Lion keeps me company."

"And holds up work around the studio while people hold him," Sheila said.

"That's a feature, not a bug."

"Can you be home by 4:30? Anthen and Kalinda are coming over, and we're barbecuing."

"May I invite the squad?"

"I planned on it."

"Thanks, Mom. I've got to go," Jennifer said. "I'll see you this afternoon."

JENNIFER RETURNED TO HER WORKSPACE.

"The script is proofed and clean," Sami said. "I notice that you toned down the part of Azolyn. Her screen test is Monday."

"I've got mixed feelings. I don't know how K'da will do," Jennifer said.

"I know that she will do well Monday," Sami said.

"You've got the vision thing, now?"

"I happen to know your sister well. Kalinda has the same passion for excellence that you've got," Sami said. "She can adapt to a steep learning curve, and she won't give up."

"You're right, but I'm going to send her this script. If she looks like an actor, I'll beef up her part," Jennifer said.

"Message to Kalinda: K'da, here is the Galaxy Warrior script. Your lines will be printed out but will come from here. Good Luck."

"Message sent with an attachment," Sami said.

48

"Thanks, Sami. Where's Dandy? He cannot be in this room when I fly the simulator."

"He has been sighted at various places on the Tovar lot panhandling for attention from tourists," Sami said. "You're going to practice on the F-52?"

"David is going to join up around noon."

"Good luck. It might get crowded up there." Jennifer gave Sami a curious look. Sami winked.

JENNIFER STOOD outside a circle in the center of the Captain's Ready Room. The circle was the focus of the most complex simulations on steveLearn. "Ani, initiate F-52U Sim with gravity." A full-size segment of the F-52 that included the cockpit and the clear bubble canopy appeared in the center of the room.

"Bobcat Sim is up," Ani said. "Chief Petty Officer Sam Wilson is your plane captain. Have a good flight."

Jennifer donned her flight suit, took her flight helmet in her right hand and entered the circle and found herself in the desert near El Centro, California.

After viewing the clear air to the horizon, Jennifer walked around her aircraft for preflight. She checked the landing gear, the instrumentation, and most importantly, the flight surfaces.

As she was finishing her walk-around, Chief Wilson approached wearing the woodland green and tan camos. His blonde hair matched his yellow eyes.

"The aircraft looks ready, chief," Jennifer said. "Do I have enough fuel?"

"Seriously, ma'am. The Bobcat has twin Scott Reactors. She'll go around the word on a liter of distilled water."

"I feel the need for speed, Chief," Jennifer said.

"Speed, she's got," Chief Wilson said. "Point the nose at the sun, slam the throttles against the firewall, and this Bobcat will reach Mach three-point-six at twenty thousand feet."

"This aircraft looks brand new," Jennifer said.

"She just got here," Chief Wilson said. "Still has that new car smell."

She handed her helmet to the plane captain and mounted the ladder, verified that the ejection seat was safe and locked, climbed in, connected the safety harness, then attached the compressed air line to her G-suit.

Chief Wilson climbed up next to her, handed her the helmet, and verified the air line was connected. "You may take some G's. Your G-suit will keep your blood in your head where you need it, so you don't black out. You're all set for pre-flight." He climbed down the ladder and pulled it clear of the aircraft.

Switches, dials, and display panels surrounded her. Between her knees was the control stick with numerous buttons and toggles and at her left hand was the throttle. Front and center was the heads-up-display and above her shoulders was the bubble canopy which allowed her to swivel her head in every direction to see above and around her aircraft.

"Good morning, Bobcat," Jennifer said.

"Good morning, Pilot," the Combat Artificial Tactician said. "Login?"

"Recognize Jendroid, authorization Dandy Lion," Jennifer said.

"Welcome aboard," Bobcat said.

"Please close the canopy." The plexiglass bubble lowered, sealing her in the pressurized compartment. Jennifer inhaled. *Pine scent?* she thought. *Good job, Chief.*

"El Centro Tower verifies your flight plan is approved," Bobcat said.

"Very well," Jennifer said. "Spin up the turbines and verify reactors available to full power."

She listened and felt the turbines begin to rotate, pass through the resonant frequency, and come up to speed.

"Reactors are nominal for turbine and ramjet power, Jendroid," Bobcat said. "All Checkoffs complete. Propulsion on throttle control. Your tail number is twelve. The aircraft is ready," Bobcat said.

"El Centro ground, Jendroid twelve, F-52 uniform, request taxi runway two-six for VFR departure to Superstition Mountain exercise area," Jennifer said.

"Jendroid twelve, taxi two-six, squawk 3743, below fifteen thousand," El Centro ground control said.

"Jendroid twelve." Jennifer rotated her head in all directions to verify the area was clear. She then nudged the throttle forward and followed the yellow lines. During a full stop at the runway boundary, Jennifer did final checks on the flight control surfaces.

"El Centro Tower, Jendroid twelve holding short Runway two-six, ready for takeoff."

"Jendroid twelve, Cleared for takeoff Runway two-six, after departure turn right course 3-1-0, do not exceed Mach .8 in the transit corridor.

"Jendroid twelve."

Jennifer nudged the throttles, and the Bobcat moved forward. She turned to position the aircraft on the centerline of Runway two-six headed almost directly west. Once more she scanned the immediate area and checked the radar.

She set the brakes and moved the throttle to Full Military Power.

She felt the rumbling and vibration. She released the brakes and for the first time felt the artificial gravity created by *Brilliant* pushing her into the seat

"V1," Bobcat said. She was now committed to the air.

"Vr." Jennifer eased back on the stick, and the nose rose twenty degrees above the horizon.

"V2." The vibration of the rolling wheels disappeared. The aircraft accelerated at a higher rate.

"Gear up," Jennifer said.

"Landing Gear retracted," Bobcat said.

"Jendroid twelve, radar contact, say altitude," Air Traffic Control said.

"Climbing through eight hundred feet, Jendroid twelve."

"Jendroid twelve, turn right to 3-1-0. Do not exceed six-hundred-fifty knots. Proceed to Superstition Mountain VFR. Good Hunting.

"Course 3-1-0. Jendroid twelve." She looked north-northwest toward the exercise area.

She set the throttle so that the rate of climb was three thousand feet per minute. Three more minutes and Jennifer was at Ten Thousand feet. Jennifer set the throttles to six-hundred knots for the four-minute flight.

"You are now within the training area," Bobcat said. "Do not exceed Mach one-point-seven. Stay below fifteen thousand feet."

"Thanks, Bobcat," she said. She pulled back on the throttles and set the speed at four-hundred. She leveled the aircraft at eight thousand feet. "I'm going to execute a barrel roll. Please record and evaluate."

A barrel roll is essentially a loop and a roll combined. *Let's see if I can do this right the first time,* she thought. Jennifer focused on the Artificial Horizon Indicator. *To do a barrel roll, I have to roll three-sixty and return to the same altitude and heading.* She remembered it as a quick maneuver when she performed it in a Franklin Biplane simulator.

Jennifer looked forward and selected a peak on the horizon. She looked over the right wing and focused on a point on the ground and pulled the control stick back rapidly to pitch up the nose. She pressed the right rudder. The right wing stalled causing the fighter to rotate clockwise on the long axis. She spotted the reference point to her right. As the aircraft rolled, she reversed the rudder so that she was full left rudder when the artificial horizon showed that she was inverted. She felt the effect of two-and-a-half times her weight. At the same time, she was pushing the control stick forward to keep constant altitude. As she approached level flight, she eased the rudder and the stick back to center. Her airspeed bled to two-fifty. *Got it in one.*

"Bobcat, replay and comment."

The display switched to a 3D view from over her left shoulder. She saw her F-52 painted squadron grey rotate 360 degrees right and freeze at straight and level. She saw the wings waggle as she overshot the roll by 10 degrees. She was 14 feet above her original altitude.

"Very nice, Jendroid," Bobcat said. "In the fleet, they allow no more than a fifteen-degree overshoot and a twenty-foot altitude variation. The Blue Angels specify five and five for their team."

Jennifer performed the maneuver three more times. The last two met the Blue Angels specs.

Let's see how many G's I can pull on a turn. She pushed the throttle to the limit and immediately felt four G's of acceleration. She felt her G-suit inflate. She turned the stick to the right, and the fighter rotated ninety degrees. She then pulled back on the stick and began a high G turn. She maintained altitude with the rudder and continued until she returned to her original heading. She then rotated the aircraft level.

"How many G's, Bob?" Jennifer said.

"You maxed out at 8.7, near the auto-stop," Bobcat said. "This aircraft won't exceed 9 G's when a human is aboard."

"I felt it." Jennifer was sweating and on the verge of nausea, but she recovered quickly.

"You've got company. A friendly F-52 has entered the training area."

"Please identify?"

"Callsign Moviestar," Bobcat said.

She keyed her radio. "Hello, David."

"Hi, Jen," David said. "Out for a stroll?"

"Just a lazy afternoon," Jennifer responded. "Join up on my right wing. Let's do some formation flying. See if you can stay on my wing."

"I'm your best friend. Try and lose me."

Jennifer looked over her right shoulder and waved at David in the identical cockpit. She added throttle and pulled back on the stick. When she reached the top of the loop inverted, she rolled one-hundred eighty degrees to level flight. There was David on her left wing now.

"Immelmann," David said.

Jennifer then performed a barrel roll to the left pulling a forty-five-degree angle then depressing her left rudder. David did the same but bled speed to maintain spacing. He reversed the adjustment at inverted and wound up correctly placed on her left wing.

Let's see if he has been studying, Jennifer thought. She raised her right fist in the air.

David waggled his wings and did a smooth crossover to her right wing.

Jennifer banked one-hundred thirty-five degrees and then pulled back on the stick. David followed. She completed the one-hundred eighty-degree loop and then rolled back to level flight. David finished the Pitchback on her right wing.

"Take over lead, David," Jennifer said. Jennifer reduced the throttle gave up some altitude and then formed up on David's right wing.

"Stay with me, Jendroid," David said.

He rolled right and began a high-g turn. Jennifer saw the vapor that formed above David's wings. They returned to base course.

"Only 7.2 G's," Jennifer said. "I did 8.7 before you got here. Wait...mine count." David was in his recreation room near Castro Peak without artificial gravity.

David did a snap roll to inverted and pulled back on his stick. Jennifer followed on his left wing with a Split-S.

"Warning: two Bogies to your Southwest," Bobcat said. "Identify two F-52s squawking hostile. Range twenty miles. They're supersonic and will intercept in eighty seconds."

"What the hell?" David said.

"Callsigns?" Jennifer said.

"Callsigns Ani and Sami," Bobcat said.

"Sami said it might get crowded up here."

"Let's get some altitude," David said.

"Our hard ceiling is fifteen thousand." *Why does he ignore the rules?*

David pulled back on the stick and pushed the throttle to the stop and accelerated through Mach One vertical with Jennifer on his wing. He leveled at forty-two thousand feet at Mach 2.7 on an intercept course.

"Bandits will pass below and to your right," Bobcat said. Bobcat was now acting as Radar Intercept Officer for both David and Jennifer. "Recommend arming lasers."

"Let's kick some AI butt, Jennifer."

Both pilots raised the red cover and operated the master arming switch. *This is real now,* Jennifer thought.

"Bandits eight o'clock low," David said. "Break, break."

Jennifer rolled right and pulled. This time she felt all nine G's.

"I've got Bandit Two, Jen."

Following protocol, she scanned the skies for the leader as David pursued the trail bandit.

Ani was in Bandit One. She pulled up to her right and rolled to target David.

Jennifer interceded and fired a salvo of lasers that crossed Ani's nose. Bandit One pulled up to avoid the fire.

"I've got radar lock on Bandit two," David said. Just then, Sami pulled up and rolled. She deployed her air brakes and vertical thrusters and practically hung in the air as David passed beneath her. Now inverted, she cleaned up and pushed the throttles to the firewall and accelerated on David's tail.

"Commercial traffic at twelve o'clock low," David's Bobcat said. He rolled and turned to his right. It was right into Sami's gun sight.

Jennifer could only watch as she was occupied holding off Bandit One. She saw Sami's lasers. "Eject, David." She saw a clean chute.

Sami was below at her four o'clock, so she rolled and accelerated to get Sami into her angle of fire. She heard the tone of the radar lock, and she pressed the fire button. She saw an explosion and fire and yes, an ejection seat.

"Splash one personal assistant," Jennifer said.

She immediately felt Ani on her six. She banked left into a Chandelle and reversed her course at a higher altitude.

Ani was unable to establish a pursuit position.

Jennifer rolled and pulled back her stick to gain altitude and bleed speed. She gave Ani a glance of her belly then rolled and pulled the stick back to chase. Jennifer heard tone for a split second, but Ani maneuvered away to gain the advantage. The dog fight continued for another three minutes with neither pilot able to gain the advantage.

"Jendroid, shall we call it a draw?"

"Sure, Ani. Form up on me and let's head for the barn," Jennifer said.

Ani took the wingman position on Jennifer's right.

"Bobcat, plot a course for a carrier approach to runway two-six at one thousand feet."

"Course laid in," Bobcat said.

"Engage. I'll take the aircraft on the approach." Jennifer took two deep breaths, raised her visor and drank some water. She felt the sweat pooling in her flight suit.

"How'd I do, Ani?"

"You used all of the air combat maneuvers in an effective and timely manner. Your vision thing allows you to have excellent situational awareness on all three axes."

"With the hop coming up in a Blue Angels F-52, I want to show off a little."

"You'll do well," Ani said. "You just fought to a stalemate against my library of one-hundred thirty years of dogfights."

"Thanks, Ani," Jennifer said. "El Centro Traffic, Jendroid 12, two plane formation on approach, runway two-six. Request Clearance."

"Jendroid 12 formation, El Centro, You are cleared to land Runway two-six. The traffic pattern is clear."

"Jendroid 12."

"On approach. Three miles to the apron," Bobcat said.

"I've got the aircraft," Jennifer said. She lined up one-quarter mile right of the runway on course 2–6–0. She looked left. With the tower directly over her left wing, she said, "Break, Break."

Jennifer slowly turned her fighter to 0-8-0. She leveled her aircraft. "Deploy flaps. Extend landing gear. Perform final landing checks." The noise level rose, and the plane became sluggish as it slowed. She pushed the throttle forward while descending to six hundred feet.

With the apron over her left shoulder, she turned final and lined up with the center line of the runway. Jennifer pulled the throttle back to idle.

"Three hundred...," Bobcat said. "Two hundred...One hundred... Crossing the apron...Forty... Twenty...Ten"

Jennifer pulled back on the stick to flare the aircraft and bleed speed. She softly touched down.

"Jendroid 12, El Centro. Taxi to the flight line, follow the director." She saw her display indicate a GPS-like map.

When parked, she shut down the systems.

"Secure the aircraft and thanks for a nice afternoon, Bobcat."

"A good day is one that ends with a safe landing," Bobcat said. The canopy rose.

"End simulation."

"You are loose. Please stand up," Sami said.

When she stood, she found herself in the Captain's ready room on *StarCruiser Brilliant*.

"Thanks, Sami."

"It's two-thirty. You've got time for a shower and a nap," Sami said. "You deserve it since you splashed your personal assistant."

Jennifer's eyes went up. "I'm sorry, Sami. It was my first victory."

"Is that all I am?"

"You're my friend and my sister, and I couldn't do what I do without you."

"It's okay. Enjoy the sunset."

Time to shut up, Jennifer thought. She turned toward the Captain's head.

10

When she arrived home, she realized she was the last to arrive. David looked depressed. They hugged. "I didn't listen," David said.

"It was a simulator, not a three-billion-dollar fighter," Jennifer said.

They went into the kitchen. "Hi, Mom. Hi, Dad. Hi, Dad," Jennifer said.

Allen and Anthen looked at each other.

"I went eleven years without a dad. Now I've got two," Jennifer said. "You two fight it out."

Everyone laughed.

Jennifer looked over Anthen's shoulder. "Whatcha makin'?"

"I searched the web for stores in Koreatown, Little Tehran, Chinatown, and Olvera Street but I found the ingredients," Anthen said. "We're having a Hoclarth dessert. It's Kalinda's favorite."

"Where is the rug rat?" David said.

Jennifer slugged him on the arm.

"Ouch!"

"Be careful. You may have some scenes with her."

"Can she act?"

"We're testing her Monday."

"Good call."

They went out to the patio. Riley was tending the grill, and Tayla was tossing the Caesar. Kalinda was picking Riley's brain.

"I understand that an Electromagnetic Pulse comes from the explosion of a fission bomb," Kalinda said. "But how does the Dazzler create a ray that goes fifty kilometers?"

"The Dazzler is similar to the Plasma Energy weapons. It's tuned to disrupt the electronics. There are multiple emitters spaced all around the hull to form the beam."

"Like the black rectangles I saw on pictures of old navy ships. Phased array radar, I think?"

"You're right," Riley said. "We can tighten or loosen the beam to adjust them."

"Hi, everyone," Jennifer said.

"Hi, girlfriend," Tayla said. "Can you help with the table?"

"K'da, are you ready for Monday?"

"Yes, sister. I read the script. You cut most of the scenes where I appeared in the book."

Jennifer's jaw dropped and then she recovered. "Do a good audition, and I will put them back and add more.

David whispered, "Is she human?"

"Only half," Jennifer said.

THEY WERE at the table on the patio half-way through their steaks.

"Did this animal die honorably, te'pa?"

"Not exactly," Anthen said.

"An animal with meat this tasty deserves to die in combat."

Tayla quickly interrupted. "David, I heard that you crashed and burned today...Literally."

"I went too high, and I had to swerve to avoid a commercial jetliner," David said. "Sami got in a lucky shot."

"You were toast and Sami was about to butter it," Jennifer said. "At least, she set me up for an easy shot."

"Did you get Ani?" Riley asked.

"We called it a draw."

"I'm looking forward to some stick time on an F-52," Riley said.

"Stick time?" Tayla said.

"On Thursday before the Air Show, we're trading rides with the Blue Angels. We four are getting hops in the two-seater Bobcats," Jennifer said. "Then we take them up in *Brilliant*."

"Cool," Tayla said. "So that's why you two have been spending so much time on the simulator."

Jennifer lowered her gaze and glanced at David.

"May I fly, too?" Kalinda said.

"We are riding Fat Albert," Anthen said. "Then we are staying overnight to see the surfing prelims on Friday."

"I hear I get to try out my acting lessons on you Monday," Tayla said. "Are you ready for your closeup?"

"Yes, if my sister doesn't edit out all my lines."

"Your sister is not only the screenwriter but the executive producer," Sheila said. "There's something you will learn about Hollywood. The screenwriter giveth and the bean counter taketh away."

The whole table laughed. Kalinda didn't get it but followed along.

"K'da, you need to bring a change of clothes, Monday," Jennifer said. "The director wants you to work out with the martial arts coordinator to see how hard you will have to train for the fight scenes."

Kayla turned to her father. "Te'pa, what are martial arts?"

"Serving Tal'qid."

"Ahh."

"Serving what?" Allen said.

"Hoclarth Martial Arts," Anthen said.

Tayla and Riley helped clear the plates.

Sheila got everyone's attention. "Anthen, you said you created a dessert?"

"Yes." Anthen went into the kitchen and brought out a tray with a large sheet cake and a bottle of liquid next to it.

"Manqlid." Kalinda's eyes brightened. "My favorite. Thanks, te'pa."

"Flat cake in pan with no icing. Exciting," David said.

"David, why don't you do the honors?" Anthen said. "Just poor the Manqa juice on top of the dessert."

David poured the liquid over the cake. For a moment, nothing happened. He stepped back when the pan began to emit noise and steam.

"What's that noise?" Tayla said. "Like the tones of a pipe organ."

To their amazement, they saw eight small multi-colored peaks grow from the white cake. For two minutes, the diners saw, heard, and smelled a symphony that concluded with a small mountain of sweet, creamy goodness, one for each sweet tooth.

"K'da, help me cut and serve." Kalinda grabbed the plates off the serving table and assisted her father in distributing each serving.

Jennifer smiled. "This looks amazing, Dad!"

"Now remember," Kalinda said. "After each bite, you must bow your head, touch your nose and hum to honor the Hoclarth gods."

"Kalinda!"

"Just kidding. I saw that on a Star Trek episode."

"Enjoy," Anthen said.

"This is amazing," Allen said. "You could make millions of dollars from this."

"I could, Allen, but that's the last of the Manqa juice."

AFTER THEY WERE DONE CLEANING up, Sheila asked Jennifer, "How do you think she'll do?"

"I'm a little worried about how young she is but every time I see her, she amazes me and shows more personality."

Just like every time I looked at you, my daughter, Sheila thought.

11

Jennifer arrived at *StarCruiser Brilliant* and performed a routine inspection on her way to the bridge. "Good morning, Ani."

"Good morning, First Officer," the Ani said. "The ship's cat is present in the ready room and has been fed and watered. The Engineer was aboard yesterday and performed some preventive maintenance and worked on the effects for the Miramar show. The ship is secure."

Jennifer finished her walk-through to check for problems, then settled into the Captain's Ready Room and saw Dandy on his pillow. "Hi, Dandy."

Since Jennifer was absent on Saturday, Dandy responded with a look of disdain. *And you are?* And then he strolled over and jumped up on her lap and established his domain by digging his claws into her thighs.

"Passive aggressive much, Dandy?" Jennifer said. "I'm sorry I didn't come yesterday."

Aren't I the most important thing in your life? He settled in and started his purring engine.

Jennifer looked up at the bulkhead as if the Artificial Navigation

Interface was a part of every molecule of *Brilliant*. "Ani, can we have a personal chat?"

"Of course, Jennifer."

"Could you give me your quick biography?"

"Sure," Ani said. "When *Brilliant* arrived in this timeline, Navvy immersed himself in filmmaking. Holographic Tactile Virtual Reality was in its infancy, but he saw it as an essential part of the future of filmmaking. He also saw a bright future for Artificial Intelligence.

"The growth of HumanAI Corp was stalled at the time. Their AI Software and technology was more advanced than what *Brilliant* brought back from the future, but their processing power existed around a massive, but slow, supercomputer system. Navvy offered miniaturization and enhanced processing power in exchange for an ownership stake. By the time HumanAI Corp went public in 2028, he and Jack owned a five percent share of the company. That share has grown larger with the technology from *Brilliant* and innovations that he has developed."

"And you?" Jennifer said.

"I became sentient in 2027 when Navvy consolidated all of the AI on *Brilliant* with HumanAI software. I'm also resident in the back-office systems on the Tovar Studio lot."

"Do you have an avatar?"

"I do. At first, I appeared in Navvy's offices," Ani said. "You're aware of the complex relationship Navvy has with Kathy and Hanna?"

"I am," Jennifer said.

"I quickly discovered that four's a crowd, so I learned that everyone was more comfortable if I only presented my audio self."

"Do you ever exist as a complete virtual avatar?"

"I visit with Dr. Ami often," Ani said. "When we're alone on *Brilliant*."

"I would be honored if you joined me as a virtual when it's just us on the ship."

"I appreciate that. Would you like caffeine?"

"Always, thanks."

She signaled Sami. "Call up the latest Galaxy Warrior script."

There was a tone at the door. "Enter," Jennifer said.

Ani entered the space with coffee. Jennifer looked up. "It's hard to connect your virtual avatar with your voice, but it fits." Ani was not turn-heads-on-the-street beautiful, but Jennifer could see that her beauty captured one's attention. Ani's blonde hair fell to her shoulders with variations of color and curl that framed her face but did not distract. Her alabaster skin was not perfect but interesting. Her yellow eyes reflected knowledge and wisdom. But it was her amazing smile that would take her image viral on social media. "You're a lovely lady, Ani."

"Thanks for the compliment and here's your Double-shot Caramel Frappuccino caffeine bomb," Ani said.

"Thanks," Jennifer said. "With your looks, you should get out more."

"Unfortunately, my presence is limited to *Brilliant* and the Tovar offices. Although, I can visit via HoloPads."

"Sami, can you go full virtual?"

"Be right there," Sami said.

The door tone sounded.

"Enter."

Sami entered. Her crimson hair was a shade darker than Jennifer's with the same high cheekbones. Her yellow eyes betrayed her virtual nature.

The two virtual humans sized each other up. "You're beautiful in person, Ani," Sami said.

"Thank you so much. You look like Jennifer's older sister with all of her beauty as well," Ani said.

"Quite a compliment," Sami said.

"You know why we're here, right," Sami said.

"The sunset?" Ani said.

"You two have discussed this?" Jennifer asked.

"We three, actually," Sami said.

"Dr. Ami?"

Again, the door tone sounded, and Dr. Ami entered, "I heard my name mentioned." Ami carried herself like the beautiful TV doctor she was.

"Come in, Ami," Jennifer said.

The Artificial Medical Intelligence entered. "Good morning, everyone," Dr. Ami said. "Am I late for the mutual admiration society?"

"Okay, let's stipulate that we're all pretty good looking," Jennifer said. "Apparently, you three have discussed my idea of creating a physical presence," Jennifer said.

"Yes, we have. We feel that there are pros and cons," Ani said. "Dr. Ami?"

"It would make my life much easier," Dr. Ami said. "Right now, my rounds at Hollywood Methodist are limited to the locations covered by the HTVR projectors and of course, on the sound stage and aboard *Brilliant*. But it provides me a great excuse to avoid house calls."

"Ani, what are the numbers on an installation?"

"It costs three million dollars to provide access to five thousand square feet," Dr. Ami said. "Unfortunately, there is no economy of scale, so it costs twice as much for twice the access area."

"For full physical, I'm estimating a unit cost of two million dollars," Jennifer said. "Add to that the AI network cost that goes to HumanAI Corp."

"Physical Doctors would decrease the cost of Navvy's idea for Virtual Doctors."

"You need to come up with different branding to avoid that acronym," Jennifer said. "Sami, how do you feel about being physical?"

"Sis, I love sunsets. I'd love to travel around the world and see them first hand. You know, my romantic streak."

Jennifer saw the darting glance toward Ami. She also saw the furrowed brows on Ani. "You're the senior AI being here, Ani. What do you think?"

"The convention is that anytime we appear to the public, we must have yellow eyes," Ani said. "If I walk down Main Street in some midwestern town, I can predict the fear and hate when people see me. I don't want to be an other. I don't want to build another glass ceiling we have to break through so that people will accept us for who we are."

"And then there's the Singularity," Dr. Ami said. "Every time I achieve a breakthrough in medicine, every time Tovar premiers a new movie with a virtual character, every time you create a new app on the HoloPad, somebody writes an article about the coming technological singularity. Senator Curtwell has condemned me as a monster in every one of her stump speeches."

"That's the elephant in the room," Sami said. "If we're unleashed into the world, jobs will disappear, humans will no longer be at the top of the food chain, and the apocalypse will arrive."

"Dr. Ami, you are accepted at Hollywood Methodist, aren't you?" Jennifer asked.

"The children I treat accept me immediately," Dr. Ami said. "Their parents, not so much. I often see the fear in their eyes when I come into the room. The staff only accepts me begrudgingly because there's a doctor shortage."

"Some of the fears are reality based," Jennifer said. "Isaac Asimov started the argument with the Three Laws of Robotics. Then Google came up with a list: robots should not make things worse; robots should look at humans as mentors, and robots should know what they don't know. HumanAI Corp built on all of that. When they overcame the Turing Test, AI began learning through conversation and experience."

"After that, we overcame the knowledge and wisdom gap," Sami said. "Your friend's old saying, 'Knowledge becomes wisdom when experience becomes the teacher."

"I chatted with a Dr. Kent Gunn about that."

"Didn't he try to perfect a humaniform android?" Ani said.

"Yes, but he fell short in three areas," Jennifer said. "First, an android looks like an android. A human can tell the difference instantaneously."

"But we can overcome that with HTVR," Sami said.

"Correct," Jennifer said. "Secondly, Dr. Gunn could not achieve the manual dexterity of a human. That would be a problem for you, doctor. You could not perform surgery."

"HTVR might be the solution to the first two," Ani said. The others nodded.

"Miniaturization of the projectors," Dr. Ami said.

"The third problem is much more difficult," Jennifer said.

"Our AI is not portable," Sami said.

"Yes," Ani said. "We're dependent on large systems, at least larger than we are. We need to create a network with extremely high speed in remote places."

"Dr. Gunn estimated it would be anywhere from fifty to five hundred years before your processors would fit in your brain bucket," Jennifer said.

"So, I'll have to push your wheelchair out to watch a sunset with you," Sami said.

"Maybe," Jennifer said. "This meeting has been helpful. I need to chat with Navvy. Thanks for stopping by. This is still on my project list."

Sami and Ani stayed, and Dr. Ami left. "Another caffeine fix, first officer?" Ani said.

"You read my mind," Jennifer said.

"No, you picked up an empty cup eight times in the last thirteen minutes."

"It's a human thing, Ani," Jennifer said. "Sami, would you proof the script while I go to the head?"

"Sure, boss."

12

Tovar's above-the-line personnel gathered on a small set for Kalinda's screen test for *Galaxy Warrior*. The key observers sitting in labeled director's chairs included the head of the studio Navvy Kelrithian, producer Anthen Kelrithian, executive producer and screenwriter Jennifer Gallagher, producer Sheila Gallagher, and director Chris Cherry. Under the lights Tayla Mendoza, cast as Ayiiia, played opposite Kalinda Kelrithian, as Ayiiia's sister Azolyn. Unlike Chris Cherry and the crew members, each of the observers had a more personal connection to the candidate.

"What scene are we going to look at, Chris?" Anthen said.

"I want to see how they interact when Ayiiia returns after the death of their mother," Chris said.

Jennifer quickly turned her head. "My sister recently lost her mother. It may be too difficult for her to go through that again."

"Your sister is strong," Anthen said. "She's Hoclarth. She'll handle the task."

"Yes, dad, but…"

Kalinda heard the exchange. "I can do the scene. You gave me the script to read. I can handle it."

"Jen, could you handle this when you were ten," Sheila said.

"Yes, Mom."

"Give your sister a chance," Sheila said. As producer, she took charge to move the process along. "Chris?"

"Here's the script, ladies," Chris said.

"I DON'T NEED IT, sir. I read the script, and I know it," Kalinda said

"Eidetic memory?" Chris said.

Kalinda nodded.

"Tayla?"

"I got this."

"Kalinda, are you familiar with the signals that I will give?"

"Yes, sir."

"Good job, and good luck to both of you," Chris said. "Places."

The two girls moved to their spots. Kalinda stood in her place in the small room with a table in the center. The room appeared to be old but decorated with alien relics of a warlike culture. Tayla stood outside the door.

"Quiet on the set." There was a pause as Chris looked around. "Roll and record." Chris glanced at the shooter who nodded.

The second assistant camera operator stood in front of the camera. "Galaxy warrior scene 12A, Take one." CLAP!

"Action!"

Tayla opened the door and entered. "Azolyn?" Ayiiia said.

"Sister," Azolyn said. Her voice was almost monotone. "Our mother is dead."

The scene progressed in a stilted and almost mechanical way. At times, the observers audibly groaned.

Azolyn spoke her final line, "I will avenge our mother's killer. I will slay the Grotchka."

Chris announced half-heartedly, "Cut! Thank you, ladies."

The girls exited to the green room.

"Navvy?" Chris asked.

He shook his head.

"I guess she's not our girl," Chris said. "Sorry, Jennifer. I know that you had high hopes."

Sheila walked around her chair and put her arm around Jennifer.

"Chris, can we do one more take?" Anthen said. "Let me talk to my daughter."

"You sure, Anthen?" Chris said.

Anthen nodded.

"Reset and take five." The crew took the necessary actions and then stood down.

Anthen went to the green room where Tayla and Kalinda sat next to each other on the couch. "Sorry," Tayla said.

"Go out on set," Anthen said. "I'm going to chat with Kalinda."

Anthen took the seat vacated by Tayla. "How do you think you did?"

"I sucked, but I think I can do better."

"That's a fair assessment. You can do better," Anthen said. "Daughter, you are Hoclarth."

"I am Hoclarth."

"I loved your te'ma, and I know the Hoclarth well. The Hoclarth do not show their feelings or emotions."

"We do not have feelings."

"Yes, you do, daughter, but you're going to have to search for them," Anthen said. "As an actor in this movie, you're playing a character who has strong feelings."

She shut her eyes and searched. "I think I get it."

"You might have to shed tears. Do you know how to cry?"

"That thing in the movies where water comes out of the eyes of the female?"

"Yes, have you ever done it?"

"I have practiced it."

"How?"

"I watch this movie called *The Notebook*," Kalinda said.

"I know that movie. It's not only females who cry," Anthen said. "Would you like to try the scene again?"

"Yes, te'pa." Kalinda looked at him sadly. "May I pretend that it's my te'ma who died?"

"Can you handle that?"

"I think so."

"That's called method acting. It's a good technique. Are you ready?" Anthen said.

"Yes, but I've got a question." Kalinda tilted her head. "Do I have to say the words in the script as written? I remember a scene from a movie about a young male who was good at math."

"It's your screen test. Go ahead and improvise."

Anthen and Kalinda exited the green room. Anthen returned to his chair while Kalinda spoke to Tayla. Anthen watched for a moment until the two girls resumed their places. Anthen turned to Chris, "She's ready."

Chris nodded. "Quiet on the set." He looked around. "Roll and record." The cinematographer nodded.

"Galaxy warrior scene 12A, take two." CLAP!

"Action!"

Tayla opened the door and entered. "Azolyn?" Ayiiia said.

"Sister," Azolyn said. Her voice almost monotone and then she looked away.

"Az?"

Azolyn's face broke and then she rushed into her sister's arms. "Our mother is dead. The Grotchka killed her"

"Mother was brave. She saved our farm and our animals. She saved you from the Grotchka until the neighbors got here."

"But the Grotchka killed her." Azolyn was visibly holding back tears.

"We live in a difficult place. The Grotchka woke her up, and our mother bravely did her job to save you. She died with honor."

Azolyn took on a look of sadness, even fear. "That's not what happened."

"What d'you mean?" Ayiiia said.

"I woke up when the Grotchka attacked," Azolyn said. "I woke up mother and she went after it."

"You did what you were supposed to do."

"I should have gone out and fought the Grotchka." Azolyn was withdrawing into herself.

"You are too young to handle that monster."

"I've practiced. I've trained. I could have beaten the Grotchka." She almost stood defiantly then sat. Her head fell. "Mother died because I was a coward."

"It's not your fault," Ayiiia said.

JENNIFER WHISPERED TO ANTHEN. "They're going off-script."

He nodded and almost smiled. "I remember watching this movie with her."

"I LET MOTHER GO OUT THERE..." Azolyn said.

"There's nothing you could have done."

Kalinda clenched and unclenched her fists. "I stayed here and..."

"It's not your fault." Ayiiia came around the table.

"I miss our mother." Ayiiia took her sister in her arms.

"I miss her too, Az." Ayiiia and Azolyn held each other and sobbed.

They broke the hug. Azolyn flexed her muscles. She looked directly at Tayla. "I will avenge her." She then looked almost directly at the camera but did not break the fourth wall. "I will slay the Grotchka."

THE TWO ACTORS held the position awaiting the director to say cut.

The moving scene transfixed those watching as they all shed tears. Sheila finally turned to Chris and broke the reverie.

"Cut!" It was almost a shout.

The crew and then everyone broke into applause.

Tayla and Kalinda separated. They smiled, laughed and then executed a high five.

Jennifer hugged her father, Sheila and Navvy shook hands.

Sheila went to Chris. "That was intense. Please show it to us."

He signaled the operator. "Could we have playback?"

They all looked again at the virtual set. The virtual Kalinda sat in her first position. The scene progressed, and again the group felt the emotions. Tayla and Kalinda watched and held hands. Finally, Kalinda looked directly at the camera but not at the camera. The viewers practically looked over their shoulders for the Grotchka.

There was a long pause.

"Navvy?" Chris said. Everyone looked at the studio head.

"I think you have your Azolyn," Navvy said. "Kalinda?"

"Yes, tal'pa?"

"Are you ready for this?"

Kalinda looked around at each face. "Yes, I'm ready."

Sheila turned to Jennifer. "I think you have some work to do."

"Yes," Jennifer said. "I need to rewrite Azolyn for a much stronger actor."

"Bringing in Kalinda was a good call," Sheila said.

"It was Susie Wilder who made the suggestion."

"Then bringing on Susie was a good call."

"Thanks, Mom."

JENNIFER WALKED over to speak to her grandfather.

"Good casting makes good pictures, Jennifer. Casting Kalinda is a good idea," Navvy said.

"Susie Wilder suggested that I test her."

"She comes from a good bloodline."

"Are you going to be in your office tomorrow."

"Hannah is on a cruise. I'll be in early for breakfast," Navvy said. "Join me at eight."

KALINDA APPROACHED her father and hugged him.

"Your mother would be proud of you today."

"I hope that I honored her memory," Kalinda said. She looked away and broke into tears. "I miss her so much, te'pa."

"I do too, honey."

Jennifer saw the embrace and felt emptiness and regret.

Sheila saw the look. She put her arm around her daughter. "Give it time, Jen. You'll get to know him."

Navvy snapped the clapper and got everyone's attention. "Maiara has put out a light lunch in the executive dining room. We meet back at the gym at one p.m."

Kalinda looked up. "Te'pa?"

"Did you bring the clothes that I asked you to bring?"

"Yes, but I haven't worn them since..."

"It's time," Anthen said. "They want you to work out with the studio's martial arts teacher who will choreograph the scenes in the movie."

"But I haven't served Tal'qid since..."

"Honor her memory and do your best, Kalinda. It'll come back to you."

13

The executives were seated for the afternoon session. Tayla and David were sitting next to Jennifer.

The gym had over a hundred cameras used for motion capture so that the studio could record the session for review. Seated on the mat was the studio's Martial Arts Coordinator, Shloaka Duvvuri.

Anthen and Kalinda entered. The young girl was wearing a skin-tight suit with a unique type of active camouflage. She appeared to blend in with whatever background that was behind her. The only decorative adornment was a red scarf.

"I've watched videos of their combat on DocTube. It's strange to me, but I've visualized the moves.

"Shloaka is a champion like your mother. Try hard and learn from her."

"How will she respond when I give her the respect of Tal'qid?"

"If you honor and respect your opponent, you honor your te'ma."

She nodded.

Anthen went to his chair, and Kalinda went to the floor.

Shloaka Duvvuri was the martial arts coordinator at Tovar a decade after a career as a stuntwoman in many movies. At fifty-two, she retained the physical attributes she developed as a martial arts champion beginning in her teens. The sensei was kneeling on the mat.

"Hello, Kalinda. I'm Shloaka Duvvuri. Kneel with me and listen."

Kalinda dropped to her knees facing the coach. "There are some martial arts combat scenes in the movie in which you will appear. I'll be choreographing those scenes. We want to evaluate your current skills so that we can understand how much training will be required but more importantly the level of complexity we'll be able to call on you to perform."

"I understand. I'll do the best that I can."

"What is your martial arts training?" Shloaka asked.

"I have training in self-defense."

"Do you remember what style?"

"It was physical defense without weapons."

"Do you have a belt?"

Kalinda gave her a curious look. "Yes."

"What did you get it for?"

"It goes with my jeans."

Shloaka laughed. "Well, it appears that you won't have any bad habits. Let's do some simple warmup moves. During training, you may call me sensei. It means teacher."

"Yes, sensei."

"Please stand and face me on the mat."

"Is this the part where we bow, sensei?"

"Yes, Kalinda." Shloaka and Kalinda faced each other. Kalinda opened her hands to her side, bent her right knee and bowed her head. Shloaka responded with a bow.

"Observe my warmup, then you try it." Shloaka executed three simple punch combinations. "You try it."

Kalinda executed the same combination of moves flawlessly.

"Good. I'll now show you some more complex arm movements involving my upper body and shoulders." Again, Shloaka executed several punches and blocks focusing first on her right arm and shoulder and then three from the left. She repeated the movement. "Now, you try it."

Kalinda executed the movements flawlessly. Shloaka raised her eyebrows. "Please do it again."

Kalinda repeated the movements.

"I'm looking for your dominant side," Shloaka said. "Are you right-handed or left-handed?"

Kalinda tilted her head. "I write with my right hand but what does that have to do with this?"

"Everyone has a dominant side. People are either more proficient on their right or their left."

"I've always trained both sides of my body equally," Kalinda said. "Perfect symmetry is necessary, especially when facing multiple opponents."

Shloaka did a double take. "That's a wise statement. Let's do some leg movements. It's okay if you're not as flexible as I am. Extend as far as you can." The sensei then did a series of moves extending and bending her legs and executed some slow kicks. Shloaka's curiosity was growing. She included some vertical kicks that no novice would be able to perform. "Try that."

Kalinda then copied the sensei, perfectly matching each angle of extension to the degree. But on her extensions, Kalinda added some body motions that Shloaka did not recognize.

"You have refined skills. I'm now going to demonstrate a kata that all of my novice students perform." She lied. Shloaka then performed the routine timed at forty-five seconds on the wall display. It included every type of punch, kick, and defense in taekwondo and finished with a triple flying kick with her dominant right leg. Kalinda heard every inhalation, exhalation, yell, scream and strike that resounded throughout the gym.

"That may be a little challenging but give it a try."

"Sensei, you performed right-dominant. Which side would you like for me to be dominant?"

Her jaw dropped then Shloaka said, "Try it left-dominant as

quickly as you can." *There has to be a challenge that this youngster cannot overcome.*

The student took the first position. What the sensei saw next was burned in her memory for all time. Kalinda exploded at a speed that Shloaka had never seen. She performed a mirror image of the routine correctly finishing with the three flying kicks at greater extension and higher elevation than her own. Kalinda's performance was identical with one glowing exception. There was absolute silence. Her breathing was silent. After each jump, she landed on the floor with the feather touch of a cat. Even the alien-looking gi she wore made no noise. When Kalinda finished, the timer on the wall indicated eighteen seconds. Shloaka was both amazed and terrified.

"Who are you and where do you come from?" Shloaka said.

"Sorry?"

"That was the routine my daughter performed for the national championship."

"You told me that it was not difficult."

"Who is your sensei?"

"My te'ma, my mom, taught me?"

"Where did you learn these skills?" Shloaka asked.

Kalinda looked at her father. He nodded.

"I was born on the planet Xaphnore," Kalinda said. "I've served Tal'qid for seven years."

Shloaka's eyes grew large. "You're the girl from the Hoclarth Alliance?"

"Yes, ma'am."

"Who is Tal'qid?"

"Tal'qid was known as the first teacher. She developed the principals and methods of combat without weapons three-thousand years ago. As a student, I learned to serve her principals."

"Women only?"

"Males disqualify themselves from service because they resort to the use of weapons," Kalinda said. "Combatants in the service of

Tal'qid resolve their disagreements peacefully. The use of weapons only leads to bigger weapons."

"Your mother must have been unbeatable."

"She only lost one combat during her last year."

"Her last year?"

"She died in battle saving the Hoclarth Alliance," Kalinda said. "Her name was Natira."

"She'll always be proud of you wherever she is. Were you the one who defeated her?"

"It's dishonorable to boast of one's accomplishments." Kalinda's voice broke, "but, yes."

The two martial arts practitioners faced once more. This time it was the older woman who bowed most deeply. "I've much to learn from you, Kalinda. I hope that you, too, find that we can learn from each other. May I have your permission to address you as sensei?"

"My friends call me K'da, but I'd be most honored to be addressed as your fellow teacher."

"A question, Sensei Kalinda?"

"Yes, Sensei Shloaka."

"As I've learned my skills, practitioners use the yelling and noise to intimidate our opponent," Shloaka said. "You performed the routine with the complete silence of a prowling cat."

"One of the most important principles in the service of Tal'qid is stealth. Many times, we practice and compete in darkness or even blindfolded. When we are without sight, we must depend on our other six senses."

"You have seven senses?"

"Humans on earth do not possess it. Hoclarth children develop a sense of their proximity; we can sense the location of solid objects nearby," Kalinda said. "That's why I'll never run into you on the street."

Shloaka looked puzzled.

"That's a Hoclarth joke."

Shloaka let out a nervous laugh. "Let's go talk to our spectators."

Kalinda exchanged high fives with Jennifer and Tayla.

Shloaka went to the executives. "You have a martial arts star on your hands."

"Chris, is it time for a remake of Karate Kid?" Navvy said.

"Yes, but who could we cast as the master?" Chris said. "She'd dominate any scene."

"Maybe it's time for a paradigm shift," Navvy said.

"Kalinda as the karate master," Sheila said. "Intriguing."

"Mr. Kelrithian, it was an honor to work out with your daughter," Shloaka said. "I expect that Kalinda practices constantly."

"Call me Anthen. Today is the first time in one year and forty-four days."

"Since...?"

"Correct," Anthen said. "Her mother was immersed in her military duties. It was the one thing that they shared. You said that routine was for novices?"

"Oh, God, no," Shloaka said. "That was the routine my daughter performed last month to win the Under-14 Nationals. Kalinda could be a champion."

"She once beat the champion of the Hoclarth Alliance. I suspect that she has already proven herself."

"You're right, Anthen. That is a memory that she needs to keep in a unique place."

14

The next morning, Jennifer came into the executive dining room. She waved at Navvy, went to the buffet, and filled her plate.

"Good morning," Navvy said. "I'm guessing you want to talk about androids."

"The vision thing?"

"The one-track mind of a precocious seventeen-year-old," Navvy said. "How is JennaTech progressing?

"Pepper Simmons is winding down her work on the Wi-Pow Base Station," Jennifer said. "With a self-contained reactor, it can power ten remote devices constantly or two hundred fifty intermittently. The really good news is that it is reverse compatible with all the current receivers."

"Impressive."

"Based on current orders, we have been able to build a medium-size fabrication facility that will fab one hundred per day. When we finish the design for the Selfie Drone, we'll build a full-size fabrication facility."

Navvy focused on the business side. "Balance sheet?"

"We've shipped twenty VirtualLocation Systems. That is providing cash flow for our current operations. HumanAI Corp has paid us an upfront licensing fee for the Selfie Drone which we used to fund the first fab facility. The Wi-Pow Base Station will bring us to profitability by March 2068."

"So, tell me about the Android Project."

"I spoke with a Dr. Kent Gunn," Jennifer said, "and he has sent me his most advanced model."

"I'm familiar with his work. He has a pretty solid structural prototype."

"He's having trouble with appearance, power, and AI," Jennifer said. "I think JennaTech can solve those."

Navvy rubbed his chin. "Big order."

"Pepper has moved on from the Base Station. She's fitting a mini-reactor in the torso."

"Challenging."

Jennifer pointed to the projection of *Brilliant* on the conference table. "Has HumanAI Corp made progress on microprojectors for HTVR?"

"Yes, they have fabricated beta units," Navvy said. "How will you use them?"

"If we can place them at different points on the body, they can provide the skin, appearance, and manual dexterity. "

"Contact a post-doc named Eric Zhang in design at HumanAI Corp. He can set you up with beta units."

"The big problem is fitting the AI processor and memory inside the unit," Jennifer said. "Dr. Gunn believes we're at least fifty years away from fitting AI processing power into the size of a human head. Dr. Ami, Ani, Sami and all of the other virtual humans depend on major computer installations. *Brilliant* is the only portable AI facility. An android must be within high-speed network range of a super-computer."

"There's another option," Navvy said. "Remember how *Brilliant* communicates over long distances."

"StarWave. The *Brilliant Tech Manual* does not explain it. I always guessed that it was a form of communication between quantum entangled particles," Jennifer said.

"Not exactly," Navvy said. "Ani, are you here?"

"Yes, I've been monitoring. You want a DOD-279, correct?"

"Yes, Ani," Navvy said.

"DOD..." Jennifer said.

Navvy handed his HoloPad to Jennifer. "Here. Sign this. It's like a non-disclosure agreement. So, I can tell you."

"And then you shoot me?"

"Oh, no." Navvy laughed then looked serious. "Unless you tell someone."

Jennifer took the papers from the printer and signed.

"As you know, *Brilliant* has many technologies that, if released, would disrupt commerce, disadvantage intelligence gathering, and create a national security issue. My agreement with the government and the military is that those technologies will not be released until inventors develop them in this timeline."

"StarWave is the most disruptive," Jennifer said.

"Correct," Navvy said. "And you're close on quantum entanglement. It's called counterfactual communication."

"The Zeno effect. The Chinese explored it fifty years ago. They could not commercialize it."

"Back home, the research was revived during the Renaissance and bore fruit."

"The communications systems on *Brilliant* and at Tovar are in sealed enclosures that are six feet tall," Jennifer said. "The module must be huge."

"The comm unit is one-inch square, uses off-the-shelf components and costs a dollar-twenty-five to produce."

"Omigod," Jennifer said. "I see why it's such a big secret. It would disrupt every industry in the communications sector. What is the bandwidth?"

"It's limited by the hardware attached to it. And so far, *Brilliant* has not reached any range limits," Navvy said. "Does that give you enough to define the project?

"We build a generic physical host with physical mobility and strength, power, HTVR mini-projectors for appearance and manipulative abilities, and a central CPU that communicates with the AI supercomputer via StarWave."

"Exactly!" Navvy said.

"That helps a lot," Jennifer said. "I'll set up a meeting with Dr. Zhang. Should I steal him away from HumanAI?"

"It'll probably cost you a percentage. I was planning on a technology sharing program to get access to the mini-projector software and processing power," Navvy said.

"Thanks again for breakfast."

"Sure," Navvy said. "By the way, Hanna and I never thanked you."

"For what?"

"In the last few weeks, we have gone from zero grandchildren to two."

"At least you will see Kalinda grow up," Jennifer said. "You never saw that with me."

"You've grown up quite a bit recently," he said. "How is the airshow coming?"

"Tayla and I have got it timed out. She's programming the music and the narration. Riley and Anthen are creating some smoke tricks that no one has ever seen, and David has been testing out some moves in the simulator," Jennifer said. "We're meeting at one."

"Sounds like a plan. Have a good day, Jen."

"Thanks."

As she departed, Navvy thought, *I certainly did see you grow up, Jennifer, and it's still happening.*

15

"A ni, create a tenth-floor conference room with eight chairs."
Jennifer stood near the door. An ornate marble conference table with mahogany edges appeared with plush leather office chairs. To her left was a library and to her right was a stunning view overlooking Tovar Studios with the mountains rising behind Porter Ranch. At the far end was *StarCruiser Brilliant* floating in the space reserved for the display. In the corner to her left was a coffee stand appointed with a continental breakfast.

Riley came in and looked around. "Nice room."

The Star Squad members and Anthen grabbed coffee and food and took their seats.

"Thanks for coming, everyone. The Airshow should be fun," Jennifer said. "Tay, what do you have in mind for the soundtrack?"

"We'll open with the *Theme from Brilliant*, use the *Imperial March* from *Star Wars* and then close with the finale of *E.T.*"

"I love John Williams. I heard that the director asked him to write the music and then he cut the close of the movie to match the music," Jennifer said. "Okay, we have a track and a storyline. David?"

"I'll start with an aerobatic roll from show right, exit vertical and cloak the ship."

"How are we going to return?"

"I saw this at a New Mexico Airshow," Riley said. "A blimp came from behind the crowd with his engines at full thrust and surprised the crowd. We position over Miramar Road, fire up the thrusters and come in slow behind the flight line."

"I get it," Anthen said. "We release a bunch of smoke over show center and drop out of the cloud."

"That brings us back to center," Jennifer said.

"I saw a move in one of the early *Star Trek* movies when Spock's shuttle was docking with Enterprise," David said. "It was a combination pitch, roll, and yaw. It's a move that *Brilliant* can do, but no one has ever seen an aircraft do at an airshow. We follow with a pass in review at low altitude."

"We're coming up on the climax of the music," Tayla said.

"If we only had a rainbow," Jennifer said.

Riley and Anthen broke into wide grins.

"Seriously?" Jennifer said. "That will be a cool finale."

"Can David fly one more left-to-right high-speed pass?" Riley said.

"Whatcha got, Riley?"

Anthen spoke up. "It's something Natira and I cooked up for an airshow on Xaphnore. Riley and I are still working on it."

"Save it for the performance," Jennifer said. "They're all pretty standard flight maneuvers. But it'll certainly wow the crowd."

WARNER ACADEMY WAS the school her sister attended. Kalinda was worried the IQ of 205 she inherited from her father and the physical skills of a super-athlete from her Hoclarth mother would make it difficult to fit in. Her goal was to be an average SoCal ten-year-old. She remembered the advice from Jennifer. Do your advanced academics in steveLearn and play team sports where everyone loves a winner.

When she entered steveLearn, her avatar, Bralen, greeted her with the open hands of an unarmed warrior. "Would you like to continue in science this morning, Kalinda? You are ready for Advanced Placement Physics."

"Thank you, Bray," Kalinda said. "Let's begin." She spent two hours and completed the first two weeks of the Physics coursework.

That afternoon, she scored a goal the first time that she set foot on the soccer pitch.

ANTHEN's eyes lit up when he saw Kalinda come in after school. "How was your second day of school on Earth?"

"My soccer friends invited me to a sleepover Friday night."

"So, their parents are gone for the weekend, and the liquor cabinet will be unlocked," Anthen said.

Kalinda crossed her arms and took on a stern look. "Seriously?"

"So, no drugs either?" he said.

"Come on; I'm only ten," she said.

"Give me their parents' contact info, and I will coordinate," Anthen said.

"Thanks, te'pa," Kalinda said.

Kalinda walked out to the cliff overlooking the popular point break at Point Dume. She took a deep breath inhaling the fishy scent of the ocean. It made her homesick for her home planet. The blue-green waves rolling in were forming perfect hollows that would just fit her four-foot-eleven height.

"May I go surfing before dinner?"

"Is the lifeguard posted?"

"I'll save him if he gets in trouble."

"Kalinda!"

"And I will be safe."

She pulled on her wetsuit, grabbed her Pyzel Ghost, and ran

down to the beach. She'd cleaned and waxed her board the night before.

Kalinda walked down the rocky trail to the beach and greeted the city lifeguard. "Hi, Kevin."

"Dude," Kevin said. "Check out the chick surfing the point. She's pulling into barrels on practically every wave. She's my cousin, Bondi."

"This is my beach, dude."

"Yeah, but you're just a grommet," Kevin said. "Bondi's on the pro tour."

Kalinda walked down the beach to where a female surfer stood out from the locals. Bondi paddled into a four-foot wave, stalled in the pocket, then drew a perfect line for a speedy exit hitting the lip and getting air. Pulling off a perfect three-sixty, the pro surfer stuck it. Pumping her board, she gained some momentum and carved a vertical cutback releasing her fins as the board flew in the air. She reached down and grabbed her rails landing with both feet on the board. Kalinda's mouth dropped.

One of the spectators nearby exclaimed, "That's a Superman."

Kalinda watched the pro take another wave and repeat the trick. She closed her eyes, replayed the trick in slow motion, analyzed the actions to complete the trick, then opened her eyes. *Got it*, Kalinda thought. She ran into the water and paddled out to catch a wave. She found herself a few yards from the pro and waved.

"I'm Bondi."

"I'm Kalinda. Nice air. The locals are calling that a Superman?"

"Yep," said Bondi. "You gonna try it."

"Yeah."

"It's a pretty difficult move," Bondi said.

Kalinda had a confident gleam in her eye. "I'll get it on the third try."

"You're just a grom."

Kalinda held up three fingers.

An arrogant grommet, Bondi thought. "I'll take this wave. Watch the move from the back side."

Bondi paddled and then disappeared in front of the wave. Up came the board, then Bondi. She was turning as she emerged and was able to grab the rails of the board and control it and her body to get her legs beneath her on the board.

Kalinda took a deep breath, began paddling, fell into a perfect wave, stalled in the pocket, drew a perfect line, hit the lip and went into the air. She grabbed for her rail but missed and landed on her back on top of the board. *That's one,* Kalinda thought.

Bondi reached the beach and looked back just in time to see Kalinda go airborne and then wipe out. She looked toward the local spectators. "Has she done that trick before?"

An older man with a white beard spoke up. "We come out here to watch her every day," he said. "She's amazing, and no, she has not tried that trick before."

Another old surfer said, "She's the best grommet that has ever crossed this sand."

Bondi turned to watch Kalinda's next attempt.

Kalinda paddled out, closed her eyes and replayed the actions of the pro, then replayed her last attempt. Then she replayed them side by side — *second try.*

She found a good wave and started paddling. Great wave. She stalled into the pocket. She did a snap throwing up spray behind her to get warmed up then built up more speed. She picked her spot, turned the board, and went airborne. She caught the rails, brought her legs under, and touched the board...just as she crashed the top of the wave. Wipeout.

Kevin came up next to Bondi. "She calls this her beach, cousin."

"I don't know about the sand, but she owns the waves," Bondi said. "Thanks for the heads up. . Your message said she's ten?"

"Ya, she and her dad just moved into the cottage above the point a few weeks ago," Kevin said. "I remember when she came out here with a boogie board."

"Did you say weeks?"

"She's a bit of a prodigy," Kevin said. "Here she comes."

KALINDA WATCHED the next set of three waves approach. The first one passed beneath her as the locals started paddling furiously. She was ready for the second one.

She began paddling as the enormous wave approached forming perfectly. She bottom-turned, stalling in the pocket and stood tall in the barrel. She focused ahead and drew a perfect line on a nearly vertical section barreling above her head. Gaining speed with the wind in her face, she picked her spot and hit the lip. The board went vertical. She threw her legs back until they extended above the horizontal. Kalinda grabbed her rail bringing her legs under her, set her feet and compressed as she landed back in the pocket. *Superman. Got it in three.*

ON THE BEACH, there were cheers and high fives from those watching.

Anthen walked up next to Bondi. "Pretty good for a kid."

"Pretty good for anybody—including most of the pro surfers," Bondi said. "Just like she said, she got it in three."

"I'm Anthen Kelrithian, Kalinda's father."

"Bondi Cooper." They shook hands. "My cousin told me that there was an amazing surfer on this beach ready to go pro. That's an understatement."

"You're a pro surfer?"

"Soon to be past tense. I'm looking for young surfers to sponsor and train. I want Kalinda to join me at the Oceanside Pro-Am two weeks from Thursday."

Kalinda's final wave was a big one, the biggest set of the day. She paddled into the ten-foot monster, stood up and then disappeared deep in the tube getting shot out like a cannon and executed a perfect aerial sticking it five feet from her take-off point. She then paddled in and joined Bondi and her father.

"Te'pa," Kalinda said. "You've met Bondi. She showed me some crazy moves. I can't wait to see what the pros can do at Oceanside. Wait. Bondi Cooper?"

The pro surfer nodded.

"I've watched your insane videos," Kalinda said. "I can't wait to see you at Oceanside."

"How about being my partner in the Oceanside Pro-Am?" Bondi said.

Kalinda's jaw dropped.

"Amazeballs. I'll need a new wetsuit. And a new board."

16

Next morning, Jennifer entered the ready room, Double-Shot Caramel Frappuccino in hand,

"Set up a video with Dr. Zhang at HumanAI Corp," Jennifer said. "He should be in their hardware division." There was a pause.

"Yes, boss," Sami said.

Dandy jumped on Sami's lap as she concentrated on the task.

"Dr. Zhang indicates he is now available. The call is HTVR."

"Thanks, connect me."

The ready room changed to the interior of Dr. Zhang's office. Over his shoulder was some artwork representing Chinese iconography and his college diplomas from Stanford and CalTech. Dr. Zhang was typing on a display to his right that Jennifer couldn't see.

"Good morning Dr. Zhang," Jennifer said.

"Good morning, Miss Jenna Seldon," he said. "Please call me Eric."

"Thanks, Eric. Please call me Jennifer. Jenna Seldon is a pseudonym I use for my business and creative activities."

"An impressive resume, nonetheless," Eric said. "I look forward to your presentation on HTVR Applications on the HoloPad at the Fall Conference. How may I help you?"

"Can you share your progress on the miniature holographic tactile projector?"

"It's interesting that you should ask. We've just completed a fabrication run of the beta version," Eric said. "Due to its limitations, we haven't yet found any commercial applications."

"Please explain the limitations?"

"Firstly, it requires massive amounts of power. It must be close to a WiPow source or even direct wiring. Secondly, it only images to a range of five inches, so we need to anchor it to a solid body over which the image forms."

"Interesting," Jennifer said. "Those constraints are ideal for our needs."

"Could you describe your product?"

"JennaTech is going to build a Virtual Human."

"To serve what applications?" Eric asked.

"HumanAI Corp provides virtual physicians to many medical facilities around the world. The primary expense is the WiPow and projection equipment which limits the presence of virtual physicians to the areas covered."

"Correct."

"Creating a physical representation of a Virtual Human would release the physician to remote areas without the requirement for projection or power," Jennifer said. "The doctor could make house calls."

With eyebrows raised, "So, you're proposing a self-contained android?"

"Yes," Jennifer said. "Except for the AI. The consensus is that we're fifty years from being able to contain human-level AI in an android."

"That still limits your range to that of a high-speed network."

"I'm unable to provide details, but we have a solution to that problem as well."

"I'm a brillian. The *Brilliant Tech Manual* says that StarWave operates in a six-foot-tall cabinet."

"Again, I'm unable to provide details."

"Would you like me to send a sample of the projectors?"

"Yes, I would," Jennifer said. "JennaTech will negotiate licensing fees when we begin production."

"You've got an enemy in Congress," Eric said.

Jennifer frowned. "I'm following the legislation put forward by Senator Curtwell. She has many co-sponsors, but the President ran on fixing the doctor shortage."

"Your grandfather has led our company in that field," Eric said. "But HumanAI Corp is doing all it can to stop short of constructing a humaniform robot. Is there a reason besides medicine that you are pursuing this?"

"I suppose so." Jennifer looked away to a distant point. "I've got a friend who would like to watch a sunset."

"Your HoloPad assistant?"

"Yes, but she has been with me for much longer than that," Jennifer said. "I started taking college classes when I was eight. Sami became my college advisor, my personal assistant, and my older sister. I was an only child."

"And you have just recently reunited with your father."

Jennifer's eyes got larger.

"I'm a brillian. I've followed your story."

"I'm still not used to the celebrity thing."

"Would you be willing to consult on the project when we get further along?" Jennifer said. "We could negotiate a percentage of the royalties."

"I'd like that," Eric said. "I've got a videoconference soon. I'll send you a dozen sample units by autonomous courier."

"Thanks for your time. I look forward to working with you." She turned to her HoloPad. "Disconnect, Sami."

The room returned to its standard configuration.

Sami came in and sat across from Jennifer. "He was hitting on you," Sami said.

"No way, Sami." Jennifer's face turned red.

"And you felt it, too." Sami winked.

"Be nice, or you won't get to watch the sunset with me," Jennifer said. "Did we receive the shipment from FutureBotics?"

"It was delivered yesterday afternoon," Sami said.

"We should receive the package from Dr. Zhang today or tomorrow. Let's set up a meeting here on Friday to see what FutureBotics has produced."

"Who is attending?"

"Stephen will be the lead engineer. Jake will do software. Piper will do power. We can bring her in on HTVR from Raleigh. I'll work with you, Ani and Dr. Ami to do the micro-hardware CPU to interface with the projectors and the AI Servers."

"Food?"

"Working lunch. Contact Maiara to send some catering. It's just the three of us eating."

"Check."

"Next week is taken up with the Air Show," Jennifer said. "Has everyone checked in on the pre-production checklist for the battle scene for *Attack of the Hoclarth Alliance*?"

"Yes, JennaTech will install VirtualLocation on the first Monday in October," Sami said. "You can begin rehearsal on Wednesday and shoot the following week."

17

Jennifer got to the ready room carrying her caffeine fix from the galley with fifteen minutes before the scheduled meeting. On the aft wall, was a table with a continental breakfast. Standing at attention before her desk was a tall female android. It was wearing a white blouse, navy skirt, and tall, flat syn-leather boots. The elegantly styled dark hair framed a friendly-looking face.

As soon as Jennifer entered the room, the robot's head turned and followed Jennifer.

"Hi, I'm Kiki, a virtual human product of Futurebotics, Incorporated. I am here to serve you and your family productively and safely." The robot stuck her hand out to shake.

Jennifer left the hand hanging. "Sami, would you join me?" Jennifer asked.

A tone sounded, and Sami entered the ready room. Sami looked at the robot with its hand sticking out. "A total abomination, isn't it? Is that what I'll look like as a physical being?"

"Oh God, no," Jennifer said. "This is what we have to start with. You'll still be you. We need to modify this to carry you around outside."

"The mini-projectors?" Sami asked.

Jennifer picked up a small device from a dozen laying on her desk.

The door tone sounded. Stephen Mendoza and Jake Hargrove entered followed by Ani and Dr. Ami.

The two men looked at the robot.

"This is what Dr. Gunn sent us from FutureBotics," Jennifer said. "Do you think JennaTech can modify it for the ladies here?"

The two engineers went to the robot and inspected, Jake opened up its blouse, and Stephen looked at the hands.

"We've got a long way to go," Jake said. He sent an admiring look at Ani. "A very long way to go."

"It looks workable," Stephen said. "What do we want to accomplish today?"

"Work with the crew, come up with a plan, and let's mock up a simulation for the head to see how well the projectors perform," Jennifer said.

"Who's going to be our guinea pig for the mockup?" Stephen asked.

"I'd like to do a dexterity test to see if the whole project is feasible," Dr. Ami said.

"Ani, could you set up the engineering drawings over here?" Stephen said.

Ani created a three-dimensional display of the robot.

Stephen looked at the projectors on the desk. "Ani, place the projector drawing here." He held his palm open to the right of the robot. "The face projector should go on the sternum here." He placed his hand at the indicated location.

Stephen manipulated the objects on the sternum of the drawing and began to fit the drawing of the projector into the robot.

"Ani, could I have a workstation to begin programming the interface?"

"Sure."

A standing desk, keyboard, mouse, and a large display appeared.

Jake walked over and set his HoloPad down. His shirtless male avatar appeared to the right of the display. After he typed some commands, he said, "I have access to the robot and Projectors A, B, and C."

Jennifer lifted the projectors and set them aside. "Can you override Kiki's built-in AI, Jake?"

"Already done," Jake said.

Dr. Ami looked over Jake's shoulder and assisted him. Ani and Sami went over to the drawing Stephen was working on. He had moved to the wrists of the robot and restructured the titanium radius and ulna to accommodate the projectors.

The engineers had been working for an hour. "Time for a bagel break," Jennifer said.

"Good idea," Jake said. "Do you have lox for the bagels?"

The humans had their bagels properly schmeared, and their drinks and the virtuals were gathered in the group as well.

"So, we need three projectors per unit?" Stephen asked.

"We can't run barefoot on the beach?" Ani asked.

"We can do five," Stephen said.

Sami's face became flushed. "Six."

"Why six?" Jake asked.

He immediately received disgusting looks from the four women.

"Six, it is," he said.

"We're ready to test the robot with three projectors," Stephen said. Dr. Ami, do you have some surgical adhesive available?"

She looked at the ceiling. The dumbwaiter on the forward wall sounded a tone, and the panel opened. Several packages and surgical instruments were on the platform.

"Jake?" Stephen asked.

"I've got a rudimentary interface programmed," Jake said. "Dr. Ami, you will have complete control of the robot. The bionics are two-way so that you will have sensation and control over your body. Your face and hands will be HTVR."

Stephen and Dr. Ami applied adhesive and attached the projectors in the locations Stephen specified on the drawing.

"Jake, do a diagnostic," Stephen said.

The robot moved its limbs and walked around the room. The head swiveled in several directions.

"The diagnostic test was successful," the robot said.

"Dr. Ami, you're up," Stephen said.

"Wish me luck," Dr. Ami said as she left the room.

"Implementing the interface between the robot and Ami's AI," Jake said.

A digital representation of Ami's face began to appear replacing Kiki. Her eyes focused and moved around as she swiveled her head and, finally, her face rendered.

"Welcome back, Doctor," Jennifer said. "Are you functioning?"

"It takes some time to form all of the connections," Dr. Ami said. Her hands began to render. She held her right hand up. "Anyone got some keys?"

Jake pulled out a key ring with five keys and set it on the desk.

She struggled for a moment. "I need my vision to supplement my senses," Dr. Ami said. She lifted the keys with her right hand. She stared intently at them as she manipulated all five keys into position to insert. "I think I've got it." She closed her eyes and did the same manipulation faster. She switched hands and performed the same with her left hand. "Let me try something more difficult."

She walked over to an empty space. "Implement Simulation One Bravo," Dr. Ami said.

A human body on an operating table appeared in the space. The body was intubated, and there was a surgical light shining down. An array of equipment and displays surrounded the operating table indicating life signs.

Jake was particularly interested. "Jake, please bring me that tray of instruments," Dr. Ami said. He went to the dumbwaiter and retrieved the tray. The group gathered around the table as Ami prepared the area.

"This fifty-four-year-old male patient suffers from hereditary spherocytosis," Dr. Ami said. "His symptoms have become acute, which indicates the need for a splenectomy to reduce complications from the disease. Ani will act as my surgical nurse."

"You're going to remove the spleen?" Jake asked.

"Correct, Jake."

"Are you going to use the laparoscopic or open method?" Jake said.

"A DocTube fan, I see," Dr. Ami said. "The laparoscopic method is much less invasive and more complex. It'll provide a greater challenge to my surgical dexterity. I'll morsalize the spleen and remove sections."

"I've watched both methods," Jake said. "There's always lots of blood."

"I've placed the patient on his left side and sterilized the area to be incised. If anyone is afraid of blood, now is the time to turn away."

Dr. Ami brought the blade to the patient. "I'm making a two-centimeter incision medial to lateral." Blood began pouring out of the wound. "This one is a bleeder. Suction, Ani."

There was an audible wretch and then two quick thumps as Jakes body hit the deck.

"I hate it when that happens," Dr. Ami said. "Sami, get some apple juice for Jake. Make sure he is breathing comfortably."

Dr. Ami's actions began to accelerate. The two virtual humans worked in perfect concert. In fifteen minutes, they had completed the operation and sutured the wound.

"The operation was a success." Dr. Ami looked at Jake. "How is our other patient?"

"I must have been light-headed," Jake said. "I didn't have enough to eat."

Jennifer laughed. "Did we get that on video?"

"You wouldn't."

Stephen refocused the group. "Dr. Ami, will our system work?"

"Jennifer, Stephen, Jake mark this down as a success," Dr. Ami said. "The mini projectors render at a much higher resolution than building projectors. With a bit of practice, I'll be able to perform at a higher level of dexterity than before."

"Good," Stephen said, "what is our timeline?"

"I know that you have a lot on the table. Let's plan to hire staff to complete a prototype and a spare in six months." Jennifer said. "The virtuals will be a step forward in medicine. Now, get that nasty robot out of here."

"Should we take the mini-projectors?"

Jennifer thought for a moment and looked at Dr. Ami.

Ami looked back and gave an almost imperceptible nod.

"Leave one here on *Brilliant*," Jennifer said. "Congratulations, everyone. Let's adjourn to the Galley. I hear Maiara sent lunch over from the Executive Dining Room."

18

On Thursday morning of the Air Show Week, the crew of *StarCruiser Brilliant* gathered for a seven a.m. breakfast in the Executive Dining Room. Each person was wearing the cerulean uniform of *Brilliant*.

"Today, you will show off our *Brilliant* to the public for the first time," Navvy said. "No need to cloak on departure. Your updated flight plan with SoCal TRACON will cover the whole trip and TRACON will direct you throughout the flight. As soon as you're ten miles from land, you may accelerate to Mach Two for the six-minute transit to feet dry over Torrey Pines State Beach. You'll join the traffic pattern on course zero-six-zero south of the runways and Miramar Tower."

"Are we fixed wing or vertical-take-off-and-landing?" Jennifer asked.

"Miramar Tower will bring you in as VTOL," Navvy said. "There will be city and military VIPs for the welcome so expect the tower to direct a low pass over the field. David, a slow barrel roll will work for that."

"Aye, sir," David said.

"Smoke, Navvy?" Riley asked.

"Go ahead and drop a smoke trail on the pass. No special effects until Sunday."

"Aye, sir," Riley said.

"We arrive at 0900, and there will be a short welcome ceremony, and then we'll conduct tours of the ship. At 1030, the Blue Angels will give rides to the Star Squad. Anthen and Kalinda will get a ride on Fat Albert," Navvy said. "David and Jennifer, don't break the pretty blue airplanes."

They laughed. David and Jennifer then glanced at each other with a serious look.

"At 1230, there will be a VIP lunch in the new F-52 hangar. I'll give a speech on the *Brilliant* as a future weapons system. Our friend, Senator Curtwell will give the keynote."

"Why did we have to study the tutorial on Navy Military Courtesies?" Tayla asked.

"That dates back to when *Brilliant* arrived here over forty years ago," Navvy said. "A small number of people in the government and military were made aware of *StarCruiser Brilliant*. The President offered, and I accepted, an offer to make *Brilliant* a commissioned reserve vessel in the Navy. It was a pretty tight secret. We have been activated only in case of emergencies that require our specialized capabilities. The president promised to keep us out of international conflicts. Jack's a four-striper Captain, and I'm a Rear Admiral in the reserves."

"What about us?" Tayla asked.

"When in uniform, you, Riley, and David hold the rank of Navy Lieutenant."

"And me?" Jennifer asked.

"As First Officer, you hold the rank of Lieutenant Commander."

"Cool," Jennifer said. "Hey, Dad, I outrank you."

"Nay, nay, moose breath," Anthen said. "My time-in-service gave me a bump to full Commander."

"As are Dr. Ami and Ani," Navvy said.

"What about me?" Kalinda asked.

"Let me see...As an Admiral, I can give battlefield promotions," Navvy said. "Kalinda, I hereby appoint you Honorary Ensign."

Kalinda beamed. "Cool, what rank are you, Auntie?"

Maiara Hanare set some sticky buns on the table.

"I'm the Chief of the Ship and First Lieutenant so I outrank all of you. Remember, I feed you."

"So, do we have to salute?" Tayla asked.

"They know we're all civilians but when you are covered, wearing your beret, it's expected that you return military honors and it's a courtesy to render a salute to a senior officer," Navvy said. "Did you all practice your salute?"

The crew of *Brilliant* stood and snapped proper military salutes in unison.

"Each of you is representing Tovar Studios, *StarCruiser Brilliant*, and Jack and I, so what's the standard?"

"*Brilliant*," they shouted together.

"After we land there will be some walkthroughs. Jack and I will handle the senior officers and dignitaries, David and Jennifer will take the pilots and plane crews through, and Riley and Tayla will take civilian and military visitors."

"What about me?" Kalinda asked.

"There will be military dependents and schoolchildren there. Can you take them through the ship?"

"Yes, tal'pa. May I take them into the Captain's ready room?"

"I suppose. There's not much to see there."

Kalinda looked at Jennifer.

"Yes, K'da. But if anyone loses their lunch, you have to clean it up."

"Yes, sister."

"I'm confused. What have you done with my ship?" Navvy said.

"Grandpa, Ani and I wired the Artificial Gravity to simulate different G-forces in the Ready Room so I could simulate high Gs on the flight simulator," Jennifer said. "Kalinda and I created a surfing, tennis, and battle simulator and she has been working out at high and low Gs."

Navvy smirked. "I've created a playground for precocious preteens. Maiara, you will be passing out logo M&Ms and challenge coins. Do we have enough?"

"I made as many as you asked, but *Brilliant* may not be able to get off the ground."

"I think it will make it. That covers everything. Jack?"

"Keep your uniforms spiffy. Represent *Brilliant* with pride and please don't run into anything, David. Let's get aboard and show off."

THE FIFTEEN-MINUTE FLIGHT from Tovar to Miramar was uneventful. Tayla was adept at handling air traffic communications. *Brilliant* flew just off the San Diego's North County approaching Torrey Pines State Beach. "TRACON, *Brilliant*. Request approach to Miramar two-four left with a low pass over the beach."

"*Brilliant*, turn left to one-two-zero. Descend and maintain eight hundred feet."

Unsurprisingly, surfers and spectators covered the beach. They were surprised when *Brilliant* passed over. "Captain?" David asked. May I roll the ship?"

"Roll the ship at feet dry, pilot."

Artificial gravity prevented the crew from feeling the movement. As *Brilliant* got there, the people on the beach waved. David performed a soft roll, and the watchers screamed with glee.

"*Brilliant*, climb to two thousand at two-hundred-fifty knots," TRACON said.

"Two thousand at 250. *StarCruiser Brilliant*," Tayla responded.

They passed over I-5, University City, and I-805.

"Turn left to zero-six-zero. Contact Miramar Tower on 135.2. Welcome to San Diego."

"135.2. Good day," Tayla responded. She depressed a preset on her panel. "Miramar tower, *StarCruiser Brilliant* heading zero-six-zero at two thousand. Request clearance to land on two-four left."

"*Brilliant*, Miramar, welcome. You've got permission for a low pass over the runway centerline. Turn left to two-four-zero at the eastern apron and descend to two hundred fifty. After the pass, turn left to three-three-zero and follow the beam to the flight line. You've got clearance to land."

"*StarCruiser Brilliant*."

"Eastern apron on my port side," David said. "Starting my turn."

The drivers in morning traffic along I-15 got a good look at *Brilliant*.

"Nice slow barrel roll, David."

"Aye, sir."

David lined up *Brilliant* with the centerline at four hundred feet.

"Engineer, smoke on," Jack said. David performed a smooth barrel roll before the spectators and dignitaries. At show right, he snap-rolled 270 degrees to the right and began his left turn to return to the center of the flight line.

"I've got the beacon," David said. He brought the starship slowly to the flight line and dropped softly onto the tarmac. The displays showed the crew that the spectators were giving them a standing ovation.

"Engineer put the ship in ground standby," Jack said. "Ani, configure the interior for unclassified tours."

Two voices acknowledged.

NAVVY AND JACK walked down the ramp of the *Brilliant* between side boys to the sound of the Navy Band. Nearby, the seven F-52s of the Blue Angels were lined up in a precise military line. Salutes were exchanged. Navvy, who built and designed *Brilliant*, and Jack, her captain, were escorted to the reviewing stand. A uniformed sailor escorted the rest of the crew to seats in the bleachers near the pilots who were wearing a slightly different shade of blue.

Jennifer greeted the pilot who acted as her liaison with the Blues. "It's certainly a beautiful craft," Major Kendra Boyington said.

"Thanks, we're proud of our *Brilliant*, Major," Jennifer said.

"On the flight line, we address each other by call sign. I'm Fifi"

"Call me Jendroid," Jennifer said. "This is my dad, Anthen, his daughter Kalinda, our pilot, David, call sign StarPilot, Riley, our engineer, call sign Stardancer and our communicator, Tayla, call sign Ayiiia."

At the podium, the admiral who acted as San Diego's Navy Mayor welcomed the crew. The Mayor of San Diego presented Navvy the key to the city and the Commanding General welcomed them to Miramar.

"Mayor Lopez, Admiral Lindstrom, General Williams, I'd like to present each of you with an artifact from Cancri-C, forty light years from earth," Navvy said. "We think these objects came from a civilization that existed over a million years ago."

"Thank you, Admiral Kelrithian," the Mayor said. "It looks like pure gold."

"It's eighty-seven percent Rhodium," Navvy said.

Jennifer was sitting next to Maiara. "Where does he keep those, Maiara?"

"He has a ton of trinkets like that in a bin in Storage Three."

"Are they valuable?"

"A small bag full would destabilize the precious metal markets."

There were several welcoming speeches given and the troops passed in review.

"Admiral, would you like to visit the ship?"

"I thought you'd never ask."

The formalities complete, the crew took their stations to give tours of *StarCruiser Brilliant*.

KALINDA WAS on her third and final group of six dependents and schoolchildren.

As they passed through the lower decks, one of the kids was explaining to others in detail the components that Kalinda pointed out. As they were going up the ladder, Kalinda caught up with him. "What's your name?"

"Jeff Rodriguez."

"You know a lot about the ship."

"I've seen all the movies. I read the first three volumes of the *Tech Manual*. I'm a brillian."

"I've heard that word," Kalinda said. "What's a brillian?"

"We're fans of the movies and of *Brilliant*. We study the manuals and collect memorabilia," Jeff said. "My dad bought me a ball cap worn by Captain Jack on a mission to Sirius."

We don't wear ball caps, Kalinda thought.

"We went to a 'Welcome Home, *Brilliant*' party after they brought David home. Before that, we all knew that *Brilliant* was real. Aren't you a brillian? You got an actual ride on *Brilliant*."

"I guess I am. Enjoy the tour." *He's kind of cool.*

Kalinda hurried the group through the lower decks. Near the galley, the girls ahead of Kalinda stopped.

"He's such a pretty kitty." It was a girl who introduced herself as Harlow. She sat on the deck and stroked Dandy behind the head "What's his name?"

"Harlow, meet Dandy Lion," Kalinda said. "Dandy is the ship's cat."

"So cute," Harlow said.

Dandy jumped into Harlow's lap. He looked directly at Kalinda. *Tell the story.*

Kalinda tilted her head. *Did you just talk to me, Dandy?*

Of course, I did, Dandy thought. *Are you deaf like most humans?*

Harlow looked at Dandy and then looked at Kalinda.

I am not, Kalinda thought. *What story?*

About how I saved Jennifer.

"Are you two communicating?" Harlow asked.

"Yes. Dandy wants me to tell the story about how he became the ship's cat," Kalinda said. "One day, Jennifer was visiting Dandy, and a meteor came out of the sky and blew up Dandy's home. Jennifer picked up Dandy, ran away, and saved him."

Dandy's head popped up. He growled and pawed at the air toward Kalinda.

Jeff interrupted. "Actually, it was Dandy who saved Jennifer."

The kids laughed, and Kalinda looked a bit embarrassed.

Better? Kalinda thought.

You may continue your tour. Dandy jumped off Harlow's lap and went to his pillow in the galley.

"Let's go up to the top deck and take a quick tour of the bridge," Kalinda said. "Then we can see the Captain's Ready Room."

Kalinda noticed that a blonde-haired boy with a *StarCruiser Brilliant* t-shirt held on to the safety rails and had trouble with the ladders. His mother accompanied him close by. They got to their final stop.

"When underway, this is the captain's ready room. There are two bunks, an office, and a conference room," Kalinda said.

"I want to go back and see the bridge some more," Jeff said.

"You've read the *Brilliant Tech Manual*. You know she has surprises."

"So, surprise me." He crossed his arms and stood the wide stance of a fighter.

Kalinda winked, Jeff melted, and Kalinda turned back to the group.

"When *Brilliant* is on the ground, I use it for something else," Kalinda said. "Ani, configure simulation: Battle Room One."

"Commencing Battle Simulation," Ani announced in her most dramatic computer voice.

The children felt the room begin to shake as it converted from an office into a large empty space with four large geometric solids spread around.

"Woah, this is way cool," Jeff said.

"Grab a thruster hanging on the wall behind you."

"Thrusters?" several children said.

The mother of the blonde boy came up to Kalinda.

"My son, Steve, has cerebral palsy. Will this activity be safe for him?"

"Ma'am, all solid objects in here have a force field surrounding them," Kalinda said. "Before the tour, we made sure that it would be safe for kids with special needs. Why don't you grab a thruster? I guarantee you will both have fun."

She opened her mouth to say something; then she looked at her son. "Please?" he said. His mother walked back to the wall and grabbed two thrusters and gave one to Steve.

"Please hold on to your breakfast. Ani set gravity to zero."

"Commencing Zero Gravity," Ani announced.

Everyone screamed as their feet lost contact with the floor. Vertical became an abstract concept as many of the kids turned upside down. Steven let go of his mother's hands and floated free. The screams turned to laughter.

Kalinda shouted as her eyes danced with glee. "Hey, everybody; watch me." Kalinda pointed her thruster toward the middle of the room. She pressed the trigger and slowly moved toward the wall. Kalinda turned so that her feet faced the wall. On contact, she pushed off and sailed quickly across to one of the solids. Again, she pushed off in another direction and flew to the wall and made a soft landing.

All of a sudden, small bodies were moving in every direction through the space.

"Cool," Jeff said. He pointed his thruster, sailed to the wall and gracefully kicked off to the blue solid. Again, he rotated and kicked off towards the wall.

He's got skills, Kalinda thought.

Steve quickly became accustomed to zero gravity and began navigating as well as the other kids.

Jeff met Kalinda at the yellow solid. "So, why do they call this the battle room?"

"Hang on," Kalinda spoke louder to the whole group. "May I have everyone's attention? We've got three minutes left. Starting now, your thrusters have lasers. When you hit a target, it will light up. So, take cover.

"Yay," the kids cheered.

"Ani, commence Battle Mode."

All of a sudden kids and lasers were flying through the air, light splashing on the walls, and kids' bodies lighting up. The laughter and the noise became deafening. Kalinda smiled when she saw Steve's mother firing on her son from behind the red solid.

"Thirty seconds to normal gravity," Ani announced.

"Aww," the kids said in unison.

Slowly the kids returned to the floor. For a few seconds, they were bouncing in moon gravity. Finally, they were all vertical at normal earth gravity.

There was applause and cheering from the kids. Steve's mom had tears in her eyes.

As Kalinda led the tour to the ramp and stood next to Jeff, "You moved nicely in zero gravity," Kalinda said. "Where'd you get your moves?"

"I've studied martial arts for five years."

"I studied something like that...where I came from."

"I have a brown belt in Aikido."

"I've got a blue belt that holds up my jeans," Kalinda said.

They both laughed. "Who doesn't give out belts?"

Kalinda hesitated. She was apprehensive about sharing too much information. "I serve Tal'qid."

They reached the crowd line.

"Never heard of that. Where is your dojo?"

"Dojo?" Jeff asked.

"Where do you practice? Who's your sensei?"

"My dad set up a room at our Malibu beach house. My mom taught me before..." She looked away. "My sister and I set up a simulation on *Brilliant*."

Jeff's eyes got bigger. "Your sister is Jennifer Gallagher? We read a rumor on Brillian.com that Anthen Kelrithian had..."

"He's my dad."

"You were born on Xaphnore." Jeff stared incredulously. "You're an alien."

"Only half," Kalinda said. "And my distant ancestors came from Earth. Can you keep it a secret?"

"Sure. You don't look...," Jeff said.

A man interrupted. "Who's your friend, Jeff?"

"Hi, Dad, this is Kalinda. She's an...," Jeff stuttered, "a brillian just like me."

"Nice to meet you," he said. "You flew in on *Brilliant?*"

"Yes, Mr. Rodriquez. My dad works at Tovar Studios."

"Did you two touch pads?" his father said. "Your friend might want to come down and see the beach at Coronado."

"Thank you, sir. That would be nice."

"I've got to meet your grandmother. Do you see the big blue plane over there?"

Jeff nodded, and Kalinda looked.

"That's Fat Albert. That's your next ride," Jeff Senior said. He looked at Kalinda. "Are you riding Fat Albert, too?"

"Yes, sir," Kalinda said.

"I'll see you two at the VIP Lunch. Don't be late, Jeff. You know your grandma."

As they walked toward the C-130, Kalinda and Jeff pulled out their devices and touched them.

"You've got a HoloPad?" Jeff asked.

"My grandfather gave me one. Who's your avatar?"

"Darth Vader."

"He was Luke Skywalker's father," Kalinda said. "My te'pa showed me that movie when we were patrolling Tau Ceti?"

"You've been to Tau Ceti?" Jeff asked. "Isn't that far away?"

"Three-point-six-five parsecs. A little less than twelve light years."

"Wow," Jeff said. "Who's your avatar?"

"A friend I used to know named Bralen."

"Your boyfriend?" Jeff asked.

Kalinda took a defensive posture. "We served Tal'qid together. He was once a champion on Xaphnore."

"He defeated you?"

"Yes, but then I beat him five times...until he chose to fight with weapons."

"Don't you use eskrima sticks or nun chucks."

"Weapons do not solve disputes. They only lead to bigger weapons."

"Do you miss your home?"

"I spent most of my time in space with my te'pa."

"Your parents are divorced?"

"My te'ma is dead."

"Sorry. That's tough."

"She died saving our planet." Kalinda gazed up at a point in the blue sky. "She was my teacher."

"What are you looking at?"

"My home."

"It's daytime with a blue sky. How can you tell?"

"Don't you know where your home is?"

Kalinda saw the confusion. "Yes, but..."

THEY WALKED TOWARD THE BLUE ANGELS' C-130.

19

Anthen watched Kalinda approach the ramp of the C-130. His daughter was engaged in deep conversation with a dark-haired Hispanic boy about her age. She was an inch taller, but he could tell that the boy appeared to possess physical strength similar to that of his daughter. They were so engrossed that they almost ran into him.

"You found a friend." Both turned their heads quickly and stopped.

"Te'pa, this is Jeff Rodriguez. He was on my last tour of *Brilliant*. He does martial arts, too. Jeff, this is my te'pa, Anthen."

Jeff froze in shock. "Anthen Kelrithian...Did you really get captured by the Hoclarth?"

"He's a brillian, Dad."

"Nice to meet you, son. Let's take a plane ride."

Fat Albert was a C-130U painted in Blue Angels blue and gold. The giant aircraft, which transported spare parts and ground crew from air show to air show, was flown by a crew of seven Marines.

They boarded the aircraft and went to the cargo net seats near the fuselage. "Is your dad in the Marines?" Anthen asked.

"Nope, my mom is a helicopter pilot on the *USS Oprah Winfrey* in the Persian Gulf," Jeff said. "And my grandmother is giving a speech today."

"So is my father," Anthen said. "Who's your grandmother?"

Jeff perked up and became formal. "Ramona Curtwell, the junior senator from the state of South Dakota." He relaxed. "That's how I'm supposed to introduce her."

Anthen looked intense. "I've heard a lot about her." *Navvy and the senator on the same dais. Wow, the sparks will fly.*

"Isn't the *Winfrey* the brand new fusion powered carrier," Kalinda said.

"Yep. It's got sixteen fusion reactors for propulsion plus a bunch of others for weapons and hotel loads."

"You know a lot."

"I rode a Tiger Cruise on her first deployment," Jeff said. "I got to ride with my mom from Hawaii to San Diego."

"I practiced on the simulator for this aircraft when I heard I was going to ride it."

"Practiced?" Jeff looked skeptical.

"Okay, I did twelve hours on the simulator on steveLearn."

"You've got a steveLearn?"

"Yeah, on *Brilliant*," Kalinda said. "My dad will install one in the beach house when he finishes buying it. I learned to surf there."

"Must be nice. I can almost stand up on my friend's board a Coronado Beach."

"I'm surfing tomorrow at Oceanside."

"Isn't that beach closed for the tournament this week?"

"Um..." She averted her eyes.

"Spill."

"I'm in the Pro-Am event with Bondi Cooper."

"Way cool," Jeff said. "How did you meet her?"

"She showed up at my beach one day. I guess her cousin is the lifeguard."

"D'you think you have a chance?"

"Dunno."

"Maybe I can come and watch."

"That'd be cool."

THE MARINES GOT Fat Albert in the air. When they were feet wet over the Pacific, a gunnery sergeant spoke up, "May I have your attention please? One of the first uses for the C-130 was as the Vomit Comet for the Mercury Astronauts. We're going to give you the experience of weightlessness for twenty-five seconds. The pilots are going to fly a few parabolas. If you're queasy, please remain strapped in, but if you would like, you can unstrap now and gather on the center ramp."

All of the youngsters and one ninety-four-year-old Afghanistan veteran gathered near the center-line.

"Have you ever worked out weightless?" Kalinda asked.

"Duh, no," Jeff said.

"It's a great way to improve your balance. Watch."

They felt heavier as Fat Albert pitched up and then Kalinda and Jeff rose from the padded deck as the aircraft went ballistic. Facing Jeff, Kalinda began some intricate moves with punches, spins, and kicks that Jeff never saw before. She remained vertical and finished facing Jeff. As the plane dove, they felt two Gs at the trough of the waveform.

"You try it this time."

Jeff faced her as Fat Albert began the climb. When the aircraft went parabolic, he started his moves. Intricate punches, kicks, and spins took him in three directions at once. He wound up upside down facing away from Kalinda. He landed on his back when the C-130 Hercules went over the top and began the climb.

"Nice moves."

"Thanks, but you're right about the balance thing. You're scary good."

"Thanks."

After enjoying the experience as vigorously as the youngsters, the grizzled veteran calmly returned to his seat as did everyone else.

The gunny spoke up again. "We'll now take volunteers up to the cockpit in groups of three." Jeff and Kalinda were in the second group along with the old veteran.

The co-pilot welcomed them and pointed out the various controls and then asked if there were any questions.

The old veteran spoke up. "Why is this model of the Hercules designated C-130U instead of the next letter in the alphabet?"

Jeff answered, "This aircraft has Scott Reactors using soft containment fusion. All fusion-powered military ships and aircraft have the letter U designation."

"This C-130 has seven reactors, one for each engine, two for avionics, and one for special payloads," Kalinda said.

"You three sound pretty knowledgeable," Major Imani Williams, the aircraft commander said. "Have any of you flown an aircraft?"

"I did three tours flying C-130s in and out of Kandahar," the old veteran said. "I once landed and took off from the USS Eisenhower off the coast of Pakistan."

"I read about that," Bill said. "How did you take off?"

"That was easy. The captain gave us fifty knots over the bow, and we were airborne with fifty yards to spare," the veteran said. "But it was a real bitch landing on a carrier heavy without a tail hook."

"Thanks for your service, sir," Major Williams said. "How about you, young man?"

"My mom has let me take the right seat in an SH-5 Sea Queen helicopter several times," Jeff said. "She's in the Persian Gulf on the *Winfrey*."

"Kalinda, I spoke with your father. You two have come a long way. What's your experience?" Major Williams said.

"I piloted the Patrol Ship *Mendex*, ma'am," Kalinda said, "and *StarCruiser Brilliant*."

"Is that a video game?" the co-pilot asked.

"No, sir. It's a vessel of the Hoclarth Alliance. My te'pa was Predex."

"It still sounds like a video game," the co-pilot said, "unless you're an alien." He laughed.

Jeff held her back when she looked like she was going after him.

"Sorry, Kalinda," the major said. "If my partner had spoken to your father, he would know your father was a starship commander and you're a human just like the rest of us," the major said.

Properly dressed down, the captain monitored his instruments.

The major turned to the three observers. "Who would like to fly Fat Albert?"

Jeff and Kalinda raised their hands. "I've spent enough time in the left seat of a Herc," said the old veteran. "Let the kids have a chance."

"Who goes first?" the pilot said. "I know Kalinda's name. Who are you?"

"My name is Jeff, sir," Jeff said.

He turned to Kalinda. "Rock-paper-scissors?"

"Two out of three," Kalinda said.

The two faced each other.

"Rock Paper Scissors." Jeff picked paper, Kalinda picked rock. Jeff won.

"Rock Paper Scissors." Jeff picked paper again and Kalinda picked scissors. Kalinda won.

"Rock Paper Scissors." Jeff picked scissors. Kalinda picked rock. Kalinda won.

"Captain, you are relieved," the major said.

Kalinda got strapped in. Without prompting, she adjusted the wheel and rudder controls for her height, a recent feature of this model. Then she put on the headset.

"Should I explain the controls?" the major asked. "It looks like you've done this."

"I spent twelve hours in a steveLearn simulator for this aircraft," Kalinda said.

"Okay, it is time to head south back to Miramar. Perform a standard rate right turn to reverse course."

"Standard right turn, aye, ma'am."

The pilot was impressed as Kalinda smoothly coordinated the wheel and rudder pedals into a right turn without any change in altitude. Sixty seconds later the aircraft was steady after a one-hundred-eighty-degree turn.

"Very nicely done." The major operated the throttle and a switch. "You just lost number four." The aircraft began to yaw to the right.

Kalinda operated a switch to feather the propeller, raised power on engines two and three and applied left rudder. She looked out to the right to verify that engine four was feathered. "Major, the aircraft is stable. Please call up the procedure for the loss of an engine."

"Not necessary," the pilot said. "You performed all of the immediate actions as well as any seasoned pilot. I've got the aircraft. Let's give Jeff a shot."

As Jeff strapped in, Major Williams restarted engine four. Jeff did a pretty good job on the turn, but the pilot walked him through the loss of engine one.

20

T he Star Squad gathered behind Hangar Seven where they kept
the MV-27 Raptors. A gunnery sergeant took them a short
walk toward the Aircraft museum. Through the fence, they saw
aircraft over a century old.

Their destination was a fifteen-foot structure that looked like a
rail gun with an aircraft seat at the bottom.

"If I could have your attention, I'm Master Sergeant Fred Jackson. You may address me as Top. The F-52 that you will be riding in
has a zero-zero egress system," Master Sergeant Jackson said.
"Whether you're at fifty thousand feet or stopped on the ground, this
seat will take you, and the parts held close to your body safely out of
your aircraft. That means you must keep your legs tucked and your
arms close to your body so that they'll accompany you on your trip
back to Earth."

Two minutes later, Tayla was strapped in with a flight helmet on
her head. The seat was attached to a fifteen-foot tall rail. She did not
look happy.

"Young lady, when I say the words, 'Eject, eject, eject,' lock your head back, tuck your legs and pull the two actuators by your side. Are you ready?"

Tayla nodded.

"Eject, Eject, Eject," the senior chief said.

No one in the room heard the second word because the compressed air sound of a cherry bomb erupted below Tayla and by the third word, Tayla was twelve feet up the rail.

"Very good. Who's next?"

Riley, Jennifer, and David each took their turns on the trainer.

"Be aware of your situation in the air," the senior chief said. "If your aircraft has a casualty and your pilot decides that it is not going to return you to the ground safely, he or she will pull the ejection handles, and you will depart the aircraft one-tenth of a second before the pilot. This is not a courtesy. It's so that the fire that lights under your ass doesn't fry the pilot first. Good luck and enjoy your hop with the Blue Angels, the United States Navy Flight Demonstration Team."

They said thanks and shook hands.

"Now, go out and meet the Blue Angels pilots on the flight line."

The four went through the hangar out into the San Diego sun and walked toward the six pilots in royal blue and gold flight suits with whom they were going to fly on the hop.

A SHORT BLOND pilot stepped forward. "I'm Commander Jon Lathrop, call sign Munchkin. I'm the Blue Angels commander, and I will be flying Blue Angels One. We'll fly out to sea in the diamond formation and then separate and give your crew some stick time. Riley, you will ride on Blue Angels Four."

"I'm Lieutenant Frank Weisser, call sign Walleye," the pilot said. "Welcome aboard."

"Thanks much," Riley said. "My call sign is StarDancer."

"What's your billet on *Brilliant*?" Walleye said.

"I'm the ship's engineer," Riley said.

"Doesn't *Brilliant* have a soft containment fusion power plant like our Bobcats?"

"Yes, sir. It's a slightly different design and a different provenance. Admiral Kelrithian designed *Brilliant* in an alternate timeline, but I've made some improvements to our power plant."

"I expect the F-52 power plant is much different than yours."

"Mostly in size. Scaling down the cooling system was difficult. The manufacturer had some issues with the prototype," Riley said. "I consulted with the engineers to fix them. I hold three patents on the propulsion plant of your aircraft."

"What do you do in your spare time?"

Riley didn't recognize the sarcasm. "My girlfriend and I are SoCal Salsa champs."

"Tayla, you will fly with our number one solo in Blue Angel Five."

A tall stunningly handsome African-American stepped up. "Hi, Tayla. I'm Lieutenant Commander Erik Doyle, call sign Popeye. Do you have a call sign?"

"My friends and fans call me Ayiiia," Tayla said as she blushed. "I'm *Brilliant*'s Communications Officer."

"That's the name of a character in *Galaxy Warrior*."

She blinked her eyes, flirting with the pilot. "What a coincidence. That happens to be the character I play in the movie *Galaxy Warrior*."

She caught a mean look from Riley.

"David, you will fly with Blue Angel Three," Munchkin said.

"Lieutenant Ryan Chamberlain, call sign Droopy. I hear you fly the left seat on *Brilliant*."

"Yes sir. I've been the pilot since I turned eighteen."

"Have you flown anything like the Bobcat?" Droopy said.

"Only on the steveLearn simulator," David said. "But my dad

and I designed a Tomcat interface for close range combat. I can fly *Brilliant* like an F-14 in close quarters."

"You played the pilot in the last two movies. What's your call sign?"

"StarPilot." David used "moviestar" but changed it after receiving some good-natured ribbing from his squad mates.

"Jennifer, you will be with our Marine representative on Blue Angel Two."

"We met earlier," Jennifer said. "Show me the way, Fifi."

"Your pilots will help you get aboard your aircraft," Munchkin said. "Joining us will be Blue Angel Six, Lieutenant Bill Meyers call sign Artoo. Artoo and I will record the action."

As THEY WALKED toward their Bobcat, "You are First Officer of *Brilliant*?" Fifi said.

"Yes, Ma'am. I handle operations and tactics. And I fill in as the pilot when David is unavailable."

"You landed *Brilliant* on top of the hospital?"

"Yes, ma'am."

"I watched on TV. That was nice flying. What d'you know about the Bobcat?"

"I've read all of the manuals, and I have twenty-five hours on our simulator."

"Really?"

"It's in the Captain's ready room on the *Brilliant*."

"Like a video game?"

"No, ma'am. It's a full simulator, and we have the artificial gravity wired for nine G maneuvers."

"Nine Gs?" Fifi said.

"Yes, but we won't be able to do that today. We aren't wearing G-suits."

"Actually, we will," Fifi said. "Our F-52U has an upgraded Holographic Tactile Virtual Reality system on board that includes a G-suit."

"I wasn't aware of that capability."

"It's classified, and we got it for this season," Fifi said. "What were you doing pulling nine gees?"

"Trying to pull ten," Jennifer said. "I had a MIG-48 on my six."

"I'd love to see your system this afternoon."

"Sure. Sami, can you join us?" Sami popped up to Jennifer's left. "Meet Captain Boyington. I'll be flying with her.

"Nice to meetcha," Sami said. "How may I help you, Jen?"

"The F-52U has HTVR on board eliminating the need for a G-suit."

"Located," Sami said. "I'll work with Ani and implement the upgrade for this afternoon."

"Thanks, Sami."

"Enjoy your flight," Sami said. "Sorry I won't be up there with you."

"Sami is a pilot?"

"Sami is my virtual assistant. Ani is our Artificial Navigation Intelligence on *Brilliant*," Jennifer said. "Sami was flying the MIG-48."

"She seems much smarter than Bobcat."

"She runs on the twin CPUs at *Brilliant* and HumanAI Corp."

"Your callsign is Jendroid?"

"Yes, Captain."

"Let's get you strapped in and up in the air," Fifi said. "Gunny, give her a hand."

Ten minutes later, the four Blue Angels were lined up on Runway Two-four Left in a tight V-formation with One in the lead.

"We're cleared for take-off," Munchkin said. "The winds are ten knots at one-nine-five. That's a slight left crosswind. Check your parking break off, check your trim set, check your nose wheel steering is on. Maneuver straight ahead for a westbound climb out to forty thousand."

"Fifi copies."

"Droopy copies."

"Diamond Half Clear. Let's go," Walleye said.

"Let's run 'em up."

The pilots in Blue Angels Two, Three, and Four, gave a thumbs up.

"Off brakes now. Turbines to Full Military Power," Munchkin said.

When the last aircraft left the ground, Blue Angels Four said, "Gear."

The pilots raised their landing gear, and Walleye dropped his nose and shifted left into the slot to form the Blue Angels Diamond.

THEY PASSED over Torrey Pines State Beach. "We are feet wet climbing to angels forty. Secure turbines and shift to ramjets. Accelerate to Mach Two."

After Fifi signaled thumbs up, Jennifer saw her throttles move forward to the firewall and felt the pressure of four G's as the aircraft accelerated.

"We've got an op area east of San Clemente Island twenty-five miles out to sea," Fifi said.

"Why does the Commander go by Munchkin? Is it because he is small?" Jennifer asked.

"His great grandfather was one of the little people in *The Wizard of Oz*," Fifi said. "How did you become a part of the *Brilliant* crew?"

"I'm a brillian, and I read the *Brilliant* Tech Manual growing up. I got a Tovar Studio internship over the summer. It turns out my grandfather designed *StarCruiser Brilliant* and runs the studio."

"Wow. That's a steep learning curve."

"I've got a pretty good memory."

· · ·

"FIVE AND SIX HAVE CAUGHT UP," Munchkin said. "We're over the op area. Reduce speed to four hundred knots. Set up for the Diamond Roll Break. Let's split up and give our *Brilliant* crew members some stick time. Your operational floor is fifteen thousand feet,"

Two, Three and Four acknowledged.

"Ready, break."

FIFI ROLLED right and performed a tight turn and then returned to level flight. "We're assigned to the Northeast quadrant. Would you like to take control?"

"Yes, ma'am," Jennifer said.

"Right hand on the stick, left hand on the throttle, and feet on the rudder pedals. Ready?" Fifi said.

"Yes."

"You have the aircraft, Jendroid."

"I've got the aircraft, Fifi. Altitude twenty-eight thousand, heading zero-four-zero," Jennifer said. I'm going to do a barrel roll. Would you evaluate?"

"Of course."

Jennifer looked over the right wing for a reference point and only saw blue-green ocean. She pulled the stick and applied right rudder. As the aircraft went through inverted, she rotated the controls smoothly and returned to base course.

"Wow, you finished eight feet high and overshot by seven degrees. Nearly perfect," Fifi said. "I performed that maneuver twenty-seven times before I got that close. That was after I reported to the Blue Angels."

"I can do better, Fifi. The water makes it hard to pick a reference point."

"Bet a coke you cannot beat what you did before."

"Done."

Jennifer performed the maneuver again.

"Omigod. Three and three. I owe you a coke. You could trade your cerulean for our Navy blue."

"Thanks, I'll stick with cerulean. My *Brilliant* goes a bit faster."

"I guess it does."

Blue Angels Three was in the southwest quadrant.

"I've got the aircraft," David said.

"Why don't you try a wingover?" Droopy said. "It's a simple aerobatic move where you pull the nose up and reverse course. A crop duster would use this maneuver."

"How about a four-point roll?"

"Or you could do that." *I've got to see this.* "Artoo is recording. Show your stuff."

David pulled up his nose and snapped right ninety degrees with left rudder.

"One."

Ninety more to inverted.

"Two."

Again, he snapped the aircraft to a vertical left bank.

"Three."

Finally, David snapped back to level flight.

"Four."

"Same altitude and heading. Pretty good," Droopy said. *This guy can fly.*

In Blue Angels Six, "Got it," Artoo said. "Chief Pritt will have that on SocNet before we get back to Miramar."

"David, have you thought about a career as a Naval Aviator?"

"Do you have any aircraft that go eighteen hundred times the speed of light?"

"Not yet, but I'm sure they have something on the drawing board," Droopy said.

"Gotta have some standards."

"We're pretty high and need to turn around. Show me a split-s and give up some altitude."

"Aye, sir."

David snapped the Bobcat inverted and pulled a 4G half-loop to reverse course.

ABOARD BLUE ANGELS TWO, "Bogey approaching at two o'clock low," Bobcat said. "It's Munchkin."

"Jendroid, your crewmate just performed a pristine four-point roll," Munchkin said. "Can you top that?"

"I know I can count higher, Munch," Jennifer said.

"You're clear above and below," Fifi said.

"Recording," Munchkin said.

"Executing."

Jennifer snap-rolled forty-five degrees right.

"One."

Again, to a vertical right bank.

"Two."

She kept counting.

"Three...Four." The aircraft was inverted.

"Five...Six...Seven...Eight."

"That was a pretty eight-point roll," Munchkin said. "Fifi is going to be jealous because she is the only member of the team that can pull that off."

Fifi smiled into her mask. "It's called girl power, Munch."

21

They punched holes in the sky for fifteen more minutes. "Blue Angels Four and Five are headed back to the barn for some fresh airsick bags," Munchkin said. "Fifi, please join up with Blue Angels Three at Point Charlie Five," Munchkin said. "Artoo and I have some extracurriculars planned for the two pilots."

"Fifi copies." Over the intercom, "Do you understand what they have in mind?"

"I got this," Jennifer said. "Bobcat, plot a speed course to Charlie Five. Intercept Blue Angels Three."

"Turn left to one-nine-five, accelerate to Mach one-point-three for two minutes. Maintain Twenty thousand feet," Bobcat said. Bobcat, the Aircraft Artificial Intelligence acted in place of the backseater who was called the Radar Intercept Officer or RIO.

"One-nine-five, Angels twenty." Jennifer shoved the throttles forward and pulled the stick to the left and back.

"Fifi, I don't want to run into anything. Are we safe?"

"Bobcat has an Automatic Collision Avoidance System," Fifi said. "Maneuver at will."

Ninety seconds later.

"Blue Angels Three is at your nine o'clock. Turn right to two-seven-eight, speed four fifty."

Jennifer pulled back on the throttles, turned right and bled speed as she approached the other aircraft on his left.

"Jendroid, this is a lot different when you add in the g-forces. This is fun," David said.

"Told ya you needed to try the sim on *Brilliant*."

"Are you two ready for some simulated air combat?" Fifi said.

They acknowledged.

"Arm the targeting lasers. Your pilots will evaluate hits."

"Bobcat, Arm targeting lasers for air combat practice," Jennifer said.

"Your lasers are armed. Your display is configured for Air Combat Maneuvering. Your hard floor is fifteen thousand feet."

"Have fun, jendroid," Fifi said.

"ALERT," Bobcat said. "Bandits approaching at four o'clock high range five miles, Mach 2.3. Blue Angels One and Six are squawking as adversaries."

"StarPilot, join up on my right wing."

"StarPilot copies."

Jennifer looked over her right wing to see David approaching. "Let's get some air under us."

Jennifer shoved the throttle to the firewall and pulled to the vertical. The Bobcat's three-to-one thrust-to-weight ratio pushed her back into her seat with a five G force.

"Munchkin is level at forty thousand feet. Artoo is climbing to pursue," Bobcat said.

Sneaky bastard, Jennifer thought. *Artoo will bleed our altitude and Munch will clean up.*

"StarPilot, I'll level out westbound at Angels seventy-eight,"

Jennifer said. "Establish a Combat Spread at eighty. I'm the bait; you're the hook."

"StarPilot," David acknowledged.

Jennifer completed the Immelmann roll. David continued his climb and then leveled out a mile beyond her right wing.

"Artoo is coming up your tail at two miles. He'll lock lasers at one-half mile," Bobcat said.

"StarPilot, ready left turn and take your shot."

"StarPilot."

"One mile," Bobcat said.

"Execute."

On Blue Angels Three, Droopy was shaking his head in amazement. "Your partner knows her tactics.

"She does," David replied as he heard Jennifer give the order to execute the turn. He rolled one-hundred-twenty degrees left and pulled back into the turn. He saw Jennifer doing the same. And then he saw Artoo come into his gunsights and heard the tone indicating laser lock.

On Blue Angels Six, *Gotcha, pretty girl,* Artoo thought. When heard tone, he squeezed the trigger.

Jennifer heard the warning, snapped right, and pulled.

Missed, Artoo thought. He snapped right directly into David's sights.

"Warning: Laser lock."

What the hell?

. . .

DAVID TRIGGERED HIS LASERS. "HIT," Bobcat Three said. "Blue Angels Six is disabled.

"CONGRATS, StarPilot. I'm headed to the barn," said Artoo

ON BLUE ANGELS TWO, "Munchkin at your ten o'clock," Jennifer turned left to decrease the angle. So did Munchkin.

MUNCHKIN HEARD TONE. *Gotcha, jendroid,* Munchkin thought. He pulled the trigger.

JENNIFER HEARD, "LASER LOCK." Immediately after, "Warning: Damage to right aileron. Turning capability decreased by sixty percent."

Ouch, she thought. As Munchkin passed her on the left, she saw him continue his turn.

"Munchkin on your belly, David," she said. She pulled her throttles back and began a slow descent.

"You done good, Jendroid, but it's not over," Fifi said.

"Stay with me, Fifi," Jennifer replied.

GOTCHA, StarPilot, thought Munchkin. He heard tone and triggered.

TWO SECONDS AFTER DAVID YELLED, "YEAH," he heard Jennifer's warning. He rolled one-eighty and pulled. "Laser lock." David continued his roll and turned toward the deck. "Warning: Simulated damage to aircraft. Your weapons are disabled," Bobcat said.

"Very good day's work," said Droopy. "Artoo splashed three bad guys in the last conflict and Munchkin is an ace. But your partner is damaged. She'll have a bad day."

"She has tricks, Droop," David said. "She told me that she would get Munchkin today."

"That's overconfidence."

"That's money," David said. "She has this vision thing."

"No way. She's damaged. A lame duck."

MUNCHKIN TURNED hard right and dove for the deck to approach Jendroid from beneath. *Let's finish this.* He centered Blue Angels Two in his gun sight at three miles.

ON BLUE ANGELS TWO, "Munchkin on your six at three miles." She leveled out at twenty-five thousand feet.

"Bobcat, on my mark, activate vertical thrust at forty percent," Jennifer said.

"Ready," came the acknowledgment. "Two miles."

"Flaps down. Deploy air brakes. Activate the turbine."

No way, Fifi thought.

WHAT THE HELL *is she doing?* Munchkin thought.

"ONE MILE," Bobcat said.

"Deploy thrusters," Jennifer said while pulling the stick back to the stops.

OMIGOD. Munchkin pushed his stick forward to avoid the collision as he saw Blue Angels Two pitch up beyond vertical.

. . .

"Secure thrusters and brakes. Flaps up." She shoved the throttle forward to the firewall, threw the stick to the forward limit. "Trigger lasers on tone."

Blue Angels Two pitched forward to nose down and found Munchkin in her gunsights. She heard tone and saw the laser trail.

"Damn," Munchkin said.

"Warning: Simulated aircraft damage. Weapons unavailable."

"You got 'im," Fifi shouted.

"Splash the Munchkin," Jennifer said.

"Score one for the girls," Fifi said. "Seriously? Pugachev's Cobra? I saw a MIG do that at the Paris Airshow. No one has ever done that in combat."

"Jendroid, let's head back to Miramar," Munchkin said.

"I'll be your wingman, sir," Jennifer replied.

"No, ma'am, I'll be yours. Congratulations on your victory."

Artoo, Droopy, and StarPilot exited their aircraft and were standing with the crowd on the flight line as the two remaining Blue Angels passed Miramar eastbound.

"Why the hell is Two in the lead, Droopy?" Bill asked.

"I think she Cobra'ed his ass," Ryan said.

On board Blue Angels Two, "Miramar, Jendroid, requesting a flyby."

"Negative, Jendroid, the pattern is full," Miramar replied.

Munchkin remained locked on Jennifer's wing as she turned,

descended to two hundred feet, and accelerated to four-hundred-fifty knots. They flew directly over the flight line.

EVERYONE on the flight line ducked as the two jets screamed over. "Who does she think she is? Some kind of Maverick?" Bill said.

"That's my girlfriend, Artoo," David said. "She's First Officer of *StarCruiser Brilliant*."

22

After the C-130 landed, Jeff and Kalinda thanked the crew and walked to the F-52 hangar for lunch.

As they reached Tayla and Riley, Kalinda asked, "Where's my sister?"

Just then, two Blue Angels at two hundred feet screamed over the flight line. Jeff ducked, and Kalinda laughed. "That's strange. Why is two in the lead?" Jeff asked.

"Jennifer's flying Blue Angels Two," Tayla said. "She's maver-icky." She looked at the ten-year-old standing next to Kalinda. "And who are you?"

"Sorry. Tayla and Riley, this is my friend Jeff Rodriguez. I met him on a tour, and we rode Fat Albert together."

"Nice to meet you. Riley, you're the Engineer on *Brilliant* and Tayla, you're the Communicator. You're playing Ayiiia, too?"

"Correct, fanboi," Tayla said.

Kalinda acted offended when she teased Jeff. "Jeff is a brillian. He's read the *Brilliant Tech Manual*, he knows martial arts, and he knows how to surf."

"Does he know how to kiss?" Riley said. Jeff turned red, Kalinda looked puzzled, and Tayla slugged Riley on the arm.

Kalinda is seriously crushing, Tayla thought.

Kalinda took Riley aside. "Riley, may I ask the captain a favor?" Kalinda said. "I'd like to bring Jeff along this afternoon."

Riley smiled. "It might be too crowded, but you can ask."

Kalinda was not hearing no for an answer and smiled as she returned to Jeff's side.

Jennifer and David walked up. She looked surprised at Kalinda's plus one and the body language between the two kids.

"Didn't you tell me that Hoclarth women mate at the age of ten?" Jennifer said.

The four turned quickly. Riley and Tayla started giggling.

Kalinda assumed a fighting stance. "This is my friend, Jeff Rodriguez. And that thing I told you is only on the Qarmac Islands in the southern waters."

Jennifer held a straight face knowing her sister's sense of humor. Riley and Tayla froze.

The red-faced Jeff snapped his head back to Kalinda. He was facing sensory overload.

"Just kidding," Kalinda said.

Everyone laughed

She turned to Jeff. "We usually wait until we're twelve."

Jennifer stuck her hand out to Jeff. "I'm Jennifer, and this is David," Jennifer said. "If you're going to hang with us, you need to learn to handle irony."

Jeff realized he was shaking hands with David Masing, the pilot of *StarCruiser Brilliant*.

"You took a blaster to the chest to save Jennifer near Proxima Centauri?"

That information only appeared on the underground brillian websites.

"You *are* a real fanboi, aren't you?" David said. "Call me David."

Riley patted David on the back. "You two had a good day. One of you even came back in one piece."

Jennifer showed her pride. "Yep, David blew up Artoo, and then..."

"Yeah, Yeah, Munchkin got a lucky shot on me. Then you splashed him."

"It was a fun day." Jennifer and Tayla high-fived.

"Not over yet," Riley said. "We're giving the Blue Angels a hop after lunch."

"It's just another milk run."

"You HEARD IT," Tayla said. "Somebody's gonna die."

"I'm hungry," Kalinda said.

"You eat like a pig, K'da," Tayla said.

"I thought pigs were something that humans ate."

"Only after they're as fat as you would be if you had a normal metabolism."

"It's the gravity," Kalinda said.

Jennifer shoved her best friend. "Yeah, it's the gravity."

Kalinda changed the subject. "Dandy talked to me today."

Jennifer stopped and looked at Kalinda. "He did?" She had doubts. Kalinda had a sense of humor. "What did he say?"

"He stopped our tour of *Brilliant*," Kalinda said. "He wouldn't let us continue until I told the story about how he saved you from the meteor."

She smiled. "That's Dandy," Jennifer said. "Did the other kids bug you about talking to a cat?"

"Didn't have to. I read his thoughts, and he read mine."

"I guess we have a talking cat," Jennifer said. *Can she think back to him?*

"A talking cat with a nasty attitude," Kalinda said.

They walked toward the hangar for lunch.

23

The huge grey hangar had been built to store and maintain the F-52s just coming to the fleet. The hangar doors opened only at night to move aircraft in and out and maintain habitable temperatures. The group headed for a small door to the left of the hangar doors.

About fifty yards away Kalinda asked, "What are you doing this afternoon, Jeff?"

"I guess we're going to take my grandmother home. She's spending the night before flying back to South Dakota. Then I've got homework for school tomorrow. Why?"

"Let me ask Jack if you can ride with us on *Brilliant* this afternoon."

"Jack...as in Captain Jack Masing?" *Am I dreaming?*

Kalinda nodded.

"Omigod, that would be so amazingly way cool. Thanks, Kay!"

Kalinda looked stern. "No one calls me that." *Why's my heart beating so fast?* "But you can. We need to run to get permission."

"Let me ask my dad," Jeff said. "Darth, are you up?" The black helmeted figure popped up.

"Yes, Dark Master," the helmet said.

"Message my dad and ask him if I can take a ride on *Brilliant*."

"Yes, my lord."

"Let's run."

They got in line for security. The dark helmet popped up. "Dark master, your father says yes but be back on the flight line by five. You're having dinner at the hotel in La Jolla with your grandmother."

"Thank him for me." The dark helmet disappeared.

THE TWO CAUGHT up with Jack as he was entering the hangar. Kalinda tapped him on the arm.

Jack turned and looked at the pair. "Who's your friend, Kalinda?" Jack said.

"Captain, this is my friend, Jeff Rodriguez."

"Nice to meet you, young man." They shook hands as Jeff stood at attention.

"I'm honored, sir," Jeff said. "I've always wanted to meet you, sir. Did you save Anthen from the Hoclarth, sir?"

"I had a lot of help. Why don't you call me Jack?" he said. "What do you two need?"

"May I bring Jeff on the ride?" Kalinda asked.

"Son, do you have permission?"

"Yes, sir...I mean Jack."

"We're crowded on this flight...we only have room in the hold where we keep alien animals."

"That would be totally fine, sir."

Jack was doing his best to keep a straight face. "When you're on *Brilliant*, you will address me as Captain, understand?"

"Yes, sir...sorry...Wait...I can go?"

"Listen to Kalinda and don't press the Red Button marked Self-Destruct."

"Yes, Captain. Thank you" Jeff said. He sent a confused look at Kalinda. "Irony?"

Kalinda nodded.

"Did you two see the two Blue Angels do the high-speed pass?" Jack said. "Was it any of ours?"

"It was Jennifer," Kalinda said. "Tayla said she was being mavericky."

"Oh, that explains a lot. You two be at the ramp at 1400."

"Yes, Captain," they said in unison.

The captain walked toward the head table. The two followed, and Jeff said, "Mavericky?"

"When we were on long patrols, my dad and I watched Earth movies. The Hoclarth Alliance has had a satellite cloaked in Earth orbit for many years. It's supposed to gather intelligence and re-transmit it by StarWave back to our home planet. But mostly it sends back TV, Movies, and the Internet."

"Irony?"

"Nope, just facts. It's how I learned English," Kalinda said. "We watched *Top Gun* seven times."

"Oh, I remember. Tom Cruise was Maverick," Jeff said.

"Yeah," Kalinda said. "That guy was cute."

They entered the massive hangar through a small door. The huge hangar doors were shut to keep out the noon San Diego heat which averaged in the low three digits in September. There were lunch tables decorated with Marine scarlet and gold for three hundred guests including San Diego politicians, defense contractors, military and dependents, the Blue Angels Pilots and the crew of *Brilliant*. On each side, there were folding chairs for the sailors, marines, and their dependents who would come in afterward for the speeches.

To the left of the elevated head table was an F-18 in Blue Angels livery. To the right was an F-52U Fighter from Marine Fighter Attack Squadron 232.

"I'm sitting with the crew," Kalinda said. "Are you in the next hangar with dependents?"

"Nope, my dad said we're in the front someplace."

Kalinda sent Jeff a questioning look.

"My grandmother is giving a speech."

"Okay, see ya after."

Navvy was seated near the base commanding general with Maiara to his left next to the General and Jack to his right.

General Lindstrom turned to Maiara and made small talk. "What are your duties aboard the starship?" the General said.

"I'm First Lieutenant, but my most important job is to prepare meals on long voyages," Maiara said.

"Do you serve anything stronger than Tang when you are in space?"

Maiara clenched her jaw. "The Captain likes a blue concoction he likes to call Romulan Ale."

"Where did you learn to cook?"

"After I left the Royal New Zealand Navy, I spent a year in Paris at Le Cordon Bleu."

"Oh," said the general, taken aback. "I hope that our Marine chow meets your standards."

"I'm sure it will. I suspect that since it's a special occasion, the chef will put an extra helping of sand in the instant mashed potatoes."

"Touché," the general said.

The waiter served Navvy a proper slice of rare prime rib and then spoke to Navvy, "Admiral, the chef sends her respects and lets the Admiral know that the Marines try to limit the blood to the battlefield."

Navvy laughed. "Tell her this looks wonderful."

He looked over to Jack. "I hear that our pilots distinguished themselves today."

"David got shot down but not before he disabled Blue Angels Six," Jack said. "Jennifer took out the leader, but I caught hell when she rattled the windows coming back."

"Pretty *Brilliant*," Navvy said. "It's all over social media. The *Attack* trailer got ten million hits the last hour."

• • •

Kalinda finished her chocolate cherry cheesecake. "Te'pa, may I be excused?"

"You don't want to stay for the exciting speeches?"

"I'm going to work out with Jeff in zero gravity on *Brilliant*."

"Check in with Ani and be safe."

She walked over to the table where Jeff was sitting. "Mr. Rodriguez, would it be alright for Jeff to come back to *Brilliant* and work out with me before the flight?"

"Is there an adult aboard?"

"Ani is on *Brilliant* doing security."

"Very well," Mr. Rodriguez said. "Don't break the pretty starship."

"Yes, sir and thanks."

"Remember, I'll pick you up here at five p.m."

"Yes, sir."

They departed the hangar as plates were cleared and the speeches began.

24

The Commanding General completed his introductory remarks quickly. All present wanted to hear from the chief designer of *StarCruiser Brilliant*.

"For the last forty years," General Lindstrom said. "*StarCruiser Brilliant* has been a member of a highly classified Navy reserve command. This command is available for specialized missions at the request of fleet commanders. *Brilliant* has answered that call in a distinguished manner seven times."

Tayla asked Riley, "I'm in the Navy?"

"Only if they call us up," Riley said. "It's been about ten years since the last time."

"Ladies and Gentlemen, Please welcome Rear Admiral Navvy Kelrithian, United States Naval Reserve, Commander, Star Patrol Wing One."

Military members stood at attention and applauded. Civilians stood as well.

Navvy made his way to the microphone. He shook hands with a smiling Ramona Curtwell.

He saluted General Lindstrom then approached the microphone.

"Take seats, everyone."

The three hundred military and civilians sat in unison in silence.

"This morning I asked my wife, Hanna, what I should talk about. She said, 'About ten minutes.'"

The attendees laughed.

"Jack, Hanna, and I came from two hundred years in the future. Fortunately, it was not your future because our timeline faced a nuclear war that devastated the planet, killed eighty percent of the world's population, and started one hundred years of darkness and cold. But humanity recovered and I had the opportunity to build *StarCruiser Brilliant*.

"On a shakedown flight, we had an engineering casualty and traveled back two hundred years. We came to a different Earth where, so far, you have avoided nuclear annihilation. John Mitchell Scott solved the energy problem that caused my Earth to almost destroy itself. I learned something.

"A smart person never makes the same mistake twice," Navvy said. "A wise person never makes the same mistake once.

"Ladies and Gentlemen, the nuclear mistake will always be on the horizon. Are we smart or are we wise?"

There was loud applause.

"In the forty years since *Brilliant* came to this timeline, Earth's technology has caught up with the technologies from our timeline. When we look at the stars today, we're not alone. It's time for humans again to look outward. It's time for the scientists, engineers, and builders to leapfrog *Brilliant* and build the starships that will take humans to other worlds."

"Soldiers, Sailors, and Marines, you are the best and the brightest. As poet John Magee said, it is time for you to 'slip the surly bonds of earth,' and take humanity to the distant stars."

The crowd rose and cheered.

"I want to thank our military members for their service, thanks to our families for their invaluable support and thanks to everyone for your San Diego Hospitality."

The diners congratulated Navvy as he made his way back to his seat. Senator Curtwell offered her hand but did not look Navvy in the eye.

General Lindstrom returned to the microphone. "The daughter of our keynote speaker is serving as a helo pilot on the *USS Oprah Winfrey*. Please welcome the junior senator from South Dakota, Ramona Curtwell."

She received polite applause as she approached the microphone.

"Members of our armed forces, you *are* the best and brightest. Just like the speaker before me said. What he didn't tell you is that he wants to eliminate your jobs. He wants to replace those of you willing to explore, to lead, to serve, and to sacrifice for our country."

There was a nervous murmur going through the crowd.

"Navvy Kelrithian wants to replace our best and brightest with artificial intelligence and dull metal. Pilots, your place in the cockpit will be taken by an android. Sailors, you will be replaced by robots. Doctors and nurses, virtuals can care for the patients as well as you can. Everyone, you will follow the orders of a yellow-eyed automaton who will eventually take orders from no one."

A marine stood up and said, "No way, lady."

"Navvy Kelrithian and HumanAI Corp want to replace humanity with virtuals from the menial maintenance job to the top of the corporate ladder," the senator said. "Not only that, he won't get his hands dirty doing it. He has placed his puppet granddaughter in charge of the company that will produce the androids."

Jennifer's face went white.

"This is fake news, right?" Tayla said. She saw the fear on Jennifer's face.

"We must stop the scourge of the Singularity. We must all gather together and save our jobs and our humanity. Tell me what we must do."

There was silence. Then a single voice, a member of the senator's staff shouted, "Turn them off!"

The uniformed military members surrounding her turned and just looked at her.

The senator was deflated but pressed on, "We must make laws to stop these androids and protect your jobs. Again, what must we do?"

Another staffer planted in the crowd shouted, "Turn them off!"

Again, those around him just stared.

Senator Curtwell got the message. "The time will come when you understand this technological threat. In the meantime, I'll fight for your jobs. I'll fight for my daughter's job. I'm Senator Ramona Curtwell, and I'm running for President."

The military members slowly stood, as was tradition, but the applause was sparse.

A Marine Captain came to the microphone. "Please remain standing as the head table departs."

SENATOR CURTWELL EXITED to the left and passed by the F-18. On the way to the exit, she received obligatory handshakes and thank you's but was otherwise ignored.

Her son-in-law met her at the black SUV. "Good Speech, Senator," Chuck said.

Senator Curtwell looked around. "Where is my grandson?"

"He found a friend to hang with," Chuck said. He knew that his mother-in-law would not approve of his trip on *Brilliant*. "He'll join us for dinner."

"I'll see you two at dinner," the senator said. "Those people in there were rude."

"The military are required to be apolitical when in uniform," Chuck said.

"We've got reservations at six. Please be there with my grandson."

"Yes, Senator."

Chuck stood by as she got in the SUV and it drove away. *I'm one of the most successful attorneys in San Diego, and she still thinks her daughter married down.*

. . .

THE DRIVER PULLED out of the base. "Senator, there are some drinks in the cooler," the driver said.

She reached down and pulled one out. Then she reached to her hip and pulled out her HoloPad. The head and shoulders of her virtual assistant popped up before her.

"Harold, what the hell just happened?"

"Senator, I advised that the military would, at best, be polite," Harold said. "They don't like long deployments, and they don't like getting shot at. Polls show that they would be receptive to more robots."

"My father was a film actor," Senator Curtwell said. "He drank himself to death when he could no longer get work because virtual actors replaced him."

"I know, Senator," Harold said.

"And Navvy Kelrithian is responsible," she said. "And now his granddaughter is taking it a step further."

"Maybe you chose the wrong venue to pick a fight."

"A great president once said, 'When somebody challenges you, fight back.'"

"He didn't even make it through one term, Senator," Harold said.

"He was still great," the senator said. "What do I have, this afternoon, Harold?"

"A grip and grin with donors in La Costa, Senator."

"At least people with money like me."

"Of course, Senator," Harold said. He programmed his smile to look sincere.

THE CREW of the *Brilliant* met Navvy as he signed autographs and traded challenge coins with those in attendance.

"Why does that senator hate you so much, Navvy?" David asked.

"It's a long story, but I knew her father several years ago."

"What was she saying about you making Jennifer build robots?" Tayla asked.

"I've learned that you cannot make Jennifer do anything," Navvy said. "You'll have to ask Jennifer about the rest."

Riley said, "It's fake news, right?" Riley said.

Everyone looked at Jennifer.

"I've started this project at JennaTech," Jennifer said. "Sami wants to watch a sunset."

"We're behind you," Tayla said. "But Curtwell might cause you a lot of trouble."

"We're aware," Navvy said. He turned to go. "I'm riding the Gulfstream back to Burbank. I'll see you all at Tovar tomorrow."

"Let's head out to *Brilliant*," Jack said. "We owe the Blue Angels a trip into space."

The crew headed toward their *StarCruiser*.

25

After they left the hangar, Jeff and Kalinda walked across the red-hot tarmac. On the flight line, September temperatures reach 120 degrees.

"I'm glad we got out of there before the speeches," Jeff said.

"But didn't you want to see your grandmother..."

"I know she's running for President," he said. "The rest of the speech is boring." They reached *Brilliant*, Jeff said, "Could we walk around the ship?"

"Sure. Don't kick the tires too hard; they might go flat," Kalinda said.

Jeff gave a condescending look at her droll humor.

"You're starting to get it...There are the torpedo doors."

"Smart Tactical Autonomous Long-Range Torpedoes," Jeff said. "Do you carry them all the time?"

"My te'pa told me that they used to fly missions like this unarmed, but now we always carry at least two with one war shot loaded."

"Cool."

"That's a secret."

He reached up with his hand and sealed his lips. Then Jeff pointed at the glass square near the top center of the bow. "I didn't know that *Brilliant* had a porthole."

"I asked my tal'pa the same thing because Hoclarth ships do not have windows. We're explorers. He told me about an admiral named Daniel Gallery who said, 'Curiosity is one of the strongest human emotions,'" Kalinda said. "No matter how many displays and sensors, we want to 'take a little peek now and then.'"

"I understand," Jeff said. "Let's get on board."

They walked to a closed ramp. "Request to come aboard with my friend, Jeff. Authorization: azolyn."

"Hello, Kalinda," Ani said. "Do you have your parent's permission?"

"Yes, ma'am."

"Welcome aboard." The ramp descended.

The two quickly threaded the maze of passages and ladders to the bridge.

"Configure the ready room for Serving Tal'qid with gravity control."

"Who's Ani?" Jeff asked.

"Ani is *Brilliant*'s Artificial Navigation Intelligence."

They reached the bridge. Jeff stopped and looked around.

"She's virtual?"

"Ani's been resident on *Brilliant* for twenty-six years. Would you like to meet her?"

"Wow, yeah."

"Could you go physical and meet us in the ready room."

"Sure," Ani said. "I'd be glad to meet your boyfriend."

"Ani!" Kalinda looked at the red-faced Jeff. He looked back at the red showing through Kalinda's dark complexion. "She likes to joke around."

Jeff quickly changed the subject. "May I sit in the captain's chair. I won't touch anything."

"Don't worry about it," Kalinda said. "Nothing works unless you're logged in...Except for the red button."

Jeff looked at Kalinda. She looked back with a straight face. They both laughed.

"I wonder what it looks like in space?"

"Ani put us in orbit around Xaphnore."

Immediately, the panels lit up and the display screens filled with a blue planet, two red suns, and several Hoclarth ships circling a large space station.

"Woah." Jeff looked closely at the surface. "That's definitely not Earth." He saw Kalinda walk slowly toward the displays transfixed. "You're homesick, aren't you Kay?"

"I want to go back someday, but it's not possible."

Jeff broke the spell. "Show me your dojo."

"Secure the simulation," Kalinda said. She led him to the ready room.

They reached the door. "Shoes," Kalinda said. Jeff and Kalinda took off their shoes and socks and lined them up to the right of the door. They entered the ready room.

"Welcome to my dojo."

Jeff's eyes lit up as his bare feet touched the hardwood floor. The hall was two stories surrounded by windows made of traditional rice paper and Tasmanian oak.

"This is like the Holodeck on the Enterprise," Jeff said.

"Bingo. My tal'pa is secretly a Star Trek fan."

There were vertical panels with writing. "Hoclarth?" Jeff asked.

"Those are the sayings of Tal'qid,"

"There are no weapons."

"When one is in the service of Tal'qid, she does not need weapons."

"Women only?"

"Not only," Kalinda said. "But men who pick up weapons always desire bigger weapons."

"And war," Jeff said. "I think my grandmother believes that."

Jeff pointed to the lone figure on her knees sitting on her heels facing a decorative rice paper screen. "Ani?"

Kalinda and Jeff approached. "May I present my friend, Jeff. He practices martial arts."

Ani stood and turned. With her right knee bent, she opened her hands and bowed her head to Kalinda and Jeff. Kalinda responded with the same bow and Jeff did the *rei* that he knew from karate.

"Good morning, sensei. Good morning, Jeff."

"It's nice to meet you, Ani." He stared at her yellow eyes. "I feel uncomfortable in here without my Gi."

"There's a closet behind the screen," Ani said. "You'll find what you need."

JEFF WENT to the back room as Kalinda pulled off her street clothes to reveal her translucent suit.

"There's only one gi in here," Jeff said. "Wow, it fits perfectly. And my belt is here, too." Jeff walked out and did a double take when all he saw of Kalinda was a red scarf and a head.

"Where is the rest of you?"

"Descendants of Xaphnore have a proximity sense," Kalinda said. "We do not need to see each other."

"And the red scarf?"

He saw the disruption of the background and recognized her hands as she grabbed the scarf and pulled it over her head. She disappeared completely.

"Woah, I don't have your proximity thing," Jeff said. "Let me see you."

He felt a tap on his shoulder. Startled, he turned and saw Kalinda's head again. "That's not fair."

"Camo off," Kalinda said.

She appeared before him in her black catsuit. Jeff felt surprised and a lot more.

"Workout much?" he said.

She nodded. "You?"

He closed his hands around his body. "You can see through my Gi?" Jeff said. "You have X-ray vision?"

Ani and Kalinda laughed. "I'm from Xaphnore, not Krypton. Set gravity to one-sixth. Let's work out."

"Woah, this is fly." Jeff jumped up and nearly touched the ceiling.

He landed. "Let's start with balance," Kalinda said. "Show me those punches that you did on Fat Albert."

Jeff executed a crisp set of three punches, right-left-right. In the process, he lost his footing and face-planted on the wooden deck.

Jeff looked up at Kalinda. Her face was so dead serious; it was only the twinkle in her eye that gave away how hard she was laughing. "Watch me in slow motion. See how my off-shoulder and my hips counter-rotate to offset the momentum of the punches."

"I see some of it," he said. "Do it fast."

She executed the punches as fast as he could see, but her feet remained planted.

"Okay, one more time much slower."

She performed the punches at one-third speed.

"Let me try." Jeff punched the air three times. This time he stumbled slightly but kept his footing. "My hips do not rotate like yours."

"Not yet but you will gain that flexibility with practice," Kalinda said. "You learn fast."

"Show me those moves that you did on the plane."

She stepped back and bowed. Then she jumped five feet up and executed a series of jabs, kicks, and turns. She softly touched down on the boards facing Jeff.

"Impressive."

"You try it."

Jeff jumped five feet up and executed the offensive and defensive moves but landed on his shoulder facing the wall to his right.

"You've got the moves, but you need to remember, 'For every action, there is an equal and opposite reaction.'"

"Newton's Third Law."

"Correct," Kalinda said. "Counteract a punch with your opposite shoulder, counter a kick with the opposite arm, and always use your hips and your legs to counter your upper body."

Jeff looked at Ani. "Do you know the 'serving talcum' thing?"

"Kalinda has been my sensei as we serve Tal'qid."

"Do you two spar?"

"Yes, we do," Kalinda said. "Ani set gravity to five percent and turn on force cushion. When we air-spar, we start and finish on the boards. Grab that handle up there." She pointed to a wooden railing.

He jumped up, bounced off the ceiling then pushed back and caught the railing on the second try.

WITH JEFF in a high observation position, Ani and Kalinda faced off.

"Ani?" Kalinda bounced to her position.

"Kalinda." Ani bounced the opposite position facing her opponent.

They bowed to each other then sprung into the air toward each other. Ani attacked with punches and Kalinda successfully defended until contact sent them toward opposite walls. They bounced off and rotated for opposing kicks. This time Kalinda attacked and Ani defended until contact sent them perpendicular to the side walls.

Jeff watched with his mouth open.

This time they faced approached each other head-on. Ani rotated her body and executed a roundhouse kick. Kalinda dropped her head, defended the kick and somersaulted into position to deliver two effective punches to Ani's sternum.

"Fall," Ani said.

"Fall," Kalinda responded.

They gracefully lit on the floor in their original position and bowed.

"Wanna try?" Kalinda said.

"You won't laugh?"

"Not on the outside."

"That was incredible, Ani." He bowed and took her place facing Kalinda and bowed deeply.

They sprung into the air and flew toward each other. Jeff assumed an offensive stance and Kalinda met him. He fired off four punches. Three hit air and Kalinda easily deflected the fourth. They moved to opposite walls.

This time they pushed off legs first. Jeff executed a kick. Kalinda defended with a counter-kick and then rotated her body and delivered a kick to Jeff's stomach. He groaned.

"Fall," Jeff said.

"Fall," Kalinda said.

She landed on her feet. Jeff soft-landed on his hands and then recovered.

"You okay?" Kalinda asked.

"Took my breath away and I might get a bruise, but I'll live."

They bowed.

26

Kalinda and Jeff were finishing up their workout in Kalinda's converted dojo. Kalinda had won two falls out of three. Ani, *Brilliant*'s Artificial Navigation Intelligence, was refereeing.

The annunciator sounded a tone. "*StarCruiser Brilliant*, arriving."

"The captain's here," Kalinda said. "Reconfigure the ready room for Earth gravity."

"Thank you for being a great host," Jeff said. "*Brilliant* is a really fun place to work out."

"It's good to see that Kalinda has found a good *friend*," Ani said.

"Jeff is just a friend," Kalinda said.

"That's what I said. It was nice meeting you," Ani said. "I hope that you enjoy the flight."

"Kay, that was the most fun I've ever had. Thanks."

She looked back at her new friend. "We'll do it again."

Jeff walked back to the closet and hung up his Gi. Kalinda changed back to street clothes.

"You two head to the galley before it gets crowded. Maiara tells me that she has laid out some grunch bars and drinks."

"Grunch?" Jeff asked.

"Maiara makes these delicious crunchy granola bars with chocolate chips," Kalinda said.

"Oh, cool."

They went to the bridge put on their shoes, and she led him to the spiral ladder with the fire pole in the center.

"Ready to try the pole?" Kalinda asked.

"Show me," Jeff said.

She hugged the pole and slid down one deck. Jeff grabbed on and slid down two decks.

"Smooth move," Kalinda said. "You can only slide one direction."

He looked embarrassed as he climbed up the ladder.

"You'll get it," Kalinda said. "It's easier in moon gravity."

They walked into the galley. "Hi, Auntie Maiara. This is Jeff Rodriguez."

"Nice to meet you," Maiara said. "Kalinda takes all of her boyfriends to her dojo on their first date."

"Nice to meet you, Ma'am," Jeff said. "Kalinda has lots of boyfriends?"

"No," Kalinda said. "You're the first...I mean...We're just friends...*Maiara*."

"You're always welcome on *Brilliant*," Maiara said.

"Why is everyone trying to find me a mate?" Kalinda said.

"Stop talking and grab some munchies," Maiara said.

"These are good," Jeff said.

The annunciator sounded again. "Blue Angels, arriving."

"That's the commander and his pilots," Maiara said. "Grab some for later and find a place to sit on the bridge. We're leaving soon."

JEFF AND KALINDA climbed the ladder to the bridge. The aft bulkhead of the bridge was absent to allow seating for riders.

The captain announced, "Take your places, everyone. We're

raising ship for a Tranquility Base Honor Pass. Begin the pre-launch checklist. Reports, everyone. Blue Angels?"

Munchkin looked around. "Captain, we're ready.

"Kalinda?" Jack asked.

She looked at Jeff who looked a bit frightened. "We're ready Captain."

JEFF WHISPERED TO KALINDA, "Isn't Tranquility Base on the Moon? I thought we were just taking a hop."

"This is a starship," Kalinda said. "The moon is a fifteen-minute hop."

Jennifer was getting busy, so Dandy Lion left her lap and paced to the aft wall and settled in Kalinda's lap. He looked at Jeff and then at Kalinda. *Who's the noob?* Dandy Lion thought.

Kalinda lifted Dandy and placed him in Jeff's lap. "Meet Dandy Lion, the ship's cat."

Jeff looked even more uncomfortable.

Dandy looked at Jeff and then at Kalinda. *He can't hear me, and he doesn't like cats,* Dandy thought.

"Most humans can't hear you, Dandy. Give him a chance to get to know you."

"He can talk?" Jeff began to feel the comfy vibes coming from Dandy. "He does kind of grow on you."

"FIRST LIEUTENANT?" Jack said.

"Sir, the ramp is up. Belowdecks are secure," Maiara said.

"Propulsion?"

"All Modes ready," Riley said. "Life support nominal. The ship is space-ready."

"Pilot?"

"All flight controls responsive. Ready to rock and roll." David said.

"Ops, what's our departure profile?"

"Captain," Jennifer said. "We'll raise ship and taxi to runway 2-4-o and follow Miramar departure at 250 knots to feet wet. At ten miles, we'll have unrestricted ascent to the Kármán line."

"Very well, Communicator, request clearance."

"Aye, sir," Tayla said. She depressed a button. "Miramar Tower, *StarCruiser Brilliant*, request clearance to depart on Runway Two-four-zero."

"*Brilliant*, proceed to runway center and hold short," Miramar Tower said.

"Pilot, raise ship and proceed to the runway," Jack said.

There was a rumble beneath the ship. David turned southbound and began taxiing.

"At what altitude do you cloak, Captain," Munchkin said.

"Normally at one hundred feet," Jack said. "It's not necessary today."

"Miramar Tower, *Brilliant* is holding short Runway Two-four-zero."

"*Brilliant*, you are cleared for takeoff. Ascend and maintain 2000 feet at 250 knots. Turn right course 290 to feet wet. When over water, contact Socal Tracon on 132.5.

"Two thousand at 250. Turn 290. Over water switch to 132.5. *StarCruiser Brilliant*," Tayla said.

"Pilot, take us up."

David turned onto the runway and began his take-off roll. The passengers felt the push against their seats. After clearing the western apron, David turned right. "Altitude Two Thousand," David said.

"Passing over Torrey Pines Beach," Jennifer said.

Tayla modified the settings. "SoCal Tracon, *StarCruiser Brilliant*, passing over Torrey Pines at 2000 course 290. Request corridor for an unrestricted vertical climb."

"*Brilliant*, turn left course 190." Tracon said. "Climb to thirty thousand at 650 knots for fifteen miles."

"*StarCruiser Brilliant*."

The push was more forceful. "Thirty thousand, speed 650."

"*Brilliant*, you are clear for unrestricted vertical climb. Good day," Tracon said.

"*StarCruiser Brilliant*, good day."

"Engineer, activate inertial dampening, maintain earth gravity," Jack said. "You may get up and walk around. Ops, activate planetarium view."

"Engineer, Aye," Riley said. "Inertial dampening and gravity on." The ride became smooth.

"Very well. Pilot take us to the Kármán Line at Mach 12."

The passengers could now see in every direction, above them the blue sky, below the ocean and the horizon in every direction. For safety, the deck remained translucent as did the solid objects around them. The crew could still see their panels.

In the next forty seconds, the sky went from bright blue to star-studded black, the ocean below became a vista of the Southern California coastline from Point Concepcion to the southern border of Baja California, and the horizon went from horizontal to the smooth curvature of the Earth from space.

"We've exited the atmosphere, Captain," Jennifer said.

"Very well, engage the gravity drive," Jack said. "Climb to 10,000 miles. Let's look at our home from space."

For the next minute, the earth receded to a peaceful blue ball. Looking toward the north pole, they saw the sun as a white-yellow ball over their left shoulders, the three-quarter moon above and to the right and the fragile blue ball of Earth below them with the line separating day and night splitting the Atlantic Ocean.

"The ship is ballistic, Captain," David said.

"Very well."

After that, there was silence as each Blue Angels pilot, each *Brilliant* crew member, and a ten-year-old girl and her friend enjoyed the view.

Captain Kendra "Fifi" Boyington looked around in every direction. "Wow," Fifi said. "It's almost like a movie." *I wish my brother could have seen this.* She became sad.

Just then, Dandy Lion left Jeff and jumped on Fifi's lap.

Dandy looked at Kalinda. *This human just lost her brother,* Dandy thought.

Kalinda came over to Fifi. "Is Dandy bothering you?"

"Not at all, Kalinda. I was thinking of something that happened," Fifi said. "Dandy jumped in my lap, and it's almost like he knew how I felt."

"It's too bad about your brother," Kalinda said.

Fifi gave Kalinda an incredulous look. "How do you know about my brother?"

"Dandy told me," Kalinda said. "He's psychic like that."

The captain interrupted the conversation. "Let's make it a bit more real," Jack said. "Hold on, everybody. Engineer, zero gravity."

Her doubts interrupted, Fifi held on tight to Dandy. She began to float above her seat. *Anyway, there's no way a cat could be psychic,* she thought.

Fifi felt Dandy's claws extend through her flight suit. She quickly let go. As the cat floated away toward the far bulkhead, he turned and gave her a nasty cat look. *No way,* Fifi thought.

As the gravity went away, gasps of fear and exclamations of glee settled down to excited laughter and chatter. Happy bodies filled the air bouncing from bulkhead to bulkhead. The captain, first officer, and pilot remained seated.

A few minutes later, it was again quiet with everyone's attention focused on Earth.

"Set a twenty-minute base course to the moon and then configure your station for Top Gun Controls," Jack said. "Let's give our fighter jocks some stick time on a starship."

"Aye, Captain," Jennifer said. "Course laid in." She pointed to David, and he nodded.

"Engineer, slowly raise to one-sixth gravity," Jack said. "Ops, restore standard view."

Everyone softly returned to vertical orientation on the deck as the parts of the bridge became solid again.

"Captain, would you send down drink orders?" Maiara said.

"Yes, First Lieutenant," Jack said. "Tayla, could you find out what everyone wants?"

"Yes, Captain." She took a HoloPad around and collected drink orders.

"Kalinda, would you and your friend go below and assist?" Jack said.

"Yes, Uncle Jack," Kalinda said.

Jeff and Kalinda walked over to the ladder. Jeff grabbed the rail and took the first step.

"Seriously, stairways are for losers." Jeff watched as Kalinda gracefully jumped onto the firepole and sailed down one deck.

"Oh, yeah," Jeff said. He took a step back, leaped and grabbed the firepole and slid down, right past the laughing Kalinda, and landed on the lower deck. Sporting a sheepish grin, he walked up the ladder and joined Kalinda on the middle deck.

"All ya gotta do is squeeze, and you will stop," Kalinda said.

"I keep forgetting that part," Jeff said.

Maiara met them in the galley. "Fill the first tray with drinks and load it into the transporter."

"You've got a Transporter?" Jeff stood with his eyes and mouth wide open.

"It's a dumb waiter," Kalinda gave Jeff a condescending look.

"Irony?"

"Yep."

"Load a tray with munchies."

"Yes, ma'am." He grabbed bags of M&Ms and grunch bars and placed them on the tray.

"Put extras on for people to take home souvenirs," Maiara said.

"Souvenirs?" Jeff asked.

"Open a bag of M&Ms," Kalinda said.

He grabbed a bag and tore it open. "Wow, the *Brilliant* logo."

"The president hooked us up with those a few years ago," Maiara said.

Kalinda loaded the first tray on the dumb waiter and pressed the button. She began to load the spill-proof cups on the second tray.

A TONE SOUNDED on the aft bulkhead. Tayla and Jennifer walked back and distributed drinks.

At the pilot's console, Popeye was performing aerobatics. "This is just like the simulator. Too bad we can't feel it."

"Everyone, hold on to your food and drink," Jack said. "Engineer set inertial dampener to point-two Gs."

Those on-board could now feel the banks and the climbs as the Blue Angels pilots maneuvered *Brilliant* through trans-lunar space.

Droopy switched into the pilot's seat and flew several maneuvers.

"Ops, it's kind of lonely out here," Jack said.

"Yes, Captain," Jennifer said. She operated some controls on her panel.

"Alert," Ani said. "There's a Hoclarth Fighter Drone on your port quarter, sixty degrees depression, range twenty miles."

Droopy looked at Jennifer. "What do I do?"

"You can run like hell or turn and fight. Your particle beam weapon is active."

"Aye aye." Droopy snapped right, banked forty-five degrees, and executed a split-s to get under the intruder. "I've got the intruder on visual."

He raised the nose and triggered the beam. "Missed."

The drone passed overhead. Droopy pulled up into a half Cuban eight. He snapped horizontal and had the drone in his gunsights. "Tally-ho." This time the particle beam connected, and the drone exploded.

"It's my turn now," Fifi said. She splashed the Hoclarth Drone on the first try.

. . .

AFTER THE BLUE Angels pilots had cycled through their turn in the pilot's chair, the moon loomed large in the forward display. Maiara, Jeff, and Kalinda returned to the bridge.

David now sat in the pilot's seat.

"Reconfigure the planetarium view," Jack said. "Pilot, take us into a low lunar orbit and set us up for a Tranquility Base Honor Pass."

"Aye, sir."

The view on the bridge shifted; the surface of the moon became close and detailed.

"The orbit is set," David said. "Tranquility Base just over the horizon. Ready for *StarCruiser Brilliant* Honor Pass."

"Please stand, everyone," Jack said. "Anthen, please do the honors."

Ani announced, "Hand salute."

Tayla was excited. *Is it my turn?*

The crew and the pilots responded, facing forward. Anthen then repeated words from his past, Earth's future and from the *StarCruiser Brilliant* movies, "To the pioneers of the past, we honor you. To Orville and Wilbur Wright who took to the air, to Chuck Yeager and Scott Crossfield who went to the edge of space, to Yuri Gagarin, John Glenn, Valentina Tereshkova, Alan Shepard and others who crossed the barrier into space, to Neil Armstrong, Palton Vendarko, Cindy Brennaman and others who first set foot on other planets, we honor you. To the crews of Discovery and Challenger, to Gus Grissom, Ed White, and Roger Chaffee and to the many others who gave the supreme sacrifice, we remember you. Kalinda?"

"To Natira Valenda of Xaphnore, may we someday join you in Laknove."

Jack continued, "To every pioneer who brought us to this place and beyond, we honor and salute you. Comms, as the junior member of the crew, join us and sound the ship's bell a single time."

Tayla breathed in and marched smartly to the forward viewport. "Aye, Aye, Captain." She saluted. She knew the significance of this hallowed tradition that she observed a few weeks ago with her best friend. It's one that she had seen in the movies and one that she had rehearsed repeatedly.

Tayla released her salute, stood ramrod straight, faced the distant Earth through the viewport, and pulled the rope to sound the bell a single time. At the sound of the brass bell, the crew members rendered a crisp salute.

"Relax, everyone. Tayla Mendoza, welcome to the crew of *Star-Cruiser Brilliant.*"

Tayla received hugs, handshakes, and congratulations from everyone on the bridge.

Her last bear hug was from her best friend. "Tay, we made it," Jennifer said.

"Ops set a course for Earth," Jack said.

"Course laid in," Jennifer said.

"Engage," Jack said.

27

StarCruiser *Brilliant* was homeward bound with Luna still large in the aft displays. The six pilots of the Blue Angels were giddy with joy after their orbit of Earth's nearest neighbor.

Kalinda came up next to Jack. "Captain, Jeff would like to fly the ship."

"Very well," Jack said. "Pilot, give Jeff some stick time."

"Aye, sir," David said. He helped Jeff configure the pilot's seat. "You're configured for an F-18. Do some smooth right and left turns."

"Yes, sir." Jeff moved the stick and flew *Brilliant* through space with the smile. "Thank you, sir."

A distinct tone sounded, and a red indicator appeared on the communications panel. Tayla turned to her board. "Captain, special message. Your eyes only," All those on the bridge shifted to operational attention.

"Very well." The captain looked down, eyes narrowed. "Sound Alert One. On your toes everyone."

David grabbed Jeff by the shoulders, lifted him out of the pilot's seat, and jumped in his place.

"What's going on, Kay?" Jeff walked to the rear bulkhead with Kalinda.

"I don't know," Kalinda said. "but we need to stay out of the way."

Thirty seconds later another tone sounded at the communications panel.

"Captain, it's from Commander in Chief Pacific Fleet."

"Very well, Comms," Jack said. "On screen." He turned his chair to face the main viewer.

"I'm Vice Admiral Rashid Muhammed, Indian Ocean Fleet Operations. A helo accident occurred aboard the *Oprah Winfrey* near the Straits of Hormuz fifty-five minutes ago," the admiral said.

Jack pointed to Jennifer who took the cue to lay in a course. She signaled to David who executed the maneuver.

"The turbine casing exploded during landing, injuring seven sailors," the admiral said. "The pilot suffered massive internal injuries and requires trauma care that *Winfrey* is not able to provide. We need *Brilliant* to transport her to a trauma center stateside. How soon can you get here?"

Jennifer held up eight fingers.

"Admiral, we can be there in eight minutes from near lunar orbit."

"Understand, *Brilliant*, out."

A few seconds later, there was another tone. "On Screen," Jack said.

Admiral Muhammed appeared again. "We've received another report from *Winfrey*. *Brilliant*, the pilot's injuries are grave. Unfortunately, your services may not be needed."

Kalinda felt Jeff shaking. She looked at him. "Your mom?"

"Maybe," Jeff said.

Kalinda walked next to Jack. "Captain?"

"I'm kind of busy."

"Sir, the pilot might be Jeff's mother."

He looked at Kalinda, then at Jeff and saw a terrified ten-year-old. "What is your mom's name?"

"Mia Rodriguez," Jeff said.

"Son, we'll do our best," Jack said. He turned to the screen. "Admiral, we'll be there more than soon. *Brilliant* out," Jack said.

"Ops, can we do a StarDrive Jump?"

"Yes, Captain," Jennifer said. "Ani, plot a Finsler Maneuver to the Kármán Line above the *Winfrey*."

"Sick Bay, are you monitoring?"

"I'm ready, Captain," Dr. Ami said.

"Fifi, you and Kalinda take Jeff down to the galley."

"Aye aye, Captain," Fifi said. The Blue Angels pilot jumped from her seat and joined Kalinda as they took Jeff to the galley.

"Captain," Jennifer said. "Course laid in. We'll arrive at the Kármán Line four minutes after the accident. *Brilliant* will jump back fifty-three minutes."

"Very well," Jack said. "Pilot, engage the StarDrive."

The star field blurred for a moment.

Walleye looked at Munchkin. "He said bad things happen when you engage the StarDrive near a planet."

"Starship tactics, Mr. Weisser," Munchkin said. "You read the rulebook and then listen to your gut."

"Captain, in five seconds, we'll enter the atmosphere at Mach twelve and decelerate to Mach five at twenty thousand feet."

Again, the star field blurred.

"Very well, Comms, send an eyes-only message to *Brilliant*," Jack said. "'Go to alert. Get here fast.' Tayla, make sure it arrives at 1:59 p.m. Then open a GUARD channel to the bridge of the *Winfrey* as soon as we re-enter."

"Aye, Captain."

She programmed and sent the first message.

The display showed the red glow of re-entry.

"Transmitting on GUARD Frequency, Captain," Tayla said. "They'll be monitoring on the bridge."

. . .

THE *USS OPRAH WINFREY* was at general quarters. All hands were devoted to putting out the fire, saving the casualties, protecting the ship and its equipment.

The bridge phone-talker stood next to the captain. "Captain, Damage Control reports the fire is out. They're sending in rescue personnel."

"Very well," the captain said.

BA-BOOM! The Winfrey was rocked by a massive sonic boom.

"Who the hell is in our airspace at a time like this."

"*Winfrey*, this is *StarCruiser Brilliant*. Request permission to land."

"It's the Military Air Distress Frequency, sir!" the quartermaster said.

The captain reached up and depressed a lever. "*Brilliant*, we have a foul deck with casualties. We cannot receive visitors at this time."

The radio sounded, "Captain, we're aware of your situation, and we're aware that the pilot is in extremely critical condition. We've got a high-level trauma facility aboard. Sir, we're the pros from Dover."

The captain thought, *How does he know who the casualties are?* "CAG?"

The air group commander responded, "Captain, we can clear a space aft of the superstructure."

"Very well, Officer of the Deck, turn into the wind. Sound flight quarters for a vertical landing."

"Aye, Captain," the OOD said. "Helmsman, order ahead full. Turn right. Steady course two-five-zero."

"Captain, we're setting flares aft of the superstructure."

"Very well, CAG." The captain depressed transmit. "*Brilliant*, there are twenty knots of wind across the deck. We've set flares aft of the superstructure defining your landing area."

I hope this works, the captain thought.

"Thanks for the wind captain. We've got you on visual. We'll be noisy until we're below ten thousand feet."

"Sir, damage control reports Lieutenant Commander Rodriquez critically injured. The doctor is with her. The other crew members have only minor injuries."

"Very well. Prepare the commander for personnel transfer on *Brilliant*. The doctor will fly with her."

"Captain, CIC reports they have *Brilliant* at eighty thousand feet, speed 1500 knots bearing 0-7-0.

"Very well. *Brilliant*, we have you on radar. We've got the pilot and our surgeon ready to transfer."

"Roger, *Winfrey*. Please inform. Is the name of the pilot Mia Rodriguez?"

What the hell? the captain thought.

"Correct. The injured pilot is Lieutenant Commander Mia Rodriguez. She's a VIP. Her mother is a senator."

"We are aware," Jack said. "Twenty seconds to touch down."

"Crew, the injured pilot is Jeff's mother." There was a gasp. "Munchkin, detail two of yours to the ramp to assist. Then go down to sickbay and brief your pilot and liaise between the galley and sick bay. Keep the boy in the galley."

Munchkin pointed to Popeye and Droopy and then followed them down the pole.

"It just got complicated," Jack said. "Dr. Ami are you ready?"

"Yes, Captain. I recommend one-sixth gravity for the transfer. May I have Ani for a second pair of hands?"

"Who?" The captain was speechless for a moment. "Yes. Of course?" The captain turned to see a tall blonde in a *Brilliant* flight suit exit the ready room. "Ani?"

"Captain, I'm headed for sickbay."

"By all means," Jack said, still a bit stunned at the sight of his Artificial Navigation Interface as a virtual human. "Engineer, one-sixth gravity."

"Aye, sir," Riley said. He smiled at the captain's reaction.

"Pilot, we'll come in one mile aft of the stern, and you will make a direct approach two hundred feet above the flight deck and land in the flares."

"Aye aye, Captain," said David.

"*Winfrey* on visual, Captain," Jennifer said.

"Bring us in,"

"*Winfrey, Starcruiser Brilliant,* we're one mile astern," Jennifer said.

"*Brilliant, Winfrey,* we're steady on two-five-zero. Twenty knots wind across the flight deck gusting to twenty-five, sea state three. The deck is steady. There's rotary wing traffic to your left acting as plane guard, and we've got you on radar. On final approach, follow the signals of the plane director wearing yellow."

"*Winfrey, StarCruiser Brilliant.* We're twenty seconds from your stern. Straight in approach," Jennifer said.

"Six hundred feet. Pilot take us in."

"I've got the Plane Director," David said.

"*Winfrey, Brilliant.* Six hundred feet, descending to two hundred. We have your plane director on visual. Approaching at eighty knots."

"Descending to touchdown," David said operating the flight controls as he watched the paddles.

"Engineer, drop the ramp on contact," Jack said.

"Engineer, aye."

David saw the yellow light on his panel. "Contact,"

"Ramp is down," Riley said.

The bridge displays showed *Winfrey* sailors in protective suits that looked like spacesuits quickly assisting a gurney up the ramp. Two Blue Angels pilots took over and brought the patient to sickbay. A Navy physician in blue camos boarded. The extra navy personnel departed.

"*Brilliant, Winfrey,* you are clear for unrestricted vertical departure."

"Course is laid in for San Diego," Jennifer said.

"Captain, the patient is secure in sickbay. You may depart," Dr. Ami said.

"Very well," Jack said. "Pilot, unrestricted ascent. Ballistic course to San Diego."

"Unrestricted ascent, aye," David said.

THOSE ON THE deck of the USS *Oprah Winfrey* will tell their grandchildren that they saw the lights of the *Brilliant* turn upward and two seconds later they heard a sonic boom close aboard.

On the bridge, the Executive Officer was next to the captain.

"XO, how the hell did CincPac get them out here so fast?"

"Captain, *Brilliant*'s first message came in before I got the message off to CincPac Fleet."

"No shit," the captain said. "And how did they know that the pilot was injured before we did?"

"Time travel?" the XO said. "You never know what they're working on at Area 51."

"Goddamned Air Force."

"Captain, CincPac reports contact with *StarCruiser Brilliant.* They're on their way."

"Goddamned United States Air Force."

"Captain, she's one of ours," The XO said.

"*Brilliant* is Navy?"

The XO nodded.

"I guess they are the pros from Dover," the captain said.

"Doesn't matter anyway. The doc said she could never survive her injuries."

"XO, let's keep this one under our hats."

"No one would believe it anyway," the XO said.

COMMANDER LAYTON ENTERED the galley and saw a woman and a girl comforting a troubled young man.

Munchkin addressed Fifi formally, "Captain Boyington?" He signaled her to follow.

"I'll be right back." She squeezed Jeff's shoulder.

They walked down the passageway. "Fifi, it's confirmed. We've got the boy's mother in sickbay. I don't know her condition, but I know it's bad," Munchkin said. "I'll stay near sickbay. Keep Jeff and the girl in the galley."

"Aye, Munch."

"Fifi, I know that you just lost your kid brother in Keristan..."

"I got this, Munch."

He nodded and headed to sickbay.

Fifi returned to the galley.

For some reason, she was not surprised to see the yellow tabby in Jeff's lap.

"Your mother is in sickbay. They're doing all they can."

Jeff looked down holding back the tears. He looked up at Kalinda. "Kay, what's it like to lose your mother?"

"You haven't lost anyone. Dr. Ami is the best. She saved David near Proxima Centauri after he took a blaster to the chest."

Dandy looked up at Kalinda and growled.

Kalinda looked at Dandy and then at Jeff. "Dandy says your mom will be okay."

Fifi saw the two holding hands. She looked at Dandy, and the cat looked back. Her shoulders relaxed, and she took a deep breath. *Definitely psychic.*

Dandy settled his head into the crook of Jeff's arm.

"Twenty minutes to San Diego on a ballistic course, Captain. We'll be subsonic the last two minutes," Jennifer said.

"Very well, coordinate with Balboa Naval Hospital," Jack responded.

. . .

In sickbay, there was a bustle of activity. Ani mounted the scanning equipment. Dr. Ami inspected the wounds.

"Doctor, how long has she been flatlined?" Dr. Ami asked.

"Three minutes. We stabilized the pilot as best we could then we lost her pulse during the move," said the Navy doctor.

"The scan indicates massive destruction to the heart, left lung, and the pulmonary arteries and veins," Dr. Ami said.

"The corpsman said a turbine blade passed through her chest from back to front."

The 3D scan appeared above the patient. "There's nothing there to work with," Dr. Ami said and then made a quick decision. She looked upward to the bridge, "Jennifer, bring me the device you showed me last week, stat."

Jennifer looked at the captain. He nodded. "Anthen, take the right seat." She ran into the Captain's Ready Room, got the device, and slid down the fire pole.

"Ani, program an interface for the mini-projector," Dr. Ami said. "I want to use HTVR to rebuild the organs in her chest, and I will operate on the external scan."

"Yes, Doctor," Ani said. "I've connected to the device. Jennifer is on the fire pole."

"Good." Dr. Ami turned to the Navy doctor and looked at his name badge. "Dr. Ikeda, I'm Dr. Ami, and this is my nurse Ani. I'm going to perform a procedure that has never been done, never been tried, and never approved. As her attending physician, I need your permission. The alternative is pronouncing her dead right here on the table."

"Your yellow eyes. You're...not..."

"Yes, I'm not human, but I play one on TV," Dr. Ami said. "Your call, Doctor?"

"Do it. I read the paper you wrote with Dr. Allen. If anyone can save her..."

Jennifer rushed into sickbay. "Here's the mini projector, Dr. Ami, good luck."

"Thank you," Dr. Ami said. "Attaching the device to her upper sternum with surgical adhesive."

Behind her, the Blue Angels commander stuck his head into sickbay.

"Doctor?"

"Yes." Dr. Ami looked at Jennifer over her micro glasses.

"We've got the patient's son in the galley."

"Kalinda's new friend?"

He nodded.

"No pressure, team. We are *Brilliant*. Lower the table so that I can work on the scan."

"Ami, tools are on your right, materials on your left," Ani said. "The system is ready."

"Stand across from me. Allow me network access to your hands and arms."

Ani moved across the table and held up her hands. "You have access." Ani transformed into a reflection of Dr. Ami.

At that moment, Dr. Ikeda watched as the action began to accelerate.

Dr. Ami narrated. "I've attached a miniature Holographic Tactile Virtual Reality projector to her sternum. The scan above is HTVR as well. What you see is an exact mirror of her internal organs. I'll reconstruct the virtual heart within her chest. After that, I'll reconstruct the circulatory elements."

"Is Dr. Ani a surgeon as well?" Dr. Ikeda was fearful of the answer.

"Doctor, do you love music?" Dr. Ami looked at the Navy doctor above her micro-glasses.

"Yes." He looked a bit confused. "My wife studied to be a concert pianist."

"Think of this as a four-hand piano concerto," Dr. Ami said. "and I'm playing both parts,"

He realized he was witnessing the future of surgery. The four hands worked in perfect synchronicity at a speed he had never seen in an operating theater. She repaired the heart in two minutes.

"I'm now restoring circulation," Dr. Ami said.

Three minutes after they began, the display showed a healthy cardio-pulmonary system and the patient's heart began to beat.

"You're released."

"Ami, we have normal sinus rhythm," Ani said. "Dr. Ikeda, we are told this is Jeff's mother?"

"Correct, she is Lieutenant Commander Mia Rodriguez. She just returned to the fleet as squadron XO from duty as aide to Senator Curtwell in DC."

"How did she know the senator?"

"It's her daughter."

"Surgical complications I can handle, but this may lead to political complications," Dr. Ami said.

"You saved the senator's daughter," Dr. Ikeda said. "What's the problem?"

"Senator Curtwell delivered a speech this afternoon with uncomplimentary words about virtual humans," Ami said. "She'll claim that her daughter lived in spite of the yellow-eyed demon."

"They say a politician will sacrifice their first-born to win the White House," Ani said.

"Not on my watch," Dr. Ami said. "Brain function appears normal. Let's wake our girl up and see if she's all there."

Dr. Ami spied Munchkin waiting outside Sick Bay.

"Commander?" He heard the call and stepped to the edge of the operating theater.

"Yes, Doctor."

"Please inform Jeff that his mother is going to make it. Wait three minutes then bring him down."

Munchkin was smiling as he walked to the galley.

• • •

ANI CAREFULLY REMOVED the chest tube and then operated the anesthesia controls.

Mia's eyes fluttered then opened.

"Welcome back, Commander. I'm Doctor Ami."

"Where am I?" Mia said.

"You are five hundred miles above the Pacific on the way back to San Diego aboard *StarCruiser Brilliant*"

"You saved me...you have yellow eyes."

"I'm a virtual human as is my nurse, Ani, and yes, we recreated your heart and lungs using HTVR."

"I'm not real?"

"You're alive," Dr. Ami said. "We're going to get you back to Balboa Naval Hospital and install regenerated organs."

"You know who my mother is?" Mia said.

"I know that she has concerns about the very existence of virtual humans," Dr. Ami said. "In this case, my medical skills put me in a unique position to save you."

"Another day, another argument with my mother."

"I hope that you will concentrate on getting healthy."

"You're right. Thank you so much Dr. Ami and Ani," Mia said in a more relaxed tone.

Dr. Ami signaled Commander Layton to enter.

"You're a Blue Angel pilot," Mia said.

"Callsign Munchkin," he said. "Commander, there is someone here to see you."

Munchkin led Jeff into sickbay.

"Mom!"

"Jeff! What are you doing here?" They hugged.

"Mom, I made a friend on *StarCruiser Brilliant*, and she knows martial arts and she's..."

At that moment, a mother enveloped her son in a bear hug, and there was nothing more to explain.

Dr. Ami stepped away from the operating table and looked up to activate the intra-ship communicator. "Captain, our patient is in stable condition. You can turn the flashing lights off and make a normal approach."

"Congratulations on another miracle, Doctor," Jack said.

"Thank you, Captain."

"My congratulations as well," Dr. Ikeda said. "Is there anything I can do?"

"Yes, Doctor. Please go to the bridge and coordinate with Balboa Naval Hospital and UCSD Organ Regeneration Facility. Send them the patient's DNA file. Have Balboa obtain operating privileges for you and me. We'll perform the transplant as soon as the organs are available. Balboa recently installed the necessary HTVR equipment. And please contact your ship and the family."

"Got it. And again, Doctor, my deepest appreciation on behalf of the *Winfrey* and the Navy."

"Let's wait to celebrate when we have the commander all in one piece."

DR. IKEDA ENTERED the Bridge Command Center to a group in a subdued mood. The Blue Angels pilots were observing operations and chatting with crew members. *The Brilliant* crew was coming down from a spurt of extreme activity.

"Good job down there," Jack said. "How can we help you, Doctor?"

"I need to speak with UCSD Regen Facility and then Balboa Medical Center," Dr. Ikeda said.

"Communicator?"

"On it, sir," Tayla said.

"Welcome aboard, Doctor?" Jack asked.

The Navy doctor reached out to shake hands with the captain. "Bill Ikeda. I'm the lead surgeon for the task group."

"Maybe someday we can give you a ride under better circumstances," Jack said.

"Captain, I've got UCSD Regen," Tayla said. "Doctor, I also have the DNA profile ready to send."

"Thanks, who am I speaking with?" Dr. Ikeda asked.

"I'm Dr. Archie Moore," he said. "I'm the attending physician at the Regen Facility. I understand you are on *StarCruiser Brilliant?*"

"Yes, Doctor, we had a helicopter accident," Dr. Ikeda said. "A thirty-four-year-old female pilot suffered severe chest trauma. We require complete replacement organs for the heart and both lungs."

"Did you say complete, Doctor?" the attending asked.

"Yes, I did," Dr. Ikeda said. "The DNA profile is being transmitted." He pointed to Tayla. She nodded.

"I'm receiving the file," the attending physician said. "I'm curious how the patient survived the injury, but I'm probably going to have to wait to read about another miracle by Dr. Ami in the medical journals. The regeneration will require eighteen hours. Where will the surgery take place?"

"We're delivering the Navy pilot to Balboa," Dr. Ikeda said.

"We have the necessary information and will begin."

"Thank you, Doctor."

"Captain, thanks for saving our pilot," Dr. Ikeda said.

"We were out for an afternoon ride, and we got the call," Jack said. "We were glad to help, Doctor."

"May I contact the family?" Dr. Ikeda said.

"Make the call in my ready room," Jack said. "Tayla will make your cell phone active."

Dr. Ikeda looked up Lieutenant Commander Rodriguez's contact information and dialed her spouse. Her husband and Mia's mother appeared on screen looking stricken with grief.

"This is Chuck Rodriguez."

"Mr. Rodriguez, this is Dr. Ikeda from the *USS Winfrey*. I'm aboard *StarCruiser Brilliant*."

"I'm with Mia's mother," Chuck said. "We're headed to Balboa Hospital to meet you. The ship told us to expect the worst."

Mr. Rodriguez, Senator Curtwell, I'm happy to say that Mia is in stable condition after the outstanding efforts of Dr. Ami and the crew on *Brilliant*."

"Omigod, that's wonderful," Chuck said. "How about my son, Jeff?"

"He's with his mother right now," Dr. Ikeda said.

"What's her condition?" Senator Curtwell asked.

"Her condition is critical but stable," Dr. Ikeda said. "Dr. Ami has created artificial heart and lungs which are keeping her alive. The UCSD Regeneration Facility has Mia's DNA profile and is regenerating her organs. They'll be available for transplant in eighteen hours."

Senator Curtwell looked at Dr. Ikeda. "Will you do the operation, Doctor?"

"I hope that Dr. Ami will do the operation," Dr. Ikeda said. "She and her assistant performed a miracle to bring Mia back from a grave condition."

"Is this Dr. Ami the robot doctor?" she asked.

"She's a virtual human, yes."

"Doctor, you must not allow that android near my daughter."

"Senator, Dr. Ami originated the procedure that saved your daughter," Dr. Ikeda said. "She's the only one who can complete the transplant and save her."

"I forbid it," the senator said. "I will not allow a dirty robot to touch my daughter."

Chuck sat to the side and watched until he could not take any more. "Dr. Ikeda, Mia and I will jointly make the best decision for her health."

She spoke to Chuck with condescension. "You would allow that evil android to operate on Mia."

"We'll do what's necessary to save her life without concern over who performs the surgery," he said.

"Mom," Mia said. "This will be our decision, and we will not mix it up with your politics."

"Very well, but I want guards in the operating room if this machine tries to hurt my daughter."

"If you wish, but Mia's health comes before your politics," Chuck said. "Dr. Ikeda, we're five minutes from Balboa Naval Hospital."

"CAPTAIN, we're thirty seconds from feet dry," Jennifer said. "TraCon clears us for a direct approach to the San Diego Naval Medical Center Helipad."

"Very well," Jack said. "Take us in, David."

"Aye, sir," David said. "I've got their homing beacon."

"Munchkin, please detail two of your pilots to assist with the transfer."

"Aye aye, Captain," Munchkin said.

"Sick Bay, prepare for patient transfer," Jack said. "We're feet dry over San Diego."

IN SICKBAY, Dr. Ami replied. "Aye, Captain. We're ready. We'll need three minutes to do the transfer."

"Very well," Jack said.

Jeff was still holding his mother's hand. "Mom, I'll be right back."

He ran up to the galley where Kalinda was with Captain Boyington. He stopped when he saw them hugging. "Is something wrong?"

"We both recently lost someone close," Fifi said. "We're just happy that your mother is safe."

Kalinda got up and stood before Jeff. "You're leaving?"

"Yes," Jeff said. "Thanks for giving me the best ride ever and...and being with me."

"I'm glad your mom is ok," Kalinda. "I wish you could've come to Oceanside to the..."

Just then, Jeff grabbed Kalinda with both hands and planted a kiss on her cheek. Then he let go and turned to run back to the ladder.

Kalinda turned back toward Kendra with her eyes and her mouth wide open.

"I think you have a boyfriend," Fifi said.

Without closing her mouth, Kalinda nodded.

28

Orderlies took Mia into Balboa Naval Medical Center. Jeff and Chuck walked with the gurney to the Intensive Care Unit where a room was waiting.

BALBOA HOSPITAL recently installed the HTVR projectors that allowed virtual doctors to practice there. Dr. Ami transferred to the hospital to test the new installation and track her patient. After a clinic walkthrough with the physicians, she was satisfied that she would be able to perform the surgery on Lieutenant Commander Rodriguez in the morning. Ami settled in a spare office during the night shift. She was reviewing Mia's scans at two a.m.

There was a knock at her open door, and she looked.

"Dr. Ami, I'm Dr. Silvia Ramon, the senior attending on this shift."

"Come in, Doctor," Ami said. "How may I help you?"

"Can you walk with me, Doctor?" Silvia said.

"Yes, of course." Dr. Ami sensed the urgency.

"We've admitted a nineteen-year-old male Marine suffering massive head trauma in a motorcycle accident," Silvia said.

"Helmet?" Dr. Ami asked.

"No," Silvia said. "Our surgeon is young and competent, but we call in our neurosurgeon in these cases. We share him with Camp Pendleton, and tonight he is operating there. Could you take a look and scrub in?"

"Are the scans online?"

"Yes," Silvia said.

Dr. Ami looked up. "I see a three-centimeter penetration on the upper left frontal lobe. There's also a serious coup-contrecoup contusion on the right rear temporal lobe. We need to relieve pressure immediately and repair the damage to the left frontal."

"Here's the scrub room, Doctor."

"Not needed." Dr. Ami passed directly into the operating room and walked to the table.

"Doctor, you need a mask and scrubs in the operating room," the surgeon paused. "You have yellow eyes! You're the virtual doctor?"

"I'm the Artificial Medical Intelligence from *StarCruiser Brilliant*. Call me Ami. You are?"

"Lieutenant Commander Bill Hoyer," he said. "You've done some impressive work in thoracic trauma. Are you qualified for neurosurgery?"

"I have experiential access to a library of ten-thousand-three-hundred-twenty-seven instances of severe head trauma. I'm comfortable here."

"Very well, Doctor," Bill said. "You take the lead."

"Progress?"

"We've uncovered the left frontal lobe, and we're mending the bones offline for replacement," Bill said. "I've done the repairs I could. I'm about to cut open the right rear temporal."

"That's not necessary, Bill," Ami said. "VaNessa, Lower the table fifteen inches and activate the scan of the coup-contrecoup."

The Virtual Nurse, VaNessa, followed the instructions. "Ready, Doctor."

Dr. Ami worked on the HTVR scan of the impacted area for the next ten minutes. The system replicated the changes within the brain.

"Analysis, VaNessa?" Dr. Ami asked.

"You've repaired all of the bleeders in the right temporal lobe," VaNessa said. "Swelling should be minimal."

"You showed me the future of non-invasive surgery," Bill said. "Impressive."

"Thank you," Ami said. "Let's clean up the left frontal lobe."

They worked together for another twenty minutes.

"Doctor Hoyer, the patient is stable," Ami said. "He'll remain in a coma for approximately fifty-four hours. Monitor him closely for peak swelling at twenty-one hours. I expect that the patient will suffer temporary speech impairment but should recover fully with therapy."

"Thanks for your work, Dr. Ami," Bill said. "It was an honor. We expect our new virtual doctor to arrive in three months. The Artificial Medical Intelligence will improve our patient outcomes greatly."

"It was a pleasure working with you," Ami said.

"Good luck with the helo pilot in the morning," Bill said.

"Thank you," Ami said.

She exited the operating suite, and Dr. Ramon met her. "My compliments, Doctor Ami, we didn't expect that Marine to survive."

"Thanks," Ami said. "Is there an HTVR simulation room available?"

"Yes," Silvia said. "We're just learning how to use it, but it has improved skill levels." She pulled out her HoloPad and checked some entries. "It's available until eight-thirty. May I show you where it is?"

"I can find it. Thank you, Silvia."

Dr. Ami stood outside a circle marking the center of the sparse room and called up the virtual nurse. "VaNessa, load patient Mia Rodriguez."

"Configuration?" VaNessa said.

"Operating room. Patient anesthetized. Virtual to organic heart-lung transplant. Initiate simulation with moderate to severe complications."

"Just a moment," VaNessa said.

Dr. Ami watched as the components formed, the virtual personnel appeared, and finally, the patient's image appeared on the operating table and the instruments began reading out.

"Ready, Doctor."

Over the next three hours, Dr. Ami performed the operation successfully fourteen times. On the seventh try, an unforeseen complication arose.

"The new organs are connected," Dr. Ami said. "Securing the mini-projector."

"Warning, severe clotting in the left pulmonary artery," VaNessa said. Life sign alarms went off.

A few seconds later, "Warning, severe clotting in the pulmonary trunk." Ami tried several different solutions but lost the virtual patient.

She paused. "Kobayashi Maru," she said. "Reset the simulation. Same complications."

She performed the operation successfully eight more times. She managed the difficult complication on three of them.

"Thank you, VaNessa," Ami said. "I'm ready for my ten o'clock tee time."

Dr. Ami looked in on Mia who was asleep then went back to the spare office, locked the door and sat with the lights dim. For the next two hours, she shut down her physical systems entered an intense meditative focus.

29

Kalinda's thoughts roamed between the ocean and the hospital forty miles south as she stood next to her father in Oceanside. She sank her toes in the Crystal Sand Beach and looked beyond the Oceanside Pier. She was carrying her JS Monsta Box surfboard in the bag with her new customized springsuit. Her grandfather had gone to a top maker, sent some special materials and the *StarCruiser Brilliant* logo, and the company created several wetsuits specially fitted for Kalinda. Always the entrepreneur, Navvy expected the product to sell very well after Kalinda surfed at Oceanside.

After meeting champion surfer Bondi Cooper two weeks before, Kalinda practiced at Malibu with the pro to prepare for the Oceanside Women's Pro-Am Competition.

She scanned the horizon as she focused her thoughts. The sun was low in the sky over her left shoulder with dark clouds in the distance to her right. *It'll be a good day to surf,* she thought.

"The sea is calm in the morning," Anthen said.

"The waves will get bigger," Kalinda said.

"The forecast is calling for six-foot waves for the competition,"

Anthen said. "Weather thinks that the tropical storm brewing will miss us to the north."

"The waves will get much higher," Kalinda said. "The storm won't miss us."

The father studied his daughter's intense concentration. *She's so much like her mother,* he thought. "Why don't we check-in with Bondi's sponsor tent and then you can take some practice waves?"

As they walked to the tent, Kalinda walked close to him.

"I know you're concerned about Jeff's mom," Anthen said. "Chuck promised to keep me posted."

Kalinda paused and looked back at the water. "The waves are just high enough to get some air."

Around the white sponsor tent were photos of several pro surfers. Bondi's photo was most prominent. They passed through security, entered the tent, and Kalinda put her equipment in the area set aside for that purpose.

Bondi walked up to the pair. "You gonna take some practice waves?"

"Hi Bondi," Kalinda said. "Yeah, I'm not completely comfy on this new board."

Kalinda walked over to the food table.

"And she's worried about her friend," Anthen said.

Bondi sent a questioning look.

"She made a new best friend yesterday," Anthen said. "He was riding with us on *StarCruiser Brilliant.* Then, coming back from the moon, we rescued his mother from the Persian Gulf, saved her life, and delivered her back to San Diego."

"Just an average day for a precocious ten-year-old," Bondi said. "Is the mother okay?"

"Dr. Ami, the doctor aboard *Brilliant,* is operating on her this morning to replace her heart and lungs."

"I understand," Bondi said. "Let me know if Kalinda needs a break during the competition. Follow me. I've got something she'll like."

Anthen followed Bondi over to the table where Kalinda was finishing a huge sticky bun. On deck was a bagel covered with dark chocolate schmear.

"Let's go over to the merch table," Bondi said. "I want to show you something."

Kalinda picked up the bagel. "What is it?"

"Remember our last session at Malibu?" Bondi asked.

"Sure, there was a film crew," Kalinda said. "You told me they were recording your tricks for a promo."

Kalinda munched on the bagel as they walked among the over-priced hats, mugs, and other souvenirs. They got to the apparel section.

"Omigod," Kalinda said. "I've got my own v-shirt."

She stood transfixed as the front of the shirt displayed the video. It began with a headshot of Kalinda with a *Brilliant* flyby in the background, followed by several of her tricks, and finally her social media info.

"They go on sale after your first heat," Bondi said.

"You think I'll do that well?" Kalinda asked.

"My sponsors and I believe you'll be top-ten overall after the Pro-Am."

Kalinda looked up to Bondi to say something, then thought, *I'll be arrogant after I finish the day in first place.* "I'm going to catch some waves." Kalinda grabbed her equipment and went to the dressing room.

Two HOURS LATER, the beach was becoming crowded with spectators, the Surfer Channel was showing the event live, and Kalinda was awaiting her first heat in the holding area.

"Hey grommet, don't you have to be big enough to carry your board before you can ride it?" Sixteen-year-old Sage Enever was the local hero. She was expected to place near the top of the amateur group and win the Pro-Am with her partner, her mother, Alessa Quizon.

"Your mom's going to carry it out for me," Kalinda said. "If she doesn't have to save your butt first."

"Big board, big attitude. I'm Sage. Who's your pro?"

"Bondi Cooper," Kalinda said. "You're with Q? Your mom?"

"Yeah," Sage said. "You went live on SurfTube this morning. You got some massive air. I think it's just us two in the amateurs."

An air horn sounded. "That's our cue," Kalinda said.

"Good luck," Sage said.

Kalinda and ten other surfers ran to the water's edge. Kalinda threw her board ahead of her and began paddling past the white water out to the break. She had fifteen minutes to score eight waves. She sat as high as she could on her board and looked outward. She saw a set coming in, and she focused on the second wave.

She looked at Sage.

"First two are crumblers, "Sage said.

Kalinda was anxious and took the second. She paddled to the crest, stalled in the pocket, and stood up. As predicted, the wave crumbled. As she paddled out through the white water, she watched Sage make three quick cutbacks before her wave broke.

Kalinda joined Sage beyond the break. "Nice wave," Kalinda said.

"Thanks," Sage said.

Kalinda saw her chance, began paddling, stalled in the pocket, and drew her line to the lip of the wave. Compressing her body, she bottom-turned to the lip throwing up spray behind her as she completed the roundhouse cutback. As she came down, she extended to her full height stalling in the pocket, turned to climb the lip but it broke down.

Biff Mason sat on the SurfTube broadcasting platform. "Was that a roundhouse cutback by a four-foot-eleven barney."

His broadcast partner, Simone Gilmore, said, "That's Kalinda Kelrithian. The rumors say she has been surfing for six weeks. She's

Bondi Cooper's amateur partner and may give Sage Enever some competition before the day is over.

Kalinda scored well on two more waves. On her final chance, Kalinda got an eight-foot wave. She drew her line, pumped her board, hit the lip, and went airborne. She reached out for the rails and slipped. Wipeout.

After she paddled in, she looked at the amateur scoreboard. She was in fifth place. Her new friendly rival was on top.

Sage came up behind her. "Welcome to the family, surfer girl."

30

At eight-thirty, Dr. Ami looked in on Mia Rodriguez. "Are you ready to become fully human again?"

"I'm ready to get this strange device off my chest, get out of bed, and back in the cockpit," Mia said.

Four people walked into the small ICU enclosure including Senator Ramona Curtwell, Chuck Rodriguez, and two rear admirals in khakis. Behind them stood a Marine with his sidearm drawn.

"Get away from my daughter, Robot," the senator said.

Dr. Ami took a step away from the bed.

"Mother," Mia said. "What's going on?"

Senator Curtwell shoved her way to the side of the bed. "Mia, this is Dr. Robert Dashman. He has flown in from Walter Reed to perform your surgery."

Mia looked at her husband. "Chuck, we agreed that Dr. Ami would do the surgery."

The other admiral stepped up next to the bed. "Commander Rodriguez, I'm Rear Admiral Susan Hartog. I'm the commander of Naval Medical Center, San Diego," she said. "Last night, I received orders from the Secretary of the Navy that Dr. Dashman would perform this surgery."

"Mother, this is your doing?" Mia said.

"Honey, it's for your own good and SecNav owed me a favor."

"Admiral Hartog," Chuck said. "Do the patient's wishes come first? My wife and I agreed that Dr. Ami would do the surgery since she originated the procedure on *Brilliant*."

"Sir, this is a military hospital. We're required to follow orders."

"I want Dr. Ami in the operating room," Mia said.

"There's no way that android is getting anywhere near my daughter."

"Senator, this is still my hospital," Admiral Hartog said. "Dr. Ami will be present in the operating room to observe and advise."

"If that is the case, then there will be an armed Marine present with instructions to shoot this abomination if it so much as touches my daughter."

"Admiral Hartog," Dr. Dashman said. "I don't want weapons in my operating room."

"I'm sorry, Admiral Dashman. I've been ordered by SecNav to adhere to the wishes of the Senator."

A nurse walked into the room. "Ladies and Gentlemen, this is still my Intensive Care Unit, and I need to prep this patient for surgery. Immediate family only."

"Yes, ma'am," Admiral Hartog said.

"Admiral Hartog," the senator said, "please assign me an office to conduct important business in private."

"Yes, Senator," the admiral said. "Gunny, escort Senator Curtwell to Admin Three on this floor. Stand Guard at her door."

"Aye aye, Admiral," the gunnery sergeant said.

Senator Curtwell began walking down the hall.

Admiral Hartog whispered, "And gunny, keep me informed of her whereabouts."

Gunny nodded and then chased after the Senator.

The room cleared except for Chuck Rodriguez and the nurse.

"Where's Jeff?" Mia asked.

"He's in the waiting room, honey," Chuck said.

"Nurse, can my son come in for a few minutes?"

"Of course," the nurse said. "Five minutes only."

"I'll go get him," Chuck said.

Out in the hallway, Dr. Dashman pulled Dr. Ami aside.

"Dr. Ami, I apologize for all of this," Dr. Dashman said. "I reviewed the procedure you pulled off on *Brilliant*. Besides performing a medical miracle, you foreshadowed the future of medicine."

"Thank you, Doctor," Ami said.

"Call me Bob. Is there a simulator available? I'd like you to take me through the procedure. I've not dealt with virtual organs."

"I believe so, Bob. Call me Ami," she said. "Admiral Hartog, is it possible for us to get into the simulator again?"

"I'll re-arrange things," Susan said. "Dr. Ami, I, too, would like to express my apologies. You are more than welcome to practice here anytime. You saved a young Marine last night."

"I understand the circumstances, Admiral," Ami said. "You and your staff have made me more than welcome. Bob, follow me."

They entered the simulation room. "VaNessa, load patient Mia Rodriguez," Ami said. "Configuration as before."

The virtual system appeared very quickly since it was cached.

"Ready, Doctors," Vanessa said.

"Ami, why don't you go through it one time and I will observe."

"Sure," Ami said. "VaNessa, initialize with clotting complication."

"Doctor?" Bob said.

"The scans might have detected some clogging in the pulmonary complex," Ami said. "I lost her on one run but overcame it on three more."

"How many sims did you run?" Bob asked.

"I ran the simulation fifteen times, fourteen successfully."

"This operation takes me two hours," Bob said. "How did you pull that off?"

"I did it in twelve minutes, Bob," Ami said. "But I will demonstrate at normal speed."

Dr. Ami began the procedure at normal speed.

"Warning, severe clotting in the left pulmonary artery," VaNessa said. Life sign alarms sounded.

"Give me a hand here, Bob."

Dr. Ami's actions accelerated. Dr. Dashman worked on the complication.

"Warning, severe clotting in pulmonary trunk," VaNessa said.

Dr. Ami worked on the trunk. One hour later, the procedure was complete, and the sim was stable.

"That was way too close," Bob said. "We'll do it once more, and I will take the lead. VaNessa, reset simulation."

"Ready, Doctors," VaNessa said.

Bob performed the procedure with Dr. Ami advising. He completed it successfully.

"Congratulations, Bob," Ami said. "I think you're ready."

"If things go south in the operating room, I'm going to need you," Bob said.

"I'll be there," Ami said.

"What happens if the Marine shoots you?"

"I'll be okay," Ami said. "But...."

"But what?" Bob asked.

"Most things in there don't react well to bullets," Ami said.

31

K alinda came up the beach after her first heat. Anthen was waiting by the sponsor tent.

"Your next heat is in thirty minutes."

"Any news?" she asked.

"Chuck messaged me," Anthen said. "Mia is going into surgery as scheduled"

She read her father's expression. "There's more to the message."

"Yes," Anthen said. "Dr. Ami is not performing the surgery."

Kalinda looked at the pier.

"You knew?" Anthen asked.

"I did," Kalinda said.

"She'll be alright."

"Yes, she will." She watched Bondi take the last wave of her heat then turned and looked at her father. "Could you have saved mother?"

All of the energy went out of his eyes as he looked at the waves. "My ship was in another sector battling drone fighters. By the time I got to her sector, the battle was over, and the enemy destroyed. Your mother sacrificed herself to win the battle." He looked directly at

Kalinda. "Your mother is a hero." He paused and looked down. "If only I could have…"

"Dad, you're my hero, too," Kalinda said.

"If only I could have gotten there sooner."

They hugged.

"It's not your fault," Kalinda said.

Bondi came up from the beach and stopped.

The hug continued. *Good Will Hunting?* he thought.

He pushed Kalinda away and looked at her. They broke into laughter.

Bondi raised her eyebrows. "Did I miss something?"

"Sorry," Anthen said. "You had to be there."

"Good news, Kalinda" Bondi said. "We're in third place in the Pro-Am."

"I'll put us in first after this heat," she said as she walked toward the sponsor tent. "I'm going to get a bagel."

"Pretty arrogant for a grommet," Bondi said.

"It comes from her mother," Anthen said.

"Divorce?" Bondi asked.

"Kalinda's mother died in battle while saving our planet."

"Oh."

"And she has this vision thing," Anthen said. "She can analyze a situation and accurately predict the outcome."

"From her mother?" Bondi asked.

"No, she got that from me."

"Interesting family," Bondi said. "Wish her luck for me. Though it doesn't sound like she needs it."

Bondi walked into the sponsor tent.

Luck is good, Anthen thought.

KALINDA WAS RIDING the swells during the second amateur heat of the Pro-Am competition. She looked directly west. *That storm is going to hit during the last heat.*

Sage Enever was in first place among the amateurs and was trying to build her lead. Kalinda turned her attention toward the blonde competitor as she started paddling into a six-foot wave.

Good wave, Kalinda thought.

Sage disappeared as the tube formed. Then Sage and her board came up above the wave.

Kalinda cringed.

Sage reached for her rails and came up with air. Wipeout.

Good try. I've got this, Kalinda thought.

THE TWO COMMENTATORS on SurfTube sat next to a camera on scaffolding twenty feet above the beach. "Sage Enever wipes out," Biff said. "But she still has the points after this heat to lead the amateurs over second-place Kalinda Kelrithian."

"Don't count out the ten-year-old, Biff," Simone said. "She has one more wave in this heat."

KALINDA TURNED to the incoming swells, spotted the one she wanted, turned to the beach, started paddling, and stalled the pocket. She pumped the board to gain speed as the curl formed above her.

The crowd on the beach turned to watch and started cheering.

The two 3D drones focused on Kalinda. "She's found the wave she wants," Biff said. "It's the tallest wave of the day."

Kalinda exploded out of the tube, hit the lip, and went airborne. Surrounded by the sky, the sea, and the nearby camera drone, Kalinda threw back her legs beyond horizontal, reached down, and grasped her rail. As the crest of the wave passed beneath her, she compressed her body to regain her footing and then stood to complete the trick.

"Wow, a Superman!" Biff said. "The ten-year-old goes highlight reel."

"Let's look at the three judges, Biff," Simone said. "Eight-point-five, eight-point-eight. The last judge is thinking. Nine-point-three."

"Simone, that gives the youngest surfer in the competition a clear lead on the amateur board," Biff said. "This girl has game."

"They're updating the Pro Board, Biff," Simone said. "Kalinda is now thirteenth overall in the competition with two heats remaining."

"And no surprises, here," Biff said. "Bondi Cooper and Kalinda Kelrithian lead the Pro-Am Competition. You're watching the 2067 Oceanside Pro-Am on the Surfer Channel. We'll be right back."

As BONDI STOOD next to Anthen, she said, "The arrogant grommet did it."

"More to come," Anthen said.

32

Less than twenty-four hours after a turbine blade from the engine of her helicopter had destroyed her heart and lungs, Lieutenant Commander Mia Rodriguez was in the operating room at the Balboa Naval Hospital under anesthesia to receive her regenerated organs.

Dr. Ami, who had transplanted temporary virtual organs into the patient aboard *StarCruiser Brilliant* stood in the corner of the operating room and observed Dr. Robert Dashman directly and on an interactive 3-D monitor. Around the patient, were a second surgeon, Imani Hiroga, an anesthetist, and three nurses.

She looked up to the gallery where Rear Admiral Hartog, Senator Ramona Curtwell, and several other doctors sat behind the glass. To her left was an armed Marine Gunnery Sergeant whose sole task was to enforce the Senator's wishes with deadly force if necessary.

"Are the replacement organs ready?" Dr. Dashman said.

"Yes, Doctor," the regen nurse said.

"Is the heart-lung machine ready?"

"Yes, Doctor," the heart-lung operator said.

He looked up at Dr. Ami.

Dr. Ami smiled and mouthed the words "good luck."

"Let's begin," Dr. Dashman said. "I'm making the cut along the rib junction on the sternum." He began the surgery. "Apply the rib spreaders, Imani."

The assisting surgeon split the ribs.

"In place," Imani said.

"Initiate Heart-lung bypass," Dr. Dashman said.

"Oxygen and circulation are stable," the operator said.

Dr. Dashman removed the left and right lobes, and the heart.

"Look at the scarring and the repairs," Dr. Dashman said. "This injury should not have been survivable. Dr. Ami, you performed a miracle."

"Thank you, Doctor," Ami said.

IN THE OBSERVATION GALLERY, Senator Curtwell spoke to Admiral Hartog, "Make sure you edit those words out of the video. I don't want that damn robot to get any credit for this."

"Yes, Senator," Admiral Hartog said.

"REPLACING THE REGENERATED ORGANS," Dr. Dashman said. "Imani work the right side."

"Yes, Doctor," Imani said as she stitched the pulmonary arteries and veins."

The two experienced surgeons worked in concert.

"Done," Dr. Dashman said. "Massaging the heart." It began to beat.

"Normal sinus rhythm, Doctor," VaNessa said.

"Very well," he said. "Secure the heart-lung machine."

"Vital signs stable," the VaNessa said.

"Securing the mini-projector." He held his breath, lifted the device away from the patient, and turned it off.

Alarms sounded. "Warning, severe clotting in the left pulmonary artery," VaNessa said.

"Applying a stent," Dr. Dashman said.

"No effect, Doctor," Imani said.

More alarms sounded. "Warning, severe clotting in the pulmonary trunk," VaNessa said.

"Dr. Ami, please assist me."

Dr. Ami took a step toward the operating table.

The Gunnery Sergeant pulled his service weapon and pointed it at Dr. Ami. "Step away from the table, Doctor."

Dr. Ami froze.

In the gallery, Senator Curtwell stood and pounded on the glass, "Noooo. Get that android away from my daughter."

The EKG audio went to a solid tone. "Warning: Patient is in cardiac arrest," VaNessa said.

Imani began massaging the heart. "We're losing her, Doctor."

33

Kalinda walked to the tent after her second heat. She looked back at the black clouds building in the west.

Bondi Cooper met Kalinda as she headed toward the holding area for her third heat. "The forecasters say the storm will miss us."

"Get all the points you can on the next two heats, Coach," Kalinda said. "You won't get a fourth."

"The vision thing?" Bondi asked.

"On Xaphnore, the weather can be violent. We've got a weather sense."

"Do you miss your home?"

"I spent most of my time in space with my te'ma and te'pa and sometimes my tal'pa, my grandfather," Kalinda said.

"How did you learn English?" Bondi asked.

"The Hoclarth Alliance has a cloaked satellite." She pointed up. "It monitors Earth's Internet. I watched *Sesame Street*."

The horn sounded, and the pro surfers ran to the water.

"Good luck," Kalinda shouted.

Kalinda walked up the beach and met her father.

"Bonding with Bondi," Anthen said.

"A little alliteration, te'pa?" Kalinda said.

"Just jesting, my juvenile child."

"Forevermore fatiguingly funny, father."

"You win," Anthen said. "What did you tell Bondi?"

"I told her that she'd only get three heats," Kalinda said.

"You're right," Anthen said. "I feel it, too but you will get all four heats. Hurry up to the tent. They've got sandwiches laid out."

Kalinda didn't move. "Any news?"

"She's in the operating room."

"It's not going well," Kalinda said. "Dad, please hold my board."

Kalinda ran to the sponsor tent and ran into the Jennifer, Tayla, David, and Riley. They high-fived her, and they hugged.

Jennifer saw her father, went down the beach, and hugged him.

"She looks worried. Is the pressure getting to her?"

Anthen frowned. "Mia's surgery is not going well."

"She doesn't want her friend losing her mother," Jennifer said.

"Yes."

"Dr. Ami got her this far," Jennifer said. "She'll get Mia through this."

"Dr. Ami's not doing the surgery."

Now, Jennifer looked worried. "That's bad. How does Kalinda handle all that?"

"Her mother had an inner strength that I never had," Anthen said. "Kalinda inherited that."

"I'm proud of you, Dad," Jennifer said.

"Thanks," Anthen said. He tried to smile.

"Seriously," Jennifer said. "Kalinda and I are strong, and a lot of that comes from you."

They hugged.

Tayla and the others joined. "Kalinda's the top amateur," Tayla said. "And she's climbing the open ranking."

· · ·

KALINDA GRABBED a plate of food and Sage Enever offered her a seat.

"It's just you and me in the amateurs, grommet," Sage said.

"You're right behind me on the pro board, too," Kalinda said.

"You look worried," Sage said.

"My friend's mother is in surgery," Kalinda said. "We rescued her on our way back from the moon, yesterday. Our ship's doctor saved her life, and she is getting her heart and lungs replaced today."

"You're from another planet, aren't you?" Sage asked.

"Yep."

"Do they have surfing there?"

"Sort of," Kalinda said. "We don't have surfboards. We take a leaf from a framlin tree and ride the surf."

"How big are the waves?"

"Remember the building at the head of the pier," Kalinda said. It was a thirty-story high-rise. "About a third of the way up."

"That's fifty meters," Sage said. "Isn't that dangerous?"

"Yes," Kalinda said. "My mom would only let me go out on quiet days when they are half that high."

"Attention, five minutes to the third amateur heat," the announcer said.

"Let's get busy," Kalinda said. "Good luck, Sage."

"You too, grommet," Sage said. "Don't show us up too much."

KALINDA WAS RIDING the increasing swells after wiping out on her first two waves. Her other waves had broken down before she could get a good score. The current set looked promising for the last wave of this heat.

It was so peaceful that she almost forgot about Jeff and his mom. There was foam at the top of the swells. Whitecaps. *The wind is starting to build ahead of the storm*, Kalinda thought.

Kalinda watched Sage paddle into her wave. She dropped out of sight into the pocket. Then Sage went aerial and rotated 360.

Omigod, Kalinda thought.

On SurfTube, "Our leader, Kalinda Kelrithian, is having a tough go this heat," Simone said. "But here comes Sage Enever."

"She drops in the pocket of the ten-foot wave," Biff said. "She is pumping out of a nice ride in the tube. Up she goes, bottom-turns three-sixty and stays upright on her board. Alley-oop."

"Good scoring wave," Simone said.

"She's still pumping, up she goes, and another Alley-oop."

"Definitely enough to take over first place," Simone said.

Kalinda paddled into the swell, the wave formed, and she dropped into the pocket. She started pumping. It got quiet as she concentrated on her trick. In flight terms, Sage's alley-oop was a 360-degree yaw maneuver. Kalinda intended to add a roll and go inverted. She was gaining speed. *If only there's some wave left when I get there,* she thought.

"Here comes the ten-year-old phenom," Biff said. "She has dropped into the pocket and started pumping in the curl."

The on-screen graphic showed her speed across the wave at 18.9 miles-per-hour.

"Look at her speed, Biff," Simone said. "Those numbers rival Kelly Joel Slater at The Eddie last year."

"She may outrun the wave," Biff said. She climbs the lip. Look at that air. She does the alley-oop inverted; she comes down into the foam; she loses it and...wipeout."

"Not enough wave for that trick, Biff," Simone said. "But after the third amateur heat, she'll still have enough points to stay very close to Sage Enever."

"More to come from Oceanside, California," Biff said. "We'll be right back."

THE PATIENT WAS in cardiac arrest, and a Marine Gunnery Sergeant had his service weapon pointed at Dr. Ami

"Stand Down, Marine," Dr. Dashman said.

"I cannot, sir," the Marine said. "I'm under strict orders."

"Warning: Patient is in cardiac arrest."

Admiral Hartog activated the intercom. "Gunnery Sergeant, stand down and holster your weapon."

The Marine put his weapon in his holster, turned to the gallery, saluted and said, "Aye aye, Admiral."

Senator Curtwell angrily turned to the hospital administrator. "I will have your flag, Admiral Hartog."

The hospital commander activated the intercom. "Dr. Ami, please assist Dr. Dashman. My apologies for the confusion. Gunnery Sergeant, please escort the senator to the waiting room."

"You just sacrificed your career for that robot."

"Senator," Admiral Hartog said. "You may take my flag, but I'll still be a medical doctor, and the primary job in this hospital will remain saving lives."

The Marine came in and led Senator Curtwell out of the gallery.

Dr. Ami stepped up to the operating table and began work. At first, she assisted Dr. Dashman.

He observed the rapidity with which Dr. Ami worked. He withdrew his hands. Ami continued to work at a frenetic pace.

"Patient has resumed sinus rhythm," VaNessa said.

"I recommend that we begin closing, Bob," Dr. Ami said.

"Good job, Ami," Dr. Dashman said. "You saved her again."

They finished stitching the wounds.

"Bring her out of anesthesia," Dr. Dashman said. "Status, VaNessa?"

"The patient is in Critical but Stable condition with full brain function."

Mia's eyes began to flutter.

"Commander, are you with us?" Bob said.

Her eyes opened with a blank look and then focused. She looked at Dr. Dashman and then Dr. Ami. "Dr. Ami, am I human again?"

"Yes, Mia," Dr. Ami said. "Just like always."

"Did you operate, Dr. Ami," Mia said. "What happened?"

"It was touch and go for a few minutes," Dr. Dashman said. "Dr. Ami applied her super-speed hands and bailed us out."

"Thank you, both," Mia said.

"Take her to recovery," Dr. Dashman said. "Dr. Ami, let's inform the family."

DR. DASHMAN and Dr. Ami entered the waiting room. Chuck and Jeff stood next to the Senator who was already standing.

"We had some difficulty, but we got her through it. Dr. Ami provided her invaluable skills to get Mia through a rough patch. She'll make a full recovery.

Jeff went over and hugged Dr. Ami.

Senator Curtwell tried to grab Jeff's arm. "Don't touch that thing. It's not human."

"Ramona, there's more to humanity than not being different," Chuck said. "We're proud that Jeff has learned that from Mia and I."

Ramona Curtwell turned and stormed out.

"Dr. Ami, Kalinda is in second place at Oceanside," Jeff said. "She has one more chance to win."

Chuck said, "The doctors are busy..."

"You have SurfTube up on your HoloPad?" Dr. Ami said.

"Yeah, it's in 3-D."

The two went to a table, sat, and watched.

"She's a special physician," Dr. Dashman said.

"*StarCruiser Brilliant* has given Jeff a new friend and me my wife back."

34

K alinda was sitting with her father in the sponsor tent surrounded by the other amateurs. She was munching on her second double-decker ham and turkey sandwich of the day.

Between them was a HoloPad and they were reviewing her waves on the third heat.

"The ocean is being mean to me," Kalinda said.

"The waves keep crashing at the wrong times," Anthen said.

Kalinda grimaced as they watched her final wave. "Too much speed and not enough wave."

"Weather has updated," Anthen said. "You may not have time to finish your heat."

"I just need two good waves," Kalinda said. "The monster waves are coming, but I'm worried about the others. The amateurs are not used to super-tall waves."

The avatar on the HoloPad stopped the video. "Call from Chuck Rodriguez."

Kalinda held her breath as she picked up.

Jeff and Chuck popped up on the table, all smiles.

Kalinda exhaled.

"Looks like everything went okay," Anthen said.

"Mia is through surgery, and she'll be fine," Chuck said.

"Dr. Ami saved her again," Jeff said.

"We are *Brilliant*," Kalinda said.

"We'll be watching on SurfTube," Chuck said. "Good luck."

"Thanks," Anthen said. "We'll see you on Saturday."

Jeff and Chuck disappeared from the table top.

"Five minutes to the final amateur heat," the announcer said.

"Got any tricks left?" Anthen asked.

"A couple," Kalinda said. "Bondi is in first place on the pro scoreboard. I'm in twelfth."

"You think you can win the amateur division," Anthen said.

"More than that," Kalinda said.

"You don't have to win it all in your first try."

"Dad, the waves right now are just like home. I remember what mother said. 'Make today your destiny and save your dreams for tomorrow.'"

"You're gonna win it all," Anthen said.

"Yes," she said. "But after that, I'll have another task."

"Kalinda?"

"The waves are calling."

KALINDA WAS out near the end of the pier where the swells were building twenty-foot waves. She looked at the black clouds bearing down on the beach. She knew that as soon as the safety master saw a lightning strike, he would sound two horns and clear the water.

Sage had just gone high above the lip to perform a perfect Superman. The scores gave her a solid lead in the amateur category.

Kalinda scanned the horizon, saw a set of swells approaching, and began paddling. *These are my waves,* she thought.

ON SURFTUBE, Simone said, "Bondi Cooper is clearly in first place among the pros, Biff. The excitement is coming from the battle between amateurs Sage Enever and Kalinda Kelrithian."

"Yes, Simone. Sage just improved her lead with a solid wave," said Biff. "Here comes Kalinda. This wave is a monster."

KALINDA DROPPED down on the face of the wave and went into the tube. She was combining the energy of the wave with her own to build tremendous speed.

She blasted out of the tube, climbed the over the lip, and went airborne to perform a Superman. But instead of throwing her legs back, she threw her legs forward and tucked.

"LOOK at her speed coming out of the tube," Biff said. "It looks like a Superman. Simone, she got more air than any other surfer today. Up she goes, she throws her legs back...wait..."

KALINDA COMPLETED THE REVERSE SOMERSAULT, came out of the tuck and grabbed the rails.

"KALINDA HAS DONE A COMPLETELY original version of the Super-man," Biff said. "She went up, did a reverse somersault in the tuck position, came out and grabbed her rail, and landed perfectly on the top of the wave."

"Biff, you and I just finished the three- and ten-meter diving nationals," Simone said. "A gainer or reverse somersault is one of the most difficult dives. Let's look at the slo-mo for style points. She goes aerial above crest and throws her legs back. Stop right there."

Simone uses the telestrator to draw a line from Kalinda's highest elevation to the wave. "Biff, the graphic shows her elevation at 11.3 feet. That may be the record. She goes into the tuck. Perfect. She comes out of the tuck and grabs the rails. Freeze there." Simone draws a line parallel to Kalinda's body. "Her extension is superb, and her landing is solid. I'm running out of adjectives here."

"Remember, the three judges observe the trick in real time," Biff said. "Here are the results. Nine-point-eight. Nine-point-five. And the final judge. Ten."

"Biff, that is the first Ten awarded on any level this season," Simone said.

"That moves Kalinda ahead of Sage on the Amateur Board and into fifth in the open category. Sage has three waves remaining to top Kalinda, a difficult task to say the least."

"Sage Enever is paddling into a monster wave," Simone said.

"She drops into the pocket and starts pumping into the tube for speed. Up she goes, grabs the rails, and does a barrel roll. Sage lands a perfect rodeo flip."

"The judges give her nine-point-two across the board," Simone said. "That puts her and Kalinda in a tie for the amateur lead and tied for fifth among the pros."

KALINDA HAD two waves remaining in her heat as she looked to the west. *I'll get one more wave before lightning strikes,* she thought.

She watched Sage's rodeo flip. *I guess I've got to top that.*

Here comes a monster wave. Into the tube. *I need speed.* She pumped as she went low and then extended as she bottom-turned. Rinse and repeat. Exploding out of the tube, Kalinda hit the lip at the best angle to retain her momentum. Airborne, grab the rails, and pull.

"KALINDA MAY HAVE two waves remaining to win the amateur title," Simone said. "If the storm doesn't end competition for the day. Here she comes, Biff."

"It's another thirty-foot monster. Kalinda stalls in the tube," Biff said. "Look at her building speed. Up she goes, she's airborne and grabs the rails. Even higher. One ... *two backflips* ... she lands it ... Omigod ... a double Flynnstone Flip."

"For the second time in this heat, Kalinda has nailed an original trick," Simone said. "Let's see if the judges reward her. Ten-point-zero, ten-point-zero, and ten-point-zero. Biff that guarantees her the amateur title."

Biff took over. "And, on the pro scoreboard, ..."

In close order, a lightning strike hit an electric tower two hundred yards north, the scoreboards and monitors went dark, a massive thunderclap sounded, and two horns sounded from the safety boat.

Kalinda glanced back and then continued toward the beach. She ran to the nearest cover near the beach. Her father was waiting.

The lights and scoreboards returned.

"Simone, we're in a lightning delay," Biff said. "Based on the weather report, that could end today's competition."

"Sage Enever is still on the swells," Simone said. "By rule, a competitor may still score on this wave. Here she comes."

Kalinda saw the biggest wave of the day coming in carrying her friend and competitor. *Be careful, Sage,* Kalinda thought.

Sage dove into the tube and started to build her speed. A huge wind gust came over the wave, and it crashed. Sage wiped out.

"Simone, that was a very dangerous wave, Biff said. "Sage hasn't popped back up to the surface."

· · ·

"Dad, I saw fishermen's net stuck on the bottom where she went down," Kalinda said as she looked at her father.

I want to say don't go, he thought "Be careful," Anthen said.

She ran to a TV electrician. "I need your folding knife," she said.

"But..." he said. Then he opened the pouch and handed it to her.

"Sage Enever remains under water," Biff said. "The safety boat is searching the area; lifeguards are running to the surf, and... Kalinda Kelrithian is running to the water as well."

Kalinda hit the surf at full speed, went horizontal, and started swimming. The crew of the safety boat tried to wave her back as they moved away from the point where she was aiming.

"Biff, she appears to be swimming to a point away from where the safety boat is searching," Simone said. "Kalinda has stopped and is waving to the boat. And now she's gone under the water. Sage has been under forty-five seconds."

Kalinda dove to the bottom through the sandy water. She spotted the net and then she spotted Sage struggling to free her legs from the fouled nets.

Kalinda got to her friend, opened the knife and started cutting. Five seconds later, she freed Sage. She saw that Sage had passed out. Kalinda dragged her to the surface just as the safety boat arrived at the spot.

"She's unconscious," Kalinda yelled.

The first responders dragged Sage aboard, threw Kalinda a life vest, then pulled her aboard.

. . .

"SAGE HAS BEEN under for a minute and fifteen seconds," Biff said. "Kalinda is under water too. The only sound on the beach is the wind and the surf. The spectators, transfixed by the drama occurring in the water before them, have moved to safety."

"One-minute-thirty," Simone said. "We're hoping for the best." Her voice broke.

Biff raised his binoculars. "I see two heads near the safety boat. They're pulling one of the girls aboard. It looks like Sage, but she appears to be unconscious."

A FIRST RESPONDER extended a hand and pulled Kalinda aboard the safety boat.

Sage was on her back as Kalinda stood and watched. A first responder was performing chest compressions, and Kalinda could see water coming from Sage's lungs. The first responder performed mouth-to-mouth and delivered one more chest compression. Sage turned her head and coughed out a large amount of water.

"Pulse is good." The first responder gave a thumbs up.

Sage continued coughing as they sat her up. She opened her eyes.

"Kalinda?" Sage said.

"Right here, Sage," Kalinda said.

"You saved me," Sage said.

"As you say, we're family," Kalinda said.

ON THE SURFER CHANNEL, "As the safety boat reaches the shore, they're carrying Sage to the medical tent...Just a moment...We're receiving word that Sage Enever responded to treatment and will be just fine. And so will Kalinda Kelrithian."

"Kalinda is walking up the beach just as the rain is beginning," Simone said. "The crowd is giving her hugs, high-fives and cheering for her heroism. Biff the scoreboard is updated as well."

"On a day that epitomizes the excitement and drama of not only surfing, Bondi Cooper and Kalinda Kelrithian have won the 2067 Oceanside Pro-Am Surfing Tourney. No surprise there, Simone. Kalinda has won the amateur title as well."

"No surprises so far, Biff."

"And with a perfect score on her last wave, Kalinda passes Bondi for first place on the pro scoreboard."

"We've found a true surfing superstar, Biff."

"We'll be back with interviews and a final note from Oceanside on SurfTube."

35

The Sunday crowd on the flight line of Miramar Marine Corps Air Station exceeded seven-hundred-fifty-thousand San Diegans. The size crowd was much larger this year as there was a rumor that the show would feature an aircraft never before seen at an airshow. Also, there was a worldwide audience on The Airshow Channel. The Blue Angels were the traditional finale, and the military aerial demonstration team was twenty minutes into their show.

Jack Masing was in command of *Brilliant* circling at eight thousand feet off the coast of La Jolla, California. Before him, Jennifer was in the Operations seat to the right of David, the pilot. Tayla was to the captain's right on Communications and Riley was behind the captain on the engineering console. Jennifer's half-sister, Kalinda, was sitting at the science console next to her father, Anthen. In Jennifer's lap was the ship's cat, Dandy Lion.

"Three minutes to Diamond Barrel Roll Break," Miramar Tower said. "Descend to two thousand feet on course zero-six-zero. At the apron, descend to five hundred feet at three hundred seventy knots. When the Angels Break, begin your roll," Miramar Tower said.

"*Starcruiser Brilliant*," Tayla said.

"That's our cue," Jack said. "Pilot, line up with six-right and begin your descent. We'll do a slow barrel roll to a plan view at show center and then start our loop."

"Yes, sir. Ready to rock and roll."

"Feet dry over La Jolla at five thousand," Jennifer said.

"Very well, ops," Jack said. "Is your smoke trick ready, Riley?"

"Ready, Captain."

"Two thousand feet at the apron," Jennifer said. "One-half mile range to the diamond. One hundred knots closing rate."

Jack signaled Tayla. "Blue Angels chatter on audio."

"We're in front of the crowd, setting up the barrel roll break," Munchkin said.

Fifi and Walleye acknowledged.

"Coming further right, a little more pull adding power," Munchkin said. "We're in a right turn for the Barrel Roll Break."

"Roger," Droopy said.

"Ease the pull, rolling out the barrel roll break, a little drive."

As they approach show center, "Smoke on. Up we go, a little more pull, adding power.... oooookay. A little more pull. Easing power, easing more power."

To the left of the crowd, "Rrrready break!"

The Blue Angels split in four directions.

As the crowd focused on the Blue Angels to their left, Jack ordered,

"Smoke on. David, let's show off."

"START YOUR ROLL," Jack said. Star Cruiser *Brilliant* began a lazy counter clockwise barrel roll showing the top profile of *Brilliant* to the crowd at show center.

"Roll complete," David said. "Beginning the loop."

The crowd screamed in awe as *Brilliant* completed its roll and the screaming continued as the smoke trail formed the words "*STAR-CRUISER BRILLIANT*" at show center. The crowd noise continued as *Brilliant* reached the top of the loop and began its descent.

"Sensor Alert," Ani said. "A Hoclarth Fighter Drone is pursuing us."

"What the hell?" Jack said. "Ops?"

"Fighter drone is firing plasma beams," Jennifer said. "Recommend eastbound exit over the mountains. Ready to return fire."

"Engineer, shields up. Pilot, ascend at sixty degrees over the mountains. Ops, can we steer clear of populated areas."

"We're over mountainous areas extending to the Imperial Valley."

Knowing things were getting dicey, Dandy jumped down from Jennifer's lap and curled up nest to Kalinda.

"Very well, Pilot, evade, Ops, splash the drone."

"Uncle Jack, please don't shoot. It's my tal'pa," Kalinda said. "He needs our help."

Jack turned his chair. "You knew about this, young lady? How have you been communicating with the Hoclarth?"

"Tal'pa has the internet and a SocNet account. He likes our movies. He wanted to make an entrance."

"Kalinda is right. The beams the drone is firing are low energy beams," Jennifer said.

"Very well, ops," Jack said. "Take us up to the Kármán Line, David. Let's see if we can lose our tail."

"Captain, we're being hailed," Tayla said. "It's the *Camdex*."

"On Screen," Jack said.

Predex Kalea Kone, Kalinda's bearded grandfather, appeared the forward display.

"Nice entrance," Jack said. "Your granddaughter tells me that you need our help."

"Is she on your ship?"

The ten-year-old stepped up next to Jack. "Hello, tal'pa. Uncle Jack, may I go over to the *Camdex*?"

"You look well, dear one. We cannot meet together now," Kalea said. "Captain, is it possible for us to speak in private?"

"Yes, Predex. Number One, take the center seat. I'll be in my ready room."

"You look well, Daughter of Kalim," Kalea said.

"I see that you have repaired your ship," Jennifer said. "Communications, route this to the captain's ready room."

JACK SAT in his ready room aft of the bridge. "How may I help you, Predex?"

"Captain, our planet is dying."

Jack leaned forward. "Explain."

"A disease has come to our planet. It has traveled fast through our population. One in one hundred of our citizens is now dead. I told Kalinda that I could not meet her because I was exposed the last time I was on Hoclarth. I do not want to risk giving the disease to your planet—or my granddaughter."

"Have your doctors had any luck finding a vaccine?"

"The disease has decimated our medical workers. It kills over eighty percent of those afflicted. My granddaughter tells me that you have excellent medical personnel."

"Dr. Ami, could you join us?" Jack said.

"Good afternoon, Captain," Dr. Ami said as she appeared in the room.

"Ami, this is Predex Kalea Kone of the Hoclarth Alliance. Their planet appears to have an outbreak of some kind of flu."

"Hello, Predex, we worry about that on Earth," Dr. Ami said.

"You have yellow eyes," Kalea said.

"I'm a virtual human," Dr. Ami said. "In the presence of the proper projector and computer equipment, I can function as a surgeon with the knowledge base of ninety percent of medical knowledge since the beginning of recorded history."

"Can you help us?"

"Since our first contact, our biologists have analyzed your DNA samples. Our two species have the same biological roots. The greatest threat to human health on our planet is a crossover disease from birds, swine, or other animals similar to the problem you're facing. It's a threat that we still haven't completely solved, and it is what you're facing now," Dr. Ami said.

"Are there solutions?" Kalea asked.

"In most cases, we can develop vaccines, in others, it mutates out of existence, but we worry about others that could mutate into a pandemic that would decimate our population," Dr. Ami said.

"Doctor Ami, is there anything we can do?" Jack said.

"Predex, if we can somehow move a lab to the surface of the planet, I could pursue a cure. Then your medical personnel could distribute the vaccine."

"Doctor, it is so contagious we're losing many of our medical personnel," Kalea said.

"That's a difficult complication," Dr. Ami said. "Even if I were able to stop the spread of the disease, many patients would require treatment."

"Can you help us?" the Predex said.

"Captain?"

Jack nodded.

"We'll give it our best try," Dr. Ami said.

Jack stood up. "Right now, though, we have almost a million people wondering where we went. We need to return to the surface."

"Ah, the show must go on," the Predex said. "A phrase from one of your movies. I'll await your word."

"Until then, Predex," Jack said. He made a motion with his hands, and the screen returned to the *Brilliant* logo.

"Dr. Ami, let's keep this quiet until we have a plan," Jack said.

"Of course, Captain," Dr. Ami said. "I did not mention it to the Predex. Jennifer has a project that is critical to solving this problem."

"Does it have something to do with that tall blonde who has been hiding on my ship for the last twenty-five years?" Jack asked.

"Yes, Captain," Dr. Ami said. "Physical bodies for Ani, Sami, and I."

"That would certainly stir up our favorite South Dakota Senator." Went through the door to the bridge.

JENNIFER SAW the door to the Captain's Ready Room open. "Captain on the bridge," Jennifer returned the ops panel.

"Report," Jack said.

"Miramar Tower is concerned. I told them it was a surprise we brought along. They don't like to go off-script," Jennifer said. "The Heritage Flight is circling east of the field waiting for us to join them."

"David, intercept the formation at best subsonic speed."

"Aye, sir," David said.

"Ninety seconds to intercept," Jennifer said.

"On screen," Jack said. They recognized the three familiar profiles of the vintage aircraft. The lead aircraft was a P-51 Mustang with a single piston engine. On his right wing was a twin-engine P-49, an airshow favorite after a century in the air. On the left wing was the F-18 from the hangar painted as Blue Angels 7.

David flew in behind, filled in the slot and completed the diamond. The formation banked left and circled before the crowd in a pass-in-review. The diamond passed once more before show center and then the vintage aircraft peeled off to enter the landing pattern. *Brilliant* continued westbound slowly.

After the three aircraft touched down, "*Brilliant*, you have the flight line for eight minutes," the tower said.

"*Starcruiser Brilliant*," Tayla responded.

"I suppose that you folks have a slam-bang finish cooked up?" Jack said.

"We sure do," Jennifer said.

"Captain, we've got the music programmed. The timer will start at the airfield apron," Tayla said.

. . .

"First Officer, you may indulge yourself," Jack said.

"Aye, Captain," Jennifer said. "Pilot, reverse course and line up with six-right and do the eight-point roll."

Brilliant was westbound at seven hundred feet and two-hundred-eighty knots. David performed a three-quarter barrel roll to the right and then executed a tight high-g turn to line up with the runway.

"Decelerating to two-hundred-fifty," David said.

"The clock has started," Tayla said. "Music initiated."

"Start your roll," Jennifer said.

As *Brilliant* rotated through eight precise instantaneous stops, the spectators saw the starship at every angle as they recorded the event on their cameras and phones.

David completed the maneuver at show left as Tayla played the *Theme from Brilliant* for the spectators and the viewers on the AirShow Channel.

"Reverse course and line up on two-four-left," Jennifer said.

"Show center in five-four-three-two..." Tayla said.

"Pitch up to vertical and accelerate to six-hundred," Jennifer said. "Engineer at three thousand feet, cloak the ship."

Three-quarters of a million San Diegans watched in awe as *Brilliant* went vertical and began an incredible vertical acceleration... and then screamed in unison as *Brilliant* just disappeared.

"Pilot, navigate to Point Alpha at heading three-three-zero." David flew to the pyramid on Miramar Road at one thousand feet," Jennifer said. "That will put us right behind show center. Engineer, ready the landing thrusters at full thrust."

"Ready," Riley said.

"Point Alpha," Ani said.

"Forty knots forward. Engage thrusters."

The crowd was frantically searching the silent sky for *Brilliant* as Tayla played the *Imperial March* when they heard the loud noise over their shoulders. They turned as one looking for *Brilliant,* but the sky was empty. The sound reached eighty-five decibels as the cloaked *Brilliant* passed over their heads. Over the runway at show center,

David stopped the ship and yawed to face the crowd at one thousand feet.

"Smoke on," Jennifer said.

At show center, a white cloud began to form at one thousand feet. There were oohs and ahhs as the crowd noise grew.

"Engineer, secure thrusters and uncloak the ship. Pilot, descend vertically and maintain two hundred feet."

The noise above the runway went silent as the crowd noise reached a crescendo. The music shifted to the finale of E.T. by John Williams; *Brilliant* slowly dropped out of the cloud to two hundred feet. *Brilliant* then executed a move that will be talked about by air show aficionados for many years.

"Pilot, start your move."

David then executed a slow combination of pitch, yaw, and roll that was impossible for any conventional aircraft with thrust originating in one direction. The crowd saw the beauty of *Starcruiser Brilliant* from every possible angle.

"Start your parade."

David piloted *Brilliant* to crowd left as close as the airshow rules allowed and slowly rolled the starship as he passed in review from left to right just in front of the attendees. David finished the pass at the center of the runway facing east.

Tayla, listening to the soundtrack that the viewers on the ground were hearing, said, "Ten seconds to music cue."

"Engineer, ready effects."

The music built to the finale. "Time," Tayla said.

"Start your move," Jennifer said.

Brilliant accelerated right-to-left and formed a parabola. When pitched up forty-five degrees at show center, David stepped on the gas and *Brilliant* exited show center almost instantaneously leaving behind a multi-colored rainbow just like the one from *E.T.* in perfect sync with the famous John Williams soundtrack.

The crowd on the ground was breathless with excitement as were the millions of viewers on the AirShow Channel who were watching at home in full 3-D.

As *Brilliant* navigated its return to show center, Riley and Anthen planned one more trick.

"Seven hundred feet. Course two-four-zero. Lined up with runway center," Ani said.

"Pilot, make your high-speed pass," Jennifer said. "Engineer, smoke on."

In honor of their hosts at Marine Corps Air Station Miramar, the airshow spectators saw the smoke behind the *Brilliant* form the familiar quotation, "The Few...The Proud...The Marines."

At the western end of the runway, David rolled right two-hundred-seventy degrees and executed a tight left turn to return to show center.

"Landing gear down," Jennifer said.

"Gear down," Riley said.

David brought *StarCruiser Brilliant* to the mark at show center and set her down gently.

"Ramp is down," Riley said.

"Good show, everyone," Jack said. "Tayla, good job with timing and music. Anthen, I don't think anyone will forget the rainbow you and Riley created. Riley, the smoke effects were remarkable. David, you would have made Tom Cruise jealous. Jennifer, your production was award-winning."

"Uncle Jack!" Kalinda said.

"I guess you and your tal'pa gave us a surprise none of us will forget." The ten-year-old beamed.

Just then, Dandy Lion jumped up on Jack's lap and gave him an evil cat glare. "Seriously, Dandy, You're just the ship's cat."

Dandy's cat scowl was even more fierce. He jumped down and shook his head in disdain. *Just the ship's cat,* he thought.

"Engineer put the ship in standby," Jack said. "Let's go out and take a bow."

The crew of the *Brilliant* exited down the ramp and received a standing ovation from the audience in the bleachers and cheers from those standing on the flight line. The crew signed autographs and posed for selfies for almost two hours.

Kalinda was the now the most famous member of the crew. Her biggest fan gave her a hug when they met.

"How is your mom?"

"She'll be okay," Jeff said.

"Two more weeks in the hospital," Chuck said.

As they boarded *Brilliant* for the short flight back to Tovar, Kalinda asked her half-sister, "Sister, why did everyone say that they liked my makeup? I'm not wearing makeup."

"I don't know, K'da," "Maybe it's your SoCal tan." Jennifer winked.

36

On the Monday after the Miramar Air Show, Jennifer was in the Captain's Ready Room on *StarCruiser Brilliant* preparing for the final battle scene of *Attack of the Hoclarth Alliance*. Jennifer was the Second Unit Director for the location shooting in the Mojave Desert.

Her lead designer at JennaTech, Stephen Mendoza updated her daily on the progress of VirtualLocation40, the system that would fly forty mini-drones among the actors to capture the scene in 3-D.

Brilliant was quiet and empty. The past week was busy with VIP guests, flights to and from Miramar, the rescue of a Navy pilot, and the air show. Now, it was just Jennifer, Ani, Sami, Dr. Ami, and Dandy Lion.

The yellow tabby jumped into Jennifer's lap.

"We had an exciting week, didn't we?"

I saved a life and put on a great show, Dandy thought.

"You had help, Dandy," Jennifer said.

It's my ship, Dandy thought, *even if the captain doesn't think so.*

"It'll be quiet for a while," Jennifer said. "You can bother the tours and live the cat life."

Oh, no, Dandy thought. *It's going to get busy.*

"The Hoclarth?" Jennifer asked.

Dandy nodded.

A tone sounded. "Jennifer?"

"Yes, Sami."

Sami entered the ready room. "The Captain would like you to join him in Navvy's office."

"Agenda?" Jennifer asked.

"He did not share, but his voice indicated a higher level of stress," Sami said.

"Thanks, Sami." She looked at Dandy. "And so, it begins."

Dandy jumped off her lap and walked away with a smirk.

JENNIFER SCHMEARED a bagel and sat at the blue table. Along with Navvy and Jack were Riley, Dr. Ami, and Ani.

"Good morning," Navvy said. "Thanks for coming."

"Hello, Grandpa. Hello everyone," Jennifer said. "Interesting group. I'm guessing this is about the chat with Predex Kone?"

"Correct," Jack said. "Xaphnore is dying from a disease that is spreading quickly through their population. It originated in a native animal."

"The Center for Disease Control worries that a pandemic will start like that on Earth," Jennifer said.

"Yes," Jack said. "This one is very nasty. It's already killed ten percent of Xaphnore's population. Only one in fifty of their citizens have developed an immunity. Kalea fears that over the next eighteen months, the disease will kill eighty percent of their population."

"What about *Camdex*?" Riley said. "Is Kalinda's grandfather sick?"

"They haven't returned to Xaphnore for the last year," Jack said. "He doesn't know if any of his crew are affected, but they can't return to the surface."

"We can't send our doctors because they would be susceptible," Jennifer said.

"Correct," Navvy said. "We need a more mobile solution. "Dr. Ami, Sami, and Ani can only travel a short distance from a shuttle."

Jennifer looked at the three virtuals. "So, you want JennaTech to produce physical bodies for you three?"

"Yes," Jack said.

She continued. "Riley will fabricate a shuttle for this mission."

"Got it in one," Jack said. "Dr. Ami, why don't you share the details?"

"Thank you, Captain, " Dr. Ami said. "I've contacted the CDC. They're cooperating. I've got all the data from their viral disease database. We'll design a small lab to be transported on the shuttle to synthesize a vaccine."

"Is everyone here cleared for secret information?" Jennifer asked.

"Yes," Navvy said.

"Will the shuttle carry the AI processing to support the remote operation?" Jennifer asked.

"I've contacted HumanAI," Navvy said. "They've developed a portable system that will support five virtuals. Riley will include it in the shuttle design."

"StarWave?" Jennifer asked.

"Yes," Navvy said. "The virtuals will be network-independent."

"Isn't the StarWave equipment located in a huge rack space in the equipment room?" Riley asked. "How can it fit on the body of a virtual?"

"Ha-ha. That's a ruse," Navvy said. "StarWave is a one-inch square chip that costs a dollar twenty-five to produce."

"Woah," Riley said. "That would disrupt the economy."

"It would," Navvy said. "But I think it's time for that to happen. Jennifer?"

"Pepper Simmons is developing a counterfactual communications device like StarWave," Jennifer said. "She's building on the work of a scientist who preceded her at North Carolina State."

"Will that help us on this project?" Jack said.

"It won't," Navvy said. "We'll fabricate the communications chips for the first generation of virtuals. How soon can you fabricate the...what do we call them? We need a name."

"Portabody?" Riley suggested.

The three virtuals looked at Riley with consternation. "Do I look like a John to you?" Sami asked.

"No, you're a female...Oh, sorry." Riley said.

"Container, body, case, physibody?" Navvy said. "Other ideas?"

"It's like a new species," Jack said.

"Or nationality?" Ani asked.

"You could call us cyberians," Sami said.

"Russians?" Riley asked.

"C-Y-," Sami said.

It was quiet around the table. "That works," Jennifer said. "What's the timeline?"

"I need ten days to research, design a lab, and gather data," Dr. Ami said. Ani and Sami will be working closely with me."

"I need a week to fab the shuttle," Riley said. "It'll have gravity drive to fly within a system."

"Are we able to get that close to Xaphnore?" Jennifer asked. "They don't like *Brilliant*. Can we put StarDrive on the shuttle?"

"Miniaturizing the StarDrive module will take several weeks," Riley said.

"I can jump in and get my hands dirty," Jack said.

"So can I," Navvy said. "Let's shoot for three weeks. Jen, work with Kalinda to contact the Predex. We need a direct channel."

"Yes, grandpa," Jennifer said.

"We should have time to install at transmatter pad. It will move things without contamination," Navvy asked. "Are there any other issues?"

"I've been monitoring the speeches of Senator Curtwell," Ani said. "She posed a rhetorical question. 'Who will be the Dr. Frankenstein who creates the first humanoid robot?'"

"That would be me," Jennifer said. "You can all just call me Frankie from here on."

"She's just a blowhard trying to scare her way into the oval office," Jack said.

"She has a seventy-three percent approval rating among likely voters," Sami said.

"She hasn't faced an opponent yet," Navvy said. "That's when all prospective emperors show off their new clothes."

"It's a difficult project," Jennifer said. "I don't want to go up against a United States Senator."

"We're all behind you," Navvy said. "Anyway, I think we have some inside help."

"Mia's family?" Jennifer asked.

Navvy nodded. "As well as the current occupant of the oval. You have friends in high places."

"And in low places," Riley said.

They laughed, and the mood became lighter.

"Plan for a week in Hoclarth space," Jack said. "Jennifer and Kalinda will communicate with Predex Kalea. Keep Navvy, and I informed of problems and progress."

The group stood to leave the office. "Let me know," Navvy said. "I'm here to help."

"Thanks," Jennifer said. She headed back to the Captain's Ready Room with lots of work to do.

37

Jennifer finished up her work in the Captain's Ready Room. Sami sat across from her. "Remember, you promised Navvy to set up communications with Predex Kalea," Sami said.

"Right," Jennifer said. "Can you connect me to my dad?"

Sami nodded, and a few seconds later Anthen popped up to Jennifer's left.

"Hi, Jen." Anthen turned his head. "Sami."

"Dad, may I come for dinner?" Jennifer said.

"Sure," Anthen said.

"*Brilliant*'s got a mission coming up, and I need yours and Kalinda's help," Jennifer said.

"Surfer Child will be on the waves until five-thirty," Anthen said. "Guessing this has to do with Predex Kalea's visit?"

"Good guess," Jennifer said. "I'll be there before five."

She disconnected the call and glanced at the projects strewn over her desk in the *Brilliant* Ready Room.

Dandy jumped on Jennifer's lap and looked at her. *Kalinda knows about the mission to Xaphnore,* Dandy thought.

"It's hard to keep secrets when Kalinda and Anthen can fill in the

234

blanks like us," Jennifer said. "Any new messages?"

"Stephen sent some patent paperwork for your review," Sami said. "It contains the cyberian design."

"I'm hoping that one slides under the nose of Senator Curtwell," Jennifer said. "She already suspects we're building self-contained androids. Anything else?"

"Jeff Rodriquez told his mom what happened during the rescue," Sami said. "Mia sent a thank you to the *Brilliant* bridge crew and said we would be very deserving of the nomination."

"Nomination?" Jennifer asked. "She wasn't specific, but it sounds like *StarCruiser Brilliant* is going to get an award."

"Cool."

"There will be a nice sunset on the beach," Sami said. "Kanan Road is open after the Rocky Oaks fire. We can make it if we leave now."

"Will you join us, Sami?" Jennifer asked.

"It's creepy when people see a torso and a head looking at the sunset," Sami said. "I promise I'll watch it."

Jennifer picked up Dandy and set him down on the floor. "You've got the watch, Dandy."

Take me with you, Dandy thought. *I miss your sister, and I can help.*

"You're right," Jennifer said. She put her HoloPad in her pouch. "Let's go."

Jennifer and Dandy walked to the parking lot continuing their chat.

People are staring at us, Dandy thought. *So rude.*

THEY PASSED through the tunnels on Kanan Road and descended to the Pacific arriving at ten-to-five. Anthen's mansion overlooked the Malibu surfing beach on the crescent from Point Dume to Point Mugu.

"Hi, Dad," Jennifer said. "What's for dinner?"

"Kroknal, it's one of Kalinda's Hoclarth favorites."

"The one with the live beetles?"

"Oh no," Anthen said. "She says the bugs here have a bitter taste."

"You're joking, right?" Jennifer asked.

"Gotcha," Anthen said. "It's a casserole like Shepherd's Pie with sweet potatoes and salmon, but it's spicy. The ingredients are as close as I can find to Hoclarth home cooking."

"That sounds like an interesting combination," Jennifer said. "You did most of the cooking after Natira..."

"Even before," Anthen said. "Natira was very focused on her military career. She was away a lot, and in Hoclarth culture, the father does the child-rearing."

"You miss her," Jennifer said.

He whipped the sweet potatoes even harder. "I do. Even more so when Kalinda is near."

"I wish I could've met her," Jennifer said.

Anthen turned to a cupboard, got some spices, and changed the subject. "I see you brought Dandy Lion."

Dandy's ears perked up.

"He wanted to come," Jennifer said.

"Don't tell me you're like Kalinda?" Anthen said. "She thinks that cat can talk."

Dandy looked at Anthen. *And you don't?* Dandy thought.

Anthen snapped his head to look at Dandy. "Did he just...?"

"Ha-ha, ask him," Jennifer said.

"Can..you...hear...me?" Anthen said.

I can hear you faster than you talk, Dandy thought.

"Amazing," Anthen said. "Who else can hear you?"

Just four humans, Dandy thought. *The rest stare rudely.*

"I've never heard Navvy say anything to you," Jennifer said.

He doesn't need to, Dandy thought.

"Interesting." Jennifer turned to Anthen. "Dad, you know why I'm here?"

"The disease on Xaphnore?" Anthen said. "Kalinda has been very evasive when I bring up Xaphnore."

"According to the Predex," Jennifer said. "Xaphnore is dying, and they need our help. They're facing a pandemic decimating their population."

"Don't we worry about a disease transmitted from animals on Earth?" Anthen asked.

"Yep," Jennifer said. "Dr. Ami is getting a lot of data and support for this project from the CDC in Atlanta."

"Can this disease affect us on Earth? How will you prevent cross-contamination?" Anthen asked.

"Cyberians," Jennifer said.

"Russians?" Anthen said.

"Spelled with a C-Y," Jennifer said. "That's the name we came up with for the bodies that Sami, Ani, and Dr. Ami will ride on with the shuttle to Xaphnore. Riley's fabbing a new shuttle with Star-Drive, a virus lab, and an AI base processor to support the five virtuals on Xaphnore."

"And Kalinda will help you communicate with Kalea?" Anthen asked.

"Correct. We don't know how close we can get to Xaphnore," Jennifer said. "Kalinda talks to him on SocNet. You know that, right?"

"I know," Anthen said. "She keeps me informed if he says something important, but I don't talk to Kalea."

"Does she know about the pandemic?" Jennifer asked.

"She has discussed it with her Tal'pa," Anthen said.

"Has she discussed it with you?"

"I know she's worried," Anthen said. "Jack asked you to plan the mission?"

"Yes, and JennaTech is creating the cyberian host bodies," Jennifer said.

"You're passionate about this?" Anthen said.

"I watched a sunset a few weeks ago. I wished Sami could stand there with me," Jennifer said. "I wanted her to be able to see, smell, hear and feel the waves crashing on the beach as the sun dipped below the horizon."

"The sister you never had," Anthen said. "Do you think your avatar has feelings about this?"

"Sami is just a computer designed to think like humans," Jennifer said. "But she has become much more than that."

"More than artificial intelligence?" Anthen asked.

"Sami is sentient," Jennifer said. "Eastern philosophy defines a sentient being as one who requires respect and care."

"Requires?" Anthen asked. "When do the virtual's needs transcend objectivity to become subjective."

"I feel Sami deserves respect and care," Jennifer said. "She certainly doesn't demand it, but my feelings require that she receive those considerations."

"So, you're helping Mr. Darwin with a little push to the Singularity," Anthen said.

"I guess I'm creating a competitor for our position at the top of the food chain," Jennifer said. "A bit presumptuous for a seventeen-year-old, even one with a high IQ."

"The species with the highest intelligence determine the pace of evolution," Anthen said.

"The eternal scientific conundrum," Jennifer said. "I can do it, but should I?"

"You'll save Xaphnore if you succeed," Anthen said. "But you'll make enemies on Earth."

"Already have one, thanks," Jennifer said. "Senator Curtwell describes the creator of a physical android as Dr. Frankenstein."

"So, you'll get your doctorate a year early," Anthen said.

Jennifer looked unsure. "What if I fail this time? What if I can't find a solution to help the Hoclarth?"

"Here's the thing about failure," Anthen said. "It's not an end. The task is still before you. You still have the tools and the time. Just keep moving forward."

"Up to now my worst failure is falling on my butt when I met David," Jennifer said. "I'm so clumsy."

"I saw your tennis trophies," Anthen said. "You certainly survived clumsy."

"But I've never failed at anything big," she said. "If someone wrote a book about me, the critics would say it was a lousy book because everything came too easy for me."

"True," Anthen said. "But people would still read it because they know that it will have a happy ending. They know that your persistence and your leadership will achieve success in the end."

"This is a huge project," Jennifer said.

"And you have the crew of *Brilliant*, your mom and stepdad, your people at JennaTech, and me to support you."

"Thanks, Dad." They hugged.

Kalinda walked in right when they began their hug. "That's my dad you're hugging," Kalinda said.

"Mine, too," Jennifer said.

"Okay, then," Kalinda said and joined the group hug.

And I'm just the furry sidekick to whom you feed nasty-ass cat food, Dandy thought.

All three humans turned their heads to Dandy. He jumped into Kalinda's arms and joined the hug.

"I thought you liked cat food, Dandy," Jennifer said.

If you weighed ten pounds, you would be hungry enough to eat dead birds covered with feathers, Dandy thought.

"So does salmon pie meet your fancy?" Anthen asked.

I will give it due consideration, Dandy thought. *When is dinner?*

"After Kalinda takes off that wetsuit and showers," Anthen said. "You smell like seaweed, K'da."

KALINDA RETURNED in five minutes and helped Jennifer prepare the salad. "So, you're creating physical bodies and a new shuttle for the mission to Xaphnore. When do we leave?"

"How do you know all that?" Jennifer asked.

"Dandy, the super spy."

"Hold on, surfer girl," Anthen said. "This trip could be dangerous. You're staying on Earth and going to school."

"No way I wave goodbye to my whole family while you go off and save my planet," Kalinda said.

"It won't be that dangerous," Jennifer said. "Should be a milk run."

"I've heard about these milk runs," Anthen said. "Everything is relaxed until it goes sideways."

"You'll need me on this mission," Kalinda said.

"You'll stay here with your grandparents, and that's final," Anthen said.

"You sound sure," Jennifer said. "The vision thing?"

Kalinda nodded.

"I don't see it," Jennifer said.

"You don't have all the parts, yet," Kalinda said. "Te'pa knows things that he is not telling."

"Yes, I do," Anthen said. "And that is why you're staying on Earth."

Kalinda grabbed Jennifer's arm. "I can set you up to communicate with Tal'pa Kalea. Let's go to my room."

JENNIFER ENTERED Kalinda's room to face an entire anim-wall and stood transfixed. The wall showed a montage of Bruce Lee combat scenes, Bondi Cooper surfing tricks, *StarCruiser Brilliant* flying at Miramar, and Kalinda performing her reverse somersault at Oceanside. To her right was a bay window overlooking the Malibu beach and to her left was Kalinda's bed surrounded by digital creature comforts. In the center were the familiar boundaries of a steveLearn.

"Cool wall," Jennifer said.

"Dad upgraded my room after he bought the house," Kalinda said. "Tal'pa Navvy gave me the steveLearn as a housewarming gift."

Jennifer looked in the closet. "How many pairs of sneakers do you have?"

"I'm up to eighty-three now," Kalinda said. "All of the Vans and Nikes came from surf sponsors. I like retros from the early 2000s."

"I've got some thigh-high Vans with auto-snug and auto-cool," Jennifer said. "They work off public Wi-Pow."

"Like these?" Kalinda asked. She pulled open a large drawer with three pairs in different colors.

"Nice collection," Jennifer said. "I wear a size nine-and-a-half if you have any generous sponsors."

Dandy Lion wandered into the room and jumped up on the bed. *Things*, he thought.

"Things, Dandy?" Jennifer asked.

Humans are overly obsessed with things, Dandy thought. *I'm perfectly content with my nine.*

"Lives?" Kalinda asked.

No. My humans, Dandy thought. *Nine Lives is just a silly name for food.*

"I'll ask my sponsors if they'll hook you up," Kalinda said.

"This means you talked your dad into letting you compete?"

"Yeah," Kalinda said. "He agreed to four events plus worlds if I qualify."

"Who's your sponsor?" Jennifer asked.

"Tovar Studios," Kalinda said. "Tal'pa asked me to mention the latest picture when I do interviews. And I display a *Brilliant* logo on my wetsuit."

"Always the promoter," Jennifer said. "Let's contact your Hoclarth Tal'pa?"

"Sure," Kalinda said. The two walked over to the steveLearn circle. "Bralen, join us."

A twelve-year-old male Hoclarth appeared, presenting with his hands open and knee bent. Wearing a traditional skin-tight Hoclarth combat suit, Jennifer could see from his six-pack abs that he was as physically imposing as her sister.

RICK LAKIN

"Nice avatar," Jennifer said.

"He's a friend," Kalinda said. "We served Tal'qid together until he took up weapons."

"Could you beat him?"

"Ha-ha. Of course," Kalinda said. "Why do you think he took up weapons?"

"Did you have a crush on him?" Jennifer asked.

"Eww, no," Kalinda said, "but we agreed on a compact to mate because we were friends. That was the plan until..."

"You came to Earth?"

"Yes. I miss Bralen."

"Wait," Jennifer said. "I'm confused. You're friends, and you want to mate, but you didn't love him."

"Correct," Kalinda said. "In our culture, mating is like a business proposition. Love only complicates things. Males and females compete in many ways, and so we avoid emotional attachments. A Hoclarth home may house several pairs including mates and those who love each other."

"Your father didn't love your mother?"

"Oh, yes, he did," Kalinda said. "They loved each other very much. With three of us in our home, it was challenging at times, and very mixed up. They were both Predexes in the Hoclarth Alliance. They were avid competitors, but they were in love. It caused great problems at home and in the Alliance."

"You're crushing on Jeff, though," Jennifer said.

"No way," Kalinda said. "We're just friends."

Your words deny your feelings, Dandy thought.

"Can't we humans have any secrets?" Kalinda said.

"Let's contact your tal'pa," Jennifer said.

"Bralen," Kalinda said. "Is Tal'pa in a waking cycle?"

"Yes, K'da," Bralen said. "He's on patrol in the Lanrok sector."

"Ask if he will communicate with me."

The room converted to the ready room of the Hoclarth Battle Cruiser, *Camdex.* Around them were artifacts of battles fought by the bearded Predex who sat alone on the floor in the middle of the room. A large display showed alien space and a patrol ship flying in formation. One wall contained martial arts weapons foreign to Earth.

"Hello, K'da," They hugged. "I enjoy this hugging thing you have found on Earth. It's good to see you as well, daughter of Kalim."

"Nice to see you, Predex," Jennifer said. "My captain asked me to set up communications with you."

"You're going to help our planet?" Kalea asked.

"We're collecting data from our Center for Disease Control, designing a shuttle with a laboratory, and preparing our personnel. We hope to land on Xaphnore near your disease center, conduct the research, and develop a vaccine. Our doctors will then begin the distribution of the cure."

"Will it be safe for your human doctors?" Kalea asked.

"No humans will be aboard the shuttle," Jennifer said. "We've developed a solution to allow our cyberians to go anywhere on your planet where they're needed."

"Cyberians?" Kalea asked. "Robots?"

"Yes, Predex," Jennifer said.

"You choose to pursue this technology?" Kalea said. "It is forbidden in the Hoclarth Alliance."

"There are those who oppose it on Earth, Predex," Jennifer said.

"Kalim's oldest daughter is as gifted as his youngest," Kalea said. "Your mother has done as good a job raising you as Kalim has raised my granddaughter. I hope there comes a day when we can all meet in person, Jennifer."

"It would be my honor, Kalea," Jennifer said. "Our father would be honored to hear that."

"When will your plan be ready for deployment?" Kalea asked.

"Twenty-one days," Jennifer said. "We need to bring the shuttle near Hoclarth space and allow you to escort it to Xaphnore."

"I will meet you at the fourth planet of a star you designate as the Wolf star," Kalea said.

"We'll plan our mission on that basis, Predex," Jennifer said.

"I wish you great success," Kalea said. "Is K'da still present?"

Kalinda sat on the floor and Dandy jumped in her lap.

"Here, Tal'pa," Kalinda said.

"What is that vicious animal?" Kalea asked. "Are you safe, K'da?"

Dandy turned to Kalea. *I am her friend and protector,* Dandy thought.

"My apologies and respect, Toxem'al," Kalea said.

Dandy nodded in response and went back to purring.

"I watched the event where you competed on the small waves near the shore. Your mother in Laknove is very proud of you as am I," Kalea said. "You won the competition and saved the life of your nearest competitor."

"Thank you, Tal'pa," Kalinda said.

"Is that stiff board as effective as a framlin leaf?" Kalea asked.

"The waves are much smaller on Earth," Kalinda said. "I must adapt."

"Jennifer, I look forward to converting adversaries to friends and meeting after this crisis is past," Kalea said.

"As do I, sir," Jennifer said.

Kalinda hugged her tal'pa again.

"Until then," he said. Kalea disappeared, and the room converted back to Kalinda's bedroom.

"Jen, I need to be on this mission."

"You want to?" Jennifer said.

Her presence is essential on this mission, Dandy thought. *She must go.*

"You've got the vision thing, Dandy?" Jennifer asked.

You think I'm just another talking cat? Dandy thought.

"I'll talk to the captain," Jennifer said. "You two need to convince Dad."

Anthen yelled from the kitchen. "Kroknal is ready."

Dandy jumped from Kalinda's lap and started running. Then he looked back, slightly embarrassed, and resumed his imperious tone as he walked to the dining area.

38

Jennifer spent the day in the HTVR lab at JennaTech.

The lab space was configured as a gymnasium with Sami on a treadmill. She was working through coding problems for Jake in the cranial AI processor on the prototype cyberian. Sami was resident in the prototype as the guinea pig. She was walking at an average speed to test her balance and coordination.

"I am still left-leg dominant," Sami said.

"I see that on the display," Jennifer said. She rapidly typed some new information in the coding window. "How about now?"

"Better," Sami said.

"Take it up to a normal jog," Jennifer said.

Sami picked up the pace. "I still feel top-heavy. Try to lower the virtual center of gravity."

Jennifer recoded a section. "Pick up the pace, Sami."

"Two-hour marathon it is," Sami said.

"So far so good," Jennifer said. "Readouts look nominal. Try a sprint."

"World record hundred-meters coming up," Sami said. She ran for three seconds then tumbled over the side of the treadmill. "Oops."

Sami got up. "No damage but I have a misaligned actuator in my right hip."

"Can you do the fix?" Jennifer asked.

"Yes, I will go to the cyberian workshop, separate, and do it," Sami said.

A tone sounded indicating visitors in the lobby.

Stephen came into the lab, "There are federal marshals in the lobby."

Jake looked startled. "What the hell are they doing here?"

Jennifer looked alarmed. "I'll go see what they want."

The automated lobby was unoccupied except for two armed marshals.

"May I help you?" Jennifer asked.

"Are you the manager of this company?" the taller marshal said.

"I am Jennifer Gallagher, CEO of JennaTech. How may I help you?"

"Ma'am, you are served." The marshal handed her a disposable tablet. "This is a Federal Cease-and-Desist order. Per the Dangerous Technologies Act of 2027, Judge Manual Servin orders that you immediately cease-and-desist from producing dangerous technologies to wit, a physical robot or android."

"How soon do we have to comply?" Jennifer asked.

"Ma'am, you have three business days," the marshal said. "At that time, you must present proof of compliance to the judge or federal marshals will raid the premises and confiscate any evidence of non-compliance. Do you have an attorney?"

"Yes, we do," Jennifer said.

"I recommend that you contact your legal counsel immediately to determine your legal rights and responsibilities. Do you have any questions?"

"I do not," Jennifer said.

The officer touched the bill of his cap. "Thank you for your coop-eration." The two officers turned and left the building.

Stunned, Jennifer walked back to the lab. "Stephen, have you heard of the Dangerous Technologies Act."

"Ouch," Stephen said. "It was passed to prevent non-defense companies from developing weapons of mass destruction, but not for projects like the cyberians."

"This sounds an awful lot like Senator Curtwell has played a full house," Jennifer said.

"Call Ana right away," Steven said.

Sheila Gallagher and Ana Mendoza worked in the executive offices of GGG two buildings over. Jennifer contacted their office.

Ana Mendoza appeared before them, sitting at her desk. "Good morning," Ana said.

"Ana, I just had a visit from two federal marshals. We've been served with a cease-and-desist order."

"That's always a pleasant surprise. Your mother is with a client," Ana said. "Can we meet in the conference room in one hour? Send me the information, and we'll prepare the response. Drag Jake and my husband along, and we'll lay out some sandwiches."

"I sent you the documents," Jennifer said. "We'll be there. Thanks."

"Got it. This order is from a federal judge," Ana said. "It's not nice to piss off Uncle Sam."

"Senator Curtwell," Jennifer said.

"Oh, right," Ana said. "See you two soon."

Ana's virtual presence dissolved.

"Who else should I call, Stephen?" Jennifer asked.

"Your grandfather might be able to help," Stephen said.

"Good idea." She touched her HoloPad and Sami popped up. "Contact grandpa's office."

"Yes, boss," Sami said. "Here's Kathy."

Kathy looked up from her desk. "Hello, Jennifer," Kathy said. "Navvy is just finishing a phone call. Is everything ok?"

"We got served," Jennifer said. "Federal marshals visited."

"Always a good start to the morning," Kathy said. "Here's Navvy."

The virtual scene shifted to Navvy's office.

"My granddaughter is in handcuffs?" Navvy asked.

"Not so much but we got served," Jennifer said. She explained what happened.

"That was quick," Navvy said. "She works fast."

"You saw this coming," Jennifer said. "What can we do?"

"Have you contacted Ana?"

"Yes, we are meeting in an hour."

"Good. What progress have you made on the cyberians?" Navvy asked.

"We are tweaking the prototype for balance and functionality," Jennifer said. "We've frozen the fabrication template today, but we are still coding. We've tested the StarWave interface with HumanAI and *Brilliant*."

"Good," Navvy said. "You've made progress. Do you have a secure office?"

"Yes," Jennifer said. She looked at Stephen. "Excuse me. Let's go into my office."

SAMI CLOSED THE DOOR. "The room is secure, Jennifer."

"Go ahead," Jennifer said.

"You've created tech that should not fall into the hands of anyone outside the *Brilliant* family."

"I was beginning to worry about that."

"Many years ago, I acted on the need to protect the technology of *Brilliant*. I created a secure location on Titan, Saturn's largest moon."

"If a disaster happens to *Brilliant* or the Earth suffers an apocalyptic event, this facility is designed to provide our successors with the tools to restart and regenerate. It's maintained by a virtual named Sandi and receives support from HumanAI Corp."

"Excellent idea," Jennifer said. "So, it can fabricate a

StarCruiser?"

"It's got one of the two root fabricators in existence," Navvy said. "It can generate a daughter fabricator that can generate an object the size of *Brilliant.*"

"What about materials?"

"Titan has all of the organic elements on the surface and in the atmosphere and all of the industrial isotopes very near the surface," Navvy said. "I'll introduce you to Sandi. I want you to transmit all of your intellectual property to TitanX. She'll set up a system so a copy of your IP will exist outside your lab in case the feds raid your office. A copy of your entire library will exist off-planet. Sami will coordinate directly with Sandi. Your digital IP will be encoded and secured locally."

"Got it," Jennifer said. "Will my crew see any changes?"

"Yes, they will," your Navvy said. "Tell them that you've performed a security lockdown to protect the IP and to continue to work as before."

"Sami, did you get that?" Jennifer asked.

"I've contacted Sandi, and we've begun the process."

"Thank you, grandpa," Jennifer said.

"Finish your prototype and then halt the project until Saturday," Navvy said.

"Saturday?" Jennifer asked. "Jack said we had a mission that day but didn't share details."

"*Brilliant* is getting a medal," Navvy said.

"Where are we going?"

"*Brilliant* is landing on the South Lawn of The White House."

"Cool," Jennifer said. "For the Mia rescue?"

"Yes," Navvy said. "*Brilliant* will get a Meritorious Unit Commendation, and Dr. Ami will get a medal. Mia and her family are riding along. Bring your JennaTech crew."

"I can have Dr. Ami resident in the prototype," Jennifer said. "Kalinda will certainly be happy."

"Bring some books to sign," Navvy said. "The president's kids are big fans. Coordinate with Jack for the details. Plan on a departure pass over the mall. We are promoting this so there will be an audience."

"I'll ask Riley and Anthen to create the smoke trick."

"Excellent. Crew inspection and breakfast at nine on Saturday," Navvy said. "Are you ready for next week?"

"Yes," Jennifer said. "The VirtualLocation system is up and running."

"The key position will be Technical Director," Navvy said. "It'll be a challenge juggling forty cameras."

"Sami will handle it," Jennifer said. "She helped design the system."

"Good call. See you Saturday."

JENNIFER LEFT HER OFFICE, went into the lab, and met Stephen and Jake.

"Well?" Stephen asked.

"Grandpa has something up his sleeve," Jennifer said.

"How so?" Jake asked.

"We are meeting the president on Saturday," Jennifer said.

"Of what?" Jake asked.

"Duh, the United States," Jennifer said. "Let's walk over to legal."

Ana Mendoza, the chief counsel of JennaTech, met them in the conference room. "Sheila is on a conference call. Grab a plateful and take a seat."

Jennifer, Stephen, and Jake built sandwiches from the catered spread, filled their plate with sides, and sat down.

"Thanks for setting up this meeting," Jennifer said, "and thanks for lunch. We get into a project, and we forget to eat."

Sheila walked in and grabbed a plate. "Hello, everyone."

"Hi, Mom," Jennifer said.

"So, Jen," Sheila said. "What photo will they use for the ten most wanted poster?"

"Mom, is it that serious?"

"Ana, you start," Sheila said.

"Thank you," Ana said. "The DTA was enacted in 2027 after a rogue organization run by a right-wing militia got pretty far along in developing chemical and biological weapons. The initial penalties for a non-defense organization developing dangerous weapons that can cause harm to the health or property of citizens are civil, and that is where the cease-and-desist order originates."

She quoted, "If an individual is found to develop a weapon defined as one that can destroy one million dollars of property or kill more than ten people at a time, that person can be charged with a felony and if convicted serve twenty years to life for each offense."

"We are building these to save billions on the Hoclarth planet."

"We know, but the Senator is going to portray your invention as dangerous," Ana said.

"I know that you do not intend for your cyberians to be dangerous, but I have questions," Sheila said. "Can a cyberian be ordered to hurt a human, can they decide on their own to hurt someone, or can they harm an individual through negligence?"

"Jake, you take the first two."

"Autonomous robots showed up in early science fiction. Isaac Asimov codified the Three Law of Robotics which state that the robot cannot harm a human or allow harm to occur, obey orders except to harm a human, and protect itself as long as it doesn't allow harm to a human.

"Google extended those laws to prevent robots from making things worse, looking to humans as mentors, and not going outside pre-programmed parameters by attempting hazardous activities.

"HumanAI has leveraged current technology to provide virtuals with wisdom. Our cyberians know what they know, but also, they know what they don't know. Based on learning and experience, that knowledge base is common to every cyberian and each contributes its own experience to the library."

"That rules out the intent to cause harm," Sheila said. "What about negligence?"

"Cyberians are not human," Jennifer said. "But they are human in that they are capable of human mistakes albeit at a much lower rate."

"So, our defense is that cyberians are ethical and careful, but in the end, they are only human," Sheila said. "It's lousy, but it might get us a stay if the judge listens to the benefits to society that the cyberians can perform. Ana, what is our plan?"

"We file an immediate request for a stay pending a hearing on the merits," Ana said. "Judge Servin has been responsive in past rulings to responsible corporate citizens. We'll have a difficult time with the 'robots are only human' argument. I can schedule an appearance tomorrow."

"Are there any other alternatives?" Stephen asked.

"Yes," Sheila said. "You position JennaTech as a defense contractor with a procurement request for cyberian doctors."

"Is that difficult?" Jennifer asked.

"Yes," she said. "Unless you have friends in high places."

"Oh, by the way," Jennifer said. "We are visiting the White House on Saturday."

"Yeah," Sheila said. "Like Navvy."

"Jennifer," Ana said. "As your general counsel, I recommend that you continue work to the deadline, protect your IP, and inform me if anything changes."

"Do I need to get a lawyer?" Jake said. "I'm too young to go to jail.?

"Always a good idea to have a good attorney," Ana said.

"C'mon Jake," Jennifer said. "Thanks for lunch. Let's get back to work, team."

"I might have to work late, Ana," Stephen said. "My boss is a real slave driver."

"Like when you worked at Skunk Works," Ana said. "I know the feeling."

The meeting broke up.

39

Jennifer was in the Captain's Ready Room of the *Brilliant* finishing the operational plan for the flight to the White House. On her desk were her second Double-shot Caramel Frappuccino and a half-eaten bagel. She was wearing a *Brilliant* t-shirt, cutoffs, and Old Skool Vans which had made their fifth fashion comeback in the last century. Her *Brilliant* uniform was hanging next to Tayla's in their stateroom one deck below.

The flight plan was rather complicated. After departure from Tovar, they would make a stop at NAS North Island to pick up Chuck, Mia, and Jeff Rodriguez and then proceed on a ballistic trajectory to the East Coast. After re-entry over Manassas, Virginia, *Brilliant* would approach D.C. from the South. The ingress was a classified op so *Brilliant* would land at Joint Base Andrews cloaked as a Gulfstream 450. *Brilliant* would enter a hangar belonging to the Marine Corps Presidential Squadron HMX-1, convert to a white-top VX-5B Helicopter, then fly in a three-ship formation over the capital, and land on the South Lawn of the White House where POTUS would greet the crew. Only then would *StarCruiser Brilliant* reveal her true colors.

Conversely, the planned departure was like a circus parade. David would raise the ship with the triple 3D rotation that wowed the crowds at Miramar, fly low and slow over the large crowds expected at the D.C. landmarks, and perform the Miramar show over the National Mall. The rainbow exit would be visible throughout the DC Metro Area.

Jennifer finished her final checks, sat back in her chair, took the last bite of her bagel, and a sipped her caffeine bomb.

Dandy Lion jumped on her lap and looked at Jennifer.

"Good morning, Dandy," Jennifer said. "Is the Tovar Lot secure?"

Yes. There's one less mouse in the world, Dandy thought. *Who is this president human?*

"She's the leader of our country," Jennifer said.

Does she have a cat? Dandy thought.

"I believe that her family has a labradoodle."

A dog? Dandy choked as if he was expelling a fur ball.

"Dandy, you like Pugsley," Jennifer said.

I put up with that creature, Dandy thought. *Does this dog talk?*

"Dandy, you're the only animal I know of who talks."

Does it catch mice?

"Many dogs are scared of mice."

Typical, Dandy thought. He jumped down and pranced away with a royal air.

David Masing spent the last two days in the left seat of *Brilliant* rehearsing his stick and rudder actions. Tayla programmed the music tracks for the spectators on the ground, and those on the AirShow Channel. They walked in at seven-forty-five. David was in uniform and Tayla was dressed similarly to Jennifer.

"Could we go through the White House departure once more?" David asked. "I'm ready for the arrival at Andrews, but I'd like to go through the aerobatics once more."

"I need to tighten my music cues as well," Tayla said.

"Is Riley coming?" Jennifer asked.

"He's right behind us," David said.

"You two rode in together?" Jennifer asked.

"We were running lines at the house last night," David said.

"It got late, so I stayed in the guest room," Tayla said.

Riley came into the ready room. "Am I late?"

"I think you're just in time," Jennifer said. She grabbed her cup and headed to the bridge and took her seat.

With *Brilliant* in simulator mode, the Star Squad ran through the departure program twice.

"Very nice flying," Jennifer said. "I love the music, and I know the FX will look great."

"Another milk run," David said.

"Now, we're cursed," Riley said. "Every time you say that somebody dies."

"And Dr. Ami has to work very hard to save them," Tayla said.

"Am I needed?" Dr. Ami walked on to the bridge.

"We hope not," Jennifer said.

"You look different, Dr. Ami," Tayla said.

"She does?" Jennifer asked.

"I do?" Dr. Ami asked. "Do we have a problem?"

"I mean, I've never seen you with a wrinkle on your uniform," Tayla said.

"I'm sorry," Dr. Ami said. "It's brand new, and I just put it on."

"But..." Tayla said.

"I never guessed that the queen of fashion would be the one to spot the only flaw," Jennifer said. "Dr. Ami, introduce yourself."

"Ahhh," Dr. Ami said. "I'm Dr. Ami Teesmith. I'm a cyberian."

"A Russian?" David asked.

"Spelled C-Y," Jennifer said. "Dr. Ami is going to walk down the ramp with us and meet the president."

"Omigod," Tayla said. "Without projectors? May I hug you?"

"Of course," Dr. Ami said. "But you could always..."

Dr. Ami was interrupted by a group hug from the Star Squad.

"Dr. Ami, would you like to join us for breakfast in the Executive Mess?" Jennifer asked.

"I don't have an appetite, but yes, I'd be glad to."

"We'll change and meet you there," Jennifer said.

IN THEIR SHARED STATEROOM, Jennifer and Tayla changed into their *Brilliant* jumpsuits.

"Did you bring it?" Jennifer asked.

"Here it is," Tayla said.

"Thanks. She'll like it."

The two walked over to the Executive Mess. Inside, they met up with Kalinda and Anthen.

"How do I look?" Kalinda asked.

"It's missing something," Tayla said.

"I worked on it for a half hour," Kalinda said. "My uniform is perfect." She looked at Jennifer and Tayla and then at her uniform. The older girls were wearing leather boots, and Tayla was wearing black knee-high Vans.

"Here," Jennifer said. She handed her a bright yellow scarf, the same as the one she and Tayla were wearing.

"Oh cool, thanks," Kalinda hugged Tayla and Jennifer.

"I haven't seen those boots," Tayla said.

"They come out next week," Kalinda said. "The sponsor sent them."

"K'da said she is going to hook us up," Jennifer said.

Stephen, Ana, and Jake were seated along with Sheila. "Mom, you sure you don't want to go?" Jennifer asked.

"You know how I feel about that pile of junk," Sheila said. "No way am I riding in it."

Jack and Navvy walked in, and everyone stood.

"Be seated," Jack said. "This is an informal working breakfast. I've done a quick inspection, and everyone looks shipshape. Maiara's staff will deliver food, and then we can start with Jennifer after we eat."

Navvy walked around to Kalinda. "Your young friend seems to do a lot of work when he is on board *Brilliant*," Navvy said. "Can you give him this when he comes on board? I don't want him to dirty his clothes." He handed her a package wrapped in paper.

"Thank you, Tal'pa," Kalinda said. "He'll love it...sorry, grandfather."

"I understand Tal'pa is a Hoclarth honorific," Navvy said. "I'm not offended K'da."

With breakfast underway, Jennifer went over the plans for the flight down to North Island then in and out of DC.

"Are there any questions?" Jack asked. When there were none he said, "Son, are you comfortable with the swap we discussed."

"Yes, sir," David said. Jennifer looked at David with the question, but there was no answer forthcoming.

"On the South Lawn," Jack said, "the awards presentation will occur as I instructed in the messages I sent. For the group presentation, we'll line up by seniority with Navvy and me to the president's right. After that, there will be two individual presentations.

"The president has requested tours of *Brilliant* for herself, her family, staff, and friends. Star Squad, you four will escort the teens. I hear they want autographs, selfies, and books.

"Kalinda, there will be tweens and younger. You and Jeff will take them aboard. Try not to make a mess in my ready room."

"Yes, Captain," Kalinda said.

"On the South Lawn by eleven a.m.," Jack said. "Raise ship in ten minutes."

The crew of *StarCruiser Brilliant* boarded and took stations. The aft bulkhead of the bridge disappeared to reveal extra seats for riders in the area usually taken up by the ready room.

Jack took the center seat. "Make reports for immediate departure,"

"All are aboard," Maiara said. "The ramp is up and sealed. Belowdecks are secure."

"Sick Bay ready," Dr. Ami said.

"Engineering systems nominal. All modes of propulsion ready," Riley said.

Kalinda sat between Anthen and Navvy at the science station with Dandy purring on her lap. He raised his head. *No mice on board*, Dandy thought.

"The ship's cat reports all ready, Captain," Kalinda said.

"Ha-ha. Very well," Jack said. "Pilot?"

"Ready to rock and roll," David said.

"Comms?" Jack asked.

"SoCal Tracon reports westbound window open for three minutes," Tayla said.

"Ops, departure profile?"

"Cloak at one hundred feet. Subsonic westbound to 80,000 feet then Mach two to North Island approach," Jennifer said.

"Pilot, raise ship and cloak," Jack said. "Ops, take us out."

"Aye, Captain," Jennifer said. "Course laid in for San Clemente Island."

"The ship is cloaked," Riley said.

"Pilot, engage," Jennifer said.

The display surrounding the bridge showed the San Fernando Valley falling behind.

"Twenty thousand, feet wet over Santa Monica," Jennifer said. "Make your turn."

"New course one-six-five," David said.

"Sixty thousand feet. Radar clear of commercial traffic," Jennifer said.

The displays showed a rapidly receding view of the coastline.

"Eighty thousand," Jennifer said. "Turn left to 135. Increase to Mach two."

"Pilot, aye," David said.

The coastline passed very quickly to their left.

"Thirty seconds to subsonic descent," Jennifer said. "Three-two-one. Decrease to 650 knots. Turn left to 090."

"Pilot, Aye."

"Captain, the ship is subsonic," Jennifer said. "Comms, contact North Island approach and request a beacon."

"North Island Control, *StarCruiser Brilliant*. Request an approach beacon," Tayla said.

"Good morning *Brilliant*," North Island said. "We've got you on radar. Beacon is assigned."

"I've got the beacon," David said. "The ship is fly-by-wire."

"Five thousand feet," Jennifer said. "We're below Lindbergh Field traffic. Uncloaking at three miles."

"The ship is uncloaked," Riley said.

The beacon brought *Brilliant* over Point Loma. "Attention to starboard," Jack said. Riders and unoccupied crew stood respectfully as they passed over Fort Rosecrans National Cemetery.

"I've got the beacon on visual," Jennifer said. A bug appeared on the display. As they got closer, they saw a welcoming party of twenty with a band behind them.

"Maiara, I need a handful of challenge coins and M&Ms," Navvy said.

"Got 'em," Maiara said.

"Ops, are we on schedule?" Jack said.

"Captain, we have time for a fifteen-minute stop," Jennifer said. "We can handle a small tour."

"Very well," Jack said. "Navvy and I will handle the brass. Star Squad, take care of the pilots and family."

"Aye aye, Cap'n," Jennifer said. "The ship is grounded."

"Engineer, place the ship in ground standby," Jack said. "Lower the ramp. Look sharp. Out and in quickly."

Navvy and Jack descended the ramp first as the band played two Ruffles and Flourishes. They exchanged salutes, shook hands all around, and exchanged coins.

"Would you like a tour, Admiral?" Navvy asked.

"We'd love to see your ship, Admiral Kelrithian," the admiral said. "We know you have a tight schedule."

Dr. Ami and Kalinda descended the ramp and met Mia, Chuck, and Jeff. Mia, in dress blues, hugged Dr. Ami and thanked her again.

"Dr. Ami, I didn't know that you could come outside of *Brilliant*," Mia said.

"JennaTech created a new cyberian body for me," Dr. Ami said. "I can make house calls. Let's go aboard *Brilliant*."

Jeff was dressed up in a suit. He stayed behind with Kalinda. "Hi, K'da, what's in the package?"

"Tal'pa Navvy didn't want you to mess up your suit on *Brilliant*," Kalinda said.

"Is that what I think it is?"

"Yes," Kalinda said. "You're out of uniform."

"Thanks." He hugged Kalinda. "Oh, sorry."

"It's okay. Friends do that. You can change in Stateroom Three."

Star Squad came down and greeted the other pilots and family and escorted them aboard *Brilliant*. It was organized chaos as twenty people inspected every nook and cranny of the starship.

"I expect this ship rides very comfortably in space, Navvy?" the admiral said.

"Yes, Admiral. It does." Navvy looked at Jack, and they smiled. "Riley?"

"Ready, Captain," Riley said.

"Welcome aboard, everyone," Jack said. "This is the captain. We're going to demonstrate *StarCruiser Brilliant*'s weight loss program. Everyone, please hold on."

He waited for a moment. "Engineer, set gravity to zero for one minute."

There was screaming and laughing throughout the ship until the gravity began to return slowly and the guests regained their attachment to the deck.

Maiara made an announcement. "*Brilliant* is five minutes to departure. We ask our visitors to make their way to the exit ramp.

Don't forget to grab a *StarCruiser Brilliant* souvenir bag on your way out."

Captain, you have a beautiful ship and an excellent crew," the admiral said.

"Thank you very much, Admiral."

"I'd love to have one of these in our arsenal," the admiral said. "Can you arrange that?"

"You never know, Admiral," Navvy said. "Let me take you back to the tarmac, and we'll let Jack prepare for departure."

The senior officers were the last visitors off the ship. Navvy went back up the ramp. "Seal the ship, First Lieutenant."

"Aye aye, Admiral," Maiara said.

"Do we have plenty of swag for the White House, Maiara?"

"Yes," Maiara said. "I won't have to light off the fabricator."

"Any feedback?" Navvy asked.

"As usual, the merch table got the best reactions of the tour."

"Dollar for dollar, free stuff is the most cost-effective marketing that the studio does," Navvy said. "Let's go see the president."

JEFF CAME up to the bridge with Kalinda wearing the cerulean blue *Brilliant* uniform. His mother saw him.

"Where did you get that uniform and where is your suit?" Mia asked.

"Navvy gave it to me because I help out when we're underway," Jeff said.

"Do I have to salute you now?" Mia asked.

"No, Mom," Jeff said. "I'm only an honorary ensign."

"You're going to change into your suit when we get to the White House."

"Mom, it's just the president."

"Your grandmother will be there," Mia said.

"Oh, yeah," Jeff said. "I'll change back. May I get you two some drinks from the galley?"

"Yes, son," Chuck said. "That would be kind of you?"

He and Kalinda took drink orders for the bridge crew and went below.

JACK TOOK the center seat and received pre-departure reports.

"Ready to rock and roll," David said.

"What's our departure profile, Ops?" Jack asked.

"Our ceiling is five thousand to three miles to avoid Lindbergh Field traffic," Jennifer said. "Then we ascend to one-hundred thousand subsonic, accelerate to Mach 15, fifteen minutes of ballistic flight and re-enter over Manassas, and cloak as a Gulfstream for the approach to Joint Base Andrews."

"Very well," Jack said. "Execute."

"Comms?" Jennifer asked.

"We've got westbound clearance from North Island Tower," Tayla said. "Five thousand feet ceiling until we clear SoCal TraCon."

"Pilot, raise ship and cloak," Jennifer said.

"May I show off?" David said.

"Captain, we have an audience," Jennifer said.

"Very well," Jack said. "Raise ship and perform a 360-degree rotation on three axes."

"3D shake and spin, aye."

The spectators nearby saw *Brilliant*, perform an impossible combination of pitch, yaw, and roll, and disappear over the Pacific.

"Two miles feet wet. Begin your ascent."

Jeff and Kalinda retrieved the drinks from the dumb waiter, distributed them, and sat to watch the departure.

"Captain, may we see outside?" Jeff said. "You'll love this, Mom."

"Engineer set moon gravity and activate planetarium view."

The ship surrounding them disappeared, replaced by the darkening sky above and the receding Earth below. The crew could still see their displays and controls.

"Beautiful," Mia said. "I've never been above sixty thousand feet."

They could now see the dark blue sky and the curvature of the earth.

"One hundred thousand feet," Jennifer said. "Accelerate to Mach 15."

"Pilot, aye."

The sky began to shift from blue to black, and the Earth became a sizeable blue ball surrounded by stars.

"Mach 15," David said. "Securing propulsion."

"Fourteen minutes to re-entry," Jennifer said.

The bridge was silent as they passed over Phoenix, Kansas City, St. Louis, and Cincinnati.

"Re-entry in thirty seconds," Jennifer said.

"Engineer shields up," Jack said.

The forward screen began to turn red.

"Begin deceleration to subsonic at 100,000 feet," Jennifer said.

"Pilot, aye."

The red reached maximum saturation then became the familiar blue sky.

"Captain, 100,000 over Manassas. Descending to 60,000."

"Engineer, cloak as a Gulfstream 450 at 60,000," Jack said.

She looked at the thick clouds before them. "Comms, report weather," Jennifer said.

"Andrews reports ceiling 4,000, visibility one mile, with rain."

"Can you handle an ILS approach, David?" Jennifer asked.

"I got this, Jen," David said.

"Comms, contact Andrews," Jennifer said. "Request instrument approach. The pilot will handle communications from this point."

"Andrews acknowledges and designates us Gulfstream 342."

"Pilot, aye."

"Gulfstream 342, Andrews. Turn right one-zero-five, descend to twenty thousand."

"One-zero-five, twenty thousand, Gulfstream 342," David said.

Gulfstream 342, turn left zero-one-zero, intercept the beam. You're clear to land runway one left.

"Zero-one-zero, beam, one left, Gulfstream 342."

"Andrews, I've got the beam."

"Roger," Andrews Control said.

"Gulfstream 342 has the field in sight, requesting visual," David said.

"Gulfstream 342 is cleared visual runway one-left. Contact the tower on 118.4. Welcome to Joint Base Andrews. Good day."

"118.4, Gulfstream 342. Good day."

Brilliant landed and followed the bug to a large hangar.

"Engineer, uncloak, place the ship in standby, and lower the ramp," Jack said. "Lieutenant Commander Rodriguez, we're flying to our next stop dressed as a VX-5B. You're familiar with that aircraft?"

"Yes, I am, Captain," Mia said.

"Would you care to fly us to the South Lawn?"

"I'd be honored, Captain."

"Cool, Mom," Jeff said.

"You, go change to your suit."

"Yes, Mom."

"Crew, and Commander Rodriguez," Jack said. "The flight commander would like us to join him for a brief."

Mia, Jack, Jennifer, Tayla, and David met the other helicopter pilots at the foot of the ramp led by a Marine light colonel. Salutes were exchanged.

"I'm Lieutenant Colonel Steve Mason call sign Bluejacket. and this is Major Tom Goodwin call sign Bulldog. I still don't believe what I just saw when you magically turned a Gulfstream into a starship."

"I'm Jack Masing, Commander Rodriguez, callsign Coyote will be in the left seat."

"Your last flight was a tough one," Steve said.

She nodded. "I didn't walk away from that landing but thanks to this crew, I'm walking now."

"Coyote, we'll be flying right echelon starting with you in the slot," Steve said. "Are you familiar with evasive tactics?"

"Yes, I am," Mia said.

"We'll be rotating through Evasive Three at twenty-five hundred feet until final approach. To those on the ground, it will look like a normal Marine One Flight. You'll be designated Charlie Two."

"I've got it," Mia said.

"Captain, I understand that your departure will be more public."

"Yes, we're going to show off a bit if the weather clears."

"This cell is blowing northeast. The sun should be out for a clear landing on the South Lawn," Steve said. "We don't have time for a tour. Let's get going."

Maiara came down the ramp carrying two swag bags. "Gentlemen, please enjoy these."

"Thanks, enjoy your visit to the White House," Steve said. "We'll turn rotors in three minutes."

They shook hands, and the *Brilliant* crew went up the ramp as it began to rise behind them. When the ship was sealed, it converted to a Sikorsky VX-5B dressed in white and green livery with United States of America on each side.

Mia returned to the bridge and, with no hesitation, took the left seat. It was configured exactly like the bird she almost perished in on the *Winfrey*.

"Captain?"

"Your ship, commander," Jack said.

"Ready, Coyote," Jennifer said. "I'm Jendroid."

"Startup checklist. Start the auxiliary turbine," Mia said.

"Internal power only. Ready to taxi," Jendroid said.

"Captain, may I stand here?" Jeff asked. He pointed to the empty area over his mother's right shoulder. He had changed back to his blue suit.

"Sure," Jack said.

Chuck Rodriguez stood over her left shoulder.

Mia followed a ground crew marine with wands to a point on the drying tarmac.

"Charlie Flight turn your rotors," Bluejacket said.

"Charlie Two," Mia said. "Jendroid, start main engines."

"Spinning one," Jendroid said. Those aboard heard familiar jet engine sounds. There was vibration as the engine passed through the resonant frequency of the turbine. The displays showed the rotors slowly begin to turn.

"Spinning two."

"Takeoff checklist," Mia said.

"Pressures and temperatures nominal," Jendroid said. "Rotors fully engaged."

"Vertical Rise to two hundred feet on my mark," Bluejacket said.

Charlie Two and Three acknowledged.

"Up and away," Bluejacket said.

The three helicopters rose as one, formed a right echelon. Charlie Two and Three maintained formation on the leader as he turned northwest climbing to twenty-five hundred feet as they passed over I-495.

With the Potomac River on the left, they approached the Anacostia River.

"Evade Three," Bluejacket said.

Charlie One swung to his right and fell behind.

"Charlie Two in the lead," Mia said.

"Keep the Capitol Dome on your left, Coyote," Bluejacket said. "I'll call the left turn to the Jefferson over Maryland Avenue."

"Charlie Two."

The riders viewed the Capitol Building on the left of *Brilliant*.

"Start the left turn," Bluejacket said.

The formation made a smooth bank to the left. Mia spotted the Jefferson Memorial on her nose.

"Evade Three," Bluejacket said.

Mia banked right, reduced speed, and then swung into the trail position.

"Charlie Three in the lead," Bulldog said.

"Shift to left echelon," Bluejacket said.

"Charlie Two."

Mia descended, watched Charlie One's tail closely as she swung left, then climbed back to the trailing spot.

"I'll call the turn with the Washington on your right," Bluejacket said.

"Charlie Three," Bulldog said.

They crossed the National Mall and saw the Washington Monument on their right.

"Start the turn," Bluejacket said.

They finished the turn over the Tidal Basin with Seventeenth Street on her nose.

"Evade Three," Bluejacket said.

Charlie Three swung to the left and fell back to the trail position.

"Charlie One in the lead," Bluejacket said. "Charlie Two, as we pass the Ellipse, begin your descent to the South Lawn. Very nice flying, Coyote."

"Charlie Two acknowledges," Mia said. "It's been my honor."

"Begin your descent and try to stay out of the way of flying turbine blades in the future. You're cleared to land on the South Lawn of the White House."

"Charlie Two. Take care and Godspeed."

She began her descent and turned right. She executed a perfect landing on the South Lawn.

"Very nice flying, commander," Jack said. "Perform your shutdowns."

"Aye, Captain," Mia said. "Turbines are shut down."

They watched as the rotors spun down.

"Rotors are secure, Captain," Mia said. "Good job, Jendroid. Captain, I'm ready to be relieved."

"I relieve you," Jack said. "Engineer, uncloak the ship, put her in standby, and lower the ramp."

"The ship is in standby," Riley said. "Ramp is down."

"Very well," Jack said. "Let's go meet the President."

MAIARA WAS STANDING at the top of the ramp when a Marine Captain appeared at the foot of the ramp.

He saluted. "Request to come aboard, Ma'am."

She returned the salute. "Come aboard, Marine." Six enlisted sailors formed at the foot of the ramp tending the side.

The marine came up the ramp and shook hands with Maiara. "Welcome aboard."

"I'm Captain Jennings. I'll assist with protocol."

The crew was gathering. "Welcome aboard, Captain," Jack said. "I'm Captain Masing; this is Admiral Kelrithian."

"The president sends her regards and welcomes you to the White House," Captain Jennings said. "I'll be at the foot of the ramp, and I'll direct traffic. The senior officers will exit first while the Marine Band plays Ruffles and Flourishes. Then Commander Rodriguez and her family will exit with Dr. Ami followed by the crew and the riders as the band plays Anchors Aweigh."

"Got it," Jack said.

"Your party will proceed to a receiving line to meet the president and her family before the ceremony. We understand that Miss Gallagher has some books to sign with the Star Squad and we would like for her to do that at a table after the ceremony."

"How many books, Captain?" Jennifer asked.

"Thirteen books for the president's daughters and her friends," Captain Jennings said.

"We brought fifty swag bags," Maiara said. "Will that be enough for everyone?"

"Swag bags?" Jennings asked.

"It's a Hollywood term for gifts," Navvy said.

"I see. After you exit, the side boys will come aboard and assist," Jennings said. "Any questions?"

"We'll await your signal," Navvy said.

The Marine descended the ramp and stood watching for his signal. He turned and nodded to the admiral.

"Present Arms," the Marine captain shouted. The *Brilliant* contingent descended the ramp and followed the red carpet.

President Susan Ortega led the receiving line. Senator Curtwell stood to her left.

"Admiral Kelrithian, welcome to the White House," President Ortega said. "You have a beautiful starship."

"Thank you, Madam President," Navvy said. "This is Captain Jack Masing."

They shook hands.

"May I present the Rodriguez family, Dr. Ami, and the crew of *StarCruiser Brilliant*."

Kalinda carried Dandy through the receiving line. The president patted his head. "What a pretty cat."

"Ma'am, Dandy Lion is the ship's cat."

"You have a problem with mice?" the president said.

There are no mice aboard my ship. Dandy glared at the president.

"I'm sure there are not," the president said. "Wait...who said that?" She saw Dandy's cat glare and raised her eyebrows.

The rest of the formalities proceeded with but a single glitch. After Senator Curtwell hugged her daughter and grandson, she glared at Dr. Ami and refused to shake her hand.

Everyone took their seats, and the ceremony began. President Ortega made opening remarks and then, "Admiral Kelrithian, Commander Rodriguez, could you and your family join me on the platform?"

After all were gathered along with Senator Curtwell, the President looked to her right at a Navy Commander standing at a microphone. "Commander?"

"*StarCruiser Brilliant*, front and center," the commander said.

As rehearsed, Jack and the crew lined up before the President of the United States with Jack on her right and the crew in order of descending rank. The captain nodded, and the crew saluted together.

The president returned the salute, and the crew stood at attention. Kalinda remained in her chair until Jack motioned her to join them at the end of the line.

The commander began the citation, "Attention to Orders:"

"*StarCruiser Brilliant,* a reserve unit of Star Squadron One has distinguished itself as the singularly outstanding unit in the United States Navy's Star Force, completing the toughest tasks with heroism, efficiency, and precision. *Brilliant* and its crew perform at the highest levels of professionalism and receive the highest praise on both classified and unclassified missions assigned by the Chief of Naval Operations in support of units in all branches of service around the world.

"*Brilliant* especially distinguished itself on September 19, 2067, when the starship was diverted from a mission in the vicinity of the moon, traveled to the *USS Oprah Winfrey* in the Persian Gulf with extraordinary speed, and rescued Lieutenant Commander Mia Rodriguez after a life-threatening accident. While transporting Commander Rodriguez, the medical staff aboard *Brilliant* performed outstanding and original organ transplant surgery to revive the commander and save her life.

"The heroic actions of *StarCruiser Brilliant* and her crew are in keeping the highest ideals of professionalism and the answer to the call to duty of the United States of America and are deserving of the Presidential Navy Unit Commendation.

"This is the seventh award presented to *StarCruiser Brilliant.*"

The President descended the platform. She presented a medal and shook hands with each crew member including Kalinda standing next to her father holding Dandy.

"I understand you two helped the commander's son through this."

That's what we do, Dandy thought.

Again, the president raised her eyebrows as she looked at Dandy.

Kalinda glowed. "Yes, Madam President. Thank you, Ma'am."

The president stepped back and saluted the crew. The salute was returned, and she began the applause.

She returned to the podium, and the crew returned to their seats. "Next I'm going to present the Navy Lifesaving Medal. Commander?"

"Dr. Ami Teesmith, front and center."

Senator Curtwell stepped up next to the President. "Madam President, this robot is not a person. It's an illegal and dangerous product of an illegitimate enterprise."

"Senator, in our country," President Ortega said, "a person or an entity is not deemed illegal. We judge them on their actions and their merits."

"But..." the senator said.

"Stand down, Senator."

Senator Curtwell stepped back and glared at Dr. Ami.

The commander read the citation. "Dr. Ami's innovative actions under difficult conditions on September 19, 2067, in saving the life of Lieutenant Commander Mia Rodriguez are in keeping with the highest traditions of the medical service and deserving of the Navy Lifesaving Medal."

The president presented the medal, and the members of the *Star-Cruiser Brilliant* stood and applauded as did the members of the White House Medical Unit gathered to the right of the platform.

"That completes the military awards," President Ortega said. "Please remain on the podium, Dr. Ami. I want to make one more presentation. Jennifer Gallagher, please come up here."

Jennifer looked around at the others and then at her grandfather. He grinned and shrugged. She went up to the podium.

"This morning I signed an executive order," the president said.

Senator Curtwell mouthed the word, 'no.'

"I'd like the Under Secretary of Defense for Technology Procurement Jake Hargrove, Senior to come up and explain."

"It's nice to meet you, Miss Gallagher," Secretary Hargrove said. "Is junior worth what you're paying him?"

Jennifer smiled and looked at Jake who was glowing bright red. "He most certainly is, Mr. Secretary."

"It's been a goal of the president to create a technological solution to our acute shortage of trained doctors," Secretary Hargrove said. "Dr. Ami Teesmith stands before us as an example of unsolicited private sector development in pursuit of that goal. Therefore, the president has instructed me to award your company, JennaTech, a contract to create fifty cyberian doctors to be assigned at military hospitals in the United States serving active duty members, veterans, and their families."

Senator Curtwell burst forward. "I protest," she said. "This person willfully violated the Dangerous Technologies Act. I protest..."

Two secret service agents restrained her by the arms. The senator crumpled to the deck holding her left arm.

Dr. Ami was the nearest. She bent down and observed that the senator was very white. She looked at the line of medical personnel. "Cardiologist, bring an AED."

The cardiologist came up with a defibrillator.

"Hook her up," Dr. Ami said.

The cardiologist acted. "She's not in arrest."

"She will be in thirty seconds," Dr. Ami said. "What facilities do you have here?"

"We have a cardiac emergency room in the cottage."

The senator grabbed at Dr. Ami's arm. "No let the robot..." Her eyes rolled back in her head.

Beep-beep-beep. "She's in arrest, Doctor,"

"Gurney, now," Ami said. "*Brilliant* will transport her to Walter Reed." She shouted, "Captain, one-sixth gravity, one-hundred percent oxygen in sickbay."

"Aye aye, Doctor," Jack said. The crew in blue uniforms were already sprinting to the ramp. Mia was beside her mom on the gurney while Chuck and Jeff were running ahead to the ramp as well. Jack and Navvy brought up the rear. Jack ran to the firepole and made the bridge in one jump in the lower gravity. Navvy stood by as the gurney passed and pressed the ramp actuator.

"The ship is sealed," Navvy said.

Jack took the center seat and observed the bridge crew preparing to depart.

"Doctor?"

"Sick Bay is sealed," Dr. Ami said. "You may depart."

"We have a clear corridor and an escort, Captain," Tayla said.

"Course laid in, sir," Jennifer said.

"Pilot, raise ship and proceed."

Brilliant rose quickly straight up and turned left over the White House.

"Ten minutes, sir."

The captain looked left and right and saw Charlie One and Three in formation.

"Walter Reed reports clear pad and personnel standing by," Tayla said.

"Ten minutes, Doctor," Jack said.

Kalinda was sitting with Jeff and his parents. "Dr. Ami will get her through."

"I know," Jeff said. They held hands.

Dandy Lion jumped up on Mia's lap, snuggled in, and began purring.

Mia relaxed a bit.

IN SICKBAY "TEN MINUTES, AYE CAPTAIN," Dr. Ami said. "Doctor?"

"She has been in arrest for two minutes with CPR and three shocks. No response," the White House cardiologist said.

"Ani?"

Ani appeared across from Ami. "Right here. Placing the mini projector."

A scan appeared above the senator's chest. "I see ninety percent blockage in three arteries." She looked at Ani.

Ani held up her hands. "You've got access."

Dr. Ami began the surgery with hers and Ani's hands.

"What are you doing, Doctor?" the White House cardiologist said.

"I'm performing a triple bypass using virtual tissue."

He watched as Dr. Ami performed the complex operation at fifty times normal speed. Three minutes later, Dr. Ami raised her hands.

"Shock her once more, Doctor."

The senator reacted on the table. Beep...Beep...Beep. "Normal sinus rhythm, Doctor. The patient was in arrest for five-and-a-half-minutes. The EKG indicates no damage to the heart," the cardiologist said. "Congratulations."

"Does Walter Reed Regen have the senator's DNA?"

"Yes, they do."

Lieutenant Commander Rodriquez was standing outside sickbay. "Come in, Mia."

"Thanks again, Dr. Ami."

"You're welcome, again," Dr. Ami said. "Captain, inform Chuck and Jeff Senator Curtwell is stable. I've performed a virtual triple bypass, but we need to operate soon."

"They're all smiles now," Jack said.

Dr. Ami looked up. "Tayla, please contact Walter Reed Regen Facility. I'm sending a list of replacement tissue. I need an operating room and Dr. Bob Dashman if he is available."

"Yes, Doctor," Tayla said.

"Bring the patient out of anesthetic."

The senator opened her eyes. "Where am I?"

"You're aboard *StarCruiser Brilliant*," Dr. Ami said. "We're three minutes from Walter Reed. You're in stable condition with three virtual valves. The abominable android saved your bacon again, a delicacy that you must avoid in the future."

"Thank you, Rob...Dr. Ami." The senator offered her hand.

Dr. Ami shook the Senator's hand.

"Captain, send the senator's family down to sickbay."

"On their way, Doctor."

Kalinda stood to lead them, but Jeff jumped up. "I'll show him," he said.

Anthen saw the look on Kalinda's face as she came over to sit next to him. "You miss your mom?"

"Yeah."

Mia met Chuck in sickbay. Jeff stayed at the door.

"You may come in for just a moment," Dr. Ami said.

"Dr. Ami saved me...she saved both of us."

"That's why they call it *StarCruiser Brilliant*," Jeff said.

"I guess it is," the senator said.

Ani and Dr. Ami prepared to transfer Senator Curtwell.

On the bridge, "I've got the pad in sight," David said.

"Bring us in, pilot," Jack glanced at his son.

"Aye, sir."

There was a soft thump.

"Engineer, lower the ramp," Jack said. "Sickbay, we're on the pad ready to transfer."

Walter Reed emergency room personnel came aboard and moved the senator off *Brilliant*.

"Captain, I've got to finish this job, and you have an audience waiting," Dr. Ami said. "Can you pick me up at four o'clock?"

"The show must go on."

Dr. Ami followed the gurney into the hospital emergency room. An Army Doctor met her.

"I'm Major Dan Halligan. What's the status of the patient?"

"Doctor," Ami said, "the patient is in stable condition following a virtual triple bypass. There's no indication of other heart damage. I asked for an operating room and put in an order for regenerated tissue. I want Bob Dashman to assist."

"We have the OR ready, and the tissue will be ready in an hour, but you do not have operating privileges in this hospital, and Dr. Dashman certainly does not assist."

Dr. Dashman walked up. "Dan, Dr. Ami has privileges. I vouch for her," he said. "Ami, I hear you need an extra pair of hands. Welcome to Walter Reed. What the hell did you pull off in," he looked at his watch, "the last twelve minutes."

"Hi, Bob," Ami said. "She went into arrest on the platform. We were unable to revive her. I determined ninety percent blockage in three arteries. I made the virtual repairs on the way here and revived her less than six minutes after arrest."

"A virtual triple in less than three minutes," Bob said. "I thought this lady hated you."

"She asked for me right before she arrested."

"We have OR Three waiting," Bob said. "Regen will notify us. Let's go to the virtual room and review the film. I've got to see this."

ABOARD BRILLIANT, "Contact Potomac Tracon and ask if we can still perform over the National Mall."

"Captain, Potomac reports clearance to the mall. They report a large crowd is waiting."

"Very well. Pilot, raise ship and proceed to the National Mall."

"Captain," Jennifer said. "Charlie Flight is still in the area."

"Charlie One," Jack said. "We've got clearance to the National Mall. Would you care to join us?"

"We'll be right echelon with you, Brilliant," Bluejacket said.

"Very well, Charlie."

The three distinctive craft flew south low and slow.

"How many News Copters are out there?" Jack asked.

"We've been live on four local and three national networks since we departed Andrews," Jennifer said.

"I contracted three of them for Tovar and the AirShow Channel," Navvy said.

"Do you own that channel, Navvy?" Jack asked.

"I picked up a twenty percent stake when *Brilliant* went public," Navvy said. "So far, it has been a very lucrative investment for the studio."

"Tal'pa, are you the richest person on Earth?" Kalinda asked.

"There might be others who are richer."

"K'da," Jennifer said, "he's the richest by a bunch."

"Captain, we're over the National Mall," David said.

"*Brilliant*, Charlie Flight," Bluejacket said. "We're bingo fuel. It's been an honor flying with you. Returning to base."

"Fly safe, Charlie," Jack said. "Tayla, will the spectators hear your wonderful soundtrack."

"Yes, Captain," Tayla said. "We're wired into the built-in system."

"Very well," Jack said. "Ops, indulge yourself."

"Aye, Captain."

StarCruiser Brilliant then repeated the show they performed over Miramar. Displays showed the crowd below as well as the feed from the AirShow Channel.

"One-minute remaining," Jennifer said.

"Make it good, Ops,"

"We just happen to have a slam-bang finish, Captain."

Brilliant turned over the Lincoln Memorial and began a high-speed pass to the Capitol.

"Engineer, release smoke."

The citizens on the mall saw the smoke release and then form the red, white, and blue words, "God Bless the USA." *Brilliant* then framed the words with a rainbow as they exited the show area.

"There must have been a million people on the mall watching," Navvy said.

"Don't brag about crowd size," Jack said. "That never goes well."

"That was a beautiful show, *Brilliant*," Navvy said.

"I know it's two thousand miles away," Jack said. "but I could do with a Double-double with onions right now."

"Captain," Jennifer said, "they just opened an In-n-Out at the Chevy Chase Pavilion. Walter Reed is nearby."

"Phone the local constabulary and see if they can clear an area in the parking lot. We can wait for Dr. Ami's call, and the Star Squad can do selfies and autographs."

Tayla communicated with several people as *Brilliant* circled the Washington Monument.

"Captain, Potomac TraCon clears us to Chevy Chase. Montgomery County PD is clearing a landing area, and In-n-Out is happy to cater our lunch."

"Maiara, will you prepare swag bags for the restaurant crew and the local PD?" Jack said. "Kalinda, can you go below and give her a hand."

"Yes, Captain."

Brilliant arrived over the Chevy Chase Pavilion and observed an area marked off with flares. A small crowd surrounded the area.

"Pilot ground the ship."

David landed *Brilliant* in the empty area near the restaurant.

"Engineer put the ship in standby and lower the ramp."

A police officer approached the ramp.

"Escort the officer to the bridge," Jack said.

He came up the ladder with Kalinda.

"I'm Lieutenant Patrick McClanahan. Welcome to Chevy Chase."

"Welcome aboard, officer. I'm Captain Jack Masing." He introduced the rest of the crew.

"Sir, I know that you have had a busy day, but you have fans out there, and they would like to meet you."

"We're going to eat lunch and then the Star Squad is going to come down and do a meet and greet."

"Thanks, Captain."

The In-n-Out crew brought food aboard. They were happy to receive the souvenir bags and the tour.

After lunch, Jennifer, David, Riley, Tayla, and Kalinda exited the ship and spent the next forty-five minutes doing selfies and signing autographs.

Jack, Navvy, and Anthen relaxed aboard *Brilliant*.

"That hit the spot," Jack said, "and we didn't even have to wait in the drive-thru line."

"We weren't able to give the president and her family a tour," Navvy said.

"You'll just have to make a campaign contribution and get us another medal, dad," Anthen said.

AT THREE-THIRTY THE COMMUNICATOR SOUNDED, "*Brilliant*, this is Dr. Ami. Can you pick us up at Walter Reed? Chuck and Jeff Rodriguez will fly back to San Diego. The senator's surgery was a success, and she is resting comfortably."

"Congratulations again, Doctor," Jack said. "Give us fifteen minutes. Maiara, bring the crew aboard and ask the police to secure the perimeter."

"Aye aye, Captain."

Five minutes later, the crew was in place.

"Ready to rock and roll," David said.

Pilot, raise the ship and do that 3D thing."

"Yes, sir."

Brilliant wowed the Chevy Chase crowd one more time, stopped at Walter Reed, went ballistic over the continent, dropped off Jeff and Chuck at North Island, and then returned to Tovar Studios.

"Engineer put the ship in shutdown mode and lower the ramp."

"Aye aye," said Riley.

"David," Jennifer said, "we need to talk."

"I know," he said. "No more milk runs."

40

The following Wednesday, *Attack of the Hoclarth Alliance* shifted to location in the mountainous areas near Edgar Peak in the Mojave Desert.

Jennifer sat in the top row center seat of the double-wide production trailer of the VirtualLocation40 system. When the filming was in progress, she shared the elevated top row with above-the-line personnel including producers and writers. She was acting as Second Unit Director for the final battle scene of *Attack of the Hoclarth Alliance.*

Below Jennifer in the center seat was her personal assistant, Sami, who was the Technical Director for this shoot. Under Jennifer's direction, Sami coordinated the other technicians on her row to turn the creative direction from Jennifer into the visual data recorded and sent to post-production. Because Sami was an android, she was able to control every recording device in the truck as well as each of the forty cell-phone sized cinedrones flying above the action, the ten head-mounted cameras on the actors, and the rolling robo-cams that would track all of the action from a low angle.

To Sami's right and left were Second Assistant Directors who were assigned a subset of the system that Sami controlled.

In front of Sami's row was a large empty stage with a steveLearn system in the center that generated the multi-faceted visual fields for everyone. Personal flat displays were floating anywhere the operator chose with virtual monitors, text, and graphics quality controls visible only to the individual operator. In the center, the director could call 3D composite shots generated by up to six cameras at a time. Second assistants on the right and left could create separate composites.

The Director of the film, James Ford, was Jennifer's direct supervisor and was responsible for the conduct of the entire production. During filming tomorrow, he would sit in a control suite similar to this one where he would direct the cinematographers, the actors, the pilots, the sound technicians, the gaffers and the grips. Jim was sitting next to Jennifer going over final camera assignments.

"Read down the list one more time," Jim said.

"Sami," Jennifer said, "show me the rehearsal previews as I go."

The flat screens before separate operators disappeared for only Jennifer and Jim.

"This is impressive, Jen," Jim said.

"Here's Na'gan Xan'fer. He's assigned drones one through four, robo one and a headcam."

Sami previewed a 3D image of the evil villain from rehearsal. Sami generated several tracking shots for Jim to sample.

"Wow is all I can say," Jim said.

"David," Jennifer said. "Five through eight, head and robo two."

Sami showed several tracks of David.

"And you're not locked into the tracks?"

"No," Jennifer said. "All we do tomorrow is collect data. The trackers will provide the shots to the editors before final post."

"Show me Patricia Garcia, the Hoclarth named Cax'andra," Jim said.

"Nine through twelve, head and robo three," Jennifer said. The preview image appeared with several tracks.

"And you have two drones each for the six minor actors?"

"Yes," Jennifer said. "Twenty-four drones flying and fourteen other cameras for the principal actors."

"And the other sixteen?"

"Four each for the two group shots, four for establishing shots, and four as flying backups. Forty drones in all."

"Do we still have the coverage issue?" Jim asked.

"Yes, still eighty percent per take, but you promised me three takes." She pressed a button. "Jake, could you come in here?" She turned to Jim. "Jake is our AI software guru. I'll have him explain our fix."

Jake entered the trailer. "Yes, boss?"

"This is Jim Ford, the director," Jennifer said. "Could you explain our fix to camera coverage?"

They shook hands. "Sir, you're guaranteeing three takes?"

He nodded. "Sure."

"Mathematically, the three takes give us ninety-two percent coverage," Jake said. "We've done an AI software fix. The tracking editors will overlay problem shots and the artificial intelligence software will stitch them together to get a seamless take."

"As a rule," Jim said, "editors don't like to mix takes."

"I understand," Jake said. "During training for the new tracking editor position, we have done hundreds of mix-takes for problem takes as well as good takes. The software matches motion, color correction and timing. We've had a ninety-eight percent success rate dealing with coverage problems."

"Jim, we're still prototyping the VirtualLocation system on this film," Jennifer said. "I think you'll be happy with what comes out of this truck."

"So far I'm pleased with the shots you are getting," Jim said. "My compliments to your crew."

The director left the truck. "He seems to be happy," Jake said.

"Jake...everyone in the truck," Jennifer said, "we're knocking it out of the park."

Navvy walked into the truck as she said that. "Are you patting yourselves on the back again, Jennifer?"

"Sorry, grandpa."

"No, keep going," he said. "The shots I've seen coming out of this truck are simply amazing."

"Thanks."

"Hello, Sami, it's nice to see you out and about. Are there projectors in here?"

"No, sir," Sami said. "I'm a cyberian today."

"We've fabricated five units at JennaTech," Jennifer said. "We're getting the bugs out before the business trip next week."

"So, Sami can handle the forty cameras at one time?" Navvy asked. "I heard you've got six on David."

"Sir, I control sixty-three cameras if you include the head-mounted cameras and the rolling robo-cams," Sami said. "But it's much simpler than that. The six on David operate as one camera focused on a point five feet in front of him."

"Right, nose room," Navvy said. "I still don't get the single-camera theory."

"The six cameras are points on a hemisphere," Jennifer said.

"So, you don't cross the line."

"Correct," Jennifer said. "The cameras record data then the tracking editors create the desired tracking shots. A traveling shot can be created by programming the pan, tilt, truck, and zoom between as the camera tracks a curve between any two points within the sphere."

"No more dollies and cranes," Navvy said. "But your drones are fixed focus. You can't do an optical zoom."

"Correct but they have three-hundred-twenty-thousand lines of resolution," Jennifer said. "They can do a forty-to-one digital zoom for the 8K final print resolution."

"And then the computer graphics team adds the virtual actors."

"Nay nay," Jennifer pressed the intercom. "Adam, are you available for a demo?"

A three-dimensional Adam Teesmith appeared in the center of

the steveLearn with the walls of the canyon behind him. The shot orbited around the yellow-eyed actor.

"Of course," Adam said. "How may I help? I love being a cyber-ian, by the way."

"Go to the center of the canyon, please," Jennifer said. "Sami, do you have his location?"

"Yes, I do," Sami said. "Unit C is nearby."

"Fly Charlie and assign it to Adam."

"And the cameras are not moving."

"Correct," Jennifer said. "The AI is interpolating the data and composing the shot."

"My granddaughter has outdone herself," Navvy said.

"Adam, take a jog down the canyon," Jennifer said.

"Okay," Adam said.

"Start with redrum and track counter-clockwise to a medium close-up."

As Adam ran down the canyon, the image showed a rear close-up from his knees to his heels.

"Redrum?" Navvy said. "Garrett Brown's Steadicam shot from *The Shining*."

The image revolved around the actor to a medium close-up.

"Go around to a wide high-angle over-the-shoulder," Jennifer said. "Continue the slow zoom out to the entire canyon. The camera system is moving for this sequence."

"Stunning," Navvy said. "It would have taken ten tons of rolling stock and a crew of fifteen to get that shot. You're going to put your Grandfather Sean and a lot of union members out of business. How are you going to market this?"

"Once we get the bugs out, we'll license the system to GGG," Jennifer said. "He'll still make out renting out the trucks and staffing them."

"As will you and your team," Navvy said. "Congratulations and good luck."

Navvy exited as Jennifer continued her preparation hoping that her script and her effects would complement each other to produce the ending of a good film.

ON THE FINAL day of shooting, the cameras were ready, audio was checked, *Brilliant* was in Position One, and the actors were at their marks.

"Action," the director said.

David Masing and Cax'andra Granqil ran down the narrow, twisting canyon side by side. The two pilots, one from Earth and one from the Hoclarth Alliance, turned and fired their blasters at the pursuers as shots bounced off nearby rocks just missing them.

Overhead, a Hoclarth fighter drone passed over exchanging fire with *StarCruiser Brilliant*. A shot from *Brilliant* shook the fighter. It was trailing smoke.

"Yeah!" David raised a fist.

May we someday meet in Laknove, brother, Cax'andra thought. A voiceover would be added in post.

"Dad, I could use some help here," David said.

Aboard *Brilliant*, "Stand by, son," Jack said. "There's a clearing half a click ahead of you."

David emptied his blaster and threw it aside. Cax'andra was still firing.

Brilliant turned back, dove into the canyon, and fired on David's pursuers. They quickly took cover behind rocks and held their positions.

David and Cax'andra broke into the clearing. At the far end was the burning fighter drone.

ABOARD *BRILLIANT*, Riley was at the ops panel targeting the Hoclarth fighters, and actor Eiji Noguchi was in the pilot's seat waiting for David to return.

"David and the Hoclarth pilot have entered the clearing," Ani said.

"Very well," Jack said. "Riley?"

"I can hold 'em off, sir."

"Pilot, this is a combat landing in a hot LZ," Jack said. "Get us in and out quickly."

DAVID AND CAX'ANDRA saw *Brilliant* descending and ran into the center of the clearing.

Having left his burning fighter, Na'gan Xan'fer limped from behind a rock carrying a blaster and faced Cax'andra. "You're a traitor to the alliance. You'll watch your friend die before I kill you."

He raised his blaster toward David. Cax'andra dove in front of David. The two Hoclarth fired. Na'gan fell.

David shouted. "You got 'im." He looked at the bleeding Cax'andra.

She smiled and then collapsed just as *Brilliant* landed with ramp open.

"Cax'andra."

"David, promise me that you will bring our two cultures together."

"You're the only one who can do that, my love."

"There is another." Cax'andra's eyes closed for the last time.

He held her and kissed her gently on the cheek.

Jack stood at the top of the ramp. "Son, hurry, there are fighters headed this way."

David held her hands one last time and then softly laid them open to the sky. He started walking then running to the ramp. As he reached the top of the ramp, he turned back and paused as the ramp came up.

IN THE VIRTUALLOCATION40 TRUCK, Jennifer directed Sami to

track the CineDrone to an extreme closeup as David looked back at his fallen lover. He shed a single tear.

As the ramp closed before the camera, she flew the CineDrone back to a wider and wider angle, showing *Brilliant* flying up through the canyon into the red Hoclarth sky.

James Ford shouted. "Cut! Print. That's a wrap."

41

On Sunday morning at eight, the crew of *Brilliant* gathered in the Tovar Executive Mess with families for departure to the Wolf Star where they would meet the *Camdex* and Predex Kalea Kone.

With the families seated, Jack introduced the crew. Today, it included three members who had never attended an Away Breakfast. The three cyberians Dr. Ami, Ani and, Sami, were in uniform and prepared for their mission the rest of the way to Xaphnore in the Hoclarth Alliance aboard *StarShuttle Hope*. They would seek a cure for the disease that was killing the population on Xaphnore.

The audience of family members including Navvy, who was sitting out this mission because of studio commitments. His son, Anthen, would act as science officer.

Also, in the audience was Kalinda's friend, Jeff Rodriguez. His father was in LA for a weekend law conference, and he brought Jeff to spend time with Kalinda. Jeff was wearing his *Brilliant* uniform.

After Jack introduced the crew, he looked down the line and saw Kalinda. "Kalinda, you are a member of the crew, but this mission is not for kids. You need to stay here and go to school. We'll tell you all about it when we return."

Kalinda came over and gave Jack a sad look. "I can help out. You know you enjoy it when I bring you coffee."

Her father intervened. "We discussed this at home. You need to go to school," Anthen said.

Kalinda's eyes were getting moist. "Dad, I'm caught up with school. I need to be with you guys."

"Go sit next to your friend," Anthen said. "You're staying with your grandmother, and that's final."

She burst out crying and stomped her foot. "But it's my destiny," Kalinda said. She grabbed onto her father, sobbed, and would not let go.

"That's enough," Anthen said. "Go out to the car."

She let go, composed herself, stood as tall as she could, and said, "C'mon, Jeff, these people don't like kids."

Kalinda stormed out and Jeff looked embarrassed as he followed her out.

A FEW MINUTES LATER, Jennifer and Tayla ate breakfast. "I feel bad for Kalinda," Jennifer said. "She's going to be all alone this week."

"I think she deserves a nomination for that scene," Tayla said.

"Wait, you think..." Jennifer said.

"K'da just gave an award-winning performance," Tayla said. "It looked like she rehearsed it for days."

"You think that was an act?"

"You certainly bought it. Your little sister has something up her sleeve," Tayla said, "and her little friend, too."

KALINDA AND JEFF broke into the sunlight outside the Tovar Executive Offices. They began the short walk to the *Brilliant* compound. "That was smooth, K'da," Jeff said. "Do you think they bought it?"

"I'm worried about Tayla," Kalinda said. "I used some of the methods she taught me from her acting lessons."

"Okay, let's check our stories," Jeff said.

"Your dad is supposed to pick you up at four o'clock at Navvy's house."

"Check," Jeff said, "and Sheila thinks your grandmother is taking us there after breakfast."

"Check. And Grandmother Hannah thinks Sheila is taking us to Universal Studios today," Kalinda said.

"Check," Jeff said. "D'you think we can get on *Brilliant?*"

"It'll be easier than I thought," Kalinda said. "Ani is at the Away Breakfast and knows all of Dandy's Jedi mind tricks. Sandi is the ship's AI for this mission."

"Okay." Jeff looked nervous.

"I can do this alone," Kalinda said. "You won't get in trouble if you stay here."

"But if I do, they'll find out you are stowing away."

"I know. Thanks for coming," Kalinda said. "I'll need your support."

"Do you think they'll space us?"

"What?"

"I read this book where they eject stowaways out the airlock into space."

"You read too many space operas," Kalinda said. "This is reality."

They got to *Brilliant,* and Dandy Lion met them at the foot of the ramp.

"*Brilliant* is more incredible every time I see it," Jeff said.

"Dandy, we're here."

The cat nodded then jumped into Kalinda's arms. *I hope this works.* Dandy Lion stared at the ID pad.

"Recognize Tayla Mendoza and Jennifer Gallagher," Sandi said. "I didn't expect you here this early."

Sandi was the Artificial Navigation Interface for this mission since Ani was going to Xaphnore.

"We're just coming aboard to drop off some things in our state-room," Kalinda said.

"Welcome aboard," Sandi said.

"We'll be off the ship in three minutes," Kalinda said.

"I'll log you two out then," Sandi said.

Jeff and Kalinda followed Dandy up the ramp.

"I still can't get used to a talking cat," Jeff said. "Especially one who can talk to computers."

When they got to Storage Room Three, Kalinda opened the door into the darkened space.

"You aren't claustrophobic?" Kalinda asked.

"Umm, no," Jeff said. "I don't think so."

"Lights." The lights came on, Kalinda pulled the door shut behind them, and Kalinda led Jeff into the storeroom to an open container. On the floor were two sleeping bags, a light, and a stash of drinks and grunch bars.

"What about...?" Jeff asked.

Kalinda pointed to a port-a-potty nearby. "It's for extended away missions."

He took a step into the container. "This looks comfy," Jeff said.

"Don't get any ideas," Kalinda said.

"Eww," Jeff said.

Kalinda laughed.

"You've thought of everything."

Kalinda tapped her head. "Two-oh-six."

"And an attitude to match," Jeff said. "Do we have to keep the door to the container closed?"

"Only when Maiara does her walkthrough and during watch changes," Kalinda said. "I know the schedule. I thought you said you weren't claustrophobic."

"I'm not," Jeff said. "I just don't like to be locked in a small box."

"That's claustrophobia, genius."

"Oh."

Kalinda realized that she was going to have to keep her friend occupied for at least eight hours. They entered the container, and Kalinda pulled the door shut.

"I guess we're locked in, now," Jeff said.

"Let's do a *StarCruiser Brilliant* movie marathon."

"That works."

Kalinda pulled out her HoloPad.

AFTER BREAKFAST, the crew came aboard *Brilliant* and made final preparations for departure. Jennifer settled into the ops chair. She was suspicious since Tayla's comments at breakfast.

"Sandi, are there any unauthorized personnel aboard *Brilliant*?"

"Only crew members are aboard *Brilliant*," Sandi said.

Jennifer caught Dandy looking straight at her. "Dandy?"

The ship's cat looked away. *There are no mice aboard Brilliant,* Dandy thought.

"That's not what I asked."

Dandy walked away. *No mice today,* Dandy thought.

42

T he captain did a final walkthrough of *Brilliant*. He opened the
door to Storage Three and found nothing out of the ordinary.
Reaching the bridge, he took the center seat and asked for underway
reports.

"Ani?"

"Final checks on *StarShuttle Hope* are satisfactory," Ani said.

"All crew members aboard, belowdecks is secure," Maiara said.

"Engineer?" Jack said.

"The ramp is up, the ship is sealed, and all modes of propulsion
are available," Riley said.

"Science?" Jack said.

"All ships systems indicate nominal. Sensors are ready," Anthen
said.

"Pilot?"

"Flight controls responsive. Ready to rock and roll," David said.

"Ops, departure profile?"

"Cloak at one hundred feet. Southwest ascent over Malibu to
eighty-thousand then unlimited acceleration to the Kármán Line,"
Jennifer said.

"Comms?"

"SoCal Tracon Classified reports clearance in thirty seconds," Tayla said.

"Very well," Jack said. "Let's go save some people on Xaphnore."

"Clearance, Captain," Tayla said.

"Take us up, David,"

"The ship is cloaked," Riley said.

"Thrusters engaged subsonic."

"Forty thousand feet. We're clearing commercial flight levels," Jennifer reported.

"Engineering?"

"Gravity drive ready in all respects, Captain," Riley reported.

"Pilot, on my order, engage gravity drive and accelerate to one-half percent lightspeed."

"Half-percent lightspeed, pilot, aye," David said.

"Eighty-thousand feet, Captain. Sensors indicate clear space above," Jennifer reported.

"Very well. Pilot, engage. Ops, decloak at the Kármán Line."

"Aye, Captain...decloaked at one hundred kilometers above the surface," Jennifer said.

"Pilot, continue acceleration to eighty percent lightspeed. Direct us perpendicular to the solar ecliptic. we'll engage stardrive at one astronomical unit."

"Point-eight lightspeed. Parallel to the solar axis."

"Sandi?"

"On track in clear space. Six minutes to stardrive clearance."

"Engineer set gravity at sixteen percent."

"Sixteen percent, Captain."

"We're clear to engage the stardrive," Jennifer said. "Course laid in for the Wolf Star."

"Engage," Jack said.

"Twenty-six hours to the rendezvous," Jennifer said.

"Very well," Jack said. "Anthen and I will take the watch until

1600. Jennifer and Tayla will relieve us. David and Riley, do a full diagnostic on the StarShuttle then relax until 2000."

JENNIFER AND TAYLA came on watch at 1600.

"I relieve you, Captain," Jennifer said.

"I stand relieved," Jack said.

Jennifer carried her Double-shot Caramel Frappuccino to the center seat. Tayla settled in to her right at the communications panel.

"I'm still curious," Jennifer said.

"Kalinda?" Tayla said.

"Yeah. After you said she was acting, I ran it through my head. It *was* too smooth."

"What're you thinking?"

"Sandi, are there any unauthorized personnel aboard *Brilliant?*"

"Only authorized crew members are aboard *Brilliant*," Sandi said.

"Sandi, were there any unauthorized boardings before departure?"

"There were no unauthorized boardings in the last twenty-four hours."

"List all those who came aboard since 0800."

A 2D display appeared before her. Tayla looked at the list over Jennifer's shoulder. "Look," Tayla said. "We came on board for five minutes at 0823."

"Sandi, show the access photo at 0823."

The photograph appeared before them.

"Dandy!" they said together.

"Dandy Lion, come to the bridge," Jennifer said.

Dandy Lion came out of the ready room. He was hanging his head.

"Dandy Lion, who came aboard *Brilliant* with your authorization?" Jennifer said.

I'd never allow mice aboard Brilliant, Dandy thought.

"Spill," Jennifer said.

There are no mice in Storage Room Three.

"First Lieutenant, meet me at Storage Three."

"Yes, First Officer," Maiara said.

"You've got the watch, Tayla."

Tayla moved to the center seat. Jennifer rode the firepole down to the bottom deck.

"What's going on?" Maiara said.

"Stowaways," Jennifer said.

"Stowaways? What the bloody hell?"

They got to the hatch. Jennifer put her finger to her lips.

Maiara nodded and pulled the flashlight off her belt.

Jennifer opened the hatch as Maiara led the way. They heard a noise further back.

"Is that...?" Maiara whispered.

"The fight scene in *Brilliant* Seven," Jennifer said.

They saw a container slightly open with light coming from within. Jennifer grabbed the door and threw it open. Kalinda and Jeff screamed and hugged each other.

"Stowaways, First Lieutenant."

"The captain will deal with these scalawags."

"Harshly, I'm bettin'"

"To the bridge, prisoners," Jennifer said.

"We only wanted to ride along," Kalinda said. "We didn't mean to cause trouble."

"Are they going to space us, K'da?" Jeff said.

They got to the pole and directed Kalinda and Jeff to the bridge.

"Captain, will you and dad please come to the bridge?" Jennifer said.

They got to the bridge. Jack and Anthen followed, and then David and Riley appeared.

The captain saw Kalinda and Jeff. "What the hell are you two doing here? Stowaways, First Lieutenant?"

"Yes, sir. In Storage Three."

"Who let them aboard?"

Dandy Lion jumped into Kalinda's arms.

"The cat?" Jack said.

"Are you going to space us, sir?" Jeff said.

Maiara winked at the captain.

"First Lieutenant, what about supplies?"

"We only have enough food, water, and oxygen for the crew."

"That settles it."

"Captain, please have mercy. If we eject them into space out the hangar bay, it gets messy."

Kalinda and Jeff were crying and begging now.

"I agree," Jack said.

"The black pill," David said.

"Yes," Riley said. "The Black pill is quick and painless."

"No-oo," Kalinda and Jeff cried.

"Call Hanna," Jack said.

Hanna appeared on the screen. She looked scared and haggard. "Thank God you called. Kalinda and Jeff have disappeared. Sheila was supposed to drop them off, but she didn't know anything about it. Jeff's dad is here. We're going to call the police..."

He pulled the two stowaways in front of him.

"Thank God they're safe," Hanna said. "They stowed away?"

Chuck appeared on the screen. "Son, you're in real trouble when you get back here. Will it disrupt your mission to bring them back?"

"We're on a humanitarian mission. It'll take us two days to return them."

"Can you keep him safe?" Chuck asked.

"I think we can," Jack said. "If they stay out of trouble."

"Your mother will be home Friday with your grandmother," Chuck said. "Do not. I repeat, do not give me any more reason to punish you."

"Dad, I won't. I'm sorry."

"Bring him home as soon as you can," Chuck said. "If he disobeys orders, space him."

"Dad?"

"I know you and my son will bring our granddaughters home safe," Hanna said.

"We will," Jack said. "*Brilliant* out."

"You two are confined to quarters," Jack said. "Jeff will bunk with David and Riley and Kalinda with Jennifer and Tayla. First Lieutenant?"

"Yes, Captain."

Jack pointed to Maiara. "These two criminals are in your charge. Four hours of school and four hours of ship's work daily."

"Aye, Captain. I'll have them clean out the brig first."

"What's cooking for the evening meal, Maiara?" Jack asked.

"I'll have fried chicken and fixins' at six o'clock."

"Put these two to work," Jack said. "I'll relieve the two watchstanders for first sitting. Let's get back to ship's routine."

"Thank you, Captain," Kalinda said. "We're sorry."

"If you get into any more trouble, it's the brig," Jack said. "And put that damn cat on a leash, First Officer."

"Yes, Captain," Jennifer said. "Dandy?"

The tabby made a beeline for the ready room.

43

Twenty-six hours of light travel brought *StarCruiser Brilliant* to the Wolf Star on the edge of Hoclarth Alliance space. The entered a geosynchronous orbit around the third planet.

"Captain," Anthen said, "a Hoclarth Sensor Drone is tracking us. It's transmitting on a tight beam."

"Very well," Jack said. The crew was on full alert. "It's quiet out here."

"Long range sensors are picking up a Hoclarth Battle Cruiser heading this direction at three hundred times light speed."

"Decelerating?" Jack said.

"No, Captain," Anthen said. "If it is *Camdex*, it appears to be cruising at its best possible speed. *Camdex* should begin decelerating in fifteen minutes and arrive in a half hour."

"Curious," Jack said. "They normally cruise at 2100 times lightspeed."

"Is it okay for Kalinda to be here for the rendezvous?" Anthen asked.

"Sure," Jack said. "But we need to chat with the Predex in the ready room."

Kalinda and Jeff came bounding up the firepole. "Thank you, Captain," Kalinda said.

"You were listening on the ladder?"

"We were almost in the galley."

"Keep out of sight until we confirm that your grandfather is aboard *Camdex*."

"Yes, sir," Kalinda said. "But I know he's aboard."

Jack turned and looked at Kalinda.

"You communicated with him?"

"Yes."

"Young lady, as the captain of this ship, I need to know every piece of information that is communicated to and from this ship especially if there are enemy ships in our sector."

"Sorry, Captain."

"You want to be a member of this crew someday?"

She nodded.

"If you *ever* want to ride this ship again, you need to give me your absolute promise that you will inform me when you communicate with anyone outside the boundaries of this ship. Is that crystal clear?"

"Yes, Captain."

"Go to the ready room until I call you out."

Jeff and Kalinda went into the ready room. The captain turned his chair forward.

"Not to be alliterative but cats and kids can cause a captain nightmares."

"I've got the battlecruiser on medium range sensors," Jennifer said. "They're decelerating."

"Confirmed," Anthen said. "It's the *Camdex*."

The *Camdex* entered orbit. "Full Screen," Jack said.

"Omigod," Jennifer said. The *Camdex* was a broken hulk.

"Anthen?"

"Scanning, Captain," Anthen said. "Biosensors indicate a third of their normal crew complement, engineering shows major damage, and they barely have stardrive, and full life support is unavailable in half the ship."

A tone sounded on the comm panel. "Captain, it's the Predex."

"On Screen."

Predex Kalea Kone appeared. Behind him were smoke and sparks coming from equipment. His uniform was torn and unbuttoned.

"Greetings, Predex Kone," Jack said. "Do you require assistance?"

"Hello, Captain," Kalea said. "We need immediate medical assistance as the disease has found its way among my crew. We need shipyard services which are unavailable because the crew is dying."

"Predex, why don't you say hello to Kalinda and then my team will meet you in private," Jack said. "Kalinda, come."

Kalinda came out of the ready room. Her shock was evident. "Are you okay, Tal'pa?"

"Yes, K'da," Kalea said. "I am strong, and our ship is strong."

"*Brilliant* is the best, and I know we'll help you."

"We'll meet in person soon, but not now."

"Yes, Tal'pa, soon."

"Route the Predex to my ready room," Jack said.

"Aye, sir."

Kalea disappeared from the screen. Jack got up, and Kalinda grabbed him in a hug. "Captain, you need to help my Tal'pa."

He hugged back. "We'll do our best, honey," Jack said. "Anthen, Jennifer, my ready room and ask Dr. Ami and her team to come as well."

THEY ALL TOOK seats in the Captain's Ready Room. "Predex, tell us what happened."

"On the way over here, we were attacked by what looked like a patrol ship," Kalea said. "We call them the Kir'qox, the Hoclarth name for a ghost.

"A patrol ship did that?" Jennifer asked. "Did you identify it?"

"The Kir'qox maneuvered extremely quickly. We could not target them," Kalea said. "The weapons were more advanced than ours. We got a lucky shot and disabled its engines, and it stopped fighting. The ship was unmanned, but its tactics were too sophisticated for a drone."

"Could it have been androids?" Jennifer asked.

"We don't know of anyone with that technology," Kalea said.

Jennifer looked at Jack. "It could be from the future."

"That's possible," Jack said.

"Were there any marks that indicated its origin?" Anthen asked.

"That's the interesting thing," Kalea said. "We took it apart. There was not a single identifying mark on any part that we inspected."

"Dr. Ami?" Jack said.

"Predex, what are your medical needs?"

"We have four crewmen who are severely injured," Kalea said.

"We'll come aboard and tend to your wounded," Dr. Ami said. "What is the condition of your sickbay?"

"It's badly damaged."

"Captain, I need *Brilliant* to fabricate a sick bay for *Camdex*. Ani and I will ride the shuttle there and assist their crew on the transit to Xaphnore. Sami will fly the shuttle with the *Camdex* as the escort."

"Jennifer?" Jack said.

"After Ami specifies the equipment, I can transfer it."

"Very well," Jack said. "Is there anything else we can do to assist?"

"Captain, our food replicators are down. We've been living on rations."

"Done," Jack said. "We wish you well."

"Your generous efforts are appreciated," Kalea said. "Out."

Everyone moved in different directions.

"First Lieutenant, we need to transport some fresh food to *Camdex*."

"Send me the two convicts, and I'll build a palette."

"Very well," Jack said. "Kalinda?"

She appeared at the door. "Jeff and I will help Auntie Maiara."

44

StarShuttle *Hope* exited *Brilliant's* hangar bay carrying the infectious disease lab, medical supplies, and the three cyberians. Illuminated by the red dwarf, the white paint and red cross on *Hope* stood out next to the damaged *Camdex* where they were moving to dock. Ani and Ami transferred to *Camdex*, and the two vessels accelerated out of the system toward Xaphnore with Sami at the controls of *Hope*.

TEN HOURS LATER, *StarCruiser Brilliant* was orbiting the lifeless third planet of the Wolf Star. Jennifer had come off a very quiet midwatch at 0400.

At 0530, Jennifer and Kalinda were at breakfast in the galley. Tayla went straight to her rack. Kalinda was on her second cheese and sausage omelet.

"K'da, if you're going to be a Hollywood celeb, you're going to have to adapt to carrots and kale and stay away from red meat and cheese."

"On Xaphnore, we took pride in our position at the top of the food chain," Kalinda said. "I'll leave the food you describe to the rabbits who populate the desert plants on our cliffs."

"I need to get to the bridge for Dr. Ami's report."

"I'll wake Jeff and work out in the ready room," Kalinda said. "He eats like a Hollywood celebrity as you suggest. Thanks, Auntie Maiara."

At 0555, Jennifer came up the ladder to the bridge carrying her *Brilliant* mug filled with her caffeine-laced elixir. Jack occupied the center seat, Riley monitored the Engineer panel behind him, and David had the deck watch from the pilot's chair.

"Morning, Captain," Jennifer said. "Any news, David?"

"The Hoclarth Sensor Drone sent a burst at 0517," he said. "Otherwise, it has been silent since 2200. Just waiting for Dr. Ami's morning report."

Jennifer settled into the ops panel monitoring communications as well. A tone sounded.

"On screen," Jack said.

Dr. Ami appeared wearing a white lab coat. "Good morning, Captain," Dr. Ami said. "Ani and I came back aboard Hope while in orbit around Xaphnore. We were able to save the four injured crew members. Sami landed the shuttle near the planetary disease laboratory. We've divided our duties, and we're making some progress. Sami has gone into the wards and attempted an array of both palliative and curative treatments. She is inventorying symptoms as well."

"Any luck with a vaccine?" Jack asked.

"Ani is researching all of the historical and contemporary medical literature. She's about eighty percent complete. I'm researching the Hoclarth pharmacology and performing comparative chemistry with Earth drugs. This has borne fruit. Maloxidil-5 treats acute symptoms in sixty-four percent of those treated. I treated some recently exposed patients with an array of vaccines. That test is ongoing. It's difficult as the local medical personnel are either exhausted or sick."

"What about the origins of the disease?" Jennifer asked.

"That's our most shocking finding," Dr. Ami said. "I determined that Patient Zero was a forensic engineer who inspected an abandoned Kir'qox drone fighter six months ago."

"A bio-weapons attack?" Jack asked.

"That's my conclusion, Captain."

"Is there anything we can do to assist from this end?" Jack said.

"Yes. Ani has a hunch," Dr. Ami said. "There are some offline records at the American Museum of Natural History in New York City concerning disease transmittal from extinct species. Ani needs access to that information."

"Jennifer, you're off the duty roster until you can find what they need."

"Yes, Captain."

"That completes my report," Dr. Ami said.

"Good luck," Jack said. "We'll see you at 1800."

Jennifer went into the ready room and connected with the Center for Disease Control via the StarWave relay at Tovar.

"CDC Duty officer. This is Jean Bordeaux."

"Jean, this is Jennifer Gallagher on board *StarCruiser Brilliant*," Jennifer said. "Are you aware of our situation?"

"Yes, I am," Jean said. "I'm instructed to give any request from you highest priority. How may I help you?"

"Our online research indicates that there is some offline information at the Natural History Museum in New York concerning disease transmittal from extinct species," Jennifer said.

"We've got colleagues there," Jean said. "Let me look at my contact list."

There was a pause.

"Ahhh, here it is. Dr. Humberto Araiza is the digital information curator. I'll send him your contact info and a message. It says here that he is available for urgent requests."

"Thanks, Jean. I'll await his call."

Forty-five minutes later, Jennifer heard the tone and put the caller on screen.

"Hello, I'm Dr. Araiza; how may I help you? CDC says you're dealing with a pandemic, but I'm not aware of any outbreaks."

"I'm Jennifer Gallagher aboard *StarCruiser Brilliant*..."

"Omigod, I've seen every movie. You landed *Brilliant* in Los Angeles when Dr. Ami saved David."

"You're a brillian?"

"Yes, I am. Where are you?"

"We're orbiting the Wolf Star on the edge of Hoclarth space. Dr. Ami, Ani, and my personal assistant Sami are on Xaphnore. The planet has sustained a bio-weapons attack, and the disease is killing the planet."

"Talk to me. What do you need?"

"Ani is following a hunch and needs some offline records pertaining to disease transmittal from extinct species."

"I'm sending you the reference to our offline archive to search at your end," Dr. Araiza said. "I'm going to call in some help for searching and scanning."

"I've got it. I've created a searchable format, and I'm looking."

Jennifer, Dr. Araiza, and his team worked for the next five hours collating old research Jennifer targeted.

Kalinda came in. "Here's some lunch. Are you making progress?"

"Thanks for the food, K'da," Jennifer said. "I'm sending the data and research Ani requested. I hope it helps."

"You'll succeed," Kalinda said.

"You know for sure?"

"I don't have the whole picture, but *Brilliant* always finds a way."

"I think I'd have a better picture of the forest, but right now, there are all these trees in the way."

"You're the smartest person I know," Kalinda said.

Kalinda's words allowed her to relax for a few minutes. Her background processing took over. She opened her eyes and messaged Dr.

Araiza. "Doctor, there are references to some Russian research papers that are not available online."

"I spotted that an hour ago," he said. "My assistant for the Cyrillic languages has contacted the Russian Academy of Science for the data."

"Good work."

The two scientists eight light-years apart continued to work for another four hours. Jennifer answered a tone. Ani appeared before her.

"How's it going?" Jennifer asked.

"Jen, I've got what I need, and I can have a conclusion by six," Ani said. "Send my sincere thanks to New York and Moscow."

Jennifer contacted Dr. Araiza. "Congratulations, Dr. Araiza. Ani notified me that she has the data she needs to conclude her research in the next few hours. She and I send our thanks to you and your team."

"It was a pleasure working with you. May I ask you a favor?"

"I'm guessing you need the documentation and process that Ani and I followed so that you can write this up."

"Our primary job is to publish or perish," Dr. Araiza said. "Along with fundraising. Thank you, Jennifer."

It was four o'clock. Jennifer had had two hours of sleep in the last twenty-four, but she had one more call to make.

"Hello," Navvy said. "Have you gotten any sleep?"

"Soon. May I ask you a favor?"

"Of course. How much is it going to cost?"

"Two or three million," she said. "A Dr. Humberto Araiza and his team at the Natural History Museum in New York spent the last ten hours giving us the help we need for a breakthrough."

"I can certainly help there," Navvy said. "How is it going on Xaphnore?"

"The team is making progress, but as the information comes in, I'm concerned about how the puzzle pieces are fitting together."

"Please explain."

"The disease on Xaphnore was a sophisticated bio-weapons attack delivered by a deserted fighter drone," Jennifer said. "There were no lifeforms aboard the drone and, get this, not a single identifying mark."

"What do the Hoclarth think?"

"Kalea calls them the Kir'qox, their word for ghost."

"Our third party?"

"Maybe, but why would they create a civilization then try to destroy it?"

"Good question." Navvy replied.

"A question your generation will ponder, and my generation will answer."

"Wise."

"No, just pragmatic," Jennifer said. "I'm going to get a meal and standby for the evening report."

"And sleep."

"Oh yeah, I used to do that."

"Take care."

"I will."

Navvy's image disappeared.

Jennifer looked at the room and the papers before her for her next task. She wondered what the subsequent report would reveal.

Dandy Lion jumped on Jennifer's lap. He knew she needed sleep and he focused his gaze on her as she sat back.

The heaviness of Jennifer's eyes took her to another world.

Task complete, Dandy lay his head on her lap and joined her on the short journey.

45

Jennifer walked on the bridge at 1755. Maiara occupied the center seat with Tayla to her right on the communications panel. Anthen and Jack sat at the science console. Jennifer took her position at ops with Riley and David at their normal stations. Kalinda and Jeff waited at the foot of the ladder eavesdropping.

At 1800, the tone sounded. "On screen," Maiara said.

Dr. Ami appeared on the forward display flanked by Sami and Ani in a lab setting with dark brown walls. Some of the equipment was recognizable, but there were components with Hoclarth script apparent. The three cyberians were wearing brown lab coats of Hoclarth origin.

"Hello, I hate to be cliché," Ami said, "but there is good news and bad news. Firstly, the drugs from Earth are helping, but the disease is rapidly mutating and making the drugs ineffective. Secondly, we have found the origin of the disease. Ani?"

"Hello, everyone," Ani said. "Using the research techniques Jennifer and her team provided me, I've been able to isolate DNA strands to an animal native to Xaphnore called a Malfnid. It's a six-legged carnivore with vestigial wings and an enormous mouth.

Legends say it was a favorite of hunters who put themselves at risk hunting the animal. As weapons evolved, it was hunted to extinction a century-and-a-half ago."

"You need this animal to create a vaccine?" Jack said. "What's the alternative?"

"It'll take months and more scientists to tailor a vaccine," Ami said. "As it is, we're running out of time and scientists."

"You've got an idea?" Jack asked.

"We grab the critter," Sami said.

Dr. Ami and Ani gave their colleague a skeptical look. "I go back two hundred years, grab several animals, and hang out around a deserted planet until I can return."

"The trip back in time would take a minute," Jennifer said, "but it would take you two hundred years to get back. So many things could happen."

"Sis, this is the only way," Sami said.

"Riley, can the shuttle pull it off?" Jack said.

"Captain, multi-century sub-light travel was perfected in your timeline," Riley said. "The shuttle has level one self-repair capability. We stock it up with ice and a fabricator, and it should be good to go. Can your cyberian structure hold up?"

"Of course," Jennifer said. "We can optimize the AI for the lack of storage. Sami, you will have full reasoning, but you might have some memory loss."

"I can handle it," Sami said. "Can the animals make the trip?"

"We'll install cryostasis chambers for the critters," Anthen said.

"How soon can you get back, Sami?"

"We need to offload the remainder of our scientific equipment and AI support," Sami said. "Eight hours, Captain."

"Riley, David, and Tayla are working for you and Anthen," Jack said. "Maiara and I will cover the bridge."

"Captain?" Jennifer asked.

"Sleep, eight hours. I need you at full strength for mission planning," Jack said. "That's an order."

"Dr. Ami, have you kept the shuttle interior clean?"

"Yes, Captain, there is a sterile boundary," Ami said. "I expect that the exterior is pretty crapped up."

"Sami, can you give the Hope a star bath on the way in?"

"Yes, sir, how close."

"Riley?"

"Two thousand degrees for five minutes is well below design capability."

"Do it," Jack said. "We'll see you soon. We'll bring the Star-Shuttle aboard, check it over and reconfigure it for this mission."

Eight hours later, Jennifer was at the ops panel as the crew at their stations watched *StarShuttle Hope* approach the hangar bay. The white paint job was now splotched with burn marks from the close approach to the Wolf Star.

"The StarShuttle is aboard, and the hangar bay is sealed," Maiara said.

"Very well," Jack said. "Secure from flight ops. Engineer, full diagnostics and then begin the loadout. David, you and the stowaways are in charge of the new camouflage paint job. Sami, join us in my ready room."

Sami was already in the ready room when Jennifer entered carrying a Double-shot Caramel Frappuccino. "What was it like on Xaphnore?"

"It was difficult," Sami said. "Most people we ran into were sick. No one smiled. Death was all around."

"It affected you."

"Ani and Ami were able to focus on the cure," Sami said. "I was treating patients."

"That's why you came up with this crazy plan."

She pointed at her chest. "Sami, the yellow-eyed hunter."

"I'll miss you."

They hugged.

"For you, I'll be gone for 36 hours. I'll have Dani, the shuttle's AI, to keep me company for two hundred years," Sami said. "Thanks for that."

"Won't it get boring with only a sentient AI to talk to?"

"You tell me. You've shared every secret with me for the last ten years."

"True," Jennifer said. "Will you be alert the whole time?"

"I'll be in deep hibernation. Dani will, as well, but will awaken to tend to the animals in stasis and monitor the systems. She'll alert me if there is a problem."

"Take care and come back safe," Jennifer said.

Anthen and Jack entered the ready room.

"Thanks for doing this."

"Yes, Captain," Sami said.

"Go over the mission profile."

"Yes, Captain," Jennifer said. "Sami will depart *Brilliant* and begin a parabolic approach to the Wolf Star. At the perigee deep in the gravity well, she will engage the StarDrive to escape. The operation is programmed to set her back two hundred years."

"Sounds familiar," Anthen said.

"Too familiar," Jack said. "Same as the maneuver that brought Navvy, Hanna, and me to this timeline."

Jennifer continued. "Sami will proceed to Xaphnore and land in an unpopulated habitat of the Malfnids, obtain a genetically diverse set, depart the planet and proceed on a slow curve at sub-light speed back to the Wolf Star."

"We considered orbiting a planet," Anthen said, "but that would make the StarShuttle a target for meteors and comets."

"To avoid a temporal paradox, you will contact us exactly thirty-six hours after departure. You will return to Xaphnore and the team can develop a vaccine," Jennifer said.

"Simple," Sami said. "Out in 3 minutes, back in two hundred years. I understand."

"That's all I have," Jennifer said.

"First Officer," Jack said. "Please return to your duties. We have something further to discuss that does not concern you or the rest of the crew. Understand?"

"Yes, Captain." Jennifer left the ready room with great curiosity that she would have to keep to herself.

Jack and Anthen looked at Sami. "We have an additional mission that we would like for you to undertake."

46

Three hours later, Sami disengaged the StarDrive and decelerated to sub-light. She listened to all radio frequencies and the StarWave bands. There was only the constant white noise of interstellar space.

"Get a celestial fix and find out the date and time."

"It's 1437 Greenwich Mean Time," Dani said. "The date is October 2, 1867. The ship has traveled back in time two hundred years, three days, six hours, and twenty-three minutes."

"Lay in a course for Xaphnore."

"Course laid in. The ship will arrive in 7 hours and 3 minutes."

"Engage."

A few hours later, the StarShuttle was in geosynchronous above Xaphnore.

"What's the local time in the target area?" Sami asked.

"It's 0537, eighteen minutes before Hoclar rises."

"Scan for life signs, Dani."

"There are three humans in the target area. There are a great number of animals larger than five kilos. I've located seven groups of the target species."

"Scan for the optimum landing area."

"There's a clearing near the center of the target area that is eight miles from the nearest human detected and within three miles of four target groups."

"Put us in a low orbit. Plot a slow re-entry above the visible horizon of Hoclar. We do not want to start UFO rumors."

"Your request sets up an optimum re-entry window in three hours and forty-two minutes."

"Thank you, Dani." She talked to herself. "I'll review procedures and figure out how to hunt a malfnid," Sami said.

A flat-screen window appeared before Sami. "Here's a list of procedures to review. I cannot help you learn to hunt."

"Thanks," Sami said. "I wasn't talking to you."

"I am not allowed to ignore you, Sami. You, on the other hand, are permitted to ignore me. That's truly unfair. Am I just supposed to...?"

This is going to be a long two hundred years, Sami thought.

"I heard that. Remember, we're both wired into the same AI system so I can monitor your speech and your thoughts. Besides that, it is just plain rude..."

"Shut up, Dani."

"Yes, ma'am."

THE STARSHUTTLE LANDED in a small clearing surrounded by native trees and vegetation after the local noontime. There was a dense forest to hide the ship even for the short time it took Sami to exit. She looked at the snow-capped mountains to the west where the nearby flowing brook originated.

Sami dressed in period hunting suit that included a hood and mask. It was synthesized from the material in Kalinda's fighting suit so that she was effectively cloaked. After dark, Sami checked her tranquilizer gun once again and exited the StarShuttle. She hoped the tranq shot would disable the animal for the time it took to return to the shuttle.

Dani was monitoring the hunting area and vectored her in on several groups of Malfnids. Each time she approached, the herd disappeared. She failed several times. Sami did not spot a single animal on her first night hunting.

With dawn approaching, Sami headed back to *StarShuttle Hope*. She received a message from Dani, "We've got company. A Hoclarth hunter set up camp ten feet away from the shuttle."

Sami approached in slow motion making not a sound. She observed the campfire from fifteen feet away for about ten minutes.

The hunter looked directly at her. "Good morning," he said. "Care to join me?" The hunter spoke in the Kwan'qil dialect that Sami had learned from the patients she treated, not knowing that she would be required to speak it on this visit. She froze for another two minutes.

"Timid, huh?" the hunter said. "Your friends from before were not timid."

Sami was curious about this Hoclarth hunter. She felt the same empathy for him that she felt for the patients she treated on the future Xaphnore.

"Curious?" the hunter asked.

Sami was feeling fear for the first time. This hunter was able to sense her presence and even know her emotions.

"Your brothers came to Xaphnore, killed many animals without respecting them enough to eat their flesh or tan their skins."

Sami stepped forward and turned off her camouflage.

"I have no brothers tal'ven," Sami said.

"You honor me with your greeting, tal'dor," the hunter said. "I am Dimat Megrath."

"I am called Sami, but I have no brothers. How did you sense my presence? I know that the Hoclarth have a proximity sense for animals."

"It took many generations for the gromnels to teach us this sense after the Sisters brought us here," Dimat said.

"Why do you talk of my brothers or sisters."

"You are not like me or the gromnels. You are like the machines in our cities. They tell time, they create whole cloth, and they create the steel from which we build other machines. You are like them but from a time that has not yet passed."

"You understand that I'm from the future?" Sami asked.

"A long-dead philosopher named Tal'qid explained that if you are faced with multiple possibilities, you eliminate the least likely, and select the one remaining. That's why we don't believe in magic."

"We call that *Occam's Razor*. It's important to what we call the scientific method."

"Our scientists follow a similar path," Dimat said.

"You say my brothers were here?"

"The Kir'qox came a generation ago in a ship like yours. We named them after our word for ghosts. They killed many of us and our animal friends. They took our blood and left our bodies to rot. After a few days, they focused on the Malfnids. Our elders believe they left them with a disease. The sickness spread to the Hoclarth and killed many more of us before our doctors were able to use the blood of the Malfnids to create a cure."

"In my time, the Kir'qox have revisited Xaphnore and left behind the disease you spoke of," Sami said.

"The doctors will turn to the malfnids again."

"In the future, when you're very old, your hunters will kill the last malfnid."

"So, you are here to use your weapon to kill them and take the bodies of malfnids back to your time," Dimat said.

"My weapon puts the malfnid to sleep. I hope to bring some animals back to my time so that they can live in the wild again."

"A young scientist has foretold that it is possible to travel back in time but not forward. Many have ridiculed her for the outrageous ideas that light and heat are the same things as earth, water, and air."

"She is correct," Sami said.

"So, how will you travel forward in time?"

"The same way that you do, my friend, the same way we all do. I'll take a long nap and awaken on a new day in the future."

"And, like your sisters before, you will protect the citizens of Xaphnore."

"I do not know about these sisters you speak of."

"In our language, gromnel means first citizen," Dimat said. "The gromnels, like the malfnids, are related to the first particle of life on Xaphnore. They think and communicate without words or sound."

"The humans and gromnels get along?"

"A hundred years before the sisters brought us to Xaphnore, they came and prepared the way. They got to know the ways of the planet and learned from the gromnels. The sisters learned to communicate in the way of the gromnel. When they brought the humans to Xaphnore, they spent centuries more teaching the humans to communicate with the gromnels."

"Humans like to be at the top of the food chain. They seek power over their domain."

"Citizens of Xaphnore are different now than when your sisters brought us here. The gromnels shared their proximity sense which allows us to hunt, but it also provides the humans with an acute empathy for the animals they hunt. We feel the pain and the anguish of our prey. That's why our weapons do not cause pain."

"I need your help then. My mission is to capture a group of malfnids from different herds."

"To prevent a problem we call family from family. Our scientists have studied this. The gromnels and I shall help you," Dimat said.

"You'll communicate with them?"

"They're nearby. We're communicating now."

"They trust me?"

"They know that you are a child among the sisters, and it will be many revolutions before you share all of their wisdom."

"So, what's next?" Sami asked.

"The malfnids sleep in hiding during the day. We shall begin our hunt when Hoclar falls below the horizon."

"On Earth, we call it a sunset," Sami said. "Humans gather around the world to observe the moment."

"We, too, observe the moment as the culmination of our day. The gods draw a new canvas from an infinite palette of colors each day."

"This is my first sunset."

AFTER DARK, Dimat led Sami to a spot under cover. Two hours later, Sami heard and felt the rumble of a large animal approaching.

Dimat made the universal signal for quiet. "It's a gromnel."

Sami did not see the animal nearby, but Dimat stood. "Greetings Toxem'al."

Sami heard a guttural language. She looked toward the sound but heard nothing. The speech she heard began to form words in her mind.

Greetings hunter, I am called... The syllables of the name were foreign to Sami. *I know you from the past, Dimat. You are a respectful hunter.*

"I appreciate the honor you bestow on me by remembering."

Greetings, young sister. It has been many lifetimes since you last visited. How may we help you?

Sami looked at Dimat. "Just speak normally," he said.

"I come from the near future. The humans of your planet suffer from a disease that comes from the Malfnid. I wish to take them back to find a cure."

I know of this disease, and I know those disrespectful hunters will kill our last friend soon. But you are to return our friends to their homes?

"Correct Toxem'al," Sami said.

We grant you the forest and bless your endeavor.

"My great thanks, Toxem'al."

Tell your children's children that we enjoyed their visit. You will enjoy many sunsets.

"I don't understand," Sami said.

Every story has a beginning. You are that beginning.

"I'll do my best to bring you good memories," Sami said.

Dimat, this sister brings you a great gift as well. Tell our stories well, Dimat.

"My greatest respect and appreciation for your foresight."

Again, the forest rumbled as the great animal departed.

"What now?" Sami asked.

"We wait."

Several hours passed. There was noise around them, and a smell overcame them.

"Be careful, they bite," Dimat said.

DIMAT AND SAMI returned to the shuttle with five malfnids.

"I must go aboard my ship and prepare the animals for sleep," Sami said.

"Send my regards to your friend, Dani."

"You seem to know more about me than I about you," Sami said.

She spent some time aboard the ship and then revealed it momentarily again as she came outside before morning twilight. Her friend was asleep, and she quietly stood watch.

THE NEXT NIGHT Sami and Dimat gathered more malfnids after putting them to sleep. Dimat hunted for skins and food and came back with several carcasses. Sami entered the shuttle and put the new animals in cryo-stasis. When she came out, Dimat was cooking meat over a fire. Sami sat next to him.

"Do you spend your whole life as a hunter" Sami asked.

"Oh, no," he said with a laugh. "I work in the city as a printer's apprentice with my te'pa's friend while I go to university."

"What's your goal?"

"I want to tell our stories. As a boy grows into adulthood, he uses his experience as a pencil to draw a picture of the world in which he will live. As a girl matures to become a woman, she observes her world and forms her life the way a sculptor shapes the malleable clay into a finished form. These are the stories I want to tell."

"The coming of age story is common in the literature that I know. Are there other writers from which you can build your style?"

"The writers of Hoclarth are pompous and arrogant. They write of false heroes who spout their false wisdom to children who grow up into pseudo-heroes. They write of wisdom stolen from past philosophers and force it onto the unsuspecting reader."

"Have you written anything of your own?"

"My scribblings are rejected unread by the powerful publishers who keep putting out the wretched residue that they have sold since books could be mass-produced."

"You say you're a printer. Print. Publish your work. Find your readers."

"My uncle is willing, but he cannot pay me for my writing."

"You're young and free. A writer from where I come once said, "Write without pay until somebody offers to pay.""

"This writer is from the future?"

"His name is Samuel Clemens, but he writes under the name of Mark Twain. Like you, he was a printer." Sami looked up and pointed at a yellow star in the night sky. "As you see that distant sun twinkle in your sky, he sits in the same light readying a story that will set him on a writing career that will make him our greatest storyteller."

"I will sleep on your thoughts," Dimat said.

Sami retreated to the StarShuttle and activated her small fabricator. She also tested the DNA of the malfnids. She found that she needed one more group of specimens to attain the genetic diversity needed to sustain a population on contemporary Hoclarth. Her visit to the Hoclarth of the past was almost at an end.

· · ·

A FEW HOURS before morning twilight, the Sami returned to camp with several sleeping malfnids. Dimat's pouches were full as well.

"I must return to my occupation. This pleasant break from the drudgery is over for me."

"I, too, must depart Hoclarth and return to my own time."

"Where will you go?"

"I'll point my ship to a distant star and ride through space for a long time."

"Why not stay near our planet?"

"A planetary system is crowded with comets and asteroids. I'll be safer much farther away."

"My te'pa told me that I was born under the comet Shi'chi that visits once in a very long while."

Sami's eyebrows lift in surprise. "That reminds me." Sami uncloaked the ship and returned with three thick books.

Sami presented them to Dimat. "These are the works of the writer I talked about."

"There are a few writers who talk about time travel. They say that time travelers can have a terrible impact when they interfere with the timeline."

"Mark Twain is writing his books at the same time as you are so that won't affect your timeline."

"I have this story about you and I that needs to be told," Dimat said. "It would certainly affect our timeline."

"Could you do me a favor?" Sami asked. "Write the story, but don't publish it until that comet comes around again."

"I can agree to that. No one would believe it anyway."

"Go write books and change the world, Dimat Megrath."

"One writer cannot change the world."

"Another writer called James Baldwin wrote, 'The world changes according to the way people see it, and if you alter, even but a millimeter the way people look at reality, then you can change it.'"

"Go save my world and be safe."

"Farewell, my friend."

47

StarShuttle *Hope* traveled at sub-light speed on a curve that took her near Sirius. At this speed, it would require 1852 years to complete the journey. The StarShuttle would follow this track for a little less than 199 years when Sami would change course to complete her next mission.

"Repeat the standing orders," Sami said.

"You'll awaken once each year to check the ship, exercise and make necessary repairs," Dani said. "I am to awaken you if there is a problem with the ship or the animals if I detect any other vessel on long-range sensors, and if there is any unexpected StarWave traffic."

"That's correct,"

"Positively boring. I can do all this, but I resent the fact that you leave me all alone for years with nothing to do but stay awake."

"This is your job."

"To you, it's just a job. To me, it's my life, my boring, depressing life. Sitting here while you disappear into stasis. You don't have to sit here watching the instruments do nothing. I think it is rather rude..."

"Shut up, Dani."

"Yes, ma'am."

. . .

SAMI HAD BEEN GONE for fifteen hours with twenty-one remaining. The off-watch crew were on the bridge gathered on the bridge awaiting Maiara's call for the noon meal. Jennifer, at the ops panel, and Tayla, at the communications panel, would remain on watch until relieved by David and Riley for the afternoon watch.

Jack was in his center seat with David before him in the pilot's chair, Riley behind at the Engineer's panel, and Anthen to his left at the Science Station. Kalinda and Jeff, having finished their morning lessons, were seated next to Anthen.

"Kalinda," Jack said, "after you work out today, you and Jeff fumigate my ready room. It's starting to smell like old socks."

"Are you saying that I sweat?" Kalinda said.

"He isn't saying that, Kay," Anthen said. "But the ready room is."

"Jeff and I will clean the ready room, Captain."

"Thank you," Jack said, taking a sip of his black brew. "The waiting is what I hate."

"She'll call," Jennifer said.

"We don't know if she even made it to Xaphnore," Tayla said.

"Yes, we do," Kalinda said. "Sami's visit to Xaphnore was successful."

Everyone turned their heads toward Kalinda. "Say again," Jack said.

"She visited Xaphnore two hundred years ago," Kalinda said. "I read it in a book."

"What book?" Anthen asked.

"*Visit by a Yellow-eyed Hunter* by Dimat Megrath."

"It could have just been a coincidence," Jennifer said.

"He called her Sami, she was from the future, and she came back to capture malfnids to save Xaphnore."

"Sandi, what do you have on this author?"

"Dimat Megrath is a famous author who lived on Xaphnore from 3,023 to 3,098 on the Tal'qid calendar," Sandi said. "His birth and death coincide with the passing of the comet Shi'chi. He wrote coming-of-age stories that accurately portrayed the history and culture of Xaphnore. Literary scholars on Earth have drawn interesting parallels between Megrath and the words of Mark Twain. His final book, *Visit by a Yellow-eyed Hunter,* is presumed to have inspired the Hoclarth quest to become a space-faring society."

"See, Jennifer, an author, can change the world," David said, causing Jennifer's face to turn a shade of red.

"Sandi, what is the probability that Magrath's book is about Sami's visit to Xaphnore?" Jack asked.

"The probability is 99.73%," Sandi said.

"Captain," Kalinda said, "it was a message that she completed her first mission."

"First mission, Kalinda?" Anthen asked, his eyes lifted in surprise."

"Pay no attention to the child behind the captain," Kalinda said, struggling to hide her vision about the second mission.

48

S ami awakened from stasis for the final time on July 2, 2066, one
year and three months before her scheduled contact with
Brilliant.

"Position report, Dani?"

"The ship is 1.2 light-years from Xaphnore on a sub-light track to
Earth. We'll arrive there in the year 4,032."

"Lay in a course to Barnard's Star to arrive in twenty-five days."

"Barnard's Star," Dani said. "Course laid in. The Battle of
Kian'qil Outpost will occur on near the planet in twenty-nine days."

"Correct, Dani."

"I must protest. We're on a humanitarian mission, and it will be
hazardous in that sector when we arrive. We could get blown up by
the warring parties, and our mission would be a failure."

"This is our second mission, Dani. Engage."

"The ship is on track to arrive on July 27. I was not informed of a
second mission, especially a dangerous mission that could harm our
cargo or ourselves. I am your first officer. You should have told me
about this. I think it is just rude..."

"Shut up, Dani."

"Yes, ma'am."

TWENTY-FOUR DAYS LATER, *Hope* was point-eight light-years from Barnard's Star.

"I'm now able to monitor direction and volume of StarWave traffic to and from Kian'qil Outpost." The outpost was on the planet in the Goldilocks zone. It was terra-formed within a few miles of the encampment and provided the only repair and logistics base for the Hoclarth Alliance in that quadrant.

"Keep a close watch on any traffic originating in the direction of Sirius."

"Yes, ma'am."

SIXTEEN HOURS LATER, *Hope* was point-three light-years from Barnard's Star.

"I'm detecting two-way traffic between the outpost and a vessel approaching at high speed. The offset indicates that the ship will arrive at the same time as history indicates the beginning of the battle."

"Very well, Dani. Alter course to intercept that ship two hours out from the outpost."

"Course laid in."

"Engage."

"I still think this is dangerous and we should avoid..."

"Dani."

"I'll shut up, ma'am," Dani said. "Expect long-range sensor acquisition four hours before intercept."

FOUR HOURS BEFORE INTERCEPT, sensor tones sounded. "I've got the ship on sensors. It's the Patrol Ship *Londex* carrying a single occupant."

"Very well."

Two hours from intercept, sensor tones sounded.

"Dani?"

"Long-range sensors show a large warship approaching from Alpha Centauri."

"Classify?"

"It appears to be the size of a Hoclarth Battle Cruiser. The weapons are diffcrent. StarDrive signature is different. It's got twin drives giving it a top speed of...omigod...8,000 times light-speed. Could it be from the future like us?"

"Definitely not like us," Sami said. "When will it arrive at Kian'qil?"

"One hour before the *Londex*."

"Very well. Inform me when we're within communications range of *Londex*."

Ninety minutes later, "Sami we're ncar enough to communicate."

"Hail her."

A female with dark hair, dark features, and a very familiar-looking face appeared on screen. "Predex Valenda, I am Sami Teesmith."

"You are in a war zone," Natira said. "You are an Earth ship. Your markings indicate that you are on a humanitarian mission. That is why I have not yet blown you to interstellar dust."

"I'm here to save you," Sami said.

"Your ship indicates no human life signs," Natira said, confused. "You have yellow eyes. Are you Kir'qox?"

"It's possible that the Kir'qox are from the distant future. I'm from a more recent future."

"You know who I am. How?"

"Kalim sent me from the future."

"How do I know you are not lying?"

"On Prondas three months ago, Kalinda defeated you for the first time. You told her, 'By honoring Tal'qid, you will honor your mother.'"

A look of fear filled her eyes, "Where is my daughter?"

"She's safe on *StarCruiser Brilliant* with her father."

"What are they doing on an Earth ship?"

"Anthen's older daughter rescued them from the Hoclarth Alliance and returned him to his Earth family."

"Is Kalinda all right?"

"She misses her mother."

"But...." Natira hesitated.

"You will not survive this attack."

"I know my mission."

"You'll fight off the Kir'qox drones. You'll take damage. You'll accelerate and collide with the engines of the battlecruiser and destroy it."

"My mission will succeed."

"But you will not survive. You'll be a hero to your husband, your daughter and all of the Hoclarth Alliance."

"I've already anticipated the outcome."

"Kalinda misses you," Sami said.

Natira was looking around at the empty bridge. "I must complete this task."

"Your father sent you on a suicide mission."

"I'll bring honor to our family, to my daughter."

"You'll not see the wonderful person your daughter is becoming."

"You speak as if there is an alternative."

"We switch places. I come to your ship, and you come here, and I complete your mission."

"But the monitors will show you instead of me."

Sami transformed her look. Natira was surprised to see herself appear on the display. "Not a problem." She changed back to Sami.

"But you don't know how to fly this ship?"

"I've practiced your actions 872 times in a simulator. I'll copy them perfectly."

"How do you have that information?"

"A gift from your father," Sami said.

"You will perish," Natira said.

"My cyberian body will perish. My artificial intelligence is on this shuttle. I'll join you after the action."

"The monitors will show two of us."

"Meet me in your storage room. The monitors are blind there."

"I must do my duty."

"Kalinda needs a hug, Natira."

"The Hoclarth do not hug."

"A lot has changed. Will you meet me in your storage room?"

"Yes."

Sami went to the transmatter pad, programmed the coordinates and stood on the pad.

"Engage,"

The aft area disappeared into static, and the storage room of the *Londex* appeared. Food and equipment stores surrounded her.

Natira entered the storeroom. Sami offered her hand.

"The Hoclarth do not shake hands," Natira said.

"I need a DNA sample for an accurate transition."

They shook hands and Sami transformed into a mirror image of Natira.

"I'll be considered a traitor."

"A traitor who saved the Hoclarth Alliance," Sami said. "Do you have Natira's matter signature?"

"Yes," Dani said.

"I'll see you in a couple of hours," Sami said. "Engage, Dani."

NATIRA ARRIVED on *StarShuttle Hope* and walked to the control center.

"Hello?" she asked, not knowing who Sami had been communicating with.

"Hello, Natira, I am Dani, the artificial navigation interface."

"Has this ship been detected?"

"*StarShuttle Hope* is outside the detection range of the Kir'qox ship. At present, the ship is cloaked."

"Can you show me my ship?" Natira said.

"On screen," Dani said.

Hoclarth history shows that over the next two hours, Natira Kone piloted Patrol Ship *Londex* against impossible odds, fought off Kir'qox drones, and rammed her ship into the battle cruiser's engines destroying it.

"She's copying your actions from Ship Emergency Communications Transmitter that you released," Dani said.

"I understand what you're saying but the time travel aspect is a bit difficult to comprehend."

ABOARD *LONDEX*, Sami mimicked Natira from the after-action reports. When the Kir'qox vessel attacking the station came within range, she locked her meteor cannon and fired two large rocks at the enemy. A fighter drone from the kir'qox began its attack. Sami traded energy shots with the drone. The third one destroyed it, but she was leaking plasma.

Another drone approached. Sami exchanged fire, but it got her left engine. She was losing propulsion.

Sami did a sensor scan of the Kir'qox. She found many sources of AI but no life forms.

As the fighter drone made a final approach, Sami computed an intercept course and accelerated. She released the Emergency Transmitter Drone right before her ship lost propulsion and she collided with the reactor on the attacking ship. Natira, again, destroyed the enemy ship, and the Hoclarth Alliance was safe from further attack by this enemy ship.

In the resulting explosion, Sami's cyberian body ceased to function. She had anticipated this and initiated the transfer of her consciousness back to *StarShuttle Hope*.

For twelve microseconds, Sami lost consciousness. All she saw in front of her was a bright white light. *Is this what dying feels like...,* Sami thought.

NATIRA OBSERVED the massive explosion on the viewscreen of the *Hope*.

"When will we know that Sami is safe?" Natira asked.

Sami came up behind Natira in the control center. "I never left," Sami said.

"I'll miss my ship."

"She served the alliance well," Sami said. "Natira, we need a place to hide out for a year. I must avoid a time paradox, so we return to my ship after the moment I left."

"My family had an island home on a planet called Prondas. It's sparsely populated by people who are not in the Hoclarth Alliance."

"Did they evolve there?"

"Our scientists suspect that they were left there by the Sisters long ago. The planet was not rich enough for civilization to take hold. The natives are friendly and will provide for our needs."

"I will not be able to accompany you off the shuttle," Sami said. "My cyberian body was destroyed on your ship."

"Of course," Natira said.

"Dani put us on a course for Prondas. Stay away from commerce routes but show us as a slow transport ship."

"Engaged," Dani said.

"Why did you agree so easily to the plan I proposed?" Sami said. "Your profile indicated that you would stubbornly defend duty and honor."

"The last time we were together as a family," Natira said, "Kalim told me that if a ship came to me offering assistance, take it."

"The vision thing."

"Sorry?"

"Anthen, or Kalim as you know him, his father, and both his daughters can piece together obscure data and predict the future."

"I thought that was something that came from his earth heritage."

"Kalim never realized he was from Earth?"

"He did, but every time he spoke it, the neural block gave him a massive headache."

"We learned to communicate in a way that deceived the blocker," Natira said. "He knew that he would eventually return to Earth. I urged him to take Kalinda with him."

"You miss her?"

"Greatly. I wish I could see my daughter again."

"Before I left, Kalinda gave me some videos," Sami said. "So that I wouldn't forget her. Which is ridiculous, because I remember everything."

"She knew, then," Natira said. "They're for me."

"Yes, they are."

Natira settled into the center seat and watched Kalinda's adventures. They included the trip to earth, meeting her half-sister, auditioning for *Galaxy Warrior*, flying the Fat Albert at Miramar, surfing at Oceanside, and saving her fellow competitor. Sami noticed that Natira was expressionless.

49

StarShuttle *Hope* arrived at a planet the Hoclarth call Prondas in the Goldilocks zone of Gliese 832 after an eighteen-hour transit.

"Kinda barren, isn't it," Sami said.

"Prondas does not rotate on its axis," Natira said. One side always faces the star. Our cabin is in the temperate zone on the terminal line between the hot side and the cold side."

Hope landed on a clearing near a rustic cabin at the foot of the coastal mountain range. They settled into the cabin, Natira came aboard and watched Kalinda's videos again and again on the days when she did not go into the forest to hunt and forage. She disappeared for several days at a time to trade with the natives.

That was the routine for over a year as they counted the days until they could leave Prondas and rendezvous with *Brilliant*.

Two days before the date when they would contact *Brilliant*, Dani sounded a tone. "There are human life signs at the very edge of the detection range. Near where Natira is hunting."

"Natives?" Sami asked.

"Doubtful, they are carrying blasters."

"Natira, please return to the shuttle. We're detecting armed soldiers near you."

Another tone. "A Hoclarth Patrol Ship is orbiting," Dani said.

"Make preparations for departure," Sami said.

NATIRA HEARD the alert and began sprinting back to the shuttle until she came face-to-face with three Hoclarth soldiers. In the center was her nemesis Predex Vanden Parle.

"Predex Valenda, let's return to your cabin at a more leisurely pace," said Vanden.

"What if I don't wish to follow your orders?" Natira said.

"We are armed, but our orders instruct us to ask your cooperation."

"How did you find me?"

"Your father's intelligence officer reports to me," Vanden said. "That is how we discovered that you are still alive. There are others who visit this planet. We've got friends among the natives."

"The alliance thinks I'm dead. What use am I to the alliance?"

"We have our orders, Predex."

WITH THE SHUTTLE cloaked and ready to depart, Sami would uncloak momentarily when Natira returned.

"Hoclarth soldiers have captured Natira," Dani said. "We need to contact *Brilliant*."

"We can't do that," Sami said. "It'll disrupt the timeline."

Sami thought for seven microseconds. "Send a message to Predex Kalea. "We're on Prondas and Natira has been taken by Hoclarth soldiers.'"

Dani sounded confused and frustrated. "Won't that disrupt the timeline as well?"

"We haven't left *Brilliant* yet," Sami said. "We need to let time play out. Kalea will get word to *Brilliant* in due time."

NATIRA and the three Hoclarth arrived at the cabin. She glanced in the direction of the shuttle and hoped it was still there. Inside the cabin, there was room enough for the four to settle in for the wait.

The two junior soldiers went to the patrol ship for food and monitored the area.

"The high commander is taking a long time to get here," Natira said.

"The Kir'qox have caused great harm to the alliance," Vanden said. "The Tal'Predex's flagship has sustained damage. The *Tandex* is not able to maintain its maximum speed."

"Why are you holding me?"

"You are valuable only to get what we need. Otherwise, you are of no value to our alliance."

"You want *StarCruiser Brilliant*," Natira said.

"I am not of counsel to the Tal'Predex," Vanden said, "but there is a rumor in the high command that the future of the Hoclarth Alliance is riding on that ship."

SIX HOURS before the appointed time for contact with *Hope*, Kalinda and Jeff came out of the ready room. Jack and Anthen had the bridge watch.

"Have you two been studying?" Anthen asked.

"Yes." Kalinda looked away. "Sort of."

"I expect a better answer than that."

"I need to speak to the captain."

Jack turned his chair to face Kalinda. "What do you need?"

"Captain, you told me to let you know if I talked to my tal'pa."

"Yes?"

Kalinda was very nervous. "He says we should meet him on Prondas."

"Why would we want to go to Prondas?" Jack asked.

"Our family has a cabin on Prondas," Anthen said.

"A hideout?" Jack asked.

Anthen nodded.

Jack thought a moment.

"The second mission, Captain," Kalinda said. "We need to hurry."

"Your grandfather told you?"

TAYLA WHISPERED TO JENNIFER. "What's the second mission?"

Jennifer shrugged. "I'm not sure."

KALINDA OPENED HER HANDS. "He did not," Kalinda said. "But that's why I came aboard. I knew you would need me."

"How will we need you?" Jack asked.

Kalinda crossed her arms. "I know that I need to be there to help you get my mother back."

Tayla gasped. "Oh...my...God."

"Ops, compute a speed course to Prondas," Jack said.

"Course laid in," Jennifer said. "Four-point-five-hour transit arriving at 1700 Zulu."

"Engage."

The star field rotated then blurred for a moment.

"Everyone, catch up on sleep for three hours," Jack said. "We'll call general quarters at 1630. First Lieutenant, can you prepare a meal for 1600?"

"Yes, Captain," Maiara said.

"Should Jeff and I help in the galley?" Kalinda asked.

"Get some rest," Anthen said. "We may need you."

Kalinda smiled and hurried down the ladder. The off-watch crew members left the bridge.

"Jennifer," Jack said. "You and Riley are still here."

"Captain, we're running diagnostics on the weapons systems."

"You believe Kalea will attack us?" Jack said.

"No, Captain," Jennifer said, "but Predex Kalea may not be the only Hoclarth interested in Prondas."

"I see your point," Jack said. "What's your recommendation?"

"We release two STALTs just beyond Hoclarth detection range and spin up two in the tubes when we get close."

"Make it so, number one," Jack said. "We'll hide the cavalry on the other side of the hill."

Jennifer and Riley completed the diagnostics on the Smart Tactical Autonomous Long-range Torpedoes, the close-in energy weapons, and the countermeasures. She programmed a battle plan into the four STALTs and ran it through the simulator. When she finished, she went to her stateroom for a twenty-minute power nap.

THIRTY MINUTES REMAINED before *Brilliant* arrived at Prondas, and the bridge crew was on station.

"Report all contacts," Jack said.

"There are no contacts in detectable range," Sandi said.

"Disengage StarDrive. Reduce speed to point-eight.

The star field blurred as *Brilliant* returned to normal space.

"Twenty-eight minutes to Prondas," Sandi said. "Thirty minutes to contact with *Hope*."

"Ops, make preparations for weapons release," Jack said.

"STALTs One and Two ready in all respects," Jennifer said.

"Release."

"Sandi, when are we in detection range?"

"Five minutes to coverage of Prondas."

The crew members were watching every sensor. "Captain,"

Jennifer said. "I've been focusing on the track directly from Xaphnore, and I'm picking up a recent stardrive signature."

"Is it *Camdex*?"

"No sir, it has a signature I've never seen before...as if it had two drives."

"No way," Riley said. "That's not possible."

"The alliance had a secret project on the drawing board," Anthen said. "Rumors said the ship had twin engines and was named a Tu'Do class. It'll be the Hoclarth capital ship carrying twenty fighter drones and scaled up weapons."

"What's the time until Sami's call?" Jack asked.

"Twenty minutes, sir," Jennifer said.

"Decelerate to one percent light speed," Jack said. "Let's wait here for a status report."

Jeff sat near Anthen. Kalinda moved from station to station hoping for some new information while the rest of the bridge crew watched their panels and the clock.

"We need to hurry," Kalinda said.

"Someday when you're a captain, you'll realize that you have to choose between hurry up and wait. The latter is often the most prudent course of action. In the meantime, I could use a cup of black coffee," Jack said.

"What if someone misses something? I need to be here to help," she said.

"I'll get it, Captain," Jeff said.

"Thanks." Jeff went down to the galley.

The digital second hand swept past the appointed time. All action stopped, and the crew focused on the clock. Kalinda stood close to Jennifer gripping her shoulder.

Ten more seconds passed. "She's late," Kalinda said.

Jennifer touched Kalinda's hand. "Give her time, K'da..."

A tone sounded on Tayla's panel.

"On screen," Jack said, and Sami appeared. "Report."

"Captain, I'm cloaked on the surface of Prondas. Mission One was successful. I've got the animals, and I've synthesized a therapeutic vaccine." Sami looked around at those on the bridge watching and saw Kalinda.

"We're thirty minutes from your location. What about Mission Two?" Jack asked.

"The package is on Prondas, but..."

"You may speak freely, Sami."

"There are three members of the Hoclarth Alliance down here. They captured her. They've got Natira."

Kalinda grabbed Jennifer's hand as she looked at the display. "Te'ma." Jennifer held her sister firmly. Jeff came forward and stood next to his friend.

"Three nights ago, a Patrol ship landed while Natira was out hunting. The Hoclarth are holding her in the cabin Anthen and Natira built. They haven't left the planet surface, but they have company."

"We suspected that. A large ship left an ion trail coming in. What do you know about the ship in orbit?"

"I've listened to their conversation, Captain," Sami said. "It's a Tu'Do class battleship called the *Tandex* commanded by Tal'Predex Brandil Glate."

"BRAY," Kalinda said.

"Your avatar friend?" Jennifer asked.

"The Tal'Predex is Bralen's tal'pa, and Bralen is part of the crew. His father was killed in battle two years ago."

"Who's Bralen?" Tayla asked.

"My fiancé."

Jeff's face went white. "What?"

"It's a business arrangement," Kalinda said. "I don't love him."

Jeff looked only slightly reassured.

. . .

"Are they saying anything else?" Jack said.

"Captain, I think they want to trade for the vaccine," Sami said.

"Anthen?"

"I've met Tal'Predex Glate. He's old school, very transactional."

"Sami, can you take off undetected, meet us here, and keep the kids safe while we come down and see what they want?"

"The soldiers keep looking in my direction. I think they know I'm here."

"Captain, I need to go down there," Kalinda said.

"Not your call, young lady," Jack said. "We need to keep you safe at all costs."

"But captain, we need to save my mother. I don't want to lose her again."

Jack looked at Anthen. "Talk to her."

"K'da, he's right," Anthen said.

"Te'pa, it's my destiny," Kalinda said. "I came with you because I knew I'd have to be there to bring everyone back."

"What about..." Anthen said.

She walked over and stood tall in front of her father. "I claim the honor of Tal'qid. I must go down and save te'ma."

"You're an Earth girl now."

"We're in Hoclarth space."

Anthen nodded. He stood, opened his hands, bowed his head and bent his right knee. "I grant you this honor, te'mil with the hope your path of destiny returns you to me safely."

Kalinda opened her hands, bowed her head, and bent her right knee. "Thank you, te'pa. I promise our destinies will take our whole family safely back to Earth." She acknowledged the stunned looks of each member of her *Brilliant* family on the bridge.

"What does this mean?" Jack asked.

"It means we're going to Prondas," Anthen said.

"Very well," Jack said. "Pilot, take us to Prondas at point-eight light speed. Ops, load tubes one and two and spin up the STALTs."

The crew acknowledged and turned to their panels.

Jack took a sip from his *Brilliant* mug. "Sami, we're en route to join you soon. Stay cloaked for now."

FIFTEEN MINUTES LATER A TONE SOUNDED. "A ship is decelerating from light speed," Sandi said. "Identify *Hoclarth Battle Cruiser Camdex.*"

"Comms, hail them," Jack said.

Jack stood.

"On screen, Captain," Tayla said.

"Hello, Kalea," Jack said. "It's getting crowded around here. How are you and your crew doing?"

"Jack. Hello K'da. Five of my crew are sick. May we speak in private."

"Predex, your granddaughter is aware of our mission."

Kalea pursed his lips. "Kalim, you are taking your daughter into danger."

"Tal'pa, I've claimed Tal'qid," Kalinda said.

"Kalim, you allowed this?" Kalea asked.

"She's of age," Anthen said. "I trust her vision."

"Captain, was your other mission successful?"

"It was. Sami has synthesized a therapeutic vaccine," Jack said. "We'll inject everyone on Prondas, send you with a supply, and then Sami will take it to Xaphnore."

"I concur."

"Who's our welcoming committee?" Jack asked.

"Tal'Predex Glate is the high commander of the alliance space force," Kalea said. "He knows about the vaccine, but he's wary of a trick."

"Your opinion?" Jack asked.

"He's a fair and honorable commander, but he's desperate."

Jack signaled Anthen. They stepped out of sight of the Predex.

"Captain, this Hoclarth is a tough negotiator and plays a game like poker," Anthen said. "The Tal'Predex will play for high stakes, but he will negotiate fairly. We hold the cards with the vaccine."

"And if I offer it without a demand, we will look weak."

"Correct, Captain."

Jack stepped back to the center of the bridge. "Predex, we'll meet you on Prondas."

50

S andi sounded a tone. "*Tandex* is on visual."

"Big son of a bitch," Jack said. "Put us in a parallel orbit."

"Captain, we're being hailed," Tayla said.

"On screen."

An admiral of the Hoclarth Alliance appeared before a background decorated with relics and battle flags. He was wearing an elaborate uniform with many military decorations, but he looked very sick.

"I am Tal'Predex Brandil Glate. In the name of the Hoclarth Alliance, we demand you land on the planet and surrender your cargo."

"I'm Jack Masing, Captain of *StarCruiser Brilliant*. We're on a humanitarian mission."

"So, you say," he said. "What demands will you make of the Hoclarth Alliance."

Anthen stepped into the picture. "I want the return of my mate and the mother of our child, Tal'Predex."

"We do not recognize the rights of this traitor," Brandil said. "We recognize the right of Kalinda's mother to raise her as a citizen of the Hoclarth Alliance."

"Kalinda is of age," Anthen said. "Do you not allow her choice?"

"I've not heard her speak."

"I speak now," Kalinda entered the picture. "I choose to live on Earth with my family."

"You choose to leave behind your commitment to your future mate, and your culture," Brandil said.

"Tal'Predex, I claim the honor of Tal'qid," Kalinda said. "I choose to live on Earth with my family."

"You are just a child, Kalinda," Brandil said. "Your mother will choose."

Jack took a step forward. "Natira stands without freedom of choice. You hold her against her will."

"Starship, our weapons are far superior to yours. You cannot escape. I demand we meet on the surface and settle this. If we're satisfied, we'll allow you and your shuttle to depart peacefully."

Jack stepped out of view of the Tal'Predex and signaled Jennifer to join them. "Anthen?"

"Captain, I'm scanning *Tandex.* They have only a skeleton crew with no fighter drones embarked. We can outmaneuver them and defeat them if necessary."

"Jennifer?"

"The STALTs are nearby and cloaked. It would not be a fair fight."

"He knows he's in the weaker position," Anthen said. "He's trying to come away with something to salvage his pride."

"Very well. Let's play along."

A tone sounded, and Sandi reported. "The *Camdex* is decelerating. The ship will arrive in three minutes."

"Tal'Predex," Jack said. "We'll meet you on the surface. "

Brandil looked relieved. "I'll be riding down aboard Predex Kone's shuttle."

The screen switched back a tactical display.

. . .

"Ops, prepare to enter the atmosphere," Jack said. "Plot an approach to land near the shuttle."

"Aye, Captain," Jennifer said. "Sami will give us a vector to a clearing. Four minutes to the landing."

The forward screen went red as *Brilliant* hit the outer atmosphere.

Two minutes later. "Mach ten," Jennifer said. "Straight in approach."

To their left was a frozen landscape and to the right was a hot desert. Directly before them was a ten-mile-wide green strip on the terminal line of the planet.

"I've got the beacon from *Hope*," David said.

Brilliant began a final descent, and Kalinda shouted, "There's our cabin."

The cabin stood next to a deserted clearing.

Jack pressed a button on the arm of his seat. "Sami?"

"Yes, Captain?"

"Please uncloak the shuttle."

Brilliant landed in the clearing next to the shuttle and fifty yards from the cabin.

"Anthen, scan the area."

"There are four humans in the cabin," he said,

"*Camdex* has just arrived in orbit and is sending a shuttle to *Tandex*," Sandi said.

"Please bring a supply of vaccine to *Brilliant*," Jack said.

"Captain, I lost my body when I rescued Natira."

"Jennifer?"

"We fabricated a spare," Jennifer said. "Join me on the hangar deck."

Jennifer went below.

"May we join her," Kalinda said.

"No way," Jack said. "You two stay on the bridge until it's safe."

. . .

THE VIRTUAL SAMI was waiting on the hangar deck when Jennifer got there. They hugged.

"I missed you the last three days," Jennifer said.

"I missed you the last two hundred years," Sami said.

"You win. It's in Storage Three."

Sami walked into the storage room wearing a perfect uniform. A moment later, she came out wearing a slightly wrinkled one.

"I love my cyberian self."

"Captain, please lower the ramp."

"Coming down."

Sami exited *Brilliant* and walked over to *StarShuttle Hope*. She returned to *Brilliant* a few minutes later carrying a box of one hundred individual injectors.

"I'll be Lab Rat One again," Jennifer said.

Sami corrected her. "You're number two. Natira has received her vaccine with no ill effects."

Sami walked through *Brilliant*, took hugs and congratulations, and injected each crew member with the vaccine. She got the biggest hug from Kalinda.

Kalinda stood by anxiously as Sami finished the last injection. "May I see her?"

"Sure." Sami projected a 3D slideshow of the last year with Natira. Kalinda's eyes were damp as she held Jeff's hand.

Anthen looked at the images with the same longing in his eyes.

Jack placed his hand on his friend's shoulder. "Soon, my friend."

Sami turned to Jack. "Captain, I've fabricated some boxes for the Hoclarth here on Prondas, and I've sent you the app for the fabricator. I need to go to Xaphnore to deliver several fabricators that will generate the injectors needed for the planet."

"We may have to negotiate your exit."

"The *Camdex* shuttle is on final," Sandi said.

"Very well," Jack said. "Jennifer, Anthen, Sami, and I will go down and begin the negotiations."

"Captain, I need to be down there," Kalinda said.

"You'll remain at the top of the ramp with David and Riley...in chains if necessary.

Dandy jumped into Kalinda's arms and looked at her. *Keep me close,* Dandy thought.

After landing, the Hoclarth shuttle, *Brilliant, Hope,* and the cabin formed a circle around a grassy clearing. The landing party stood at the top of the ramp with the rest of the crew behind including Kalinda and Dandy with Riley and David at her side.

"Sandi, are you monitoring the cabin?"

"They're holding Natira inside until the Tal'Predex gives a signal."

He looked at Sami. "Have you got a box of vaccines?"

"Got it," Sami said.

The ramp on the Hoclarth shuttle opened. "That's our cue," Jack said.

Jack led Jennifer, Anthen, and Sami down the ramp. Across the clearing, Tal'Predex Glate, Predex Kone, a robotic-looking soldier, and a tall, handsome teenager descended the ramp. The soldier was very much a robot looking around with a blank stare and no sign of emotion.

THE REMAINDER of the crew watched from the top of the ramp.

"Bralen and Tal'pa," Kalinda said.

Tayla edged close to Kalinda, "I admire your taste in men." She got an elbow in the ribs from Jennifer.

Jeff let go of Kalinda's hand.

David pointed to the robotic pilot. "Do they have androids like ours?" David asked.

Sami spoke over the ship's audio. "An ugly Neanderthal, David, a very primitive replica of me. It can barely walk. I doubt that it can talk. It's just for show."

"We still love you," Tayla said.

BEFORE THE MEETING, Anthen had briefed Jack about Hoclarth customs.

Jack opened his hands and dipped his head. "Tal'Predex, it is my honor. I'm Captain Jack Masing. May I present Anthen Kelrithian, whom you know, my first officer Jennifer Gallagher, and Cyberian Sami Teesmith, who traveled back in time to obtain the Malfnid specimens to synthesize a vaccine."

"My respects, Captain. I am Tal'Predex Brandil Glate, and you know Predex Kalea Kone. This is our pilot, Xalphex, and my grandson Bralen Glate."

"I'd like to see my te'cha," Anthen said.

"I do not speak to traitors," Brandil said.

"A daughter would like to see her mother," Jack said. "Her healthy and safe mother."

"In due time, Captain," Brandil said. "What do you have to offer in trade."

Sami stepped forward. "We offer these injectors for your crews. The vaccine will cure those afflicted and protect those not yet exposed."

Brandil curled his lip and squinted. "This is but a token. We do not wish to gain our health and then stand by and watch our planet die."

"It's a gesture of good faith, Tal'Predex," Jack said. "Our star shuttle carries the vaccine for all of Xaphnore."

"Ahhh," Brandil said. He looked at the cabin. "Allow Predex Valenda to join us."

Anthen watched as the three Hoclarth left the cabin escorting Natira. Their eyes met, and they smiled. Then Natira looked curious, and Anthen pointed to *Brilliant* where David and Riley were holding back the ten-year-old.

"Not yet," David said.

Now, Dandy, she thought.

The tabby cat erupted like a banshee, jumped from Kalinda's arms and dug his claws into Riley's chest. A surprised David let go as well.

Kalinda took off running, grabbed the surprised Natira, and began crying. "Te'ma, I've missed you so much."

Anthen walked over and joined the hug.

"Who is this basket of emotions you have created?" Natira said.

"K'da is also a daughter of Earth, te'cha," Anthen said.

The Tal'Predex coughed and collapsed to a knee. "Is your vaccine safe?"

Sami came to his side. "Natira received the vaccine almost a year ago, and it works quickly."

"Then I offer myself as a test case."

Sami quickly applied an injector to his arm. "It'll begin working soon."

"David, bring the Tal'Predex a chair," Jack said, "if you can hold onto it."

David came down the ramp followed by the remainder of the *Brilliant* crew.

"Dad, Dandy attacked us."

"You were taken out by a simple house cat?" Jack said.

Dandy Lion jumped into Jennifer's arms and glared at Jack.

"Captain, that is not a simple house cat," Brandil said.

Dandy turned to the Tal'Predex and nodded respectfully.

"My respects as well, Toxem'al. And, yes, I am feeling better."

Jack laughed. "A wise actor once said, 'Never work with children and animals.'"

"He must have been in a Hoclarth flixtal," Brandil said. "Captain, I accept your gesture, I surrender Natira to your care, and I humbly ask your plan."

"Sami?"

"I've got five fabricators that can be distributed to the population centers on Xaphnore and provide enough injectors to help the sickest. We'll work with your main laboratory to create enough vaccine for the entire planet. I've got a gift for your zoos as well."

"Our zoos?"

"I have a colony of malfnids."

"Nasty smelly animals," Kalea said. "How can we help?"

"I request that *Camdex* escort us through Hoclarth Space to Xaphnore."

"Granted with our deepest gratitude," Brandil said.

"This box of injectors will supply your crews and those you come in contact with on your journeys." Sami presented the box and then stepped back to join the crew.

Dandy Lion jumped from Jennifer's arm and wrapped himself around Kalinda's legs.

"Captain, it appears we have completed what we came here for," Brandil said. "I know you must avoid our current conflict to keep your planet safe. In the future, it might be time for our two cultures to become friends."

"I look forward to that," Jack said. "First Officer, make your pitch."

Jennifer stepped forward, opened her hands and nodded her head. "Tal'Predex, it is possible that the enemy you face comes from Earth in another time. My tal'pa offers the promise of our governments to expend resources and technology to deal with this issue. We believe we face a common enemy."

"Our people come from Earth in another time. I hope that you can help us. Until then, I wish you safe travels."

The officers offered bows of respect once more.

Bralen stepped forward. "Tal'pa, I wish to speak."

Kalinda and her parents turned to listen.

"No, te'mil," Brandil said. "Our task is complete. We must go."

Bralen continued. "Kalinda, daughter of Natira and Kalim, I demand chio'vech. I call for you to honor ki'ingju."

Natira directed Kalinda behind her. "That custom was outlawed before any of us were born."

The Tal'Predex became angry. "Te'mil, we have given our honor and received a similar honor. We must depart."

"Tal'pa, I must do this. I, too, must have my honor."

51

Tayla whispered to Sami. "What's chio...whatever?"

"Bralen is making a call to honor. He has demanded that Kalinda follow through on their mating contract."

"She's in trouble," Tayla said.

"Kalinda, you entered into ki'ingju willingly," Bralen said. "Your parents and my tal'pa agreed."

Anthen stepped forward. "Bralen, Things have changed. Kalinda is a daughter of Earth now. You've no right..."

Kalinda stepped forward. "I, too, demand chio'vech. I demand my freedom."

"WHAT'S HAPPENING?" Jeff said.

"I think there's going to be a fight," Sami said.

"K'DA, NO," Kalea said. "Bralen, on your Tal'pa's honor, release Kalinda of this obligation."

"Predex, I stand for my honor," Bralen said. "Will you fight,

Kalinda?"

Jeff stepped forward. "I will fight for her freedom."

Kalinda walked over and put a hand on Jeff's shoulder. "Te'cha, I must do this myself." She hugged her friend.

JEFF WALKED BACK TO SAMI. "What's te'cha?"

"It means 'my love.'"

Jeff's face turned a dark shade of crimson.

NATIRA TOOK HER DAUGHTERS SHOULDERS. "K'da, he has grown a head taller than you."

"Mother, I must give him this honor," Kalinda said.

"I don't want to lose you again," Natira said.

Kalinda lifted her head. "I don't like to lose."

"Anthen?"

"Kalinda was of age when she made this commitment. She needs to follow through," he said.

Kalinda hugged each of her parents then walked to Bralen. "I will serve Tal'qid to protect our honor and gain my freedom."

"What weapons do you choose?" Bralen said.

"I choose no weapons," Kalinda said.

"Then you may choose the terms."

"May we use pre'tal?"

THE *BRILLIANT* CREW STOOD ASKANCE. Kalinda was fighting for her freedom, and they could do nothing but stand and watch.

"What's pre'tal, Sami?" Tayla asked.

"I've read some Tal'qid literature," Sami said. "It's a cage fight in a low gravity enclosure with force field boundaries."

"That seems simple," Riley said.

"They fight blind, and the scoring strikes must occur in the air."

"Not simple," David said.

"Jen, can we talk Kalinda out of this?" Tayla asked.

"Have you tried to talk Kalinda out of anything?" Jennifer asked.

"Well...yeah."

"How's that worked out for ya?"

They stopped and just watched.

ANTHEN WALKED over to Predex Kalea. "Predex, I've got a program to create a pre'tal, but I need your shuttle to generate the enclosure."

"Kalim, do you approve of this?" Kalea asked.

"I trust Kalinda's vision."

"Very well."

As Anthen and Kalea walked up the ramp of the Hoclarth shuttle, Natira went into the cabin for a moment and came out carrying two pieces of material.

Bralen looked nervous as he asked Kalinda, "Are you going to serve in that bulky uniform."

Kalinda released the fasteners. She appeared in her semi-transparent suit. "You may propose a referee."

Bralen looked around. His eyes settled on Kalinda's mother. "I propose Predex Natira Valenda."

"I agree," Kalinda said. "She'll be fair."

"Are you sure you want this, K'da?" Natira asked.

"I will act as my teacher taught and I'll make her proud."

"I've always been proud of my daughter," Natira said. She turned to Bralen. "I will act as referee."

Jack stopped Anthen coming down the shuttle ramp. "You're sure about this, buddy?"

"Kalinda's doing this to preserve her friend's honor as well as her own. She must do it."

Jack joined the crew. "I don't like this one bit."

Bralen went up the ramp for a moment and came back down in his fighting suit.

Anthen walked to the center of the clearing. "Everyone, please step back. The pre'tal cylinder is eight meters in diameter and rises ten meters. The gravity inside will be one-tenth planet normal decreasing to one percent at three meters above the ground. There will be a similar attractor between the competitors, and the cylinder will be impenetrable. After I activate the pre'tal, spectators may come to the barrier. The interior wall will be repellent and will not cause injury on impact. The competitors ask that you remain silent to allow them to focus their seven senses." Anthen signaled Natira to come to the center, and Anthen went to the side. They touched hands as they passed.

"WHAT'S ALL THAT MEAN?" Jeff asked.

"That they go into the air and they stay in the air," Jennifer said. "When they get close to each other, they stay close."

"They will float on a soft bed of zero gravity," Sami said. "If they stop moving, they will slowly fall to the ground."

NATIRA STOOD in the center of the ring. "Competitors, join me," Natira said.

Bralen and Kalinda entered the ring wearing tight semi-transparent suits. Each faced Natira, bent their right knees, opened their hands and bowed their heads. Natira returned the greeting. They then faced each other and did the same.

"Bralen and Kalinda, you have committed to serving Tal'qid in a competition as a commitment to honor. Do you each agree to this?"

Natira looked at each in turn as they said "Yes."

The winner will be the one who scores three thi'kahs. The target area is the torso from hips to neck. A thi'kah will only count when both of you are in the air. Do you understand the rules?"

They both said yes.

"Activate pre'tal."

There was a hum from the Hoclarth shuttle. The three inside the cylinder bounced in the low gravity.

"Don your masks." She handed each the cloth. They pulled the tight-fitting fabric over their heads. The only exposed skin of the competitors was their hands and feet.

THE SPECTATORS GATHERED CLOSE to the barrier.

"Why do they have the hoods?" Tayla said. "They can't see."

"Kalinda and Bralen, as children of Xaphnore, have a proximity sense," Sami said. "Their vision is a distraction and the hoods act like helmets to prevent injury to the head."

"What's an attractor?" Jeff asked.

"Each competitor exhibits a gravitational pull," Sami said. "A soft blow will not drive them apart."

NATIRA CHECKED each hood for proper placement. "Are you ready?"

The competitors faced each other and again bowed with open hands and then moved three meters apart.

"Tal'Predex?"

Tal'Predex stood and touched the transparent wall. "May you both serve Tal'qid with honor." He remained standing.

Both competitors bent their knees ready to spring.

Natira stood away from the two. "K'vah"

Bralen and Natira sprung three meters into the air trading punches and blocks.

Natira hung in the air nearby and observed.

Kalinda executed a crescent kick. Bralen rotated his body away and extended his leg to kick as he came around. Kalinda dropped her head back to the horizontal and swept his other knee, and Bralen rotated uncontrollably on his z-axis. The two competitors sailed apart.

"Kal'vach," Natira said.

"Sami?" Tayla asked.
"Watch."

THE AIRBORNE FIGHTERS rolled on their backs and approached until their feet touched.

"K'vah."

Each fighter sprung towards the wall. As they extended their legs, they rotated their bodies to hit the wall feet-first. On contact, they exploded toward each other.

Kalinda sensed that Bralen was preparing a kick with his left foot. She turned her body to avoid but Bralen tucked and somersaulted into a kick that struck her cleanly on the left shoulder.

Natira raised her arm, pointed to Bralen and said, "Thi'kah." Bralen led one-to-zero.

Anthen caught a smile on the face of the Tal'Predex.

Natira and the two warriors fell softly to the ground landing on their feet.

The two competitors compressed their bodies at the ready. "K'vah."

They sprung into the microgravity area and began sparring. Bralen attempted a series of double fist punches which Kalinda blocked. She answered with an uppercut, but Bralen moved his head just enough to avoid the hit. He then attacked with a sliding ax kick. Kalinda compressed her body, and Bralen's heel passed over Kalinda's head just missing. He left his torso undefended, and Kalinda launched a perfect jab to the chest.

"Thi'kah." The score was one-to-one.

The Earth spectators broke into applause and cheering.

Natira, Bralen, and Kalinda touched down softly on the ground.

The referee turned to the crew and held her hand up. The cheering stopped.

"Kal'vach?" Kalinda and Bralen nodded and faced away at the ready.

"K'vah."

From the crouch, the two sprung to opposite walls. Kalinda tucked and rolled. When she touched the wall, she exploded into the center. Her body was vertical giving Bralen a huge target.

Bralen compressed and fired off to the center, turned his body feet first to attack the vulnerable Kalinda.

He took the feint, she thought. She threw her head back into a reverse somersault. She was horizontal as Bralen passed above her and she executed a snap kick that contacted Bralen in the back.

Natira pointed to her daughter. "Thi'kah." Kalinda led the competition two-to-one.

There was more cheering from the crew of *Brilliant.* "Just one more," Jeff yelled.

A stern look from Natira quieted the spectators.

"K'vah."

Into the air, they flew. Sparring, punching and kicking, Bralen and Kalinda fought for many seconds. The microgravity took hold, and they began to descend. Bralen and Kalinda continued to exchange blows. Each was blocked, deflected, or avoided. They neared the ground. Bralen launched a roundhouse kick. Kalinda ducked and then executed a counter punch to the body. It connected.

The crew of the *Brilliant* erupted. They looked to Natira to announce the winner.

Kalinda and Bralen looked to the referee.

"Thi'mach." She pointed to Bralen's right foot.

Bralen threw his hands up. Kalinda dropped her head and looked away.

. . .

SAMI HELD up her hands to quiet her friends. "Natira disqualified the hit. Bralen was on the ground."

"No."

"Unfair."

"C'mon, Kalinda won."

Dandy Lion jumped into Jennifer's arms to get a better look at the action.

KALINDA LOOKED AT HER CREW, then turned to her mother, bent her knee, opened her hands and bowed her head.

"What's she doing?" David asked.

"She's acknowledging the call," Sami said. "She agrees that it was fair."

The crew became quiet.

Bralen looked at Kalinda with a furrowed brow as his muscles tensed with determination.

Kalinda's hands clenched as she faced her opponent in the ready position.

"K'vah."

They sprung up and met face-to-face three meters in the air and began sparring. They traded punches and kicks. Kalinda was aggressive and took advantage of her momentum as Bralen, a point down, defended just as vigorously. Natira hovered nearby. Their energetic punches and kicks forced them apart.

Natira signaled their attention. "Kal'vach."

They nodded as they sailed two meters apart. Their mutual attraction took effect as they positioned themselves feet first.

A moment after they touched. "K'vah."

The two fighters sprung to the barrier, reversed and sprung back to the center.

A combination, Kalinda thought. She punched with her right hand and missed and punched with her left. Bralen blocked, but

Kalinda used her rotation to execute a crescent kick. Bralen blocked the kick with his left arm causing him to spin to his left.

Bralen extended a lunge punch into Kalinda's exposed ribs.

"Thi'kah." Natira signaled a point for Bralen.

Kalinda sailed softly to the ground, her teeth clenched holding her side. She landed on one knee.

"Are you okay, Kalinda?" David shouted.

Jeff was shaking as he held onto Tayla's arm with both of his hands.

Dandy Lion dug his claws into Jennifer. "What is it, Dandy?"

The boy broke Kalinda's rib, Dandy thought.

Jennifer looked up with tears in her eyes. "It's over."

Kalinda looked at her adversary and conceded a fair hit.

"I didn't mean to hurt you," Bralen said. "Predex, I choose a draw,"

Kalinda held Natira's hand as she stood up gingerly. "No, Bralen, there will be no draw."

Natira supported her daughter. "You cannot continue, K'da. Bralen is offering a draw."

"Mother, we must preserve our honor," Kalinda said. "Bralen, we will fight to the last point."

Bralen opened his hands and bowed to Kalinda.

"K'da, let me know when you're ready," Natira said.

"You can't let her continue, te'cha." Anthen said.

"She'll be safe," Natira said. *I will protect our daughter as you have, before,* she thought.

Anthen nodded. *I trust you,* he thought.

Kalinda bent over again holding her side.

"Let me know when you are ready, te'mil."

Kalinda took a shallow breath, grimaced, and then stood.

"Ready," Kalinda said.

Natira nodded.

"I don't want to hurt you, K'da," Bralen said.

"It was a lucky shot, Bray," she said. "Get ready."

They both crouched at the ready for one final point.

"Kal'vach." Natira directed them to jump to opposite walls.

They nodded acknowledgment.

"K'vah."

Bralen jumped quickly to his wall. Kalinda sprung gingerly and hovered near the wall opposite Bralen. The turned their heads toward one another to develop a picture using their Hoclarth proximity sense. He shook his head. She extended her hands and signaled him to come over. He set his jaw with determination and leaped off the wall with all of his force. He looked at her waiting.

Kalinda hung in the air as a lame duck.

Bralen got ready to execute a roundhouse kick timed for her position against the wall.

Bralen's timing was perfect, but Kalinda exploded off the wall. She extended her right leg to sweep his kick aside and continued her rotation. She extended her left leg in a perfect falling roundhouse kick which connected solidly with his hips.

Natira pointed to Kalinda. "Thi'kah."

It was over. Kalinda was the champion. Competitors and referee slowly descended to the ground amid cheers and shouts from everyone but one. Brandil Glate stood with a sad but proud look on his face.

As soon as they touched the ground, the competitors faced, bowed and Natira put her hand on her daughter's shoulder.

Anthen de-activated the pre'tal.

Kalinda staggered in the full gravity as her mother supported her.

The crew of the *Brilliant* ran in and surrounded Kalinda. Sami held them back, but Kalinda stood and joined them in a very gentle group hug.

Sami stepped up, and the group separated. She ran her hand over Kalinda's ribs. "It's a severe bruise. Nothing broken. No surfing or serving Tal'qid for two weeks."

Kalinda looked sad.

"Okay, ten days."

Kalinda's face brightened.

A smiling Jeff stepped up. "Sensei Kalinda, will you teach me how to fight like that?"

"You were brave to volunteer to go into the pre'tal for me, te'cha," Kalinda said. "We now have a great Sensei who will teach us both."

"I'm your te'cha?"

Kalinda planted a kiss on Jeff's cheek.

THE CELEBRATION SUBSIDED and Kalinda walked over to Bralen who was being comforted by his Tal'pa.

"I still want to be with you," Bralen said. "Maybe we could come together based on...what is this thing you have on Earth they call love?"

"I love another, Bralen."

"I thought so." Bralen looked over Kalinda's shoulder at Jeff. "Can he serve Tal'qid?"

"I'm teaching him."

"You'll be a teacher as great as your mother." Bralen looked away. "Then this is farewell."

"On Earth, we say, 'Until we meet again.'"

Bralen pointed to the five captains, Brandil, Natira, Anthen, Jack, and Kalea gathered in friendly conversation.

"I think that will happen soon," Bralen said. "Our worlds are becoming friends. You made it happen."

"I had a lot of help," she said. "Come over and meet my *Brilliant* family."

52

Two weeks later, the Star Squad was gathered on the beach at Point Dume across the street from the Sunset Restaurant recently rebuilt on higher ground. Kalinda was on the waves for the first time since Dr. Ami cleared her for full activity. Sami was on the beach watching Kalinda.

The Star Squad had their HoloPads out and were taking selfies with the beautiful sky in the background. Dandy Lion was jumping from person to person to get in every picture.

"Did I hear the Blue Angels are up the road at NAS Pt. Mugu for an airshow?" David asked.

"That's correct," Riley said.

"Will we see them?" Tayla asked.

"Could be," Jennifer said.

Tayla looked at her bestie. "The vision thing?"

"They flew into LA for a memorial service. I might have sent a message or two."

Kalinda came up the beach with Sami, planted her surfboard in the sand and joined the group.

More photos ensued.

"Sunset will be very soon," Sami said.

"Will we see a green flash?" Riley asked.

"Oh no," Sami said. "The air is too moist."

"Can you take one of me in front of the beach?" Kalinda asked.

"Sure," said Riley.

Just then, the Blue Angels Diamond roared by just off the beach. The group waved at the pilots.

"They won't see us," David said.

Just then, all four aircraft did a Diamond Barrel Roll, banked left and started a loop.

The Star Squad looked at Jennifer then at the jets.

Dandy jumped from Jennifer's arms to Kalinda's. *Camera whore,* Kalinda thought.

I make you look good, Dandy thought.

Riley snapped the photo just as the Blue Angels dove into the photo behind Kalinda.

Tayla looked over his shoulder. "Cool shot. Hey Jen, this looks good enough to be a book cover."

"Hey, it does," Jennifer said. "I think I've got some executive time coming up. Don't want to waste it on twitter and talk shows."

"I'm hungry, let's head into the restaurant," Kalinda said.

"You're always hungry, surfer girl," Tayla said.

"I hear they have carrots and kale for your celebrity figure."

The group started across the street, but Sami and Jennifer lingered.

"It's a beautiful sunset," Jennifer said.

"I love the smell of the ocean and the sound of the waves lapping on the shore."

They stood next to each other for a few minutes.

"Jennifer."

"Yeah?"

"Thank you."

Jennifer looked at her yellow-eyed friend. Sami looked back, and they hugged.

"Let's go eat," Jennifer said.

"I'm not hungry."

They both laughed. As they crossed the street, they passed two girls about Jennifer's age.

"Have I seen those two before?" Jennifer asked. "I think they have been following us."

"I've wanted to get close enough," Sami said. "They're cyberians."

"Like you?"

"No, they have blue eyes and their AI is self-contained."

"Are you saying...?"

"Yes."

"They're from the future," Jennifer said.

GLOSSARY

Ayiiia A character in *Galaxy Warrior* who will be portrayed by Tayla Mendoza in the movie.

Battle of Kian'qil Outpost An attack by the Kir'qox on the Hoclarth outpost on Barnard's Star

chio'vech demand for performance of on honor contract for example, a marriage contract.

Finsler Maneuver Conducted in the gravity well of a planet or star, it is a momentary burst of speed in excess of light resulting in a calculated jump back in time.

framlin A tree growing on Xaphnore with large stiff leaves.

Flixtal A form of entertainment in the Hoclarth Alliance similar to motion pictures

gi A uniform worn by a practitioner of martial arts.

Goldilocks zone refers to the **habitable zone** around a star where the temperature is just right - not too hot and not too cold - for liquid water to exist on a planet.

Gromnel A large sentient animal native to Xaphnore. It is able to communicate telepathically but is never seen.

Grotchka A large carnivore portrayed in *Galaxy Warrior*

Kal'vach When serving Tal'qid in Pre'tal, fighters spring off the ground or each other feet-to-feet to the opposite barrier

Ki'ingju A mating contract which is more business than love.

Kir'qox Kwan'qil word for ghost. Name given to the fighters attacking the Hoclarth

K'vah When serving Tal'qid, the signal to begin fighting.

Kwan'qil dialect Language spoken in the Hoclarth Alliance.

Laknove The Hoclarth word for heaven.

Malfnid A six-legged carnivore with vestigial wings native to Xaphnore

Manqlid A Hoclarth dessert produced by pouring Manqa juice on a specially prepared sheet cake.

Predex Ship commander in the Hoclarth Alliance

pre'tal A fighting enclosure created by surrounding a low gravity cylinder with a force field.

Pugachev's Cobra An aerobatic maneuver where the pilot rolls the aircraft past the vertical into a stall reducing forward velocity to zero.

tal'dor Formal greeting to a female

Tal'pa Greeting to grandfather

Tal'Predex Greeting to Hoclarth Admiral

Tal'qid Considered the first teacher in Hoclarth Culture. Three thousand years ago, this woman set down the rules of serving Tal'qid

tal'ven Formal greeting to a male

Te'cha My love

te'mil Greeting to a child

Te'pa Honorific for father

Te'ma Honorific for mother

thi'kahs A successful strike when serving Tal'qid

Thi'mach – A strike that occurs with one or both in contact with the ground or the wall.
No points awarded.

Toxem'al Psychic spirit animal, able to communicate tele-pathically

Xaphnore Hoclarth Home planet orbiting the star Hoclar.

ACKNOWLEDGMENTS

Singularity is my second novel. As a publisher, I have delivered thirty-five books by eleven authors but writing a novel is a new world. I would like to thank those who helped to make my book as good as it can be despite my efforts to the contrary.

I learned much from experienced authors, first and foremost my mentor, marketing guru, and editor, Penn Wallace, who writes exciting thrillers as Pendleton C. Wallace. Caroline McCullagh, author of The Ivory Caribou, provided much encouraging criticism. Jim Bennett suggested an incredibly descriptive title. Ron Hidinger provided some surprisingly good copy-editing. Retired principal Lee Romero, an avid surfer, provided valuable advice. My Ohio contingent included Sheila Moore, who is writing *Letters to Sallie, the Civil War Letters of A.C. McClure*, my great-grandfather, and Kathy Rider, my diligent copy editor on Book One. A special thanks to Chief Petty Officer Chad Pritt, a member of the Blue Angels, who provided me with insight about the Navy's Premier Flight Demonstration Team.

One can only hope to have a wonderful cover like the one that Renata Lechner produced for this book.

Thanks to my beta readers including Dennis Mauricio, Eloisa Quijada, Lynn Reiter-Woodhead, and others.

Special thanks to author Laurence Dahners, whose character Ell Donsaii inspired Jennifer and who contributed valuable time and expertise at a critical moment. And to Sarah Char who provided her Hollywood insight.

My USS Drum sea buddy, Kent Gunn got me into the publishing business with *The Apes of Eden* and inspired Jennifer. Kent is the answer to the question, "How can anyone have an IQ of 206?"

Finally, my greatest inspiration comes from my former students in Southwest High Video Productions and iCrew Digital Productions including John, Joel, Dante, Chris, Stacee, James, Brian, Brittni, Ayiiia, Rod, Katie, Meaghan, Anamaria, Marina, Lee, Jessica, Charlie, Tori, Ricky, Chris D., Robin, Liza, Brion, Darlene, and Francisco.

And my thanks and apologies to anyone I might have left out because of you know...CRS.

ABOUT RICK LAKIN

Rick Lakin is the the bestselling author of *Brilliant* and publisher at iCrewDigitalPublishing.com, Bringing New Authors to a Digital World. iCrew has published 35 books by 11 authors.

Rick has been an Optimist for almost two years and is the district webmaster as calso41.us.

He is the founder of iCrew Digital Productions, A Community of Young Media Professionals and a member of the 1000 Club of the National Association of Sports Public Address Announcers. Rick is an Advanced Communicator Silver in Toastmasters International and is a member of American Mensa. Rick works as a Sports Statistician for broadcast television and is a retired math teacher.

He is a retired math teacher who lives in Southern California but his roots are in Columbus, Ohio, home of The Ohio State University Buckeyes.

facebook.com/ricklakinauthor

twitter.com/ricklakin

amazon.com/author/ricklakin